WHO THEY ARE

FALLING SERIES

MADI DANIELLE

Copyright © 2022 by Madi Danielle

All rights reserved.

No part of this book may be reproduced in any form or by any electronic or mechanical means, including information storage and retrieval systems, without written permission from the author, except for the use of brief quotations in a book review.

This novel is entirely a work of fiction. The names, characters and incidents portrayed in it are the work of the author's imagination. Any resemblance to actual persons, living or dead, events or localities is entirely coincidental.

Designations used by companies to distinguish their products are often claimed as trademarks. All brand names and product names used in this book and on its cover are trade names, service marks, trademarks and registered trademarks of their respective owners. The publishers and the book are not associated with any product or vendor mentioned in this book. None of the companies referenced within the book have endorsed the book.

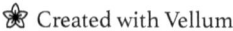 Created with Vellum

PLAYLIST

Unthinkable – Cloudy Jane
Someone Else - Margo
Love Is The Devil - Natalie Jones
Who Am I - Besomorph & Riell
Velvet - Breathe Carolina
If You Wanna Leave - Sadie
Right? - Emlyn
All Alone - Skydxddy
I'm Not Okay - Citizen Soldier
Empty - Letdown.
War Zone - Neena Rose
Heavy (Feat. Rain Paris) - Fame on Fire
Liar – Harina
Angry Too - Lola Blanc
Alive - Sia

AUTHORS NOTE

Before going into this I wanted to mention a couple things, first is the time frame. This is the second book in an interconnected trilogy, and this book takes place between the end and the epilogue of the first book, "When They Fell".

The second thing is the depiction of mental health and trauma in this book. Everyone's story with mental health and trauma is different, even the way Aylin and Nate approach their individual trauma is different. If you have experienced anything like what is depicted in this book or struggle with your mental health, know that you are not alone. Your feelings are completely valid and how you choose to handle it is completely unique to you.

If you have triggers, please heed the trigger warnings provided, though they also contain some spoilers so if you would like to avoid spoilers you can skip the next page.

Remember...

YOU ARE NOT ALONE AND YOU ARE LOVED!

<3 Madi

TRIGGER WARNINGS

Child abuse (Physical, emotional, and psychological)
Domestic violence (not between MCs)
Violence
Gangs
Depictions of mental health including depression, anxiety and trauma response.
Attempted SA (not between MCs)

"Who in the world am I? Ah, that's the great puzzle."

— *Lewis Carroll*, Alice in Wonderland

1

Aylin

Present

I really didn't need more fuel for my non stop nightmares, but about four months ago that's exactly what I got when my best friend Mel and I went on a bit of a rescue mission for her boyfriend, Zander.

HIS ASSHOLE BROTHER tried to kill him, and Mel as well, though possibly indirectly. I helped her because I know she would've done the same thing for me. When I created a distraction for them one of the guys that was helping Zander's stepbrother, Trent, chased after me.

I'M NOT sure how I managed to outrun this behemoth of a man, but I did. I got to my car with the goal of driving through the chain link fence to create more of a diversion, but as I sped toward it, the idiot rushed in front of my car.

I didn't kill him, he hopped right back up as the cops were

starting to swarm us. Then, there was the fire and the smoke coming from the building I knew Zander and Mel were in. I've never been so panicked, even though I've seen and been involved in my fair share of scary situations when I was growing up.

I grew numb to them back then.

I knew what to expect, but this was different.

This was uncertain, and I didn't know what to do.

The cops came, arrested the guy I hit, the other one that was in the building and Trent. I didn't even care until I saw the firefighters bringing out Zander and Mel, both unconscious and covered in ash, and I thought they might have been dead.

I broke down, sobbing when one of the cops came over to me, trying to comfort me, I think. I don't even remember what he was saying, all I could hear were my sobs. He held me up since my legs weren't working. His strong arms around me were the only thing I could register through my tears.

Eventually, the same cop told me they were fine, alive, but needed to go to the hospital. I had to be questioned about everything.

That wasn't fun.

It was a different officer that ended up questioning me, the one that held me through my breakdown wasn't anywhere to be seen. Once I finally left the police station I went to the hospital to see Mel.

Now, here I am months later still waking up from the nightmares of that night. Sometimes, my nightmares get tangled together and the faces are replaced with those of my parents. Sometimes it's just the nightmares of my childhood.

I can't get a break, even though I haven't talked to either of my parents in eleven years they still haunt me in my dreams.

I sit up in bed as my eyes focus on my surroundings. My small apartment that I've lived in for the last three years while I'm in grad school. It's nothing special, but it's not with my parents. It's not laced with the terrible memories, though they continue to follow me no matter where I go.

I finally get up to get ready. School started back up a couple weeks ago and today is my first day at my new clinical site. My last internship requirement since this is my final year of my Doctorate degree. It feels like it's been forever, which it sort of has with the three years of rigorous studying I've had to do.

It's about to all be worth it though, and that's what has gotten me through these last few years.

I make my way to the bathroom to tame my long brown hair, which is naturally fairly straight, but turns into a mess from my tossing and turning every single night.

Once I don't look like I have an actual rat's nest on my head I put on some makeup, not much. I like to be subtle but appear put together. Because to the world, I always look put together. Even my best friend Mel thinks I am put together, and she knows everything about me. I'm good at putting on a face, that's for sure.

My blue eyes pop against the light brown eye shadow I put on my eyelids, plus the mascara lifts my long eyelashes so my eyes appear bigger. I put a neutral nude lipstick on before assessing my small closet for what to wear.

It's my first day at my site and I need to make a good first impression and considering where I'm going, that impression needs to be a strong, professional and confident woman who knows exactly what she's doing.

I scoff. *Yeah*, I've been pretending to be that woman all through grad school, but on the inside, I still feel like the terrified twelve-year-old hiding in a cabinet, a cupboard, or under my bed.... *no*. I can't think about that right now.

Focus on confidence.

September in Oregon is still fairly warm so I opt for a simple dress, though I would've preferred to dress slightly more professional for my first day, but I know I will sweat my ass off in pants today.

The dress falls just above my knee, the dark gray material is tighter at the top because, honestly, my chest is pretty big. I've got curves, and that's not going to change. The material falls loose around my stomach since I'd prefer if the material didn't cling there. I'm fine with my body, but I don't like to draw attention to the one area that isn't my favorite.

I put on some flats before grabbing my bag filled with notebooks, and a couple of reference books I'd like to keep at the clinical site, if I have a place to put them. I've always gotten a desk, even though the room I've had to use has been shared.

This time is a little different, this one feels more like I'm walking into a real job considering I won't have someone hanging over me every second during the sessions. I'm on my own during actual sessions. I'll have check ins, but other than that it's only me.

Also, don't get me started on my thesis I have to do this year, that's another obstacle that always looms in the back of my mind.

I get in my little run-down Toyota as I make my way to the police station once again.

When I learned this was where my last clinical was going to be after everything that went down, I panicked a bit. I talked to my advisor, and explained the situation, but she didn't seem too concerned about it. She told me it would be good practice about balancing my own trauma, and not letting it affect my work. Also, a practice in boundaries since I came face-to-face with so many different officers that night. Lastly, she told me not to worry, it's Portland and the chances of running into any of them will be slim.

When someone tells me not to worry, I can't help but worry more. Call it a trauma response.

I know where to go because I was given specific instructions to head to a building around the back that is separate from the main building that I'm uncomfortably familiar with.

There's a smaller parking lot where I was told to go, and that's where I park next to the only other 2 cars here. The door isn't too far. I'm just hoping I didn't mess up already.

I look over myself one more time before heading inside, plastering on my professional, confident mask I'm so familiar with showing the world.

Once I'm inside I look around at the makeshift lobby that has a sterile feeling, almost like a hospital. White linoleum floors that are definitely older than me, white walls and two chairs that don't even have arm rests. How pleasant.

There's another door against the back wall that opens as soon as I step inside. I'm greeted by an older woman, who I can only assume is Susan Tanvers, the lead therapist who will also be my, for lack of a better term, boss this year. Technically, she's my clinical advisor, but my boss makes more sense in my eyes.

"Hello, you must be Aylin Porter?" she asks with a small smile.

She speaks strongly but friendly. I can only assume it's from years of practice in this field, feeling welcoming but not a pushover. Susan is probably in her late fifties, and she has black hair that is pulled back in a bun. I feel like she's someone who was really pretty when she was younger, but age has now caught up to her a bit. She's not unattractive, but she has wrinkles, and worry lines, that I'm sure have been caused by years of stress.

"Hello, yes, Dr. Tanvers?" I try not to gag when saying the word "doctor".

I know it's respectful, and a lot of professionals like to be addressed in their formal title, but it's something I struggle with. Years of trauma will do that to a person, especially when some of that trauma, or lack of help, came from those referred to as "doctor".

I have a pretty visceral reaction when anyone brings up my own impending title. I do not ever intend to go by "Dr. Aylin" or "Dr. Porter". Mel jokes about it, and I know it's all in good fun, I never tell her how much it bothers me. I tell her to stop, but I know she doesn't mean any harm by it.

"Please, call me Susan."

Thank God.

"It's nice to meet you, Susan, I'm excited to get to work with you this year."

She nods slightly before extending her arm inviting me into the room, which I assume is her office.

As I walk into the room, I notice it's bigger than I thought it would be, and much more comfortable than the front area. There's a desk toward the back, tucked in a corner, almost like it's hidden from the "therapy" part of the office.

The middle of the room consists of a couch that, honestly, looks comfortable. There's also a recliner, and two armchairs. The seating options are arranged in an open way to seem welcoming, with the various options so the client can pick where they would be most comfortable.

The walls have various artwork on them, nothing too bright or extravagant, a lot of neutral colors in differing designs that give the room some life, but not much of a personality. I'm okay with it though, I know how distracting some visuals can be.

"I've heard a lot of good things about you, Aylin, I look forward to the work I will see from you this year." Susan sits in one of the armchairs.

I follow suit, sitting on the couch and I was right. It's really comfortable.

"Thank you, I appreciate that," I nod. I'm not great at getting praise, it feels uncomfortable because I never know if I'm supposed to compliment them back. Be humble? I really don't know.

"I wanted to let you know how I work. I don't micromanage

so you will be conducting your sessions by yourself, and once a week we will meet to go over your notes and debrief about the clients you've seen."

This is what I was told, but I'm glad she confirmed that is what this year will look like. I don't like being micromanaged and my boss last year was the king of micromanaging, it was awful.

"I'm not sure how much you know about what we do here, but you will be seeing officers that are either out on administrative leave for a variety of reasons, or officers that are active that just need someone to talk to. A lot of them just want someone to vent to in order to not take the stress of the job home with them. Those on administrative leave or stuck on desk duty will often be looking to get cleared to return to work. We will discuss those when the time comes, and I'll help you with that decision. Of course, there's the standard things you should know, a lot of the officers you will see may bring up open cases and investigations that you are expected to keep confidential."

I nod, "Thank you, I understand. Will you continue to see clients? I wasn't given a schedule past today."

"Ah, sorry about that, I'm working my way to retirement and will likely only see a couple of the harder cases that I've been working with for a while. Those have set times weekly on Monday and Wednesday between ten and noon. Does Tuesday and Thursday all day work for you with your classes?"

"Yes, that's perfect."

This is the first year my schedule is slightly more flexible, I am a TA for an undergrad class on Monday and Wednesday mornings, 8 a.m, gross. I have my advising right after on Wednesday afternoon, my thesis seminar after that and my only real classes are in the evenings. This year is more about our thesis and clinicals since we are so close to being done.

Being a TA is what pays my bills, it doesn't pay much, but

it's enough for what I need without having to work an extra job I wouldn't have time for.

"Great, this will be our shared office, feel free to make yourself at home, I'm not too picky about things as long as you don't replace all the furniture or rearrange it too much," Susan smiles at me.

I'm glad she's nice, I'm hoping this is for real, and she's not going to turn into a witch after my first week or something.

"I know this week is a little odd since it's your first week, but I hope you're ready to jump right in, your first client will be here in an hour."

I gulp. I mean, I should've expected this, that's why I'm here, I just don't know why I thought maybe the first day would be getting my feet under me.

"Of course, I'm always ready," I smile to hide my unease.

"Glad to hear it. Are you comfortable on your own or would you like me to stick around today?" Susan asks, but I can see she really doesn't want to stick around.

I shake my head, "I feel fine on my own. Like you said, just jump in."

Susan chuckles, "I think I already like you; we will meet tomorrow at ten for our check in, and if that works for you that can be our regular check in day and time?"

I nod, "That sounds perfect, thank you."

Susan stands up, collecting her bag from the desk in the back corner, "Seriously, feel free to make yourself comfortable. I have plenty of reading material here if you're not already sick of learning."

I chuckle as she refers to the two small bookcases along the back wall of the room by the desk that are lined with books, I assume are about various psychology topics. I might look through them to see if anything stands out to me. I don't think I could ever get sick of learning. It's one of the only times my mind can truly focus on something other than what I've been through.

"Good luck. I left my number for you on the desk if you need me any other time, please don't hesitate to call. Unless it's the middle of the night, I don't want to hear from you then, please."

"Don't worry, I wouldn't do that to you," I reassure her.

She gives me one more nod before walking out, leaving me alone in this foreign room where I suddenly feel even more like an imposter than I normally do.

2

Present

I'm sitting at my desk when I'm told my sergeant wants to talk to me.

"Fuck," I mutter to myself.

I hear a snicker from the desk next to mine. I look up to meet the officer's eyes.

"Something funny, Adams?" I glare at him.

He doesn't even try to hide his amusement. "Not yet, but if you get your ass chewed out it might be."

I roll my eyes, "I haven't even done anything to get my ass chewed out about, you dumbass."

"You mean you don't think you've been caught."

I throw a pen at him as I get up to go to the sergeant's office.

He's not completely wrong, I'm going through the list in my head of shit I've done that I didn't think I've been caught doing. There's no way it's anything like that. Maybe he's letting me get off desk duty. That would be fan-fucking-tastic.

It's been two months since the incident that put me on the desk, and though it's been "encouraged" I go seek help from the psychologist, I've refused. All while I've been stuck doing paperwork while other people "investigate" what happened.

Four months ago, I had the biggest catch of my career that I really thought would lead to a promotion of some sort, or at least get me off patrol, but it didn't. Then, two months later, the "incident" happened, and I've been fucked ever since.

I knock on the sergeant's door before stepping inside. The knock was a courtesy, I wasn't actually looking for permission to enter.

Sergeant Peters is in his mid-forties with graying hair, a big build and a face that has a permanent scowl. I know it really is permanent because the one time he complimented me he still looked like that.

I was really fucking confused but accepted the compliment because I know he doesn't hand those out easily.

Today, his scowl looks more intense, and it's definitely directed at me, but I really can't think of anything I did that would warrant being called in here. I've been trying to be good.

Sort of.

I get bored sometimes, which makes it difficult.

"Greene, sit down," Peters says gruffly.

I huff quietly as I sit down in one of the chairs, opposite of his desk.

"Do you know why I wanted to see you?" Sarge asks as he holds his hands on his desk, I think he's trying to look intimidating, but that shit doesn't work on me.

"Was it my sparkling personality? Or my irresistible face that you missed more?" I kick back, folding my hands behind my head as I lean back.

"That 'sparkling' personality of yours is going to get you in trouble one day, Greene," he says seriously.

Peters isn't usually a joking man, but that doesn't mean I don't try.

"If it's not because you missed me, then no I don't know why I'm here."

"You haven't gone to see the psychologist about that Phillips case a couple months ago." I do appreciate the man cutting to the chase, but I can't stop the eye roll that comes from me.

"I thought that was optional."

"It is, with the other option being spending the rest of your career on the desk."

"Why? I'm fine!" I throw my arms up in frustration.

"That shit was fucked up, Greene, that's why."

"Yeah, I've seen a lot of fucked up, why is this any different?"

"Because people died, and you were there. I'm not arguing about this. Your options are seeing the psychologist to get cleared or continue to man the desk," he says so dismissively I only get more irritated.

"It's not the only death I've seen," I mutter.

"What was that?"

"I said when can I get this over with?" I lie.

"We just got a new psychologist, I set you a time on Tuesday."

"Wait, you already set me up with a time before you even talked to me about this? What if I said I would've been fine manning the desk the rest of my career?"

"I knew I could get you to go one way or another, now get out of my face. Tuesday at nine."

I clench my fists, I want to argue more, but I know it'll only lead to trouble. I shove the chair back as I stand up to leave his office.

"Close the door behind you," Peters calls out.

I ignore him as I walk back to my desk, leaving his door wide open.

Once I get back to my desk, I sink down into the chair as I feel Adams' gaze on me. The prick probably still has his smug smile on his face. I don't even look at him.

"What!" I snap.

"One day you're not going to be able to get out of half the shit you pull," he says, the hint of humor still in his voice.

Yeah, whatever. I don't even say anything to him. Though, he might be right.

I push back toward authority.

I take risks.

I can be pretty reckless.

But at the end of the day, I do my job and I do it well because I'm not afraid of anything, and I know a little bit of risk will pay off.

I'm also not afraid of authority, it's always easier to ask for forgiveness than permission. Plus, when I get my shit done there's no need to ask for forgiveness because everyone is usually congratulating me.

I don't need to talk to some psychologist about what happened two months ago. Yeah, they died. People die every day, it's not like I actually killed either of them. Sure, the whole situation was pretty fucked up, but I see fucked up shit every day on patrol. I just don't get why this is such a big deal.

Maybe, I'll be able to sweet talk my way to getting cleared after this stupid meeting. I'll paste on my winning smile that almost always gets me what I want, especially with women. God, I hope the psychologist is a woman, I should've asked. If not, this will be a bit more complicated, but I'll get it done. I'll be back on patrol by this time next week.

3

Aylin

15 Years Ago (Age Twelve)

"Aylin!" my dad screams from the living room.

I jump off my bed where I was doing homework, instantly shaking as I race out of my room. I know it'll only be worse if I don't get out there fast enough.

My dad is sitting in his recliner in front of the TV, his empty beer cans scattered all around him. He's only twenty-eight, since my parents were only sixteen when I was born, but he could be mistaken for forty with how badly he's aged.

I guess being a drunk will take its toll on you. Especially when you don't take care of yourself, or care enough to look after those you're supposed to love.

I stand by his chair, looking down at the floor because yesterday he was upset because I looked him in the eyes.

"Look at me you bitch," he spits.

I cringe as I raise my eyes to him slowly, still not speaking and refusing to look into his eyes.

"Where's your mom?"

I shake my head and shrug my shoulder.

"You a fucking mute?! I asked you a question!" he screams. I try to hide my ears against my shoulders.

"I-I don't know," I cry.

He knows I don't know where she is.

I got home from school and went right into my room to do my homework like he expects me to do every day. I can guess she's at work, if she's still managed to keep her job. It's not like either of them talk to me or tell me what's going on in their lives. They especially don't ask me what's going on in mine.

This has been my life for as long as I can remember. Dad's a drunk and mom is too. When they are both drunk, they remember they still have something in common, which is that they both enjoy making me miserable.

I hate this house.

I hate them.

I'm still crying, trying to hide my sobs from my dad as he takes one of his beer cans and throws it at my head. It makes contact against my temple. Luckily this time it's empty, but it still hurts. I also think it cut me.

The tears come faster, but I continue to be as silent as possible.

"What the fuck do you know then? Anything?" he taunts as I hold my hand against where the beer can hit me, the hot tears running down my cheeks.

I shake my head again. I want to run back to my room and lock the door, but I know it will only make him madder. All I can do is wait until he's done taking his anger out on me and hope he passes out early tonight.

"Of course you don't, you're as useless as your fucking mom, probably a fucking whore like her too." He starts to get up out of his chair.

I cringe at his words; I don't want him to get up, that usually means he's going to do more than throw something at me.

The chair screams against his weight as he pushes out of it.

One of these days it's going to snap when he sits in it, and he will probably blame me for that. Even though it is clearly because he's exceeding the weight limit on the thing.

He works part-time jobs, when he's able to keep them more than a month and the rest of the time he drinks and eats. That's it. *Oh*, and takes out his never-ending anger on me.

He finally stands up, unsteady on his feet. I take a timid step back in case he falls over, I'm pretty sure I would die if he fell on me. I'm still crying as I feel the blood from my head running down my hand.

"You're still standing here? If you get blood on the carpet, you'll be the one cleaning it until I can't see the stain anymore." He's breathing heavily just from standing up.

I take his words as my cue to go clean up in the bathroom, but apparently that's not what he wants because he grabs my upper arm tightly and swings me around. I cry out at the pain as his nails dig into my flesh.

"I didn't tell you to walk away from me!" he screams into my face; his spit hits my skin and his rancid breath takes over my senses.

"I'm sorry!" I scream as his nails continue to dig into me, and I can't hold back my sobs anymore, they are pouring out of me.

"You're not sorry about shit you little bitch."

"Please let me go." I feel like my bone is slowly snapping under his grip, and I'm trying to stay standing, but it's getting harder.

He continues to squeeze my arm until he decides to toss me onto the floor. The impact knocks all the air out of me, but at least my arm is free.

"If your mom isn't home in the next hour, you're going to cook dinner." He stomps away back to his chair. "Bring me another beer."

Slowly, I am able to get back onto my feet. My arm and head

are throbbing as I stumble into the kitchen to get him a beer from the fridge.

I really hope he doesn't throw this one at me.

I hand it to him with shaky hands. He snatches it, practically slapping it out of my hand.

I don't linger too long because that has also been something he's gotten mad at me for. I slowly walk to the bathroom, anticipating him to yell at me again, or come after me for walking away.

He doesn't.

He's done for now.

Unless my mom doesn't come home, then I know that will get taken out on me as well.

I lock the door to the bathroom as I start the shower. I examine the damage in the mirror. Luckily, it's just a little cut on my head. It's going to be hard to hide from teachers, but I can just say I ran into a door or something again. I don't think they believe me anymore, but I also don't tell them anything.

I learned early on this isn't how everyone's family is. I thought this was normal, everyone's parents get angry and hurt them. I thought maybe I would get older, and it would stop or get better, but I'm twelve now and it's only getting worse. I know I can't ask for help because help never comes.

Last time we had a social worker show up to the house they didn't do anything, and after they left, I was the target of both my parents since they assumed I told someone. I don't even remember what injury was caused by what anymore, I'm just used to hiding the cuts, bruises and burns while I survive.

Every night I dream about when I'll be able to leave and what my life will be like. I won't be like them, that's for sure.

I climb into the shower, sitting in the bathtub as the water rains down above me. I hold my knees to my chest as I focus on the warm water surrounding me and try to imagine I'm anywhere but here.

4

Present

It's finally time to leave work, and I decide to head down to the gym in the building before heading home. I need to let out some of my frustration that's just been building ever since I met with Peters because I was still stuck at my desk for the rest of the day.

First, I go into the locker room to change into some basketball shorts and a t-shirt I ripped the sleeves off because I didn't like how tight they were around my arms.

The gym is empty when I go in, most of the guys that use it opt for the morning or lunch breaks since they usually want to get home after work. I have no reason to rush home, I could spend all night here if I wanted to.

I connect my phone to the Bluetooth speaker to blast my workout playlist that is stacked with songs that push me to go harder. I start off with some cardio, sprinting on the treadmill, focusing purely on the music around me and the steady beat of my feet as they hit the tread.

After two straight miles I go to the weights, lifting, squatting and curling, switching between sets. Suddenly, my music is turned down and I slam the weights down to look up to see who thinks they can suddenly take over the space.

I'm about to yell at the intruder when I look up and see who it is. The invader is who I would consider a best friend and also one of my only friends at work. Mitch is standing by the speaker, his arms folded across his chest. I haven't seen him much since I got put on the desk since he's still on patrol like normal.

We've been friends since college, and he probably knows me the best out of everyone in my life.

"What the fuck, man?" I demand. We might be friends, but he didn't need to turn the music off.

"You tell me," he says, sternly, not moving.

"Uh, I was the one working out minding my own business."

"You're also the one still stuck on the desk after two months, the fuck did you do?"

He knows about what happened, and like everyone else around me doesn't think I'm fine, but they are all wrong because I really am fucking fine.

"You know what happened, and because I haven't gone to talk to someone apparently that makes me inept at my job." I snatch a towel and start to wipe my face.

Apparently, I'm done with my workout for tonight.

"Or maybe there's something actually wrong that everyone else sees and you don't."

"Or maybe everyone should stay the fuck out of it!" I get in his face because I am so beyond done talking about this with everyone.

"I'm not the enemy, Nate, no one here is," Mitch says calmly.

I storm past him without saying anything else as I head back to the locker room.

Normally, I would shower here before heading home, but I

don't want anyone else getting on my ass about my business. Plus, I really don't want to deal with anymore of Mitch's lecture he was getting ready to give me.

I grab my workout bag as I storm out of the building to my car. I throw my things in the trunk of my dark blue Camaro before I get in and drive away.

I live in a townhouse in Vancouver I was lucky to find. When I was looking at a house to buy, I learned quickly Portland would be out of the question, despite the money I got from my parent's life insurance it wasn't enough for a nice place in Portland. I looked around the surrounding towns, but this place in Vancouver came up, and it's nice to have the escape from the city, but just have a short drive when I need to.

Since I don't have to deal with the afternoon traffic I make it home in about twenty minutes, I park in the driveway before making my way inside.

My place isn't anything special, and since I don't know how to decorate for shit, I don't have anything on the walls, and my furniture consists of a sectional in the living room, some chairs at the island in the kitchen, a bed and dresser in my room.

I do have the TV mounted on the wall, so it's not on the floor or on boxes or anything. It's my basic bachelor pad, and that's fine with me. I never have women over here long enough for them to care about what my place looks like. When they come over it's for one thing because I do not want a relationship. I'm too focused on my job to deal with a girlfriend.

I head into my room which has an attached bathroom so I can shower since I'm sticky from the sweat from my workout.

I let the hot water wash over me while I think about what a shit day today turned out to be. I really don't want to talk to anyone about what happened. I don't think it's necessary at all, and it probably makes me look like some kind of sociopath that I'm so unaffected by the whole thing.

The guy was a piece of shit, he's lucky he killed himself

because I was about to do it for him anyway. It's a good thing I didn't, I bet that would've made everything even worse for me if I had.

I scrub myself of the memory, like I can still feel his blood on me.

I turn off the water and wrap a towel around my waist before going back into my room to grab a pair of boxers that I put on before laying down on my bed. I'm not even tired, more so just done with the day, and I know if I go to sleep then it'll be tomorrow. Which I can just hope will be a bit better.

It's not likely it'll be better since I don't think anything will be until after I talk to that shrink and convince them to clear me. Once that happens and my life is back to normal for the first time in months, I can focus on what's really important, and that's finally getting promoted.

Tuesday could not have come fast enough. I've been practically pulling my hair out every hour while I wait for this stupid appointment. Now, it's a little before nine, I'm standing in the makeshift waiting room of the therapist's office.

I don't want to sit down, so I'm just standing, looking around at the...well nothing really.

Then, the door on the back wall opens, and my gaze falls on a familiar pair of bright blue eyes. Except last time I saw those eyes they were crying in my arms at a crime scene.

Hell yeah, this is better than I could have expected. She's seen me before, I bet it will be no problem convincing her to clear me.

Plus, another positive is she's hot as shit. I can sit in a room with her for an hour, at least I'll have a good view. She's wearing a black skirt that hugs her hips, and a button up shirt that draws my attention to her chest. Damn, she's so much better looking in the light of day when she's not panicking about her friends potentially being dead.

A smile spreads across my face as she looks at me, it seems to take her a second before a flicker of recognition flashes across her eyes. She looks confused, but invites me into the room, following behind me as she closes the door.

I take in the office, noting the various seating options. I choose the couch so I can stretch out, get comfortable while I get this over with. I'm dreading this a bit less now that I know who I'll be talking to.

Too bad I won't be a returning client for her, maybe I can see her for other reasons. Or one other reason, because the way that skirt hugs her hips makes me picture how my hands would feel wrapped around them while she's bent over in front of me... *shit*. I should not get hard right now. Focus on this first, that later.

"Nathan Greene, I take it?" she says as she sits down in an armchair across from the couch. My focus purely on her legs as she crosses them in front of her.

"Call me Nate, sweetheart." I flash a smile her way.

She gives a tiny grin, but it's more of a courtesy. "Please just call me Aylin."

"Sorry about that, swee—Aylin," I correct myself quickly.

She shifts around in her seat for a second before her eyes flash up to mine and I think she finally remembers where she saw me last. I can't look away from her eyes, they are so bright blue it's almost hypnotizing.

"You're the cop from the night at the library," she says finally.

"Took you long enough to recognize me, guess I didn't make an impression." I stretch myself out on the couch, arms around the back and cross my ankle over my knee.

"No, it's not that, I was...distressed," she clears her throat, she seems nervous. That could work in my favor. "Look, I don't know if you seeing me is the best idea since you've seen me in a vulnerable state. I can talk to Susa—Dr. Tanvers about you seeing her."

My face falls, I don't want to see some other doctor, that takes out all the fun of this.

"No, it's okay I don't mind, it makes me more comfortable actually." I really don't want her to kick me out before she clears me.

She seems to think for a second, "I'm sorry, I think this crosses a bit of a boundary I'm not comfortable with."

"Aylin, look, I'll be good. I promise. I don't like that I have to be here as it is, but knowing you are a real human and not some robot helps already." I put on my best "innocent" face to try and convince her.

I'm not really lying, it does make me feel a bit better that I've seen her show emotion and be a real human, not some doctor in an office. It really does make me a bit more comfortable with her.

Her being drop dead fucking gorgeous also helps. Her long brown hair falling onto her chest, and those big blue eyes staring right at me. Is it wrong to want to fuck your therapist? She won't be for long so it's not that bad, right?

"Fine, but we won't be discussing that night at all, we will pretend that didn't happen."

"How are your friends by the way?" I push because I clearly can't help myself.

"They are fine, moving on."

I smile. She's flustered, I can see it in the slight pink tinge to her cheeks, and how she shifts in her seat again before meeting my gaze.

"So, Nate, why are you here?" she asks. Her voice is even and I'm impressed how well she keeps her composure when she is clearly uncomfortable to some extent.

"That's a loaded question, but the short version is I want to get cleared to go back on patrol pretty please." I bat my eyes at her, jokingly.

That little grin returns, and again I don't think it's because she's happy or finding this funny, but it's what she thinks she should do.

"Well then let's start at why you were taken off patrol in the first place," she states, holding her notebook in her lap, but continuing to look directly at me.

I groan, throwing my head back. "Shit went down, guy died, I'm here."

I look back up to see her writing something down.

"What are you writing?" I ask, trying my best to read her tiny handwriting.

"I'm just taking notes, if you're not comfortable with it I don't have to."

I shake my head. "No, it's fine, do what you need to do."

"So, tell me more about that."

I groan again, "Do I have to? I promise you I'm fine, Aylin."

She shrugs, "You don't have to do anything, you can talk about anything you want while you're here."

Anything? I smile again, I know I have a good smile, I'm complimented on it often, it's not like I'm extremely vain or anything, but I'm aware I'm attractive.

I slide myself to the edge of the couch, resting my elbows on my knees while I meet Aylin's gaze with my own. "If I can talk about anything then I'm going to talk about how absolutely beautiful you are."

Aylin's reaction is not the one I was going for. She doesn't give me the small smile she was before.

No, she's frowning.

And worse than that, she looks almost disgusted.

Did I forget deodorant or something this morning?

"Officer Greene, this is not an appropriate conversation to have with your therapist, and I already mentioned boundaries before. If this is going to continue, I will be more than happy to refer you to Dr. Tanvers so you don't have the temptation," her tone is serious and professional.

Honestly, I'm taken aback a bit. I thought she would respond a bit better than this. I'm annoyed now.

"Again, it's Nate. And I'm sorry, I'll be good."

"You said that before. Was that your plan? To come in here with your flashy smile, flirt with me and you would get what you want?"

I don't really want to answer because…yeah. That was my plan, but I got the hard-pressed therapist apparently.

"Okay, I'm sorry. I just don't think I need to be here, and I want to move on from this." I shake my head before settling back onto the couch.

"Tell me about why you don't think you need to be here?" She leans forward a little on her chair which makes the top of her shirt gap slightly.

I flick my eyes down to her chest for just a second, then meeting her eyes again before I answer.

"Because what happened wasn't even a big deal, I've seen people die while on patrol all the time, and I just don't see how this was any different."

"Why do you think other people see this time as being different then?"

"I don't know, because they just do, and I don't."

Aylin nods her head slightly. "Well maybe that's something to think about for next time. What makes this time different for everyone else, but not for yourself?"

"Next time?" I gape at her.

No, no, no. There's not going to be a next time. I don't *need* this.

She nods as she stands up, that small smile is back on her face. "Same time next week?"

"No, see, I was really hoping this could get figured out today so I could go back to normal."

"I know you did, but I think you should consider what makes this time different for everyone else. Why is everyone concerned for you? Then we can look at releasing you for normal duty."

I stand up, noticing again how I tower over her, I can't help but to think how easy it would be for me to throw her over my shoulder to do what I want with her. I stuff those thoughts down because I don't like what she's telling me.

"So, if I come back next week with an answer, you'll release me?" I'm looking down to her. She's meeting my gaze, not looking intimidated in the slightest.

"I said we can look into it, but you'll need an answer first. It was good to see you again, Nate, I look forward to next week." She turns toward the desk at the back of the room I barely noticed.

I stare at her for a few more moments, watching as she arranges the notebook she had, but didn't write in anymore after I asked about it. She doesn't look up at me again while she shuffles around a few papers. Finally, she looks up at me again.

"Anything else you need today?" That small smile is there.

I clench my jaw. *Yeah, I need to be fucking released to work again.*

"No. I'll see you next week," I murmur before leaving the office.

I thought this was going to be easy, but I guess Aylin is going to be yet another obstacle in my way. Unfortunately for both of us this is an obstacle I would also love to sink my dick into, but that's completely off the table, which for some reason, makes this even worse.

5

Aylin

Present

Thursday evening, I come home, and throw myself face first onto my couch because I'm exhausted. It's not even the end of my first full week of this schedule and I'm beat. I decide to call Mel because I haven't talked to her much lately.

Her and Zander moved to the coast where they are fixing up a house I have yet to see, and I know she's happier than she's ever been.

"Hey!" Mel answers after only two rings.

"Hey, how are you doing?" I always ask, I know what she's been through before, and even though I know she's in a much better place now I still feel it's important to ask.

"I'm better than ever, Newport is so perfect this time of year you have to come visit."

"I want to, but I don't want to intrude on the love fest over there."

Mel laughs, "You wouldn't be intruding on anything, we can keep it in our pants for a day or two."

"Can you?" I'm skeptical. She doesn't tell me everything, but she's told me enough. Which is more than I ever wanted to know.

"Well, we can try. I miss my best friend."

"I miss you too, this term is already kicking my ass."

"How is the new clinical going? Any hot cops?" I can feel her questioning look through the phone, looking for answers.

Mel always makes me laugh, she's a writer and always asks for stories from my clients. Also, if anyone is hot. I shoot her down every time because I'm not going to break confidentiality by talking about any of my clients. Plus, no one has been hot, but that's the last thing on my mind when I'm working anyway.

Well, it usually is.

Of course, Tuesday morning was another story when I saw Nate show up to the office. I didn't recognize him at first because the last time I saw him I was a bit distressed. Then, it hit me, and I remembered those strong muscular arms holding me up. I remembered that hard chest I cried into.

In the light of day, I got to appreciate his hazel eyes that wouldn't leave me the entire time he was in the office. I caught him checking me out a couple of times as well, even though his blatant flirting was obvious enough. He has dark brown hair that's buzzed short on the sides and a little longer on top. He towers over me, and his presence takes over any room he walks into.

And then he opened his mouth, and it's clear that he's selfish, and unapologetic about it. He doesn't know why he has to attend therapy to get cleared. He acted like whatever incident he was involved in wasn't a big deal. But it must be since they won't let him come back without a therapist's approval. That usually means there's more to the story he's not telling.

"Hello?" Mel's voice carries through the phone.

I realize I was too busy thinking about Nate, how frustratingly good looking he is. And how frustratingly off limits he is as well.

"Clinical is good, no hot cops, sorry to disappoint." I shake my head, standing up from the couch.

"Dammit, that's no fun."

I hear Zander's deep voice in the background, but I can't quite make out what he said, I can only hear Mel's muffled response, "I'm still allowed to ask."

"Trouble in paradise?" I chuckle as I make my way to my fridge because I'm just now realizing how hungry I am.

"Never, Zander just wondered why I would ask about hot cops." I can hear her eye roll from here.

Neither of them has anything to worry about with each other. I've never seen two people more in love and more perfect for each other. It gives me a slight pang of jealousy sometimes because I would love that. I don't have time for it right now, but it would still be nice.

The last boyfriend I had was when I was in undergrad and there wasn't excitement, there wasn't anything special, so we just fizzled out.

Since then, I've dated a little, but no one was ever worth keeping around, especially with how busy I am all the time. Plus, I have a hard time trusting people, or opening up to them. Guys usually get sick of how closed off I am, and I get tired of pretending. So, I haven't been on a date or slept with anyone in at least two years.

Mel and I continue to catch up on everything they are doing to the house, and her book that will release in a couple months. She doesn't let me get off the phone until I promise to make plans to visit soon. I let her know that we can talk about making plans another time, I'll come up some weekend. She's not thrilled with that answer but accepts it.

While we spoke, I continued to figure out what to have for

dinner. I settled for a sad microwave meal because I haven't gone grocery shopping recently since I never want to go out after I'm done for the day, I just want to go home. I make a mental note to make sure I go this weekend.

I decide to go to bed early, hoping that just maybe I won't be plagued by my nightmares. Just one night I would like to have a normal amount of sleep, but of course that doesn't happen.

My nightmares take over my mind ruining yet another night of sleep.

I WALK into the office to be greeted by Susan so we can go over my notes for the week. I'm curious what her thoughts are going to be about Nate.

He was the most difficult person I came across this week, everyone else recognized why they needed to be here, even if they weren't happy about it. Most of them actually come because they want to, they just want to talk about what they experience on the daily, so it doesn't weigh them down.

I pull out my notebook where I have taken all my notes while I sit down with Susan to go over everything.

"Was there anything that came up you had questions about?" she asks.

"Yeah, I wanted to talk to you about this one case where the officer is hoping to get released, but personally I don't think he's ready."

I go over the interaction I had with Nate while Susan listens. I left out the flirting part, I know that wasn't actually important to the session, he just wanted to try his luck at sweet talking me.

Once I'm done Susan provides her input. "I think you handled it perfectly and I agree with your decision. If he doesn't recognize the reason he is here, then he isn't ready. It sounds like he might be holding things back due to the trauma, and not because he's just stubborn. Though, that may be the case as well."

I can't handle the chuckle that comes out of my throat, I do think him being stubborn is a big part of it. That, and him not being able to stand that he might actually need some help.

"I was thinking if he is able to come next week with an answer as to what made this time different, I would try to get him to talk through the incident and gauge his reaction to see how to proceed," I explain so Susan can let me know if I should go about this a different way.

"I think that's good; I have a feeling this one might continue to give you a hard time the longer it takes to clear him so if you need my help, please let me know."

I nod and thank her before moving on to the rest of my notes from the week. Once I'm done Susan nods more.

"I think you are doing excellent, Aylin. This sounds like it was a promising first week for you, and I'm pleased with the responses you've gotten so far."

I shift uncomfortably. "Thank you."

I'm not sure what else to say. Could she just give me a pat on the back or something else instead of these compliments? Actually, no that's probably worse. I generally don't like physical touch unless I'm drinking.

I leave for the day, and the fact that it's the weekend gives me a sad pang in my chest because Mel isn't here anymore, and normally I would ask her to hang out. I could always go to Newport to see her, but it's a little too last minute.

It's okay, I decide I'm going to have a self-care weekend, treating myself to my favorite activities, especially while I prepare for the next week ahead since I think Susan is right about Nate. I don't think he's going to be someone that gives up and accepts help easily, which means I'm going to have my work cut out for me.

The fact that the man is the closest thing to a Greek God in person I have ever seen is also going to make me have my work cut out for me because I can't be attracted to him, not even a little bit.

6

3 Months Ago

I'm on my way to a call I received about a potential domestic violence situation. The caller informed dispatch there was yelling, and loud bangs on the walls. They also said there's a child that lives in the residence, so a social worker will be coming to the home as well.

As I pull up in my patrol car, calling this place a "home" is being generous. It's an apartment complex with about ten units I can see from here. All the front doors are facing the parking lot I'm in.

The building is two stories, with the second story having a railing that looks like it would fall off with a light push.

There's garbage and piles of stuff all around the two levels, and I really wonder how anyone can stand to live here.

I make my way to the door marked with the number four as indicated by dispatch. I knock on the dirty door. There's noise on the other side, a man says something before the door swings open, assaulting my nose with the stench of alcohol, smoke, and body odor.

"The fuck do you want?" the man says gruffly.

I keep my posture straight, meeting the man's gaze. He's at least six inches shorter than me, but probably at least fifty pounds heavier in pure fat. And I'm not a small man. I think all the stench from the apartment is coming from him.

"I'm here to check in after a call we received, are you the only resident?" I attempt to look around him to see if I can see the woman and child that also supposedly live here.

"Nothing to check in on, *officer*," he spits the last word at me as he glares at my badge.

Before I can speak again, I catch a glimpse of someone behind him, I assume she's his wife or girlfriend or whoever. She's blonde, stick thin and clearly terrified.

"Ma'am, would you mind if I speak with you?" I call over the man's shoulder.

"You don't need to speak to her."

"She can decide, or I can arrest you for failure to comply with a police officer."

"You threatenin' me, boy?" The man attempts to make himself appear larger and more intimidating which makes me want to laugh in his face. Also, him calling me boy is ridiculous considering I'm almost a thirty year old man.

"Are we going to have a problem?" I glare at the man, moving my hands over to where my handcuffs are kept, fully preparing to detain this asshole.

"I'm okay, officer," a small voice squeaks out, and I realize it's the little blonde woman.

"Ma'am, would you mind coming out here to speak with me?" I ask her, fully ignoring the man now.

She's hesitant as she looks to the man and then back at me. As she comes more into the light I see her red rimmed eyes, she has some small cuts on her face. She's wearing long sleeves, even though it's summer and I wonder if she's hiding the damage under her clothes.

The woman finally agrees to come out to talk to me, as she's walking out of the apartment the man is glowering at her, I see the anger in his eyes like he wants to grab her back to throw her in the apartment.

When she's almost out I hear a small voice yelling as a ball of blonde runs out to attach herself to the woman's leg, "Mommy!"

Shit, there really was a kid here, and there's no way she's older than five. The social worker should be here any minute.

I walk with the woman and the kid away from the apartment so the man can't hear us.

"What's your name?" I ask the woman as I take out by notebook to take notes.

"Rebecca, and this is Layla." She gestures to the little girl who is holding onto her mom's leg for dear life, staring at me.

"What's your last name, Rebecca?"

"Phillips."

"Is that man your husband? What's his name?"

She grimaces slightly at me mentioning the man, even before she tells me his name.

"Yes, he is, his name is Murphy Phillips."

I write down all their names, though I know I'll remember them anyway.

"Rebecca, can you tell me what happened today?"

"Nothing, Murphy was mad, so he raised his voice a little and the walls of these apartments are just so thin the neighbors can hear everything. I know it sounded worse than it was. Nothing happened."

I don't believe her.

She won't meet my eyes, she's shaking, and twisting her hands as she speaks. She's lying, and she's not even good at it. What's worse is she's actually defending that piece of shit; she doesn't want to get him in trouble.

"Rebecca, please, tell me what exactly happened so I can help you."

"That's what happened, please don't arrest him, he can't afford to miss any work. He's good to us."

There's no way he's good to this woman or this child.

"If you don't mind telling me how you got those cuts on your face?" I ask, gesturing to the various little scrapes along her cheek and forehead.

"Oh, my cat scratched me, it was silly."

More lies.

The social worker pulls up, and comes over to where we are, introducing herself as Grace. She tries to talk to Layla, but she's even more scared than her mom and won't answer much. Grace lets them know she needs to look around the apartment for any potential safety concerns.

I internally scoff at the whole place being a safety concern.

We walk back to the apartment together; Grace and I are in front of Rebecca and Layla as we approach Murphy again. Grace explains she needs to look around. Murphy is just as pissed talking to her as he was with me.

I continue to stand by, blocking Murphy from intervening with any of the women around because I don't see him as someone who is able to control himself, and if he were to try to hurt any of these women in front of me, he won't just be walking out of here in handcuffs. He won't be walking.

I think men who hurt women are the lowest of the low life forms. Why would you ever hurt anyone who is willing to put up with your bullshit? I'm not always the most respectful person on the planet, but I know you never put your hands on a woman unless it's for pleasure and she wants it. My mom raised me right when it comes to women.

Men who hurt children are even worse because they are so young and unable to do anything about it. I'm not a professional in the field, but I know the damage that trauma can do to a young child. It makes me fucking sick.

This is why I continue to glare at Murphy with the disgusted look on my face, practically begging him to try something in front of me. We continue this staring match while Grace interviews Rebecca and Layla a little more. She tries to ask Murphy some questions he gives one-word answers to.

I'm clenching my fists, fuming that there's not enough evidence to arrest this piece of shit. I know he's hurting Rebecca, and I can only assume he's hurting Layla too, or at the very least she's witnessing everything. In Oregon that's what is called a "measure eleven" crime which is an automatic felony with a serious minimum sentence.

Grace doesn't have enough evidence for removal, so reluctantly we both leave. I give Rebecca my card, subtly as I leave. I hate this part of my job. I feel like the system fails because I know in my gut something is wrong, but without the undisputed proof I can't do anything.

"I'm going to submit all my notes on this, our investigation will stay open while we get more information from Layla's school, and possibly some neighbors," Grace explains.

"I have a feeling this will be a place I'll be called back to," I say as I head back to my patrol car.

Grace nods in agreement before leaving as well.

I don't pull away from the complex right away. I continue to look at the door with a "four" on it. I know I'm going to be back here, that motherfucker isn't done, and neither am I.

7

Aylin

Present

The weekend went by too quickly, but I am surprisingly excited to have the busy week ahead of me. I feel like when my mind has too much idle time, it is to my detriment and then the memories I try to suppress, take over more than they already do.

It's Tuesday morning, and I know who my first client is going to be. I'm waiting to see if he will actually show up, half expecting him to refuse to come in, and continue to fight against this with the people above him.

I'm slightly surprised when I see him walk through the office door, I have to make sure my face doesn't show what I'm thinking because *dear God*. Even though it's only been a week since I last saw him, my memory didn't even give him enough credit.

His tall frame comes closer to me, his dark hair styled out of his face, the sides shaved short. His hazel eyes finding me immediately while his perfectly white teeth show the smile, he's throwing my way. His jaw lightly covered in stubble is sharp enough to cut glass. He walks with so much confidence it makes me question my own mask I put on to hide everything behind.

He doesn't wear a uniform like he's on patrol, he's in black slacks that hug his clearly muscular thighs, and a dark button up shirt that extenuates the muscles I know are underneath. The sleeves are rolled up to his elbows, showing his muscular forearms. Everything about him just screams physical strength.

"Good morning, Officer Greene," I say in my most even voice I can manage.

His eyes sweep my entire body quickly, and I'm slightly annoyed at his blatant perusal, but can't say much since I'm sure he saw me do the same as he walked in.

"Good morning, sweetheart," he greets as he makes his way into the office back to the couch he sat on last week.

I twist my face in annoyance. I asked him not to call me that last week, even if it sounds so perfect in that deep voice. *No, Aylin. Enough.*

"Please, call me Aylin only, we talked about this."

I make my way to the armchair, sitting without my notebook since he was clearly uncomfortable with me taking notes last week. It's harder for me to do my notes after sessions, but I can manage, I know this is something that happens. I didn't like when my therapist would take notes in front of me either.

"And I told you to call me Nate, so I guess we are even." He smirks as he situates on the couch, spreading his large body out comfortably.

"I apologize, Nate. How has your week been?"

"It's all good, I'll accept your apology because of how gorgeous you are looking today."

"Nate, boundaries. I will remind you that if you need to be referred to Dr. Tanvers then I will not hesitate to do so."

"Sorry, I can be overly honest, especially in the presence of beautiful women."

"Nate," I warn again. This man may look like a Greek God, the problem is he has the confidence of one as well and he needs to be taken down a couple notches.

He raises his hands in surrender with a light chuckle. "My week was fine, it would be better if I was back on patrol. Instead of being stuck at a desk."

"I'm sure. Have you thought of any reasons why you are currently on the desk?"

"Yeah, I guess so," he sighs before continuing. "There was a kid there. I was trying to restrain the guy and he killed himself. She saw the whole thing. That's why it's different."

I take a moment to process what he's saying. He didn't give too much information on what exactly happened. He was trying to restrain someone that ended up killing himself and a child witnessed it.

These are the times it's hard for me to keep my mask in place. My memories seep through the mental barrier I put in place to keep them out. Mental images of my dad screaming in my face, my mom grabbing me and throwing me across the room.

"You okay?" Nate's voice breaks through my memory fog, and I shake my head to clear it of the thoughts.

"Yes, sorry, just processing what you said. Who was the man?"

"Look, Aylin, I really am fine. I don't think I need to go into more about this, you definitely don't want to hear about it."

"I do, I have heard a lot of things. You can tell me everything."

Nate shakes his head. "And I've seen a lot worse and wasn't taken off patrol."

"You admitted this time is different to others though, so maybe talking through it and processing what happened is what you need."

"There's not much more to tell. I was dealing with this guy

for about a month before this whole thing happened and now, I'm here."

I frown at his dismissiveness. He's not fine, even though he wants everyone to believe he is. I'm the master of masks, his is cracked and isn't fooling me.

"You're here to process the incident in whatever way you need to."

He's silent for a few moments, just looking around the office. I continue to watch him, especially taking advantage of the time he's looking away from me to watch how his long arms are stretched on the couch, he looks like a male model sitting like that. It makes the office seem dingy having him sitting in here.

His eyes come back to me, as I meet his gaze, keeping my face still so I don't show how I have been silently appreciating every inch of this infuriating man.

"Do you ever get nervous being stuck in here with people you don't know?" he asks, breaking the tension the silence created.

"What do you mean?"

"Well, as I've said you're a beautiful woman and being a therapist you're alone in an office with officers who are mostly men, you don't know. And I know a lot of them can have a temper."

Trying to gain control of where this is going, I try to bring it back to him. "Would you say you have a temper?"

"Not one I'm unable to control, but I work in this field, with these men I know how they can be. Are you ever afraid of someone hurting you while you're all alone in here?"

I feel like he's trying to divert to something else to avoid talking about his incident, but this line of questioning has me on edge. Why is this where his mind is going unless it's something he's thought about or experienced in some way himself?

His voice isn't saying this in a menacing way though, his

smooth deep voice is almost soothing in the way he's questioning me out of concern.

"No, I'm not. People come here for help, so the likelihood of them hurting the person trying to help is low."

"Not everyone is coming here for help willingly though." His hazel eyes are boring into mine; I almost want to look away from the intensity of his gaze, but I stand my ground.

"What are you trying to say, Nate? Should I be afraid for some reason?"

He chuckles, "Nah, but I will say that I think you should know how to defend yourself and I'd be willing to teach you."

I narrow my eyes at him, I still don't understand his intentions right now. Is this still some way he's trying to hit on me or just distract me from asking him more questions?

"I think I'm okay, I can handle myself."

My response earns a smirk from him as he shifts his body on the couch, I wonder for a second if he's going to test me on what I said, but he just leans forward. His eyes continuing to bore into mine.

I'm normally an expert on reading people, but Nate is something else. He's outspoken and confident, but he's hiding behind that. I don't know what exactly it is yet, but that's not all there is to him.

"I don't doubt that for a second, sweetheart, but handling yourself and protecting yourself are two different things."

I glare at him again for the pet name. "I can protect myself, that's not something to concern yourself with. Now, don't you want to get cleared?"

I need to regain control of this room quickly, because I feel like it has all slipped through my fingers and landed right into Nate's glorious lap.

"You know I do, is that going to happen now that I told you what made this time different?"

He sits back again, his confidence exuding from him, but

that hint of something is still lingering, and I know there's more. I know he's not "fine".

"Briefly, but you don't appear to be processing any of it, for next time I think you should tell me how you plan to do that, especially if it's not talking to me."

He groans, "So, I'm not getting cleared today?"

I shake my head. "No, I think there's more to this, and you need a way to process it even after you're cleared."

"Fine, but can I come back tomorrow with my answer instead of next week?"

I raise my eyebrows at him, he's clearly looking for an easy way out of all of this. "I don't work here on Wednesdays."

"Then Thursday?"

"I think you should take more time than that to think about your answer and not just rush to something you think I want to hear, so you can get what you want."

"That's not what I'm doing, maybe I just want to see you more than once a week." He winks, and my mask of indifference stays firmly in place as I ignore the increase in my heart rate.

"If that's the case then we definitely have a boundary issue."

"Come on, Aylin, can I just come back Thursday?"

I roll my eyes, "Fine, I only have my last spot of the day which is at five."

A smile spreads on that frustratingly beautiful face of his. "It's a date."

"Absolutely not. It's an appointment," I say sternly. I let too many of his flirts slide while he's here because I know it's innocent, but I genuinely don't want to be knowingly crossing any boundaries with this man.

"Right, an appointment, see you then Aylin."

We stand up at the same time, and I'm reminded of his towering height as he makes his way to the door, and I close it behind him, finally letting my mask fall and I feel like I can take a deep breath for the first time since he walked in here.

I make my way back to the desk to write down my notes from the session and put the impromptu next session this Thursday on my calendar. I write down the notes about the little bit he shared, again leaving out the flirting, but my mind is brought back to his concern about me protecting myself.

I can't help but think there's a reason for that. I'm not sure if it's because he's hinting, I should be afraid of him or if something happened in his past to make him concerned for me, and I have a feeling there's more that he may be hiding.

8

Present

I leave Aylin's office frustrated that she, yet again, didn't clear me and is having me come back again. I'm glad she's letting me come back on Thursday instead of waiting a whole week, but I need to know what it's going to take to just get this fucking over with already.

I know flirting won't work, since it hasn't yet and honestly, I might just be doing it to gauge her reaction at this point.

Distracting her doesn't work either, it seems like she actually wants me to work through my shit. But I don't know what shit she wants me to work through since I'm fine!

Once I'm to my desk, that I despise, I sink down into the chair that has become more familiar with my ass in the last two months than it has in the last seven years I've worked here.

I can't get Aylin out of my head, I was stupid to bring up anyone trying to hurt her when they go to see her, I don't know anyone who works here that would do that. I just couldn't stop my mind from wandering about how vulnerable she is there by herself with who knows who. I know what can happen when just one person loses their shit and doesn't care who they hurt.

I've seen it too much on patrol, and then my parents were in a vulnerable spot and it left them defenseless.

There's something about her that I can see, she is strong. She's got that attitude about her, but I think it's more of a mental strength. I don't know how she would fare if someone tried to physically hurt her.

I don't know why that bothers me so much, I was serious when I said I would teach her how to defend herself. If only for my own peace of mind.

Adams looks over at me, and I'm refusing to look at him, but he feigns a cough to get my attention.

"Has anyone ever told you how annoying you are?" I ask him, still not looking over at his desk.

"Yeah, you, every day," he laughs like it's a joke.

I'm not joking. He's fucking annoying.

"Making sure you get the message." I turn my computer on to continue going through stupid files.

"Did you have another meeting with the therapist this morning? I heard it's some new chick and that she's pretty hot."

I clench my jaw and refuse to respond. I don't know why that unnerves me that clearly people are talking about Aylin around here.

"Is she hot?" he asks again.

"Adams, do yourself a favor and shut the fuck up," I snap. Something about his nails on a chalkboard voice is extra irritating this morning.

Luckily, he does shut up for a good two minutes before deciding to speak again. This time it's something I actually want to hear.

"Peters is giving a briefing on a new case connected to that one you helped bust, what was it four months ago? The drug case."

I shoot up out of my chair. "Why didn't you start with that, idiot? Where?"

He hesitates for a second before answering, "The big conference room on the third floor."

I don't even say anything as I rush to the elevator. I'm fuming. I get that I'm on the desk, but why wouldn't Peters tell me about this when it's connected to my bust.

Four months ago, a guy came in to make a report about known drug dealing, which wouldn't usually be a huge deal, it's Portland, it's all around us. He said he thought there was more involved than that and he was right.

Guy's name was Zander Wells and he had to negotiate some immunity since he was involved in some of the lower-level stuff of the operation like dealing for his stepbrother. His stepbrother, Trent Moore is quite the guy. He was able to get out of some of the early drug charges we had on him, but when he tried to burn down a building with Zander and his girlfriend Mel inside, he wasn't as lucky to get those charges dropped.

We learned later Trent was involving himself with some local gangs, trying to monopolize the market a bit and it's only the tip of the iceberg of the big picture around here. He wouldn't tell us much, as his lawyer instructed. I know there's more dealings going on around here involving gangs and I have a feeling this is what the briefing is about.

I sneak into the conference room, trying to remain unseen as I hear Peters talking to the room full of officers. I sink down into a chair in the back, lowering myself to not seem obvious.

"We need guys on the ground to find out what's really going on. It's going to be tough; these guys don't take to new people well. This is going to be a long-term assignment, and we need multiple officers going in so we can put an end to this."

I know I came in on the tail end of this, but I know what he's talking about. The gangs around here are building up their power and control. They were focusing on drugs, which is where Trent comes in, but it's becoming more than that. We hear they are going into human trafficking, and possibly even starting businesses that seem legit to hide all their various dealings. Plus, it makes it easier to launder money that looks legit to hide the less legit income they make.

They want to send officers in undercover to find out the full extent of what's going on. I know we have a couple already in, but clearly, they need more which means this is even bigger than I knew about.

Peters dismisses everyone, but I linger back as I wait for everyone to leave.

"I saw you come in," Sarge says without even looking at me.

I sit up in the chair, looking around to make sure he was talking to me.

"Greene, you're built like a fucking building, you can't be sneaky."

"Damn, I guess I should cross off 'secret agent' or 'super spy' from my life goals list then."

I thought maybe that would earn me some sort of reaction from the man with no sense of humor, but as usual it does nothing to break his steel exterior or wipe the scowl off his face.

"There was a reason you weren't informed of this briefing," Peters says sternly.

"What was that reason? Because I was the one who got the bust connected to this?"

"Because you're not ready to take something like this on."

"Yes, I am, Sarge! I was ready for a promotion to detective months ago after the bust and you know that."

I will admit that arguing with your sergeant is not usually the best idea. Though, I'm full of bad ideas today apparently if my conversation with Aylin earlier is any example.

"No, you're not, Greene. Work with the therapist. Get cleared. Then we can talk about it."

"If I get cleared, you'll put me on this case?" I'm hopeful.

"If you get cleared, we will talk."

I'm less hopeful.

"Sarge, come on, we wouldn't even have some of the info we have if it weren't for me with that Moore case," I'm essentially pleading, and this is not my finest moment.

"It was a good bust, I've told you before, but now you have other shit to deal with before jumping into something like this. It isn't just working with an informant; this is full undercover. No direct backup, and no fuck ups."

"I wouldn't have any fuck ups; I could do this, and you know it."

"Get cleared, Greene."

Sergeant Peters walks out of the room, leaving me alone, and annoyed beyond belief.

I need to get Aylin to clear me on Thursday, this is just ridiculous, and as a cherry on top, maybe if I'm not forced to see her anymore, I can see her for fun, on my terms.

9

Aylin

Present

Thursday comes too quickly. Yesterday was my busiest day as a TA for an undergrad psych class, and my advising, then thesis seminar. I spent the rest of the day working on assignments and my thesis.

I stayed up way too late working on my thesis, by the time I looked at the clock it was past midnight. I cursed myself for losing track of time, and then struggled to go to sleep as usual.

Now, I'm heading to my clinical running off of caffeine from my black coffee and my pure will to get through the day.

I didn't get ready as much as I normally would on clinical days since I opted for the extra twenty minutes of sleep instead.

I'm wearing black slacks, a simple white blouse that probably brings a little too much attention to my chest than I would prefer in a professional setting. I'm wearing simple black flats. My long brown hair is wavy around my shoulders, slightly unkempt and I'm hoping no one questions my professionalism.

I get self-conscious at times if I don't present exactly how I want to, and I feel like the teenage girl in ripped clothes hiding bruises again. That girl didn't know how to appear confident or how to make people see what she wanted them to see.

That girl hid.

I don't hide anymore.

I just show people what I want them to see.

My scars on my arms have faded enough that I can wear anything I want comfortably. Years of therapy, and distance has helped the pain behind the scars fade enough that I can forget about that time of my life for a while. At least until I go to sleep. That's when the memories never fade because my nightmares make sure I always remember.

My day continues uneventfully while I see clients throughout the day. All of the officers are nice to me, they understand why they come to see me, a lot of them by choice.

Then, my last appointment comes around and it's Nate. The one who does not understand why he's here and is definitely not here by choice.

I feel my heart racing in anticipation for him to walk through the door, and I don't know why. Everything is strictly professional despite his constant flirting. I don't think he is flirting because he's attracted to me or anything. I think he's doing it to get what he wants, and it won't work.

Nate enters the office and I can't help but be confused at his appearance. He's not wearing his usual uniform of slacks and button down. He's in gym shorts and a t-shirt. His short hair is wet, and the exposed skin on her arms is glistening, I'm unsure if it's with sweat or water. But I can't help noticing the size of his exposed muscled arms.

I could tell he was muscular under his usual clothes but, *wow*. Nate is huge. Pure muscle, everywhere. His t-shirt hugs his chest and strains against his biceps. It's taking extra effort for me to keep myself collected like I usually do because I don't think I've ever been face-to-face with a man I'm so attracted to.

It's like I'm physically pulled to him, and I can't pretend he's not the most handsome man I've ever laid eyes on. The dampness of his hair makes his locks appear even darker, and makes his hazel eyes more prominent against his tan skin

I shake my head, trying to physically shake all the lustful thoughts from my mind as he steps inside the office taking a seat on the couch as he always has. I take the time to regain my composure as I sit on the armchair, feeling like my skin is burning and my clothes are too tight like I can't breathe. I have never felt this way in the presence of anyone before.

What is wrong with me?

I situate myself, trying my hardest to keep a straight face, and to not seem affected. I feel like Nate can see something is off with me, or his natural confidence is causing the smirk on his face that brings me back to reality.

He's hot. There's lots of hot people in the world, but he's off limits and kind of an arrogant ass. I can handle this just fine.

"May I ask why you're wet?" I ask finally.

He smirks like he's thinking about a dirty joke to go along with my question.

"I went to the gym for a little before coming here and took a shower so I wouldn't kill you with my sweat smell."

I can't imagine he could ever smell bad, dammit Aylin, seriously knock it off. This isn't who I am.

"Is that a way you feel you can process difficult situations?" I ask, setting my mind right and remembering where we are and who we are.

"Working out or showering?" A smile pulls at his lips.

"Either one," I say honestly. "Processing things is individual to everyone; it's how you choose to handle it."

"Then, I guess both. Working out I guess I process anger and frustration, then I shower, and it calms me."

His answer surprises me. I feel like this is the first genuine answer I've gotten from him since he first stepped foot in here over a week ago.

"Were you angry or frustrated today when you went to work out?"

"Not really, I also just like to work out." He shrugs, and it feels like that one genuine answer I got is going to be it because he seems closed off again.

"Tell me about other ways you process difficult situations." I'm trying to get that openness back. I want it back and not even just because it's my job.

"I have lots of ways to process, sweetheart, but I don't think you want to hear about them." That cockiness is back, and I know I've lost the open honest Nate yet again.

"Nate, please, boundaries," I shake my head at him.

"Yeah, yeah, I know which is why you don't want to hear about my other ways to process. I'm pretty sure it would cross some boundaries."

My interest is piqued, ashamedly, because I want to know, possibly not at a professional level interest.

"How is that?" I keep my voice even, keeping my mask in place, though my confidence is wavering each second I'm confined in this space that is more than big enough, but I feel suffocated by his presence for some reason.

"Because it's probably not all appropriate to share, though I'd be more than willing to show you," he winks at me.

"Nate, I think this is too far. I think you need to see Dr. Tanvers." I don't like the thought of "giving up", but it's not even for him. It's for myself.

I can't continue on like this.

"No, Aylin, I just..." He throws his head back and groans in frustration. "Look, I'm going to be honest, there's a new case I learned about that I really want. It's everything I have been working toward and I need to be cleared before I can be put on it. I need this, and I know you want better answers from me. I know you expect me to have a big revelation about something, but it's not going to happen. I'm okay, I'm over what happened and I'm ready to move on. Please, Aylin, I'm not sorry for flirting with you because you're gorgeous and I can't help it, but I need to be put back on patrol."

I'm silent, unsure of what to say to his confession.

My head spins for a second while I take in everything he said.

He's being honest, I can tell, and he's desperate. I can tell that too. Nate doesn't seem like a guy that says "please" often, and he's practically begging.

I also can't help but fight the blush that rises at his admittance of flirting with me because as much as I want to believe he's doing it for his own benefit, I think he's being honest about that too. Even though it's wrong and will go nowhere.

"I understand how important this is to you, and I want to help," I say honestly.

"Then help me, Aylin, I need this."

"Look, I need to talk to Dr. Tanvers because she gets the final say in clearing you. I meet with her tomorrow. Just know that you do need to process things in life, even when it's hard and when it sucks you can't hold everything in and tell everyone you're fine. At some point it will explode because no one can stay strong all the time."

I tell him this, knowing full well what it feels like to explode, and knowing what it's like to try and stay strong all the time. It doesn't happen. No matter how strong Nate appears to be, we all have weaknesses.

"We can talk more about it Tuesday, if Dr. Tanvers signs off on it," I say, watching his face begin to flood with relief until I say Tuesday.

"How about you tell me tomorrow?" He's impatient.

"I don't see clients on Fridays."

"Just come to my desk to tell me, God knows I'm stuck there all day every day. I don't want to go through the weekend waiting."

I think for a second, I know this is stupid. I know this is a bad idea. I'm full of those in the presence of Nate, and I don't know why I can't reign myself in.

Somehow, I find myself agreeing to telling him tomorrow.

He smiles so wide it practically knocks me over, his perfectly straight, white teeth against his tan skin with genuine happiness. I'm a little weak at his reaction, and nervous that this still might not turn out the way he hopes.

I'm also slightly unnerved thinking I'm making a mistake because no matter what he says, there's something within him that I recognize in myself. I see that he's not fine, not fully. He's just good at hiding it.

It's hard to hide these things from someone who's become a professional at hiding herself.

10

Present

It's Friday, and I'm sitting at my desk waiting for Aylin to come tell me either good or bad news. I can't stop my leg from bouncing, and I'm staring at my computer screen, but not comprehending anything I'm looking at because my mind is not here. My mind is wondering what Aylin is going to tell me.

I told her where my desk was before I left on Thursday, and I told her if all else fails she can ask the front reception on the first floor, but I can see her being determined to find me herself. Or not at all because there's still the slight chance, she won't come find me and will make me wait until Tuesday anyway.

"What's your deal today?" Adams asks, leaning over toward my desk.

I barely hear him, and still, I choose to ignore him.

"Dude, you good?" he asks again.

"What? I'm fine, can you fuck off?" I snap at him.

"Did your therapist crush turn you down again?" he jokes.

I scowl at him, "I don't have a crush on her. There's nothing going on, I'm just wanting her to clear me so I can get the fuck away from you again."

Adams chuckles to himself, and I don't understand how or why this idiot seems to get off on antagonizing me.

More time passes that I'm just staring at the computer screen, and after what I think is an hour, I'm starting to really think Aylin won't come talk to me today. Maybe she will make me wait until Tuesday. *Why the fuck...*

"Is that her?" Adams shrill voice cuts into my thoughts as I look up to see who he's talking about.

Sure as shit, Aylin is walking toward my desk. Her long brown hair is flowing behind her as she walks. She's wearing jeans and a shirt that hugs her curves under a loose sweater looking thing. I stand up at the sight of her, and fuck if she doesn't look hotter now as she's walking straight toward me.

That small smile she does is on her lips, but I've learned that doesn't mean much, because she can look like that while telling me bad news.

"Hey sweetheart," I greet her. The small smile fades at my little nickname for her. I like it because I like getting a reaction from her.

"Officer Greene, I hope I'm not interrupting anything important," she says sternly, looking between me and my, now blank, computer screen.

"Not at all, I'll always make time for you," I wink at her. I can feel Adams watching the whole interaction, but I don't give a shit.

"I suppose that won't be necessary because I spoke to Dr. Tanvers who agreed to support the decision that you are clear to return to normal duty."

I barely heard what she said outside of "agreed" and "return to normal duty". Without thinking I reach out, grabbing her around the waist, pulling her toward me, picking her up and spinning her around in my arms.

"Thank you!" I beam while holding her body tightly to mine.

I barely realize I'm holding her until I feel how stiff she is in my arms. I set her down, and she's looking at me with a flushed face and wide eyes.

"I'm just excited." I reluctantly let go of her, possibly letting my hands linger on her waist a second longer than I should have.

She's staring at me in shock, and it takes a second before she regains her normal composure and says anything.

"It's okay, glad I could give you the good news. Good luck, Nate," she says before turning around and walking away quickly.

I watch as she walks away, unable to pull my eyes up from her. I also can't help but realize how good those couple seconds of her in my arms felt. She felt perfect pressed against my chest, and how it felt to have my arms around her...*What am I doing?*

I got exactly what I wanted; I don't have to continue to go to therapy. I get to go back to normal, maybe I can even get on that case.

So, why does the thought of not seeing Aylin again bother me?

"That was hard to watch," Adams voice says once Aylin is out of view.

"That was good news." I refuse to look at him as I sit back down again, ready to actually work on the paperwork I know Peters will make me finish before releasing me anyway.

"The part after the good news was painful."

"Whatever."

For the first time today, I actually do some work because I have a reason to. I want to run to Sarge's office to tell him the news and tell him I'm ready to be back on patrol on Monday, and to do whatever it takes to get on that case, but I guess he's off work today.

I decide in light of the good news I'm going to go out and celebrate tonight. It's been too long since I did anything really, and it is damn time I move past this depressing shit I've had to deal with the last two months.

Plus, the thought of Aylin is not leaving my brain, and I know I need to find a way to get her the fuck out of it. She is off limits and has made it clear she isn't interested, so I need to find someone that is.

I decide to text Mitch because there's no point in celebrating alone, and I know he will want to know about the news.

        Nate: Got good news, you up for some celebrating?

Mitch: You decide to be a monk, so I don't have to listen to you anymore?

        Nate: Ha ha. You in or not?

Mitch: Sure, I'm off at 1800.

I'm off a couple hours before him since being stuck on the desk has different shifts. I decide I'm going to work out after, then I can meet Mitch at the local sports bar for a little. Once I have had a couple beers, I might want to go somewhere else, especially if I might want to take someone home at the end of the night.

I'M WAITING at the bar for Mitch to show up. After work I worked out until I was covered in sweat, then took a shower before coming over here.

Mitch let me know he would be on his way soon, I got myself a beer and there's a college football game on the TV screens, but I'm barely paying attention since I don't give a shit about the teams playing.

A feel someone brush against my arm as she leans across the bar, trying to get the bartenders attention. I look over to see long brown hair. My heart speeds up for a second, but quickly realize this brown is much darker than Aylin's, and this woman is not as curvy as her. I take a long pull from my beer.

"This spot taken?" the woman asks, looking over at me.

"Nope," I say simply as I pretend to look at the game.

"You here alone?" She bats her extra-long eyelashes at me. I can't help but notice her eyes are not blue. She has more makeup on than Aylin ever wears.

I can't believe how picky I'm being right now. Normally, any good-looking woman shows interest in me I show interest right back, but right now all I can think about is how this girl would look next to Aylin and there's no comparison.

"Just waiting on my friend," I say simply, taking another big gulp of my beer, when I notice it's empty. I turn to order another one.

"Friend or girlfriend?" She flirts, and I offer her a small smile.

I don't know why I say what I do, I'm telling myself it's because I'm just not interested in this girl, but maybe I'm also losing my mind.

"Friend, my girlfriend is at home."

With that she takes her drink and walks away. She wasn't really my type, so I didn't want to entertain anyone that wouldn't keep my attention anyway. Plus, I still need to tell Mitch the good news, and I can't do that if some girl I'm not even interested in is hanging on my arm all night.

I get another drink when I notice Mitch walking in. I give him a nod as he comes over to my side at the bar, ordering his own beer.

"You going to tell me what we are celebrating?" he asks.

"The therapist cleared me, I can go back to normal duty." I raise my drink for a second before taking a sip.

"Congrats, man, you start Monday?"

"Not sure, Sarge wasn't in today, but I plan to ask him to put me on that big case he had a briefing about this week."

Mitch looks at me skeptically, and I don't like it.

"What?" I question.

"You think you're ready for something like that?" he asks, and I thought the look he was giving me might have been because he didn't know about the case.

"Of course I do, why not?"

"I just thought you'd want to take more time, ease back into reality first," he shrugs.

"You don't think I can do it," I narrow my eyes at him.

"That's not true, I know you can do it. I just don't know if you should."

I down the rest of my beer in one long swig, I can't believe he's saying this shit to me. I do not understand everyone's issue with me right now. A guy kills himself while you're fighting him and suddenly everyone is worried about you.

"I'm glad it's not up to you then," I say as I set down the empty bottle on the bar.

Suddenly, I'm not in the mood to do any sort of celebrating. My one closest friend doesn't believe I should do what I can to help further my career. I can't even pretend to be interested in a woman practically throwing herself at me.

Why?

Because for some reason the image of my fucking therapist flashes in my mind.

"I'm over this, see ya." I push away from the bar to head to the door.

"Come on, Nate, you're being stupid," Mitch calls after me.

"Whatever," I mutter to myself as I walk out the front door.

Since I only had two beers, I feel fine enough to drive home, which takes a little longer with the Friday night traffic, but eventually I pull up to my townhouse.

I'm annoyed at Mitch, and at everyone. I'm also annoyed at myself because all my excitement from earlier is gone, and I'm just full of frustration I have no way to release.

I should've just sucked it up and given that girl some time, that would've at least given me a release. A kind of release that I desperately need, it's been too long since I've had sex with anyone. I don't know what's wrong with me, this is never an issue for me normally.

I decide to go through my phone contacts to see if any of my past hookups are free tonight. I scroll through the contacts, and I go through the names, none of them interest me. Too clingy, too lazy in bed, tries to talk too much. I'm finding a flaw with everyone. No one seems worth calling and I feel like I must be losing my mind.

That's it, it's all the built-up stress or something. This has nothing to do with Aylin or the fact that I can't forget how she felt in my arms, or how she felt walking away. Or how her blue eyes stare right at me when I'm talking.

Why the fuck am I hard just thinking about her? There's nothing there, and there never will be. I need to get the fuck over it.

THE REST of the weekend went by uneventfully while I continued to be mad about what happened on Friday. Mitch tried reaching out to say he was sorry, and that's not what he meant.

I'm over it. I'm over all of it.

I'm walking into work Monday morning ready to get put on this case.

First thing I do as soon as I walk into the building is go to Sarge's office.

He's scowling when he sees me walk into his office, but I don't even let that stop me, not that it ever has before.

"Good morning, Sarge, how was your weekend?" I greet cheerfully, which results in him scowling at me harder, questioning me.

"Greene, what is it now?"

"Did you hear the therapist cleared me?" I grin widely.

"I saw an email from the psychologist, yes."

"So…. can I get on that case?" I smile wider.

He scowls deeper, "Greene, you haven't even started back on patrol yet and you're hounding me about this?"

"Yeah, I don't want to just go back on patrol, you know I want this."

He sighs deeply, "Look, this shit is serious. We have at least two weeks of prep for anyone going into this. This isn't something you get to give up when you get bored."

"I know that. I just want a chance to prove myself."

"Fucking hell, Greene," he shakes his head. "You can join the prep briefings and get yourself familiar with the case and with everything you would be doing. You'll be deep undercover you get that? Identity, where you live, who you associate with, all of it. This will be your life."

"I know, you won't regret this."

I stand up, I can't control my excitement. I can handle this. This is going to be my big break.

"Don't make me regret it. First briefing is today at 1400."

I leave his office without even attempting another joke, because I don't want to run the risk of him changing his mind.

Reluctantly, I go back to my desk where I don't want to be but knowing everything is about to change for the better makes it a bit more tolerable to hear Adams' annoying ass voice.

The one thing I still can't get out of my mind is Aylin. I

couldn't stop thinking about her all weekend, and I came up with a plan. Probably the stupidest plan ever to exist, but clearly, I need to satisfy some part of my curiosity so I can move on because I'm not able to do that with just thinking about her.

I decide to look up in our database of all the employees to see if I can find any contact information for her. We have everyone's name and contact information, including their email and phone number.

Luckily, she has a unique name and there's only one Aylin here because I didn't know her last name. Aylin Porter pops up. I see a phone number, I'm not completely sure if it's the number for the psych office or her personal cell, but I decide to try it anyway, and if this fails, I'll just send her an email.

"Still can't get over the hot therapist, huh?" Adams says over my shoulder.

I shove him back. "You seriously need a fucking life."

He just chuckles.

I ignore him as I pull out my phone to save Aylin's possible number in it. I won't text her now, I'll wait.

Maybe I won't text her at all, maybe I can forget about her I just need to focus on this new case, that will take away these fucking obsessive thoughts.

Yeah, I'm just saving it just in case. I'm not actually going to text her.

11

Aylin

Present

What the hell am I looking at? I'd been working on my thesis when I heard my phone ping, signaling I had a text. I assumed it was Mel, but when I actually looked, I can't believe what I see.

> Unknown: Hey, I hope this number is Aylin.
> This is Nate.

How did he get my number? I didn't give it to him, no one has it except Susan, and I know she wouldn't give it to anyone.

I'm curious to know what he wants, but this is so not appropriate. I should ignore this and block his number; I know I should. At the same time, I can't help my curiosity to know what he wants.

Maybe he just has a question. Maybe he just wants to thank me? No, that would be inappropriate, he already thanked me.

Actually, all of this is inappropriate, there's no universe

where this is appropriate at all. I know this, and I know that I'm a professional.

And yet I hate to admit that curiosity is getting the better of me. Mostly on how he got my number in the first place. Then, *why?*

I continue to stare at the text on my phone debating what I should do. Well, I know what I should do, but what I decide to do might differ from that.

And it does.

Because curiosity wins.

> Aylin: How did you get my number?

I'm shocked at how quickly he replies, almost like he was waiting by his phone for my reply.

> Nate: Perk of being a cop?

> Aylin: That seems like a blatant misuse of power, and not to mention *boundaries*.

> Nate: It's not really a blatant misuse of power when anyone in the agency can see it.

Of course, I forgot about the database that holds all employees contact information. I still stand by that's a stupid idea to have in the first place.

> Aylin: This is still crossing a serious boundary. I think we should both forget this happened.

> Nate: No can do, I have a reason for reaching out.

Oh no.

> Aylin: What?

> Nate: I just want one date with you.

Whoa.

No.

This has surpassed the line so far, I can't even see it anymore. This is beyond wrong, and what's worse is he knows it because I have tried telling him. I think his confidence is too far gone to accept that it's a no, and he's too stubborn to see why.

> Aylin: Absolutely not. Delete this number. Goodbye.

> Nate: Fine, not a date then. Let me help you with self-defense just once and if you hate it, we will never speak again.

What is with his concern about me defending myself? He doesn't know the shit I dealt with growing up, he doesn't know how capable I am. So, why is he so insistent on this?

I know I need to say no.

I know this is wrong.

I know all of these things.

But I decide I'm going to call Mel for advice, which is not something I do often. Usually, it's the other way around. I may possibly be looking for an excuse, and someone to be the devil on my shoulder because that is certainly Mel.

She answers her phone quickly, "Hey best friend!"

"Hey, so um…I want your input on something."

"Me? What did I do to deserve such an honor from you?" she jokes.

"You are always a bit more…outspoken than me, so I want that Mel."

"Should I be offended?"

"I don't think being outspoken is a bad thing," I shrug.

It's true, it's not. She always says what she's feeling and doesn't hold back. I've actually always respected her for that.

"Fair enough, give it to me."

"Okay, well, there's a cop from work that's been...persistent and I'm not sure what to do." I brace for judgment, but I know it won't happen, not from her.

"Is he hot?"

I chuckle, "Objectively, yeah he's good looking."

Like a male freaking model good looking.

"Well, what has he been persistent about and how?" She's taking this more seriously than I thought she would, though there's still her usual chipper in her voice.

"He's been flirty, and he just texted me asking for a date, which I turned down, so then he said he just wants to teach me self-defense which he brought up before like he has some weird worry about me needing to defend myself," I'm rambling.

Mel is quiet for a few seconds before she says, "Honestly that's really hot."

"It's weird!"

"He's concerned for you, and maybe he wants to show off how strong he is and how he can handle you, know what I'm saying?"

I can just picture her giving me the side eye, her green eyes narrowed in on me while her sexual innuendo is written all over her face. I can't help but laugh at the visual. I miss her.

"You think that's why? Not because he has some plan to come after me and wants to at least pretend it's a fair fight?"

"Your thoughts are morbid; I've rubbed off on you too much."

"It's a bad idea though, it's wrong and it's inappropriate," I insist, trying to get her to at least see my side of thinking.

"You're right it is— "

"Thank you!"

"I wasn't done. I was going to say you're right, it is, but I think you should take a chance and see him once."

I groan. "Who's side are you on?"

"Yours, always, which is why I'm saying to do it."

"Melody James!" I use her full name that I know she doesn't like.

"Dr. Porter!" she mocks. "Do it. I mean it. What's his name anyway?"

"Nate Greene," I say, shrugging since it doesn't matter, she likely wants to Google him or something.

"Wait what? Hold on."

I hear muffled noises but can't make out exactly what is being said until she comes back to the phone.

"I had to double check with Zander, but you know that's the cop that helped him out with the Trent shit, right?" she asks.

"Yeah, well, not really. I knew he was there that night, but that's it. Does that change your opinion?" I'm hopeful.

"Nope, Zander said he seemed like a cool guy so I'm actually more validated now."

Dammit.

"You're not helpful," I sigh.

"You love me anyway. Say yes and tell me everything." I can hear her smile through the phone.

"Goodbye," I shake my head.

"Bye!"

We hang up the phone. I look at the text exchange with Nate again, taking a few moments before I respond. This is going to be completely platonic. This won't go anywhere.

Yes, he's hot.

Yes, when he surprised me with that hug at his office, I liked the feeling of his strong arms around me.

Yes, it felt good how he held me with such ease, and comfort.

Yes, he smelled good, like fresh laundry with a natural

musk that made me want to bury my nose in his neck, and his chest, and his...*nope*. Not going there.

> Aylin: Fine. When and where?

> Nate: Tomorrow? Meet me at my desk around 1600?

I do some math to figure out the time, which is four when I guess he's off work. I don't love the idea of meeting there where anyone can see, but I guess no one really knows who I am. Plus, it's not a date. I feel like I need to make that extremely clear.

> Aylin: Fine, but this isn't a date.

> Nate: Nope, not a date.

There's no way this is going to go well for either of us.

12

13 Years Ago (Age Fourteen)

It's my first day of high school, and I'm more nervous than I usually am. I would say it's because it's my first day at a much bigger school with a lot more kids that I don't know. But I know that's not the only reason.

I'm standing in front of the mirror in the only bathroom at my house while my parents are still passed out in their room. They never wake up early enough to see me go to school, not even when they have a job that requires them to get up before noon. Which is why neither of them keep one for long.

I stare at myself in the dirty mirror, I'm wearing a camisole and shorts I slept in, which shows the bruises, cuts and burns on my skin.

Some are fresh, a lot of them are old. All of them are impossible to hide with makeup.

I fight the tears burning my eyes as I stare at myself, and all the scars adorning my body, knowing I'll have to wear long sleeves and jeans like always even though it's going to be so hot today I'll be sweating like crazy.

I refuse to let the tears fall, I cry enough when the pain is inflicted, I can't let the scars and bruises hurt me a second time. That's exactly what they would want, and if I can have control of anything in my life, I know it's going to be my resilience.

I always work hard in school because I know that's going to be my way out.

Luckily, I'm naturally smart which helps me latch onto all the information in my classes. Math, English, Science, Social Studies it all sticks fairly easily. I do my homework, even when it's hard to finish and I'm fighting sleep because I need the grades to get a scholarship to college far away from here.

Pulling myself away from the mirror after I brush my teeth and swipe a brush through my hair quickly, I go back to my room to get dressed. I don't have many clothes, it's not like my parents buy me anything. Most of my things were my mom's that she throws to me whenever I get enough courage to ask for clothes.

Of course, when this happens it isn't as simple as, "here's some clothes now get out of my face."

It usually comes with verbal lashings such as, "What happened to all your other clothes? Did you leave them somewhere or with someone ripped up when you decided to whore yourself out? Go get some yourself, you useless bitch."

Then, the few pairs of whatever gets thrown at me is whipped at me roughly until I shed a tear, sometimes begging her to stop, which only earns me a slap in the face, or a cigarette butt on my skin.

I don't know why they say the things they do to me. I'm not a whore. I've never kissed a boy. I've never had a boyfriend. I don't even have friends. I stick to myself so no one can see what really goes on in my life. I'm a wallflower, and I don't get close to anyone because I know that the people closest to you will hurt you the most.

My parents haven't taught me much in life, except that one lesson.

I used to think I loved them. A kid always loves their parents, and I just thought that was how you love. They hurt each other and they hurt me, and that's just a part of love.

As I'm getting older, I realize that's not true. That's not love. And I don't think they ever loved me.

I've never met any of my other family since my parents had me so young their families disowned them and never met me as far as I know.

I'm alone in this world.

I'm determined to get out, and not make the same mistakes they did.

I'm going to make something of myself, if only to prove them wrong that I'm not useless, I'm not worthless.

I get dressed in the tattered, old long sleeve green t-shirt and jeans that are too big they are practically falling off my waist, but I don't have a belt to keep them up. My shoes are tennis shoes that are stained and ripped the laces that are more frayed than they are solid.

I don't care how I look. I don't care what people think about me. I don't care.

Throwing my backpack over my shoulder I quietly leave the apartment, so my parents don't wake up from a door shutting or something. I'm pretty sure I have a burn on my thigh from that.

The bus doesn't have a stop by me, so I have to walk to school, not that it's far, maybe about a mile. Even though it's early the sun is already heating my skin through my baggy clothes, making me sweat.

I pull my hair up into a ponytail to help fight the heat, though it doesn't do much, and by the time I make it to school I'm drenched. I debate going to the school gym to shower in the locker room, but I have PE a little later in the day and decide I will do it then.

My first couple classes fly by as I throw myself into what the teacher says, even though it's the first day a lot of the information is about what we will be learning, and the rules and information about the new school since all my classes are with other freshmen, most of which are just as lost as I am in this foreign place.

By my third class of the day, I'm sweltering in my clothes as I have hardly had a chance to cool down from my walk here, and it's only getting hotter.

Absentmindedly, I roll my sleeves up while I write in my notebook as the teacher is talking about the project we will be starting next week that will count as a midterm instead of a test.

The teacher is walking up and down the aisle of desks when he stops at my desk, pausing to glance at my now exposed arms. He continues speaking, but I look up to see that he's still right next to me. I glance at my arms to see what he's looking at. Fresh bruises, clearly resembling fingers and some faded burn scars.

Quickly, I roll my sleeves down as he continues to walk down the aisle of desks. I'm usually careful to not let teachers see my skin. In my fourteen years I think we've had social workers come over three times. None of the visits did anything but make my parents hate me more.

After class I keep my head down as I try to scurry out of the classroom. My teacher stops me by calling my name softly. I turn to him, refusing to meet his eyes.

"Are you okay, Aylin?" he asks softly enough that the few kids still leaving the classroom probably can't hear.

"Yeah, I need to go," I practically whisper as I try to leave the classroom, but he holds his arm out, stopping me.

"I would like you to go speak to the school counselor, Mrs. Hale."

"No thank you," I say simply.

"Here's a note, you can skip your next class to go see her, please Aylin. I won't ask you anything, I just would like you to speak to her," his voice is soft, genuinely concerned, but it makes me uncomfortable.

Adults always make me uncomfortable, there's never been one I've trusted.

I take the note softly with a nod of my head before quickly walking out of the classroom.

Glancing at the note I see where her office is, and I debate for a few moments if I should rip it up and just go to my next class. Or should I suck it up and go.

I assume he emailed her or told someone about what he saw on my arm which is why he's sending me to her office. I should go, if only to let her know I'm okay and not to worry about it.

I make my way through the high school that has already been overwhelming me as I get to the office that's indicated as the counselor's office. Her name is on the door in bold letters, "Mrs. Hale".

I knock softly before it opens to reveal a woman, younger than I would have expected, maybe in her late twenties, blonde hair, brown eyes, dressed in fancy clothes. She's pretty, and I'm even more uncomfortable because I feel like she couldn't understand anything about me even if she tried.

I feel myself closing up more and more as she smiles, instructing me to come into her office as she shuts the door behind me.

"You must be Aylin?" she asks, her voice is soft, and even though I'm on edge something about her voice starts to calm my racing heart.

I don't say anything as I sit down in a puffy chair in the corner, I just nod my head. My brown hair is falling around my face, hiding it.

"I'm Mrs. Hale, it's nice to meet you." I glance up at her through my hair to see her sit in another chair, she's looking at me so I can't meet her eyes.

I just nod again.

"Do you know why Mr. Jones wanted you to come see me?" she asks.

I will be honest; I don't think I even knew what that teacher's name was.

I shake my head.

"Well, Aylin, he thought you might be hurt. Are you hurt?"

I shake my head.

"Would you feel comfortable telling me if you were?"

I wait for a second before slowly shaking my head again.

"I understand. It can be hard to trust people you don't know, so why don't we get to know each other?"

I peek my head up slightly to look at her again. She's looking at me, she has a small smile on her face. I look around the room with little decorations, but the light is soft and nice. The overhead fluorescent lights aren't on, the room is covered in what looks like Christmas lights, and it helps me feel calm. The colors around are all blue and brown. I like it.

Mrs. Hale is still just looking at me, waiting for a response, waiting for me to say anything, but I don't feel pressured to answer. I continue to take in the room around me, and I feel my heart rate going down as I feel my body physically calming, not being on the defense.

I finally meet her eyes and nod my head.

Her smile widens as she tells me about her dog, Maggie, and for the first time in my life I feel comfortable talking to an adult.

I don't tell her anything about my parents, and she doesn't ask. She asks about me, what I like, who I am, and I actually realize at one point I'm smiling.

After what feels like forever, she says I should probably go to class, but asks if I would like to come talk to her again tomorrow.

I nod my head, and I think Mrs. Hale might be the first adult I might be able to feel comfortable around.

13

Present

It's almost the time Aylin agreed to meet me at my desk, and I'm oddly excited at the thought of seeing her again. I'm usually calm around women. I can keep my composure, and everything comes naturally to me.

Not right now.

Right now, I feel like I might explode with the anticipation of seeing her again.

Adams isn't here, luckily, he left early today. Not that I give a shit, but I just didn't want to listen to any of his stupid comments.

Right on time I see Aylin coming toward my desk. She has her long brown hair pulled back in a ponytail that's swinging behind her as she walks. She's in tight leggings that hug her thick thighs, and a loose t-shirt that looks too big for her.

I stand up to walk toward her so we can head down to the gym. I'm really hoping it's as empty as it usually is at the end of the day.

"Hey sweetheart," I greet her with a smile.

She doesn't give me a disgusted look this time, just that small smile that I'm starting to really enjoy. Although I want to see her give me a full smile for once. She looks me up and down, still in my work uniform of a button up and slacks.

"Are you planning to change?" she asks, skeptically.

"Nah, I was just going to shed a few layers," I wink at her.

"Seriously?"

"No, unless you'd prefer it." I raise my eyebrows to her as we start walking downstairs to the gym.

"I'd prefer you to be as clothed as possible," she says sternly.

I chuckle, I really want to get her to loosen up, she seems so put together all the time. I want to see who she really is because no one can be like this all the time.

"Yes, I'm going to change," I tell her as we approach the door to the gym. I wave her inside, "I'll be right in."

She looks like she wants to ask me something but walks inside as I head into the locker room to change.

I take it as a good sign there's no one else in the locker room while I quickly change into an Under Armor t-shirt, basketball shorts and my tennis shoes before heading back out into the gym to find Aylin.

I watch for a few moments as she's just walking around looking at everything curiously. I don't think she knows I'm in here yet because she's just examining the weight machine, and then the dummy used for punching.

It's interesting to watch her look around like this. She's not guarded, she's not giving me one of those small smiles, she's just herself. She's just looking around, unsure, but curious.

"You ready?" I ask louder than I probably needed to. My voice makes her jump before looking over to me.

"I guess. I still don't understand why you're insisting on this so badly."

"I've seen too many pretty women get hurt, and I want to

make sure you're not one of them, so I want you to have the tools to defend yourself," I say honestly. I think back to Rebecca and the thought of Aylin in any situation where she couldn't protect herself makes my stomach hurt.

I also think about my mom for a split second before dismissing the thoughts quickly to not show Aylin more than I should.

"I don't know why you don't think I already have those tools," she says confidently, raising her chin to look straight up at me.

She looks really cute like this, hands on her hips, trying to appear taller as she has to strain her neck to look up into my eyes.

"You'll get to prove it then, but I want you to remember something. In here you're not a therapist anymore, you're just Aylin and I'm just Nate, got it?"

She chews on the side of her lip for a second, and I can't help but watch the movement, wanting to pull her lip out with my thumb before feeling how it would feel against mine.

"Got it," she agrees.

I smile, "Let's get started then."

I start off teaching her about deflections if someone is coming at her to hit her. We run through what she should do to avoid various punches, how she can duck, and how to divert a kick. She picks up on everything quickly. I'm pretty impressed.

I'm slow with my movements so she can practice, but it doesn't take long until I'm speeding them up as she's able to deflect perfectly. She's ducking and avoiding my hits. She's even anticipating what I'll do next and avoiding it perfectly, even though I switch it up every time.

"I'm impressed," I tell her.

This earns me the first real smile from her. A full smile that stretches across her whole face, her white teeth on full display.

Her bright blue eyes light up at the compliment and it makes me feel happy that I put that smile there.

"I told you I can handle myself," she says confidently. "I took some boxing classes in undergrad."

"Okay, so you're saying I should be tougher on you then?" I give her a sinister smile. I would never actually hurt her, but I could one hundred percent manhandle her a bit.

I'm tempted, but not for the sake of self-defense.

Watching her like this makes me even more attracted to her than I have been. She's tough, that's clear, and she's driven. She's got a fighter in her that she keeps hidden. I want to bring out that fighter within her.

"Go ahead," she challenges, and the look she gives me makes my cock start to stiffen in my shorts. I like the challenge she's presenting me with.

I smile as I look right into her eyes for a moment before moving toward her quickly. She moves away from me, avoiding me as I get closer, so I'm unable to grab her at first, but I know she's anticipating it. She continues to deflect me, and fight against any attempts I make. She needs to be caught off guard. She slips by me a few more times because I let her.

"Are you actually going to challenge me?" She asks with a hint of mischief in her voice. I can't help but appreciate that she's letting her guard down now.

"You want a challenge?" I ask as she stands a few feet away from me. I start to walk toward her slowly, so slowly.

"Well, I didn't come here for this riveting conversation." She folds her arms across her chest.

Wrong move on her part.

Quickly, I take advantage of her confidence as I close the distance between us, wrapping my arm around her waist, swinging her around so her back is completely against my front. I use my other arm to hold across her collarbone.

She's completely flush against me as she starts flailing her body trying to get away. She's hitting my legs with the limited use of her arms, but I just adjust my body slightly, so she isn't able to make any contact with her hits.

She lets out a frustrated groan as she continues to try to fight against me, which results in me pulling her tighter. I try not to focus on the sudden overwhelming scent of her that's something like lavender, and how I'm reminded how she feels in my arms, even though she's fighting me.

"Come on, you can handle yourself, get away from me," I say directly into her ear.

"I'm trying," she growls in frustration as I continue to keep a vise grip around her.

"You haven't even used your legs," I tell her since she's been focused only on her arms and trying to pull away from me. "You can't let panic take over you need to focus on the parts of your body you can still move and use them against the vulnerable parts of your assailant."

She takes a second, seeming to assess how I'm holding her before she brings her foot down on mine, not too hard, but I can see the purpose. I still refuse to move.

"I don't want to actually hurt you," she says quietly.

I let out a low laugh. "You won't hurt me sweetheart, you can put effort into this."

She hesitates for a second before bringing her foot down on mine again, much harder this time. "Good, but that's not the only vulnerable part you can target."

She seems to assess my hold a bit more, moving her legs around like she's feeling where exactly I am before she kicks back against my knee. This gets me to let go because it was a good hit.

Once I let her go, she turns around quickly with concern on her face like she thinks she actually hurt me. I take this to my advantage as I reach out to her again, pinning her arms behind her back, and pulling her completely against me. She yelps as our chests collide roughly.

"That's not fair," she says, looking up at me.

"Why not? You can't check on your assailant. That gives them the perfect opportunity to grab you again." I tighten my grip on her wrists I've pinned behind her back.

"I wouldn't check on an assailant, I was checking on *you*." She rolls her eyes.

"Sweetheart, you have to practice like it's real or you're not actually prepared." I pull her against me tighter. I feel her breasts pressed against me, and I'm very aware how close our bodies are to one another.

"I know you won't hurt me though," she says confidently.

"You don't know me, I just might," I threaten.

I watch her throat bob as she swallows. I feel her chest rising faster as her breathing increases. She wiggles around, testing how tightly I'm holding her. She can't get out of this easily, not with how I have her against me.

Still, she doesn't look scared. She's trying to hide what she is feeling, but it looks more like aroused than anything. *Does Aylin like a little danger?*

"What are you thinking, sweetheart?" I rasp.

"I'm thinking of how I can get out of this." She doesn't feel like she's trying that hard. Her cheeks develop a pink tinge, her eyes flick up to mine, and the look is certainly not one I recognize as someone who wants to get out of this position.

"I don't think that's true." I lean closer, so our foreheads are practically touching.

Her breath hitches, she licks her bottom lip, and I watch the movement closely.

"Well, it is," she says before stomping on my foot again, harder than before, then wrapping her leg around the back of mine at the same time she spins and ducks out of my arms.

I'm shocked she got out of that; I smile at her as she backs up away from me. She's got a smile on her face now too along with shock like she can't believe she got out of it herself.

She's breathing heavily, but I don't think it's from any sort of exertion, more like she can actually catch her breath having some distance between us. I feel the same.

"Good use of a distraction," I acknowledge.

"Told you." She stands up straight, clearly proud of herself.

"One more time, I'm not going to hold back at all so you better not either," I say seriously, and I mean it. I want to see if she can do it without giving into panic.

Aylin stands up straight before stretching her arms across her body one at a time like she's preparing. I chuckle before going toward her quickly.

I feign movements of going to hit her, though I'm not actually aiming for her so if she isn't able to block or deflect me my hand would go past her, but she doesn't falter. She's good at hand to hand with me. She's effectively moving around me, blocking and deflecting.

I'm extremely impressed by her movements, and her resilience. I decide to take it up a notch, grabbing her thighs and throwing her over my shoulder. She screams as I grab her effortlessly. She starts kicking her legs and hitting my back with her fists.

She's putting effort in, but the hits don't faze me as I carry her across the big open room as she continues trying and failing to free herself from my hold.

"You panicked," I tell her while she's still draped over my shoulder.

She stops hitting me, as I feel her press her hands against my back, lifting herself up slightly. I debate making her get out of this one, but instead I keep a firm hold on her and slowly slide her down the front of my body. I feel every inch of her soft body against mine, and when her feet hit the ground, I gently pin her arms behind her again.

She looks up at me skeptically. "You know I can get out of this one."

"Yeah, but you're not," I point out. She's not even fighting against me this time. She's completely still, her eyes looking up into mine. She's still determined, she just hasn't moved.

"Maybe I'm just biding my time." She narrows her eyes at me.

"Or maybe you don't want to get away from me." I pull her tighter against me hoping she can't feel my heart racing out of my chest. My skin buzzes at the contact and I try to control the erection that could ruin this moment.

"Or maybe you're a little too full of yourself." She's still not making any effort to move away from me. If anything, I feel like she leaned into me more.

I decide to test it, and push the boundaries to see if she will try to get away.

I lean my head down, closer this time so our foreheads are against each other. Aylin's eyes never leave mine, but I feel her breathing quicken again as she leans more against me. Our breath is mingling, the air around us feels electric. I want to kiss her. I *need* to kiss her. I feel her sink into me slightly.

That's all it takes for me to press my lips against hers, and she lets me. She kisses me back, our lips moving against each other. When I lick her lips, she opens her mouth so my tongue can enter. She tangles her tongue with mine as she lets out a soft moan. I let go of her arms so I can hold her properly. Her arms immediately reach up to wrap around my neck, to pull me closer while my hands snake around her waist as our kiss continues deeply, exploring, testing.

I move one hand up to her hair, tangling my fingers in it to pull her head back so I can deepen our kiss further. I feel my cock harden in my shorts, and I'm pressed against her so I know she feels it, there's no hiding that in thin shorts.

She pauses before pulling away from me.

Her face is conflicted, she's looking at me, searching my face and then she looks shocked as she backs away from me. Her lips red and puffy from the intensity of our kiss.

"Did I do something wrong?" I ask, afraid that I scared her away because she seemed completely fine with what was going on until this moment.

"No, well yes, this is wrong Nate. I told you, we can't do this." She shakes her head, backing away from me.

"It's fine, I don't have to see you for therapy anymore, there's no 'boundary' thing now." I try to walk toward her, but she's backing up still.

"That doesn't make it okay, I have to go, we can't do this." She turns around to walk out of the gym. I don't follow her.

I can still feel her everywhere.

I feel her lips, her tongue, her hands, her fucking body.

She wanted this too, I felt it. I don't know what she's so hung up on with this being wrong, honestly nothing has ever felt so right to me. That should scare me more than anything, but all it has done is make me want more, but I'm worried I fucked that all up.

14

Aylin

Present

I can't stop thinking about what just happened the whole way home.
Nate kissed me.
I kissed him back.
I had to leave because I could see it going further. I *wanted* it to go further and it just reminded me how wrong it is. It doesn't matter if I don't see Nate professionally anymore, this isn't okay.

I shouldn't have even agreed to meet with him today, this shouldn't have happened. None of this should have happened.

Once I get home I sink to the floor with my back against the locked door. I hold my knees against my chest while I continue to think about everything.

I want to tell Mel, but I know she will just be mad I left. She will encourage me to keep this going, even though I know it's wrong and I shouldn't.

God, if anyone found out this could jeopardize my clinical, my future. I could get in trouble. I bet he wouldn't get in trouble; he would be congratulated for getting with the new therapist. Ugh, the thought makes me sick.

There's no way I can keep seeing him, no matter how attracted to him I am, no matter how badly I do actually want him, it can't happen.

My phone goes off in my bag, and I'm hesitant to see who it is, if it's Mel then I don't think I can hold back from telling her. If it's Nate, it's worse.

Turns out it is, in fact, worse.

> Nate: Aylin, I didn't mean for that to happen, I really want to see you again, I really want you to give me a chance. I'll try my best to keep my hands to myself, but I want to see you again.

I throw my head back against the door. So much worse.

I sit there on my floor for a few more moments before my phone goes off again in my hand, and I don't even want to look at it.

> Nate: One real date, that's all I want. Just Aylin and Nate.

I don't even know why he is trying so hard with me; he seems like the kind of guy that gets distracted at the attention of a woman after five minutes, but here he is practically begging for a chance, and just one date.

I can't.

I know I can't.

The biggest reason I know I can't is because I'm too into him.

It won't end with just one date, and no matter where or when it ends, I'm going to get hurt because either I get in trouble for this whole thing, he breaks my heart, or literally anything else. There's just no way this works out and ends happily for anyone, least of all me.

No, I have to tell him no. I have to stop this before it goes any further.

It doesn't matter that that was the best kiss of my life.

It doesn't matter that I was more turned on during that entire time with him than I have been in... well, ever, and that when his hands were on me, I felt like the heat of them could burn through my clothes.

It doesn't matter that he's the most attractive man I've ever been around in my entire life.

It doesn't matter that he actually interests me and makes me want to learn all about him.

None of that matters because it ends here and now.

> Aylin: You know that's not a good idea. Thanks for today, but we shouldn't talk anymore.

I hate the feeling I have as soon as I press send. I don't get to have nice things in my life, that's just not the hand I was dealt.

I had to work extremely hard to get myself through school, I had to apply myself fully to everything in my life, I've never had anything handed to me. Now, the one time I would even consider being selfish and taking something or someone I can't have I know I have to say no. Because I know things like this aren't meant for someone like me.

> Nate: I don't think I can do that. I might just end up at your office every day until you agree.

> Aylin: Why are you so persistent? I'm sure there's plenty of other women for you to harass.

> Nate: Because you're the only one I want to harass.

I chuckle, even though I don't want to.

> Aylin: We can't. I'm sorry.

> Nate: One date. I won't touch you. I just want to know you better.

I scoff. *Yeah, right.* He doesn't want to know me better. I don't even want to know myself. I also don't believe he won't touch me, and that's mostly because I know I'm going to want to touch him. Just being around him makes me want to do things that are so out of character for me that it's almost painful to stop myself.

> Nate: One real date.

I stare at the message.
I shake my head.
No, absolutely not.
I'm saying the words.
I'm thinking them, but I'm not typing them.

> Aylin: Fine.

I throw my phone across the room so it lands on my couch because I clearly can't be trusted with it right now. I don't know what I'm doing, but suddenly my stomach flips in a way that almost feels like excitement at the thought of a date with Nate.

I slide onto the floor so I'm lying flat on my stomach while I groan. *Who am I and what did I just do?*

15

3 Months Ago

I'm staring at the dilapidated apartment complex yet again. This is the third or fourth time I've been here. Every time I'm here, Rebecca refuses to give me more information or anything that would be helpful. She insists she's fine, and Murphy just tells me to get the fuck out.

I hate having to follow certain rules because you'd have to be an idiot not to see that Murphy hits Rebecca, and yet she won't give any admission or pursue any charges. I can't do anything and it drives me insane.

This time is different though. I usually knock on their door to be greeted by a pissed off Murphy before we go through the motions.

Today, I get out of my patrol car and the front door of their apartment is swinging open, with Rebecca running out straight toward me.

"Please officer, just go, he didn't do anything I swear!" She's crying, her cheeks red and wet. Her blonde hair is tangled and a mess on her head.

I don't say anything, I just look up to the door to see Murphy standing in the door frame with his arms folded across his chest, scowling in my direction.

"What's going on?" I ask Rebecca without breaking eye contact with the jackass staring me down.

"I was mopping, then I slipped and hit my head on the counter and screamed. Murphy freaked out when he came out to find me like that, I swear, please!"

I finally decide to look at her.

She didn't slip and fall.

I know what a punch in the face looks like. Her eye is already swelling shut, she has bruises around her cheekbone, and I notice her hair isn't just unbrushed it looks like it was grabbed. Hard.

I clench my jaw, looking up at Murphy again who hasn't moved and seems pleased with the show his wife is putting on for me.

"Rebecca, where's your daughter?" I ask.

Every time I've been here Layla has come out with her mom, so the fact that she's not out here with her has me more concerned.

"Layla's at my parents' house," she says through her sobs.

I turn so my back is to Murphy because he doesn't scare me, plus I would hear him coming toward me if he tried anything. I want to make it known to him that I'm not afraid of him. I'm fully facing Rebecca as she sobs into her hands, I speak quietly so I'm sure she's the only one that can hear me.

"Can you go stay with them too?" I ask.

Her eyes shoot up to meet mine, her bruises already looking worse, probably due to her crying. She shakes her head but doesn't say anything.

"Why not?"

"I just can't. Please go."

"I need to talk to your husband first." I stand up straight

again before looking back at the piece of shit smoking a cigarette right outside the apartment.

I stalk toward him with purpose and holding back every single instinct I have to rip his head from his body.

"What did she tell you?" he asks gruffly.

"Don't worry about that, I want to know what happened from you."

"Whatever she said is what happened."

"Are we going to have a problem?" I fold my arms across my broad chest and stand to my full height because I'm aware how imposing I can look.

"Are you threatening me, *officer*?" he says the last word like he always does with a dose of sarcasm.

"You'd know if I was."

He looks me up and down before spitting off to the side. I think he tries to look intimidating to me, but it makes me want to laugh. This man couldn't intimidate me with a weapon in his hand. Which, I secretly wish he would do so I would have an excuse to kick the shit out of him.

"Leave me and my wife alone, you cops need to stay out of other people's business that doesn't involve you."

I narrow my eyes at him. "If you'd stop beating the shit out of your wife then I wouldn't have a reason to keep showing up."

"That what she tell you?" I see his irritation in his eyes as he tries to look at his wife somewhere behind me, but I adjust so it's always me in his line of sight.

"No, but you must think I'm an idiot not to see it." I'm trying to get him to admit to something, anything, but he's not.

"You don't have proof of shit, so get the fuck out of here." He stomps back into the apartment, slamming the door behind him.

I look back to Rebecca who's still a mess kneeling in the parking lot, crying. I walk up to her to try one more time to see if she will say anything about that piece of shit.

"Rebecca, please tell me something, anything and I can make sure you stay safe."

She looks up at me, and then to the closed apartment door. She looks like she might actually say something. Like she's thinking it over as she chews on her lip. She shakes her head before standing up again.

"I told you, I slipped and fell," she says before scurrying back to the apartment again without looking back at me.

I stay around like I always do to make sure nothing else happens, but like always nothing does. I always hate leaving, especially knowing I'll likely be back soon due to another complaint. The only thing slightly better this time is that Layla isn't here.

I wonder how long she's going to stay with Rebecca's parents, and I just hope that Rebecca will decide to go stay with them as well at some point.

16

Present

After finally getting Aylin to agree to a date, a real date with me we decided on Friday night. I think she wanted some time to try and talk herself, and me, out of it.

She tried multiple times to cancel, using the same excuses she already has, but I'm not budging. I refuse to.

After I kissed her my fixation has just gotten worse. I thought maybe it wouldn't be as good as I thought it would. Maybe, I was building everything up in my mind.

I wasn't.

It was better than I thought it would be, and I know I said I wouldn't touch her, but I don't know if I'll be able to help myself.

Especially when I can tell she wants me to touch her. She says one thing, but I can see clear as day in her expression and body language, she means the exact opposite.

It took more convincing for her to let me pick her up for our date. She was trying to insist that she meet me wherever we are going, but I told her then it doesn't count as a real date.

> Nate: Real date means I pick you up, I pay, I take you home, I walk you to your door and be a complete gentleman when we say goodbye.
>
> Aylin: I don't believe for a second you can be a complete gentleman.
>
> Nate: Guess you'll find out.

She wasn't completely wrong, I'm not a gentleman. Not at all, but I'm trying with her which is something completely new for me. I'm trying to be good to her since she's clearly someone who has plenty of walls that need to be chipped down in order to see who she really is.

I want to see the real Aylin.

Maybe that's why I can't stop thinking about her. Everyone I've ever known is so up front with who they are, there's never any question.

Women make their interest obvious, even when they try not to. Aylin isn't like that. She's different and she hides within herself like she doesn't want anyone to see.

But I want to see. I want to know her, and I will.

I'm pulling up to her apartment, which I know is off campus housing for the university. I question for a second if I'm at the right place. She's a therapist, but she's still in school?

I walk up to her door, I thought about bringing flowers or something to really make sure she knows it's a real date, but I also thought that's too cliché for someone like her and I don't think she would like it.

Aylin answers the door, and for a second, I think I forget to breathe. She's always beautiful, but there's something about how she's standing there in a navy dress that accentuates all her perfect curves, her long hair loose and wavy around her shoulders. I sweep my eyes over her completely until I meet her blue eyes that look even brighter. I swallow deeply before I speak.

"You look beautiful," I say with a flirty smile.

She looks down, away from my gaze as I see the pink color tinge her cheeks. She steps outside, shutting the door behind her without looking up to me again.

"Where are we going?" she asks, locking her door. I haven't been able to look away from her.

I don't think I'll be able to look away from her all night.

We get to my car, I open the passenger side for her, she gives me one of her small smiles that I've decided at this moment are my second favorite thing. My first favorite is her real smile. I've only seen it once, but it's already my favorite thing from her.

I climb into the driver's seat, still not answering her. She's looking at me, turned in her seat with her eyebrows raised because she clearly wants an answer.

"Will you accept that it's a surprise?" I ask.

Her face contorts with uncertainty as she takes her bottom lip between her teeth. I watch as she bites at her lip, dying to take it with my own teeth, especially since I know how it feels to kiss her.

Yeah, I'm not getting through the night without touching her.

"Fine," she says, turning back to sit forward in her seat.

"Are you a student?" I ask because I'm still confused about her living situation.

"Technically yeah, I'm in my last year of my doctoral degree in mental health counseling. Don't worry, I'm completely qualified to have met with you," she says this like I was actually worried about it.

Doctorate. She impresses me even more every time I see her.

Through the whole drive, I keep glancing over at her as she looks out her window with her hands folded in her lap. I take every chance I can to look at her like this, guard down, body relaxed, and I would give anything to know what she's thinking.

I park in a parking garage that's a couple blocks from where we are actually going since I know downtown Portland, and there's no way I'll find a parking spot closer.

We get out of the car; I go around to her side to take her hand as she's stepping out of the car. She looks at me skeptically but puts her hand in mine anyway after a moment of hesitation. I intertwine our fingers instantly before she can pull away.

She looks up at me as we start walking and opens her mouth like she wants to say something, but I guess she decides not to. I smile because I think she wanted to tell me how inappropriate this is but decided against it.

I squeeze her hand briefly. "Just Aylin and Nate, remember?"

She looks up at me again. "Just Aylin and Nate."

I smile, I feel like this is a first step in her potentially accepting this, so I'm happy about that.

It doesn't take us long to walk to where we are headed, which is a gaming bar. I've only been here one other time with friends, and it was fun. They have various game systems and TVs everywhere, plus board games. I know Aylin has a little bit of a competitive spirit and I want to see more of it while I try to get her to loosen up.

As we walk inside, I can't take my eyes off Aylin as she takes in her surroundings. I think this just might be what she does, it's the same interested look I noticed the other day when she didn't think I was looking at her. She examines everything around her with genuine curiosity, assessing the location with her vibrant blue eyes.

I'm just assessing her.

I haven't let go of her hand and she hasn't tried to pull away.

We go up to the bar first to get some drinks. Aylin chews at her bottom lip as she thinks about what she wants before ordering one of their specialty cocktails named after *Mario* that is mostly vodka and lemonade but has something blue in it as well.

I'm somewhat shocked she ordered alcohol, but I'm glad since that means she's giving this a real chance and not being overly cautious with me. I get a beer. Once we have our drinks, I lead her to an empty couch that's only big enough for the two of us with a game system set up to the TV.

"Ever played anything before?" I ask, picking up the controller to select a game that's preloaded on the console.

She shakes her head slowly. "No, I never had anything like this as a kid."

"Hey, video games aren't just for kids, look at where you are," I gesture around, and this earns me a small smile from her.

"I've never had anything like this as an adult either then." She looks up at me, her smile still present.

"I'll go easy on you then, sweetheart, I can't be impressing you too much on our first date," I wink at her.

Aylin shakes her head, but it looks like she does so in humor, and I can't help how happy this makes me. I can't help how happy just being around her makes me.

I pick a party game where we have to go against each other in competition. I explain how the game works, and what buttons to press on the controller. She listens and studies everything. I like watching her figure it out like it's the most serious thing in the world.

I barely pay attention to the game; I'm focused on her. Only her. I watch as she gets more comfortable with the game, getting more excited and smiling more as we play. She even wins a couple times which gets her really excited.

"I won! I guess I'm a quick learner." She smiles up at me at her victory.

"Or maybe I'm just a good teacher." I nudge her with my shoulder.

"No, I think it's all because of me." She's beaming, and I so badly want to kiss her. I want to kiss her smile and feel her again, but I'm not going to fuck this up.

She becomes more competitive, and I decide to actually start trying to win without staring at her through most of the game. I lean over her to mess with her controller.

"Hey!" she exclaims at my blatant attempt at cheating.

Her response is to get up and sit right in my lap, blocking my view of the TV. She continues to play like she's completely comfortable where she is.

I'm anything but comfortable having her right here. She wins the game, and bounces slightly in victory, her ass rubbing against my groin where my cock was already starting to harden.

I place my hands on her hips to stop her from moving. She looks back at me, a smirk on her face.

"You okay?" she asks.

I look directly in her eyes where I see she knows exactly what she's doing. "I'm great."

She nods slightly before bringing her focus back on the game where she clearly wins because I cannot think straight.

"We should have some sort of wager since you're so good now," I say to her as she moves back to her spot next to me on the little couch.

I almost grab her to force her back on my lap, but I really meant it when I said I would try not to touch her, it's just getting harder by the second. The evidence is clear as day below my waistline.

"What kind of wager?" she asks, setting down the controller while taking the last few sips of her drink.

"If I win, I want a kiss," I smile at her.

She rolls her eyes. "And if I win then I want another drink."

"I'll go get you another drink right now, pick something else sweetheart."

"If I win, you'll stop calling me sweetheart," she amends quickly.

I lean back, "Fine, but drink first. You can even pick the game."

I go back to the bar to get us both another drink. I decide to get her the same thing she already had since she didn't ask for anything else and I don't want to get her something she doesn't like by guessing wrong.

Once I'm back she has the game ready, this time it's a racing game we haven't played yet. I chuckle at her boldness.

"You sure?" I ask, handing her the drink.

"You scared?" She takes a sip of her drink, looking up at me through her lashes before I sit down.

I have to take my eyes off her because watching her lips wrap around that straw just make me think of her lips wrapped around my cock, and I think she's trying to distract me.

"Nope, just want to make sure you know what you're doing." I grab the controller confidently.

She doesn't say anything as she hits "start" on the game. I notice that she's scooted closer to me on the couch, so we are sitting against each other, thighs completely pressed together and I think I know her strategy. Distracting me. Too bad for her, two can play that game.

The game begins, the video game cars at a starting line as it counts down from ten. I lean over to speak right into her ear, "I can't wait to kiss you again."

I hear her breath hitch as my lips lightly move across her ear as I speak before pulling away. I see her move around slightly in her seat. I smirk.

The race starts, and as soon as the cars take off Aylin presses against my side harder like she's trying to push me, but not hard enough to actually make me move. She stays focused on the game. I keep glancing at her, appreciating her focus, how her eyebrows furrow, biting at her bottom lip. Her cheeks are still tinged pink.

I'm winning, but she's in second place. That's when she gets bold, moving to my lap again, only this time she doesn't just sit, she moves her hips more. She's rubbing against me while staying completely focused ahead of us.

I'm as hard as a fucking rock from her movements against me, but I'm too determined to win to let it distract me too much. She ends up starting to win, that's when I decide to get bold too, bringing my lips onto her neck, not kissing her but just running my mouth and breathe down the side of her neck.

She stops the movements she was making on my lap and hesitates on the controller long enough for me to get in the lead again right before the finish line.

"I win," I say, my voice husky because I'm so fucking turned on right now from her rubbing against me.

She turns slightly in my lap so she can see me from the corner of her eye. I watch as she hesitates to speak, she licks her bottom lip. I watch her throat bob as she swallows. "Guess you want to cash in on your prize?" she practically whispers.

I know we are in this bar and there's people around. It's not exactly quiet, but I've felt like it's only us this whole time and in this moment, I forget other people exist anywhere else in the world. Right now, it's just the two of us.

I set the controller I was holding next to me on the couch and place a hand on the top of her thigh. I feel her stiffen under my touch.

"I'm going to save my prize for a later time," I say, rubbing my thumb on the exposed skin from the hem of her dress.

Aylin slides off my lap and into the seat next to me again with a questioning look on her face that looks like there's a hint of disappointment.

Good.

I want her to want to kiss me, not just for a fucking bet.

Now, it's my turn to pick the game, I smile over at her. She's still looking at me, she doesn't say anything, but I can tell she's trying to figure me out. She has so many questions written all over her face and in those blue eyes, but she doesn't say any of them.

I continue to sneak glances at her throughout the night, sometimes when she isn't looking at me, other times I catch her continuing to examine me. I like that she seems like she wants to figure me out. I'm so naturally comfortable with her I feel like this is the most content I've been in a while. She puts me at ease. I like her. I think I might like her a lot.

17

Aylin

Present

I'm surprised how much fun I'm having with Nate tonight. I didn't know what to expect, but I didn't expect to actually enjoy myself and enjoy being around him.

He's funny and playful which are two things I've never considered myself so it's refreshing. He keeps looking over at me, and whenever he does, it looks like he's just appreciating that I'm here. His gaze isn't lustful or predatory, just happy. I like it.

I keep looking at him because I have no idea what to think about this man next to me. He makes me want to expand my comfort zone, which is why I've been a little forward, especially when it comes to being competitive.

I would never hop on a guy's lap, but for some reason with him I just throw caution to the wind and do whatever impulse I have. It also might be the alcohol because Mel has told me I get lovey and touchy when I drink.

We leave the bar after a couple hours, and I can't stop smiling. Once we are outside, I'm hit with the night air that's much cooler than it was before, since it's early October the nights get really cold.

I wrap my arms around myself as we step outside. Nate seems to notice as soon as we are outside because he wraps one of his strong arms around my shoulders, pulling me against his side as we walk. I sink into him, partly from the warmth and partly because I like this feeling of being held by him.

As we walk back to Nate's car, he breaks the comfortable silence we found ourselves in, "Would you want to go on a walk with me?"

"Isn't that what we are doing right now?" I question with a hint of humor in my voice.

"I mean a real walk," he chuckles, pulling me closer against him.

"Maybe if you have a jacket I can wear so I don't freeze." I look up at him.

I like this view more than I should. His strong jawline, the light layer of scruff on it. His dark eyelashes that any woman would kill for. I don't think I've ever seen a man in real life so perfect looking, it's almost annoying.

"I'm sure I have something."

We get back to his car and he opens the door for me again. I kind of wish he would stop trying to impress me because I like to know who people really are. I realize how hypocritical that is of me since I'm always putting on some sort of front for people, but that's because I know the real person isn't worth seeing.

Though, I've been more myself tonight with Nate than I have with anyone other than Mel in…well, probably ever I guess. I've been the quiet, questioning, slightly cautious Aylin. That is until I give into impulses. It's scary. I don't know what Nate sees, I really don't.

I hear him at the trunk before he comes back to the driver's seat. He hands me a jacket which I take thankfully. As he starts up his car, I put the oversize jacket on when I notice it says "Portland PD" on the front.

"This might be a problem," I say as Nate starts to pull out onto the street.

"Why?" He looks over at me as I point to the patch.

"Well, I would hate for anyone to assume I'm a cop," I attempt to joke.

The sides of his lips quirk up slightly, "Yeah? What's so wrong with that?"

"No offense, but you guys don't exactly have the best reputation." I glance over at him.

"Not all of us are bad though, maybe you shouldn't be so judgey." He's smiling now.

"I wasn't judging, I just said other people might assume."

"Do you often care what other people think about you?"

I think about his question for a moment. I debate lying but decide against it. I think I might want Nate to see me, because then maybe it'll make it easy when this is over. Then I'll know why, because I was myself instead of trying to be someone I'm not, to just keep him interested.

"Yeah, I do," I say honestly.

"Really? That surprises me."

"Doesn't everyone care what people think about them? Working with people it's something I see often; everyone likes to put the best versions of themselves out for the world. They hide all the bullshit, and only present the best parts."

Nate nods, I'm not sure if it's because he agrees with what I'm saying or he's processing what I said. I bite my bottom lip while I think I might have said too much.

"If that's the case then does anyone ever really know a person other than themselves?" He sounds genuinely curious.

"I think everything comes out over time. So the longer you get to know someone, the more you see them for who they really are, whether they want you to or not."

"You're making me question everyone I've ever known." He smiles at me, so I know he's not upset about the way this conversation turned.

I feel my face getting warm, I feel like this isn't really a first date type conversation, but it's okay because this is also the only date.

"So, who is the real Aylin? Have I met her, or have I met the best version you want me to see?"

"That's something you may never know," I smile at him like I'm making a joke, but it's probably the truest statement I've ever said to him. He may never know who I really am, and it's for the best.

"Good thing I like a little mystery," he winks at me. I decide to look forward for the rest of this car ride because I don't think I can handle his ridiculously good-looking face anymore without internally combusting.

"What about you? I know next to nothing about you." I'm realizing this, even though he also knows nothing about me too, but unlike him I don't like mystery. I like to know if I can trust people or not.

"You haven't asked," he shrugs.

He's right. I haven't asked and that is out of character for me. Though to be fair, he has not been the most open person when I did try to ask him things necessary for my job. The job that I'm choosing to forget about tonight.

"Then let's play twenty questions," I suggest, and immediately hate myself for the suggestion. "But we each get two skips."

Nice save, Aylin.

He glances over at me before nodding, "Deal. We are almost to where I'm taking you. You go first."

"How old are you?"

"Twenty-nine. You?"

"Twenty-seven. You can't just ask me the same question I

ask you," I glare at him.

He chuckles, "I wasn't going to do that, it was just a good question. We are here."

I look out the windows to see we are in a dark parking lot, but I recognize that we're close to the river. I tighten the jacket around myself as we both step out of the car. The air here is colder than it was in town, but I don't mind, it's nice right here. The water is lightly illuminated by the distant city lights.

We begin walking and make our way to a paved path close to the edge of the water. Nate is so close to me that we keep brushing against each other, but he doesn't reach for my hand or pull to hold me against him again.

I kind of want him to.

"I'll ask the next question," he says after we have walked for about a minute. "What made you want to be a therapist?"

Oof.

He's getting a very watered-down version, but I'm trying to tell myself that I'm not going to lie.

"I had a great school counselor in high school that inspired me to go into this field, and in college I fell in love with it." I put my shaking hands in the pocket of the jacket I'm wearing. "What made you want to be a cop?"

"Now who's copying questions?" He glances over at me.

I shrug, "It was a good question." I repeat his words from earlier and he laughs. I like his laugh. It's deep and throaty. I feel it all over my entire body giving me goosebumps.

"My dad was a cop; it was what I grew up around and he was my hero. I knew I wanted to be like him someday. I went to college for criminal justice and now, here I am."

"Are you like him? Did you do what you wanted and become like him?" I ask without fully thinking first.

He smiles, but it doesn't look like a happy smile. It looks like a sad smile.

"In some ways. He was a detective, and I'm trying to get

promoted, but I'm not quite there yet. In some ways I'm like him. I have his drive and his work ethic, but I also never saw him angry, not once. I wish I was like him in that way."

I tense. I want to ask him more about that, about him being angry. That makes me nervous, I do everything in my power to keep the flashbacks at bay. This isn't the time for that. I'm safe. Nate is safe. At least I think so.

"What about your mom?" I ask softly.

"She was a stay-at-home mom, so she was around all the time which was nice since my dad worked a lot."

I can tell there's sadness while he talks about his parents, though he's clearly fond of them. I also noticed he mentioned them in the past tense so I can assume they aren't around anymore. I want to ask, but he jumps in with his own question first.

"What about your parents? What do they do?" he asks.

"Skip any questions involving my parents," I say quickly.

He looks over at me and I keep my face calm, not wanting to show any reaction to the mention of my parents. Even without sharing any specifics, just the thought of them can send me into a tailspin.

"What's your favorite color?" he asks, lightening the mood, which I appreciate.

"Blue," I answer easily.

"Like your eyes?" he asks, and I wonder if this counts as one of his questions.

"No, darker blue. More like this dress." I gesture down to what I'm wearing.

He nods like he understands the distinction I made.

"Why me?" I ask suddenly.

Nate stops walking and steps in front of me to stop me in my tracks. I look up at him to see he's already looking down at me, his brows furrowed.

"Why you what?"

"Why are you so interested in me?" I ask softly because I almost want to take back the words. I feel like I don't want to know, or I'm worried he won't have an actual answer.

He raises his hand to hold my cheek, rubbing his thumb softly along my lips then onto my cheek before he answers. I feel like I can't breathe while he's touching me like this. I feel like I'm on fire wherever he touches.

"I've been telling you, but you don't believe me," he starts. "You're beautiful, you intrigue me, and for some reason I haven't been able to get you out of my mind since the day I met you."

His thumb grazes over my lips again. I didn't even notice I was chewing on my bottom lip until I feel him pull it from my teeth with his thumb.

I'm trying to determine if what he said is true, I'm searching his eyes, his face for any sign that what he's saying isn't the truth. All I see is his clear hazel eyes searching mine for something back.

I can barely think about anything other than how badly I want him to kiss me right now. I'm silently begging for it to happen, but he doesn't. He smiles before moving his hand down my neck, to my shoulder, down my arm until it meets mine.

He intertwines our fingers, holding tightly as he turns to start walking again.

"Do you want to go home?" he asks after a few moments of silence.

I'm a little disappointed at his question.

"Do you?" I ask.

"I don't want our date to end yet," he says confidently.

I think about that statement, unsure of what way he means it. Is that a no, he doesn't want to go home, or he doesn't want to go home alone?

I want to ask, but I hold back because I feel like asking will ruin whatever spell I'm under and I'm not ready for that to end yet. I'm not ready for reality.

"Me either," I say so quietly, I'm not even sure if he heard me.

We walk in silence for a little longer. I kind of want to ask more questions, but I'm suddenly aware of his hand holding mine and I forget how to speak.

I'm just trying to enjoy all the feelings around me. The feeling of Nate next to me, the warmth of his hand. The light on the water. The cool breeze. The flip in my stomach. The urge to pull his lips to mine.

"How many questions do I have left?" Nate finally asks.

"Honestly I lost track."

"Then how about one more each? No skips."

I swallow nervously, "Okay, you first."

"Do you want to see me again?"

I don't know.

Well, yes. Yes, I do want to see him again, but I'm still internally battling the fact that I shouldn't.

I don't know how to answer.

I don't want to lie.

I also don't want to ruin this night.

"Yes, but I don't know if we should, and you know that."

"We should do what we want because we are just Aylin and Nate."

I smile, I like the way he thinks. I like him.

I try to think of a good last question to ask him. I want to make it worth it.

"Do you still want to kiss me?"

"More than anything," he answers without hesitation as he swings me around so I'm in front of him, our chests pressed together.

He leans down, building the anticipation before his mouth is finally pressed to mine. This time it's soft, and I want more. I bring my arms up his hard chest, feeling the ridges of his muscled chest through his shirt as I bring my hands up behind his neck to pull him against me.

His arms wrap around my waist, holding me against him while his mouth moves with mine slowly, sweetly. His tongue sweeps in my mouth. I love this feeling of him. I don't want to ever break apart from this kiss. I don't want him to ever let me go.

We continue to kiss, just learning each other's mouths and enjoying the feel of one another. When we break apart, I can't help but look at him, a genuine smile on my face as I stare into his hazel eyes. He presses his lips to my forehead before moving his arm around my shoulder to hold me against his side as we walk again.

As we walk back to Nate's car, I'm somewhat disappointed this might be the end of the night. I know it's also for the best, because I might end up doing or saying something stupid. Even more stupid than the fact that I'm here right now.

Nate opens the passenger door for me, he kisses me quickly once before I climb in.

I'm really happy with how this night turned out, and that's the first thing I think as Nate drives back toward my apartment. I'm worried how I'll feel in the morning because I feel like I might be rational after I've had some sleep, and I'll likely have to go back to real life.

Right now, I don't want to go back to real life. Right now, I want to pretend that we are just Aylin and Nate.

We pull up in front of my apartment and Nate asks if I want him to walk me to my door.

I nod as we get out of the car. He comes around to the passenger side to take my hand in his as we approach the entrance to my building. My heart is beating faster the closer we get to my door.

I want to invite him inside.

I know I shouldn't.

But I want to.

I almost never do what I want just for me.

I almost never take risks anymore.

We reach my front door, facing each other before I unlock it.

"I had the best time with you tonight," he says, his hands moving to my waist, pulling me against him.

"I actually did too," I reply, wrapping my arms around his middle so I can pull our bodies together.

"You say that like you expected to not enjoy yourself?" He chuckles.

"I didn't know what to expect," I say honestly.

"Then I'm glad I was able to exceed your nonexistent expectations." He presses his lips to mine, and this time isn't soft. This time I can tell how much he wants to kiss me.

Our kiss deepens as we both become more desperate to feel each other, tasting each other and wanting each other. All logic leaves my brain, and the only thing I can think of right now is that I want this man. I want him so bad, and doing one thing for myself without worrying about the consequences won't be the end of the world.

"Want to come inside?" My voice is so breathy as Nate's lips move to my jaw, then down the side of my neck.

He kisses my neck; I feel the scrape of his teeth before he answers with just a nod of his head.

I turn toward the door to unlock it while Nate continues to hold my back against his front, his lips continuing their journey exploring my neck, down to my collarbone, my shoulder, then back up. It takes me a couple tries to unlock my door because I'm so distracted by the feeling of Nate pressed against me, feeling every hard plane of him against my back, and his hot mouth on my sensitive skin.

I finally get the door open and Nate pushes me inside with

a nip against my neck. He swings me around and presses my back to the door he just closed and instantly crushes his lips onto mine. This isn't sweet, this is hungry, desperate and needy. His tongue is in my mouth, discovering everything he can and I'm already needing more. More friction, more touching, more feeling, just *more*.

I try to move my hips to press against him but his hand is against my hip, holding me to the door behind us. He presses his thigh between my legs and I start to rub myself on him. I'm soaked and probably leaking through my underwear, but I don't care, I just need the relief. I moan into his mouth, and he chuckles as he realizes what I'm doing.

"Are you greedy or just impatient, sweetheart?" he asks against my lips.

My response is breathy as I answer, "Maybe a little bit of both."

"You want this?" He's keeping his lips just out of reach from my own. As I try to meet them again, he holds me harder against the door so tightly that my movements on his thigh have stopped and I whine.

"Maybe," I taunt, but I really do.

Since I'm letting my impulse take over tonight, I've thrown my filter out the window. I've thrown everything about myself that helps me stay guarded right out the window.

Nate just chuckles as he continues to hold me, so tight I can't move even though I try. He slides down my body, watching my eyes the whole time as he drops to his knees in front of me, his gaze never leaving mine.

"Too bad I plan on taking my time with you tonight," his voice is covered in lust as I feel his hands gliding slowly up my legs.

"Why?" I breathe out.

"Because I know you'll try to run away from me again, and I'm going to make this worth it."

He lifts my dress, slowly over my thighs until it's just barely above my hips. Then, his face is in between my legs. I feel him against me even through my underwear as I gasp.

"You're going to be begging for everything from me," he says as he slowly slides down my underwear to reveal myself to him.

"You're way too confident in yourself," I barely say as my heart is racing and I feel like I can't breathe from the anticipation.

He smiles, something mischievous shines in his eyes before he throws one of my legs over his shoulder and his mouth is on my pussy, his tongue flicking my clit and I gasp.

I feel my knee buckle and I'm afraid I'm going to fall onto him because the sensation starting where his mouth is, is quickly overtaking my whole body. He licks my entire slit and runs his tongue close to the bundle of nerves but doesn't continue with the same solid pressure he started with and I'm whimpering, my release is so close already.

I've never experienced anyone so confident and skillful, it makes me build quicker than I ever have before.

"Nate, please," I beg, and I don't even sound like myself.

"Already begging," he says as he sucks my clit into his mouth, and I feel like I might lose it.

I feel like I'm about to collapse onto the floor if Nate wasn't holding my hips so hard against the door behind me. He increases the pressure against me once again. I gasp with release as my orgasm takes over my entire body. I grip his short hair as I come down. He looks up at me, his eyes are dark with need.

"Give me another one, sweetheart," he rasps.

"I can't," I groan.

"You will," Nate growls before his mouth is on me again.

I scream out his name because I'm so overstimulated it's almost painful as he continues sucking, nipping and licking me.

When I feel the pressure of two fingers pushing inside me, I go off once again as he fucks me with his fingers, continuing the ministrations of his tongue against me. My head hits the door behind me as I cry out my second release that is borderline painful in the best way.

Nate picks me up and I wrap my legs around his waist as he carries me into my tiny bedroom. He throws me down on my bed. I yelp as my back hits the mattress. I watch as Nate reaches up behind him to pull his shirt off.

I feel like my jaw wants to drop, but I somehow hold it together while I admire his sculpted chest. His arms are huge, no wonder he can pick me up so easily because I know I am not small. His chest could have been carved from stone; it looks so smooth and strong. I bite back a moan.

This man wants me?

I don't know how or why, but I'm going to enjoy it while I can.

He leans over me, resting his hands on my thighs as he slides his hands up past my hips, up my stomach, taking my dress with his hands as they trail up my body. I feel like his hands are a fire burning their way up and I just want to fall into it fully. He reaches my chest, my nipples obvious through my thin bra.

It feels like it takes forever as his hands continue to roam my body, cupping my breasts before rolling my nipples with his large fingers through the thin fabric. His rough hands skate down my stomach to the apex of my thighs before coming back up. Nate finally lifts my dress up over my head so I'm just in my bra that doesn't leave much to the imagination.

"Fuck, sweetheart," he rasps, the noise going straight to my soaking core, throbbing with the need to be filled by him.

He reaches behind me to unclasp my bra, revealing myself fully to him. He steps back for a second to look at me before his mouth is on my breast taking my nipple in his mouth, I throw my head back in a moan at the feeling.

I love his mouth.

His mouth on my mouth, his mouth on my pussy, his mouth on my nipple.

Maybe I am greedy, and I do want it all.

I run my hands through his hair, I can barely grab onto the short strands, and I lean into him, moving my hips, silently begging him to fill me. He wasn't kidding when he said he was going to take his time because his mouth moves from one breast to the other as he bites down lightly around my nipple before soothing the sting with his tongue.

Unable to wait anymore, I reach down for his jeans and unbutton them, urgently trying to free him so I can touch him, feel him. He reaches down to help me pull down his pants completely before standing up again to just look at me.

"You are so fucking beautiful," he says, and I can't help but squirm under his praise and with the way he's looking at me like he actually means it.

I sweep my eyes up his entire body. His entire naked form and it's not fair. No human should look like this, no human on this earth should have this body. Especially with a cock that is swollen, thick and throbbing, looking at me like this. And he thinks I'm beautiful?

I reach out to wrap my fingers around him, but he grabs my wrist, pushing me back, pinning both my wrists by my head as he presses his mouth onto mine again. I feel him everywhere and I still want more. He's spreading my legs with his own. I push my hips up trying to meet his.

He lets go of me to reach down to his pants. I'm breathing heavily as I watch him take a condom out of his wallet. I give him a skeptical look.

Nate chuckles as he rips the wrapper with his teeth, "What sweetheart?"

"Did you already have that with you, or did you assume this would happen?"

"I'm always prepared, but I did not assume anything."

I watch as he rolls the condom on, biting my bottom lip anticipating his length inside me, and I feel myself get wetter at the thought.

He climbs back onto the bed, crawling between my legs as I feel his heavy cock right against me as his mouth lands on mine again. I want to feel him so bad as he rubs himself all along my pussy building my anticipation and covering himself in my arousal. I growl in frustration as I'm silently begging him to enter me.

I lift my hips, trying to push him inside of me. I'm anticipating the stretch. I saw how big he was as he was standing in front of me, and I know it's going to hurt, but in the best way. In a way I crave right in this moment.

His mouth is on mine fiercely, his tongue sweeping through my own in a way that makes me feel weak. He's almost too good at this, his kiss is claiming and powerful, and I just keep wanting more.

Then, I feel him as he begins to push inside of me. I feel him stretch me inch by inch until he thrusts hard and he's fully seated inside. We both moan into each other's mouths at the feeling. He starts to move his hips, thrusting steadily as his mouth moves from mine down my neck. He's nipping and licking along my skin.

I wrap my legs around him, pulling him further into me as the noises that come from me don't even sound like my own. I'm convinced I might be having an out of body experience in this moment. Especially as I feel his pelvic bone rub against my clit in the perfect way with each powerful thrust.

I feel yet another orgasm building, and I'm chasing it so desperately. I never orgasm more than once, and sometimes never with sex, but I'm about to come for a third time.

Nate brings his mouth back up to mine, and I'm panting in his mouth, he groans as his thrusts pick up speed, and intensity. I feel my orgasm crest and then I explode all around him. My head is thrown back with the power of my release.

I clench around him, which only makes him thrust harder. I feel he's close. I run my hands along his chest, feeling all the muscles flex while he moves inside me.

He groans with his own release, barely holding himself up on his forearms to prevent crushing me, but at this point he could just crush me and I'd beg him for more.

We are both breathing heavily as we recover. He pulls out of me and I make a small noise at the new emptiness; he rolls over next to me. I can't help but watch and appreciate this handsome man next to me because I know deep down this will be it for us.

Once I can feel my legs, I walk into my bathroom to clean myself up before returning to the bed. Nate has moved so he's propped up, sitting against my headboard. Still completely naked, and I just want to take a picture so I can have this visual forever.

I watch his eyes sweep over me, realizing I'm also completely naked. A blush rises to my cheeks as I feel self-conscious now that things aren't as...*intense*. I'm thankful for the dim light around us, knowing he can't see my faded scars that adorn my body.

"Come here," he demands, his eyes still fixated on me, and I can see him getting hard again. I don't even know how that's possible.

I hesitate, wanting to go put a t-shirt or something on first. He must notice my hesitation.

"Come here now, sweetheart."

I huff a breath before making my way back to the bed and as I start to climb on, he grabs me effortlessly, pulling me against him. Every thought I had has disappeared as we lay here, Nate holding me against him as he lifts the covers so we can settle under them together. I don't know if he's actually planning on sleeping here, but I don't want to ask.

"One more question, no skip allowed." he finally says.

I hesitate, "I don't think you can always add the exception of no skips since I had one left."

"And I have both left, but I'm willing to give them up." He squeezes me against his chest.

"Fine, what's your question?" I roll my eyes, but he can't see it.

"Will we see each other again?" he asks, and I furrow my eyebrows as I lift my head to look at him.

"You asked that earlier."

"No, earlier I asked if you wanted to see me again."

"Yes, I'm sure we will see each other again," I say, though I'm not being specific on the nature of seeing him again. Will it be in passing? More sex? I have no idea right now.

The weight of what we just did is over me, I know this is still not okay, but it felt too good. I hate this feeling.

"Your turn." He nudges me.

"I want to save my question for another time," I say, mostly because I feel my eyelids getting heavy and I can't think of anything to ask right at this moment.

"That's fine, that means we will definitely see each other again," I hear the smile in his voice, even without looking at him.

I barely notice when I drift off to sleep, soothed by the feeling of Nate's body wrapped around mine, and the sounds of his breathing and heartbeat lulling me to sleep.

I don't have any nightmares.

18

Aylin

11 Years Ago (Age Sixteen)

Last night was easily the worst night of my life.

I've been through a lot at the hands of my parents over the last sixteen years, but last night was definitely the worst.

They were both drunk off their ass, and I was just trying to study in my room when they started screaming at each other. That's nothing new, but it makes it hard to focus on my homework when it's happening.

I grabbed my headphones and plugged them into my new phone that I was able to afford after saving almost everything I've made at my waitressing job over the last three months. I started playing music as loud as I needed to so I couldn't hear them anymore.

It helped for a little. I couldn't hear them and I was able to focus on schoolwork with music, it actually helps sometimes.

Then, my door came flying open even though I know I locked it. My dad had kicked it down. He's screaming at me; I rip out my headphones so I can hear him.

"What the fuck are you doing ignoring me?!" he yells so loud I swear I can feel the sound vibrating my bones.

"I—I couldn't hear you, I'm sorry," I say softly, though I know it won't help anything.

My mom comes stumbling over behind my dad, looking over him at me, her eyes narrowing at the sight of me.

"It's because of that fucking phone, you shouldn't have it anyway!" my dad screams before grabbing it from my hand.

"No, please!" I worked so hard for that, and it's the one thing I wanted. I don't want him to take it.

"She doesn't even deserve to have anything nice since she's so worthless," my mom scoffs from the door as she sways back and forth, she's so drunk.

I hate her.

I hate them both.

My dad looks at my phone, the headphones still attached. He turns it over in his hand a few times, examining it.

"This is fancy, looks like it would've been nicer if the money helped with the bills, you fucking freeloader," he spits at me.

"I do help with the bills," I say softly, looking down at my feet.

"Don't fucking backtalk me!" he screams, throwing my phone right at my head.

I'm hit right by my eye; I feel the blood start coming down into my eye making my vision blurry. I hold my hand up to help with the throbbing.

"Why do you hate me so much?" I ask quietly; I don't even think I meant to say it out loud. Or maybe I did. Either way it was the wrong thing to say.

"What the fuck did you just say?" my mom screams as she quickly comes toward me, grabbing my hair, pulling my head back so hard it burns my scalp.

My mom used to be pretty, I see the resemblance between us. She's the same height as me, same brown hair, but unfortunately, I get my eyes from my dad, so every time I see my own I think of his. They both were attractive at some point, but apparently becoming alcoholic, abusive assholes takes your looks away.

"I just want to know why you hate me!" I scream.

Suddenly, I'm hit so hard I'm not sure if it was a fist or a slap, but my face is in agony, then before I know what's happening my whole body is pushed until I hit a wall, knocking all the air out of me.

"I should've killed you as soon as I found out I was pregnant, you useless piece of shit," she spits at me, while I'm crumpled on the ground.

I feel a foot on my side, slowly putting pressure on my ribs until it becomes harder. I scream out in pain. I'm in so much pain all over. The pressure becomes unbearable on my ribs and I scream out, "STOP!"

The pressure releases. I breathe heavily, but it hurts to take in air. I'm still on the ground, holding my body as small as I can make it. I can't hear anything, the only sounds I can make out are my heartbeats in my ear and the blood rushing in my head.

I think they leave after that, maybe because it's less fun when I'm not fighting back. That's what it seems like sometimes, but when I try not to fight back, they still do it. I don't think there's any way to please my "parents". I just want to leave. I don't know how, but I need to leave before they do finally kill me.

THE NEXT DAY at school I'm hiding my face the best I can because I have a nasty cut right by my eye along with the distinct black and purple markings already prominent on my tender skin. and bruising basically up to my temple. I also think I may have a broken rib, but there's nothing I can do about that.

I go see Mrs. Hale. I've seen her at least twice a week for the last two years and she's still the only adult I've ever trusted. She's the only person that understands me. I've never told her the extent of my parent's abuse because I'm scared.

As soon as I walk into her office this morning, I know all of that is going to change because there's no hiding the damage they did to me this time. Usually, it's able to be covered up, but not today.

She sees me, and I can tell she's trying not to show a reaction as she invites me inside her office, we sit in our same spots we always do. I'm taking in the room I'm so familiar with. She doesn't say anything at first, but I know she saw my face.

I don't know how to even start this conversation. I'm not even sure what to say. I don't think I can voice the abuse even if I wanted to, not the full extent of it anyway.

"I want to live somewhere else," I say, looking right at Mrs. Hale so she can see the physical evidence on my face.

"Is it because of your injuries, Aylin?" she asks softly.

I nod.

"Did the people you live with cause those injuries?" I notice she doesn't say parents, though she knows that's who I live with.

I nod again.

"You know I have to report this?" she says so quietly, almost like she's nervous about how I'm going to react.

I wait a moment, not fully processing how exactly my life is potentially about to change.

Finally, I nod again.

The worst night of my life led to the best day of my life, up until this point.

Mrs. Hale had to call child protective services, and when the social worker saw my injuries, she asked me what happened. I couldn't go into full detail, but what I said was enough for them. They wanted me to go stay with family, but I knew my grandparents wouldn't take me in. The options are so limited considering where we live in the small eastern Oregon town, Pendleton.

Then, it didn't seem real, but Mrs. Hale said I could stay with her. She would have to ask her boss, but she knows it's possible. Her and her husband don't have any children, only a dog. I get excited at the thought of living in a house with a dog, I've always wanted one so I'm excited to meet Maggie.

The next few months are the hardest to adjust to.

I meet her husband, Jeff. They are the nicest people I've ever known.

I move into Mrs. Hale's home. She insists I call her Sam, but it feels weird since I've called her Mrs. Hale for two years.

Their pug, Maggie, becomes my best friend. She sleeps on my bed every night and for the first time in my life I feel wanted. I feel like I belong somewhere.

The nightmares don't stop while I live there. I'm up screaming, Sam and Jeff having to check on me multiple times at night because I'm screaming so loud it wakes them up, and they don't know if I'm okay or not.

Sam gets me in with therapists and psychiatrists who diagnose me with so many big words and acronyms it's hard to even keep up. I also don't like the doctors, they look at me like I'm broken, damaged and it just makes the flashbacks worse.

I feel like I'm an experiment or something they are studying. I don't feel like a person anymore when I'm at the doctors.

At home it's better. Sam and Jeff always treat me like a person, and even better they treat me as a person they could love. It's hard to believe, and I doubt it often, but they show they care for me. The best part is that for the first time in my life I feel safe in my home.

I continue to work, saving up everything I make for college because I'm still determined to escape to go to school. I also focus on my schoolwork like crazy so I can get all the scholarships possible.

    I never hear from my parents. They had court cases for the various charges of child abuse, but I never had to go and face them. Sam and Jeff went, but I never wanted to. I don't know what happened to them, I didn't want to. I just wanted to know they would never see me again. Sam and Jeff told me they wouldn't and that's all I cared about.

19

Present

I left Aylin's apartment on Friday night after she fell asleep because honestly, I didn't want to face her kicking me out on Saturday morning, which I figured would be inevitable. Even though I wanted nothing more than to fall asleep with her wrapped around me.

I did leave her a note because I didn't want her to think I was just ditching her like a one-night stand. If there's anything I know after that night, it's that I have to keep seeing her.

I don't think I could stop if she wanted me to, and I know she wants to as well, no matter what she is trying to convince herself—and me—of.

I've never been so pulled to anyone. I like being around her, I like how she feels, I like her smile and her laugh. I like how she's cautious for me to see all of her as a person, but I'm determined.

I brought home files from work about the case to look over through the weekend. I've always been ambitious, but this is a new level because I'm determined to prove myself so everyone can see that I can handle myself, no matter what I've been through, I've got this.

It's a little more difficult to focus solely on work since I can't get Aylin out of my head. In my note I told her to reach out to me because I know she's going to have her internal battle from sleeping with me. I know she wants me just as badly as I want her, I can see it. She just has to let go a little and let herself want me.

By Sunday night I still haven't heard from her, and I haven't been able to read through all the files like I wanted to because I've been so distracted with wanting to reach out to her, or even show up at her door, but I knew that would be too far.

I decide to suck it up and reach out to her on the off chance she was just waiting for me, even though I made it clear in my note that I wanted her to make the decision.

I just can't take it anymore.

> Nate: Did you see the note I left you?

I feel like a teenager with a crush or something the way I stare at my phone waiting for her to reply. I am not usually like this; I do not know what is going on with me.

I'm surprised she replies so quickly, I half expected her to leave me on read or take hours to respond.

> Aylin: Yes.

Um. Okay.

I can't tell if she's mad, or anything. Texting can be such a bitch since you lose all the physical indicators and nonverbal communication. As someone who can read people really well, I hate texting. I know if I call her, she likely won't answer.

> Nate: Just wanted to make sure since I haven't heard from you.

I add a winking emoji so she can tell I'm trying to flirt with her. I make it pretty obvious, and I have from the start, even if she hasn't always reciprocated, she definitely did on Friday. Multiple times.

> Aylin: Because I haven't reached out. We can't do this, Nate you know that.

There it is. Exactly what I thought, she probably woke up on Saturday mad at herself for everything that happened, then spent the rest of the weekend convincing herself she can ignore me, and I'll just go away.

Like I said, I'm good at reading people.

Is it completely ethical for a therapist to fuck one of their very brief and past clients? Probably not, but it's not like I'll complain about it or tell anyone. Was it completely ethical for her to see me as a therapist after what happened with the Moore case? No, but she did it anyway. I know she will fight this, but I won't give up.

> Nate: Go out with me again.

I ignore her telling me we can't do this anymore because I don't give a fuck. I know what I want, and I've always worked for what I want.

I don't expect her to reply to me again so I put my phone down away from me so I can try to focus on more of these files, hoping something sticks.

∽

Monday afternoon comes around, and Aylin still hasn't replied to my last text from yesterday. I've been in training for the undercover case all day, luckily going over a lot of what I read already so I'm only half paying attention.

Call me cocky, I just think I'm confident, but I know they could throw me into this case without half this information and I would still get shit done. I know who the main players are, I know the gist of what we are doing. What else do they think I need?

Toward the end of the day, I decide to reach out to Aylin again, and if she doesn't respond I know she will be here tomorrow. If I just happen to go by her office, then she can try to reject me in person. I have a feeling that might be a little harder for her to do than over text.

> Nate: I really want to see you again.

I send the text on my way to the gym. I refuse to look at it once I've changed and connected my music to the speakers, throwing myself into my workout. I focus on the strain of my muscles as I begin.

My mind drifts back to her, like it always does, wishing I could at least show her how to protect herself a bit more. Call me overprotective or whatever, but I have my reasons. I have seen too many women get hurt. Plus, there's what happened to my parents.

I don't talk about that shit.

I was tempted to tell her when she asked what happened, but I couldn't do it. I don't need to tell anyone about that. She can just accept that I want her to be able to protect herself and that's it.

I want her to know how to use weapons. I want her to have the advantage in any fight. I can see that she's tough. I saw it while I had her in here. She hides it well; she hides everything well. She went through something in her life, and I don't know what it is, but I can tell.

After my workout she still hasn't replied, so I guess I'll be seeing her tomorrow because I'm not giving her up that easily. I know she wants this; she just needs a little more convincing to get her out of her head. Luckily, that's one of my specialties.

20

Aylin

Present

Nate is persistent that's for sure.
 I knew he was, but I genuinely thought after we slept together, he would have gotten what he wanted and then leave me alone.

I know I really didn't want that; I know I haven't slept with anyone in...a long time, but it was really good, and I hate that I want to do it again.

He wants to see me again, he made that clear in his note he left for me, but he was putting the ball in my court, which gave me the time to think and convince myself not to reach out to him.

Then, he gave in and texted me anyway. I've ignored his last two messages to me saying he wants to see me because I want to see him too, and I don't trust myself to keep saying no. I feel like my "no" quota is almost out with him.

It's the end of my long day at my clinical and I'm finishing up packing my stuff into my bag. I want to get out of here since I have no idea where Nate is or what he's doing. He's cleared, so he could be out doing god knows what right now, and I just want to go home.

I jump at the noise of the front door closing. My heart is slamming in my chest, no one is supposed to be here.

Next thing I know, the door to the office opens and I'm panicking because I don't know who is here. A tall figure appears in the doorway, the subtle light illuminates the features I've grown annoyingly familiar with, and my panic turns into annoyance at the sight of the dark-haired man that just walked in. It's like my thoughts of him made him appear.

"What are you doing here?" I turn back around to the desk to continue shoving my things in my bag, preparing to leave.

"You won't reply to me," his deep voice sends a shiver down my spine, and I hear him stepping closer, but I refuse to turn around.

"And you can't take the hint?" I continue to refuse to look at him, though I feel his body closer to my back now.

"I would, if I believed you really didn't want to see me again." I feel his hand come up, brushing my hair off my shoulder, exposing the side of my neck.

I turn around to face him, and dammit if those hazel eyes that feel like they could burn a hole into me could look elsewhere.

"I don't want to see you again. Good enough for you?" I fold my arms across my chest.

"No, it's not. You're lying, you have too many tells, sweetheart."

I raise my eyebrow to him. "I'm not lying, so what are my tells?"

The side of his mouth curls up in a small smile, "Your eyes don't hide what you're thinking as well as you think they do. That, and your breathing changes. You shift your position, slightly. Plus, you get the lightest pink tinge to your cheeks. All of these are small, most people wouldn't catch them, but I do."

"What makes you think these are my tells that I'm lying? Maybe you just make me uncomfortable."

"Because it's what I do. I catch liars. And sweetheart, you're not getting rid of me."

My breathing hitches, and I try to hide it. Nate lifts his hand to run his knuckles over my jaw, then down the side of my neck and onto my shoulder. I try to ignore the path of fire he's leaving behind by his touch, refusing to acknowledge any of the responses my body is involuntarily giving.

"You should go, Nate."

He steps closer to me, so our chests are less than an inch apart. I'm craning my neck to look up at him.

"Is that what you really want?"

No. "Yes."

He's looking into my eyes, searching, I can see it. I'm so focused on not showing any of my so-called "tells" that I don't feel him snake his hand around my back until he's pulling me flush against him. I gasp as our chests collide.

He leans down, his mouth brushing against my cheek, "Liar."

Before I can protest anymore his lips slam onto mine, his tongue is in my mouth, and I meet the ferocity of the kiss because damn him, of course I was lying.

Nate tightens his hold on me so I couldn't pull back if I wanted to, but I don't even want to. We kiss like we need each other's mouths, our tongues tangling together. I feel him groan into my mouth as I take his bottom lip between my teeth.

He pushes me back against the desk, lifting me so he's situated between my thighs, pushing himself against me while our mouths never part.

"You ready to admit you want me again?" he murmurs against my mouth.

I shake my head.

He chuckles as he presses his erection against my covered

center. I moan into his mouth at the feeling of him pressing against my already throbbing clit.

Goddammit I do want him again. I want him to touch me. I want to touch him. I don't want him to know he's right.

Nate's mouth leaves mine as he starts to trail kisses down my jaw and onto my neck.

"We can't do this here," I finally squeak out.

He hums against my throat where he's continuing his open mouth kisses. "So you don't want me to bend you over this desk, and fuck you until you can't remember your name?"

I moan, pulling him against me harder because I can't tell him that I want him, but I also can't stop myself from reacting, and showing him that I do.

"You don't want me to touch you here?" He slips his hand under my dress, moving my panties to the side to glide his hand over the wetness that has pooled between my legs, making my hips buck toward him. "You're saying you don't want that?"

I try to rub myself against his hand more, but he moves it away.

"Tell me you want me," he growls against my ear before nipping my neck, resulting in a gasp from my throat. "Last chance before I stop."

I debate, but he continues his kisses along my neck, up my jaw and when he reaches my lips, he ghosts over them before descending his lips on the other side of my neck.

He's trying to drive me crazy. And it's working.

I try to rub myself against his erection again in a silent plea, but he doesn't let me as he tightens his hold on my hips.

I let out a frustrated groan, "Fine, I want you."

He takes his lips off my neck to look me in the eyes again. His eyes are filled with lust before his mouth crashes onto mine again. The intensity is even more now, I'm sliding my hands up his chest to remove his shirt as I run my fingers along his corded muscles.

Once his shirt hits the floor, I barely get to touch him before he flips me around by my waist and I'm bent over the desk, just like he said he would.

Nate slides my dress, so it's bunched around my waist as he pulls my panties down my legs, running his rough, callused hands over my skin.

"I've never seen a more perfect sight, you bent over, fucking dripping for me. Are you always this wet for me, sweetheart?"

I want to slam my legs shut because it feels too personal to have him staring at me so open like this, but his hands are on my ass, squeezing as he groans.

"No, I'm not," I manage to say.

"When I was sitting in this same office with you not that long ago, you weren't soaking your little panties thinking about me doing this to you?" his voice is low and sexy, I swear I could come from just the words he's saying. To emphasize his point, he pushes a finger inside me, just barely and pumps only once before removing it, and I whimper.

"No," I say weakly.

"You didn't go home after you met with me, and touch your pretty pussy until you came so fucking hard while you screamed my name?"

I bite my lip because I would never admit to touching myself to the thoughts of Nate. Even though our night together only a couple days ago has been the only thing I think about when I find my hands between my thighs every night since then. "No," I breathe out, and even I don't believe it.

I feel his bare chest against my back as he leans down to speak directly into my ear, "Stop lying to me."

I'm about to insist that I'm not lying, yet again, but he has slid down and I feel his mouth latch onto my throbbing pussy. I yelp at the sudden contact I wasn't expecting as he begins to devour me.

"Goddammit Aylin, your taste is fucking addicting," he

growls against me, and I can't stop my moans from escaping as I try to push myself against his mouth harder. "I've needed your taste on my tongue ever since Friday."

Nate's tongue is everywhere, on my clit, at my opening, licking me all over. When he presses a finger inside me, I practically lose it. I'm holding onto the edge of the desk so hard I swear I might break it. I feel myself building as his fingers move inside me, and his tongue flicks against my bundle of nerves at the perfect rhythm.

"Don't stop," I gasp because I think he might, just to drive me insane.

I feel him chuckle against me, and that's what sends me over the edge as the orgasm takes over my entire body.

Nate continues licking me until I come down, then he presses kisses along the inside of my thighs before rising to his feet again.

His lips are against my neck again as he speaks, "Tell me you want my cock inside you. Tell me you want me to fuck you."

He thrusts his hips against me, rubbing his erection still restrained by his pants against my ass.

"Fuck me, Nate," I whimper. I blame the orgasm for the reason I actually say those words out loud.

"Do you have condoms?" He asks, his voice husky and clearly frustrated that he doesn't have one.

"I thought you were always prepared?" I taunt.

"This just shows I didn't assume anything would happen," he taunts back, biting my shoulder.

I moan, pushing back against him. "I'm on the pill, and I'm clean," I manage to say even though I'm about to lose my mind.

"I'm clean too. Thank fuck."

I hear him quickly undo his pants before kicking my legs further apart, I feel the head of him against me. He slides himself over my ass before lining up at my opening. I push my hips back, but he holds me still with one hand on my hip. I look back to see his other hand is on the base of his thick cock.

I groan, seeing the sight, his tan skin covered in impossible muscles, and his dick in his hand, as he starts to push inside me. I watch him as he watches himself slide inside me. The pure ecstasy on his face along with the feeling of him filling me brings out another moan from me.

"You're so fucking tight, Aylin, I can barely stand it," he groans, as he pushes himself all the way to the hilt, so his hips are against my ass, but he doesn't move.

"Are you going to fuck me or just stand there?" I snap because he still isn't moving.

That gets me a reaction from him as he grabs a fistful of my hair and pulls my head back, hard. I have to hold myself up as he presses deeper inside me while my back meets his chest.

"I should fuck your mouth to keep you quiet," he growls as he pulls my hair tighter. I yelp at the pain, but also feel the wetness seeping down my thighs from his words.

I like this. I want this.

"As long as you fuck something before I decide to get myself off," I shock myself with my own words. I have never been much of a dirty talker, but the only other two guys I've been with haven't either.

This is new, and I love it. I will never admit it out loud, but I think I like this side that Nate is bringing out of me, and because I know this won't last forever with him, I'm choosing to embrace it.

With that Nate pushes me down against the desk so my chest is flat against the hard wood while he pulls out of me, almost completely before slamming into me so hard I slide forward on the desk, and I cry out.

He holds me down as he continues to fuck me so hard; I swear the desk is moving with each thrust. I'm gasping and moaning with each hard slam of his hips against me. I'm not the most experienced and no one has been this rough with me or said dirty shit to me during sex. I can't believe how much it turns me on.

Each of his thrusts hits a spot inside me that brings me closer to another orgasm. I feel it building as I move my hips to meet his thrusts as much as I can with his hand holding me down against the desk.

I feel Nate press his chest against my back as he continues to fuck me so hard I swear I'm seeing stars. This new position of his body hits a spot even deeper inside me that sends me over the edge.

He grabs onto my hands, holding them above my head as I convulse under him, I'm moaning nonsense, but he doesn't stop. He continues to fuck me through my aftershocks, prolonging probably the most intense orgasm of my life, and with a few more powerful thrusts I feel him throb inside me as he explodes as well, filling me completely.

We are both breathing hard as he pulls out of me. I stay bent over the desk for a few more seconds while I compose myself before having to look him in the eye again.

I don't know what it was about all of that, but I have never been so turned on or orgasmed so hard. I've always thought I'm pretty tame when it comes to sex, but maybe that's not the case. Maybe I want more, and Nate just gave me a taste of it.

I stand up, fixing my dress, picking my underwear off the ground, but they are so wet it doesn't make sense to put them on again.

Nate leans against the desk with his pants back on his hips, next to me with his arms folded over his still bare chest, and a smirk on his gorgeous face. "Let's talk about you going out with me again."

"Nate," I start, rolling my eyes.

"Don't, Aylin. Stop fighting this." He shakes his head, moving closer to me.

I don't back away from him.

"It's wrong."

"Did that feel wrong?" he scoffs.

"No, but you know it's wrong."

"All I know is that I like you, you like me, and we both want to keep seeing each other." He reaches out to cup my face, and the touch makes me weak, or maybe it was the two Earth shattering orgasms. I can't be sure of which at this point.

"What if someone finds out, I could get in so much trouble." I try to shake my head to break eye contact with him, but he won't let me.

"No one will find out; I won't tell anyone. Just Aylin and Nate, remember?"

I hate this. I hate that I'm actually considering this. No, I'm more than considering, I'm actually fighting the agreement from coming out of my mouth because I know how stupid of an idea this is.

"Fucking in my office isn't the best way for people not to find out, you know?" I attempt to joke.

This earns me a smile from him, his perfect white teeth make me even more weak in the knees. This man is so attractive doing anything and everything, it's wrong.

"I'll try to not corner you in here again, but I will not make any promises." He holds me captive by his eyes and smile.

"Fine, I will stop ignoring you," I say reluctantly.

"That's not good enough, sweetheart." He leans closer, his lips hovering close to mine, our breath mingling.

"We can keep seeing each other," I sigh, giving in.

"Finally." He presses his lips to mine, and I melt into him because nothing has ever felt more right in my life than his lips on mine, and him holding me.

He makes me feel comfortable, safe, and alive for the first time ever, but I can't help but be scared of this.

Everything about this scares me; it's new and I don't trust

easily. I can't help but be cautious of everything and everyone, not believing for a second that I won't end up hurt in the end.

I feel like I'm losing control of everything I've held so closely my entire life to keep me safe, and it's all going to come crashing down. I'm going to slip, Nate is going to see who I really am and hate that I'm not who he thinks I am, who I want him to believe I am.

I feel like I'm Alice about to dive headfirst down the rabbit hole and descend into madness.

I wonder if she was scared?

Because I'm fucking terrified.

21

Present

The last two weeks have flown by. Every day at work I learn more about the undercover case, while I count down the minutes until I can see Aylin again, which has only been a handful of times since we are both so busy.

It's crazy how she's managed to embed herself so deeply into my life without even trying. I, on the other hand, had to try a bit to embed myself into her life, but it's been worth it.

I finally told her about this case last week because I knew I would have to tell her sooner than later considering I have no idea what that's going to look like for us. I haven't liked to think about it, but I know I'm going to figure something out. I always do.

"I'm going to be going undercover in a week or two," I whisper into her hair, unsure if she's even still awake after we fucked so hard, I think we both blacked out for a moment.

"What do you mean?" She lifts her head to face me, a sense of worry in her bright blue eyes.

"It's connected to Zander's stepbrother's case, there's some shit going on that we need officers on the ground to learn about. I can't tell you everything, but I hope you trust me." I cup her face, running my thumb along her cheek.

"That sounds dangerous, Nate." She shakes her head.

"My job is always dangerous, this is just something new, but I'll be okay, I always am." I give her a full smile.

"I know," she lays back down, resting her head on my chest, her fingers tracing the muscles there, "you are more than capable of handling yourself and I know you'll be fine."

She says the words, but I can sense the worry still in her voice. She doesn't show emotions easily, so the little peek into what she's really thinking makes me roll her onto her back, hovering over her.

"Damn right I'm able to handle myself, sweetheart. You better not forget it."

She rolls her eyes, and it makes me want to distract her again. I kiss the eyes she just rolled, her cheeks, nose, and mouth quickly as she breaks into laughter at my quick kisses.

This is the Aylin no one gets to see, but it's my favorite. Her laughing, free like whatever holds her back all the time isn't there anymore. It's a rare peek into this side of her, but when I get to, I love to see it.

Now, here we are, and they are starting to send guys into the field. We need to do this slowly to not raise suspicion, and there's only a handful of us going in. I'm one of them, next week. I haven't told Aylin that yet, but I want us to go away for the weekend since it will be the last chance we have to do so for the foreseeable future.

I decided to surprise her with this trip, but I'm sure she will be happy about it. She tends to overthink anything and everything, so I like to spring things on her at the last minute. She may act like she doesn't like surprises, but I think she secretly does.

One early morning I took her best friend, Mel's number from her phone to let her know I was planning on taking Aylin on a weekend trip to Newport to see her.

I had spoken to Mel once before under very different circumstances, and her boyfriend Zander a couple times. It felt weird to reach out but I did it anyway, for Aylin.

I was planning on us getting a hotel on the ocean, but Mel insisted we stay with them because she wanted time with Aylin as well. As much as I don't want to share her, I know she will appreciate the time with her best friend. I also remember Zander, he was a cool guy, I think we might get along well.

Before work on Friday, I packed a bag, throwing it in my trunk before heading to work since I plan to get Aylin right after, and head to the coast. She has no idea we are going anywhere; she just knows I'm coming over.

As I walk out of work, I send her a text that I know will get her mind racing.

> Nate: Pack a bag sweetheart, we are going on a trip.

I smile, knowing what her reaction to that will be. As I climb into my car I get her reply, unable to stop my laughter at how right I was.

> Aylin: What? Where are we going? I need more info than that.

> Nate: I'll be at your place soon, if you're not packed then I'm just bringing you with the clothes on your back.

I put my phone down as I make my way to her apartment.

She likes when I command her and take control. That's something I learned early on, and I love it. Sweet Aylin is not so sweet. She pretends to be, she pretends to be a few things, but I can tell when it's not genuine.

She gets this spark in her eyes when she looks at me. It's almost like she wants to break through a wall she's built and explode. I see it mostly when she wants to challenge me or fight me on something. It just makes me smile, wishing she would. She has an amazing sense of humor and is a fighter, that much I know for sure.

Aylin doesn't open up about her past, that's the one thing between us. I haven't told her much about parts of mine either. I'll share happy memories of my parents; she won't share any. She never talks about her parents or what it was like for her growing up. I know she's from Pendleton, and that's it.

I can't fault her, I haven't told her what happened to my parents, and I don't even know how that conversation would come up. One thing I appreciate more than she will ever know, is that she hasn't brought up the incident that landed me in her office in the first place. I've half expected her to ask multiple times, but she hasn't.

I'm sure both of those topics will come up at some point, but I'm fine keeping them buried for now, especially when she won't open up herself.

It doesn't take long until I'm in front of her apartment, parking on the street as I walk up to her door. I lean against the wall after knocking, waiting for her to answer.

The door swings open, the air making her long hair whip around her annoyed face, making me smile at the sight of her.

"Hey sweetheart." I grab her face to kiss her instantly because I can't help myself. Every time I see her, I just have to touch her.

She pulls away from my lips too quickly. "Nate, you can't just tell me what to do without giving me more information."

"You know you like me telling you what to do," I wink at her which earns me an eye roll. God, when she does that, I just want to pin her down and fuck her until she begs for forgiveness.

"That's different," she mumbles, heat flaring in her gaze. She's going to distract me, and I'm determined for us to make it out of this apartment at some point.

"Do you have a bag packed?" I ask to not let her derail my plans.

She huffs before reaching around the corner to show me a duffle bag she packed. I have to admit, even I'm surprised she listened.

"Good girl, let's go." I smile at her as she still looks at me with annoyance as she walks past me out the front door. I smack her ass as she walks past me, making her yelp.

"You're in an extra good mood today," she says. Once we are both outside as she locks the door.

"I get you almost all to myself all weekend, of course I'm in a good mood." I purposely drop the hint which she notices.

"Almost?" She questions as we get to my car, putting her bag in the trunk along with mine before climbing in.

I give her a smile without answering as she continues to stare at me while I drive.

"I don't get any more info than that?" she asks.

"Nope, you'll see soon enough, sweetheart." I reach my hand out to rest on her thigh as I drive.

She turns up the music as I continue to drive us out of town.

It doesn't take long before she catches on the direction we are headed, and beams over at me. Her hand that has been resting on top of mine on her thigh the whole time now has our fingers intertwined.

"Are we going to see Mel?" she asks, excitedly.

I can't help but meet her happiness while I nod.

She squeezes my hand, a huge smile on her face I can

barely turn away from, but I have to watch the road. Even though I don't want to miss a second of the happiness on her beautiful face. Happiness, I caused.

"Thank you, Nate," she says softly.

"You don't have to thank me, sweetheart. I wanted to do this."

I mean it. I wanted to do something for her, for us. I wanted to be the reason she's happy. I want to do everything I can to always keep that smile on her face.

I keep glancing over at her, seeing her eyes trained on the side of my face. She hasn't looked away; her eyes are soft with the setting sun lighting her profile making her eyes look like they are glowing.

"What are you thinking?" I ask her when she still hasn't looked away from me.

"I'm wondering what I did right in my life to get here," she says softly.

"What do you mean?"

"I usually don't think I deserve anything good, so I don't know how I'm here with you and what the catch is," she admits. Making my head snap in her direction where I can see the sadness in her eyes, like she truly believes this.

"Why don't you think you deserve anything good?"

She shakes her head, her walls coming back, that easy to read emotion leaving her eyes. "Never mind, don't worry about it. Thank you."

I feel her try to move her hand from mine, but I squeeze tighter so she's unable to. "There's no catch, and you deserve all the good in the world. I want you to know that."

She doesn't say anything in response, and that's okay. I think I just saw the first glimpse at a vulnerable side to Aylin, and it makes me wonder about what she's hiding even more.

Once we pull up to the address Mel gave me it's dark, and I'm really hoping this is the right house. It doesn't look very big.

The first level is a garage, there's a staircase to the left that leads up to what I assume is the front door.

As soon as we pull into the driveway, I see the front door fly open to reveal a short woman with long auburn hair as she runs down the stairs to greet us. I see Zander follow behind her, slower since he isn't running, but he's about as tall as me, maybe an inch or so taller so his long strides keep up with the running Mel.

Aylin and I get out of the car at the same time as I watch Mel collide with Aylin in a tight aggressive hug. They are both smiling and laughing as they greet each other.

"Hey man, good to see you again," Zander says to me, nodding.

"You too, glad it's for a different reason," I say, nodding back.

"I don't think I ever thanked you for everything by the way," Zander says as the girls are continuing their reunion.

I shake my head at him. "Not necessary at all, I think we can all move on and agree on what really matters." I gesture to the two excited women on the other side of the car.

"I can agree with you there, do you want a drink or anything?" Zander asks as I grab both bags from the trunk.

"Sounds good to me," I say to him.

"You two want to come in or are you planning on staying out here all night?" Zander jokes, Mel turns to him with her tongue sticking out.

Aylin told me about them, they were best friends for basically forever, and you can tell. You can also tell how much love is there. Even just standing here for a couple minutes, I can see how Zander looks at Mel when she isn't even paying attention to him. I've only ever seen that level of love between my parents, and it makes my chest ache at the memory.

We all make our way inside the house, Mel and Aylin not letting each other go, making me laugh. I have never had a friend I felt that close to, not even Mitch, and it makes me curious if I could get any information about Aylin from Mel, if she would tell me any little thing Aylin won't share herself.

The house is amazing, Aylin said they've been doing work on it, and I can tell. It looks upgraded, and clean. The back wall is all floor to ceiling windows looking out onto the ocean, it's beautiful. The moon is reflected in the water, you couldn't ask for a better view.

Zander shows me the guest room on the left of the living room so I can put the bags down.

"I hope you're ready to stay up while the girls talk all night," he says as we walk out into the kitchen.

"I'm ready to hear what Aylin may say about me," I say as Zander hands me an uncapped beer.

"If anyone will get information out of her it's my Mel Bell, trust me," he chuckles, taking a sip out of his own drink.

Mel and Aylin are on the couch in the living room, facing each other talking as I just watch their interaction, appreciating how unguarded Aylin is right now, I don't want to ruin it. I get glimpses of this side of her, but there's always something there. Not right now. In this moment I see her completely herself, and I can't look away.

They are speaking quietly so I can't hear, well Aylin is. I can hear Mel a little better since she's slightly louder. They both laugh, throwing their heads back like the funniest joke ever was just told.

"Nate," I hear Zander say, bringing my attention back to him in the kitchen. "Look, I don't know everything about Aylin and her past, but I know some from what Mel has told me and I don't know what you know, but understand that she's the way she is for a reason."

"What do you mean?" I ask, maybe I can just get some information out of Zander instead of Mel, that seems easier.

"I mean, she's been through some shit, and she doesn't need to go through more. I don't know what all that shit is, so don't ask. I also know that she will go to the ends of the world for the people she loves, I've seen it with them. They both would." He nods to the girls on the couch. "Don't take it for granted, and don't ever underestimate her."

I nod, "I don't think it would be possible to underestimate her, trust me."

Zander nods before heading into the living room to sit on the couch behind Mel, wrapping his arms around her. She sinks into him, while continuing to talk like he isn't even there. I want to do the same with Aylin, but I know she isn't big on shows of affection in front of people.

I think about what Zander said about her going through shit, I assumed so, but to have it confirmed makes me curious. I'm also thinking it has to do with her parents since she has such an aversion to talking about them.

I push the thoughts away for now, they aren't important. What's important is being in the here and now. I don't stop myself from walking into the living room to pull Aylin into my lap on the couch, she squeals at the sudden movement, but doesn't stop me or move off me.

I catch Mel's face directed at me like she knows this is out of character for Aylin to accept, and she's happy about it. They continue to talk with us present, Zander and I both eventually are able insert ourselves in their conversation.

Finally, after a while we all agree to go to sleep, Mel and Zander go to their room on the opposite side of the house from the guest room. I catch the wink Mel gives Aylin as we go our separate ways. It makes me chuckle and more curious about what she's said about me.

As badly as I want to ask, I really am tired, and Aylin is too. I see it as we crawl into the full-sized bed together, without much room we are having to be closely cuddled together, though I wouldn't want it any other way.

I know she isn't telling me things. I know I don't know

everything about who she really is, but right now I don't care. At this moment this is everything I could ever want, right here in my arms. My perfect little mystery.

I fall asleep to the distant sounds of waves crashing in the distance and Aylin's steady breathing against my chest.

22

11 Years Ago (Age Sixteen)

I've been living with Sam and Jeff for a few months, and I don't know how to feel. Some days I'm so glad to be out of my parent's house and out of their lives. Other times I feel like I'm fighting an uphill battle in my mind, and I don't know who I am or what I should be doing.

I started being more social now that my scars are fading, and I don't have to worry about fresh bruises on my skin every day. I've made a couple of friends, but I can tell they aren't the type of people Sam and Jeff hoped I would gravitate toward.

They are giving me space, telling me to be careful. I have a midnight curfew, and I always follow it. *Mostly.*

I will admit I've started to let go a bit as I'm figuring out who I am. I know I'm pushing my limits a bit, but I don't care. My new group of friends consists of three girls, Annie, Jasmine, and Reagan. They aren't anyone I would've talked to before, especially because they are always in everyone's business and that was exactly the type of people I used to avoid.

I don't avoid that anymore, but I also don't talk about anything from my past.

The thing with my new friends is that they love to party. There's not much to do where we live, so going to parties is really the only option we have. Yet another thing I would have never done before. I avoided alcohol like the plague since I saw what it did to my parents, but as of now I just don't care.

I don't care about anything.

We are at Jasmine's house getting ready. They have forced me into one of Reagan's dresses that I would never have considered wearing before. My ass is practically hanging out, and my boobs are hiked up to my chin.

They have a motive for putting me in this dress, and that's because Liam, a senior that we see at these parties often, has apparently said he's interested in me. He always talks to me and hangs around me when we see him, but nothing has happened. He's cute, and older, but I don't know what I'm doing when it comes to…any of this.

"Liam is going to come in his pants when he sees you, Ay," Annie says.

They call me "Ay", I don't like it, but haven't really said anything. Like I said, I just don't care.

I roll my eyes, "You don't even know if he will be there."

Reagan pops her head out of the bathroom to reply, "I have intel that he will be there."

"Intel? Who are you, the FBI?" Jasmine laughs. Reagan just shrugs before going back to doing her hair.

Reagan was right, Liam was at the party and as usual he didn't leave my side, touching me, talking directly into my ear. I kept refilling my drink because I wanted to silence the thoughts in my head screaming at me that I was going to turn into my parents.

I'll admit, that's the night I really started to spiral. I lost my virginity to Liam, and most nights after consisted of being with my friends or him, and there would usually be alcohol or weed involved.

I just. Didn't. Care.

Not about me.

Not about them.

Not about anyone.

Sam started to notice, and she tried talking to me on multiple occasions. I just waved her off because I knew what she was going to say and I didn't want to hear it.

After a particularly brutal night of partying, I wake up to Sam sitting next to my bed, a steaming cup of coffee on my nightstand with a bottle of ibuprofen. The sun from the window shining directly into my eyes, and it makes me want to curl under the blankets for eternity.

"I'm worried about you," Sam says, her voice soft.

"I'm fine," I mumble into the pillow.

"Aylin, have you been going to your appointments?" she asks gently, and I already don't like where this is going.

"Yes," I lie. I haven't. I don't like the appointments, they make me feel broken and fucked up, which I know I am. I just don't like doctors telling me over and over again.

"No, you haven't. They call me every time you skip an appointment. Please don't lie to me." Sam has the gentlest demeanor even when she's so clearly upset with me.

"Fine, I haven't, but I'm okay, I don't need to." I turn to my side to face her even though the sun is killing my head.

She sighs. "I know this has been a big adjustment for you, which is why Jeff and I have been letting you have some independence, but I feel like now is the time to intervene."

"What do you mean?"

"I don't know everything you're doing, and I don't want to, but I know it's not healthy and we are here to help. I don't want you throwing away your life because of this little rebellious streak. You experienced significant trauma, Aylin."

I cringe at the mention of my past, but she continues.

"You can't numb yourself and fight to be someone you're not, because I know this isn't who you are. You are an intelligent, strong, amazing person and I wish you could see that. Embrace that part of you, not whoever this is you're trying to be."

"What if this is who I'm supposed to be though? Isn't that what teenagers are supposed to do? Experiment and experience things to figure out who we are?" I argue.

"To an extent, but I see what you're doing, and I just can't sit back and watch it happen." She shakes her head. "Experimenting and experiencing things is okay in moderation, but that is not what you are doing."

I huff out a breath and don't say anything while I think back to what she said.

"I'm here for you, Jeff is here for you, please just think about it," Sam says before getting up and leaving my room.

After she leaves everything hits me.

They don't want me here.

They think I'm more trouble than I'm worth and they are going to end up kicking me out.

I bet Sam is calling that social worker that I've talked to a few times to come and take me somewhere else, so she doesn't have to deal with me.

I am going to end up just like my parents.

I am going to push every single person away until I'm all alone because that's what I should be.

Alone.

I can't breathe, my chest is tight as the tears are pouring down my face while the panic consumes me. I feel like I'm having a heart attack, or maybe I'm just dying.

I don't remember Sam and Jeff rushing into the room, but they are there saying things to me I can't hear because I'm just trying to catch my breath.

I think I'm screaming.

I think I'm saying, *"You want me out, you don't want me, no one wants me."*

They are comforting me. *I think.*

I don't know how long it takes before I feel like I can breathe again, and their voices become clearer as everything comes back to me. I can't stop crying. Sam is holding me as she smooths her hand down my hair.

"We want you here, this is your home, Aylin. We care," Jeff keeps saying as Sam consoles me.

Eventually, I calm down and apologize profusely about everything I've been doing. I beg them not to make me leave, I don't want to go to a foster home. I know they care about me, and they were just worried.

They tell me I'm not going anywhere; they would never do that to me. I calm down enough to believe them. But it doesn't stop the constant fear in the back of my mind that one day they will change their mind and decide I'm not worth it.

I still see Annie, Jasmine and Reagan, but I cut back on the partying because honestly, I didn't like it much anyway. I just wanted to feel normal.

Turns out Liam wasn't all that interesting without the parties, and we didn't last long after that.

Who knows who I would've been if Sam and Jeff didn't care enough to pull me from the path I was headed down, and I already knew I owed them everything, but this solidified it.

23

Present

I wake up in the morning to the sun streaming in through the tall windows that seem like they are in every room. If I told my younger self that one day, I would be waking up in a house like this I never would've believed it. I wouldn't have believed a lot of things about my life.

Even a couple months ago, I wouldn't have believed I would have just spent the night with a guy like Nate. I still don't believe any of this is real, and I know there's going to be another shoe drop soon because this isn't normal, especially not for me.

I'm nervous about him having to go undercover soon, but I'm choosing not to think about it right now. I don't want my worries or questions to ruin this weekend. I still can't believe he surprised me by bringing me here to see Mel. He got major points with her by doing this, though I already know she's a fan of his.

I turn over to see that Nate isn't in the bed with me anymore. I swing my legs over the side and stretch my arms out before making my way out into the living room to see who else is up.

Once I open the door I hear Mel's laughter and I follow the sound into the open area with the living room and kitchen. I see Nate and Zander are on the couch, Mel is standing in the kitchen nursing some coffee.

"Good morning, sleepyhead," Mel greets me, instantly pouring me a cup of coffee.

"Morning, sweetheart," Nate greets me with a smile as he stands up to come into the kitchen. He kisses the side of my head as Mel hands me a full mug.

"Here's your black coffee you psycho," she says with a disgusted look on her face. She always gives me shit about my lack of additives to my coffee, but it isn't about taste for me, I just want the caffeine.

Nate stays behind me, his front pressed against my back as we stand at the island, his arms on either side of me, caging me in. I feel a little weird having him so touchy with me in front of other people, but Mel shoots me an approving look as she goes to sit by Zander on the couch.

"How'd you sleep?" Nate asks quietly against my hair.

"Great," I say, turning around to face him. I don't know how long he's been awake, but this man never looks anything less than perfect, and it makes my heart feel crazy things in my chest. I have to look away from the intensity of his gaze.

"What's the plan for today?" Mel asks, wrapped in Zander's arms.

"I was thinking about the aquarium, have you ever been?" Nate asks me.

I shake my head.

"Fun! I wish we could go, but we have some stuff to do around here today; but we will all go out to dinner later," Mel says. I'm slightly disappointed she won't go, I don't get to see her much, but I don't doubt they have things they were planning on doing before we showed up.

"That okay with you, sweetheart?" Nate moves my chin so I'm looking up at him again.

I nod.

"You are really talkative in the morning, you know?" he says sarcastically.

I give him a small smile.

"Oh yeah, Aylin is not a morning person, you should see her hungover," Mel calls out, I shoot her a look to tell her to be quiet.

She laughs at me. My best friend, Mel, how I've missed her.

Nate chuckles, giving me some space so he's not holding me hostage against the counter, and I kind of wish he would move back. I like how safe I feel when he's close to me like that, not that I would tell him.

"Hey Nate, want me to show you what I'm working on in the garage?" Zander says.

"Oh yeah, that okay?" Nate asks me.

"Of course," I wave him off.

Zander kisses Mel sweetly before him and Nate go out the front door. I watch the two men walk out, my eyes unable to leave Nate. I don't even notice Mel saddling up next to me until she nudges me with her hip.

"The fuck did we do to be so lucky?" she asks, jokingly.

I shake my head, "I have no idea, but it's so cute to see how obsessed Zander is with you, you know?"

She waves me off. "No, you don't see how Nate looks at you. Girl, you need to open up to him more."

I cringe. Mel knows I'm holding back with him, she knows everything about me, and can always tell when I'm not being fully myself.

"I can't, he might not like who he sees if I do." I hate admitting it out loud, and Mel would be the only person I would ever dare say anything to.

"Trust me, he will. Give him a fair chance."

"I have been, that's why we are here."

"You think that, but you're really not. You need to show him every part of you."

"Who's the therapist here?" I roll my eyes, walking away to clean out my mug.

"Definitely you, I'm telling you to be reckless and you always tell me to be careful."

"And I'm being both," I shrug.

"Well, I'm saying to be less careful, and be a bit more reckless. I know you have it in you. I know you."

I chuckle. She really is the devil on my shoulder, and as much as I want to deny it, she does know me better than anyone in the world.

"You sure you don't want to come to the aquarium?" I ask her.

She shakes her head. "No, we really do have some stuff to do around here, and I want you to have alone time with your hot cop because seriously, damn girl."

"Hey, watch it, Zander would probably kick us out if he heard you say that," I laugh, he's pretty possessive of Mel, and I get why. He's lost her too many times before.

"He knows he has nothing to worry about, I can barely keep my hands off him for five minutes."

"Okay, let's not go there, I know more than I ever want to about your sex life already as it is."

"Speaking of—" Mel starts, but I cut her off.

"No! We aren't talking about me." I've never been open about my sex life. Mel has known when I date, but that's about all the extent I'll share.

Not that there's much to share to begin with.

"Come on, is it amazing? Best you've ever had? I need some

info as your best friend," she begs, making her point by sticking her bottom lip out in a pout.

I sigh, thinking before I answer, even though the answer is a resounding *yes*. I can't help but think about how we are together.

He doesn't treat me like I'm fragile, or question anything he does with me. He's confident in everything, and that's the biggest turn on I've ever experienced. Every dirty word he says to me to get me to do what he wants. The way he throws me around to the exact position he wants me in. It's more than amazing.

"Yeah, it's good," I say simply as I feel the blush on my cheeks.

"Oh, it's better than good, I can see it. I'm getting you drunk tonight, he's about to see fun Aylin." She rubs her hands together like she's plotting something.

I laugh as I walk back into the guest room to change. "Good luck with that!" I call back to her.

NATE and I drive to the aquarium. I enjoy the scenery of Newport during the day since I've never been here before. It's a pretty town, there's a river we crossed on our way here, and I can understand why Mel loves this place so much.

We head inside, getting our tickets before walking into the first part of the aquarium, it's bigger than I thought it would be. There are exhibits to see outside, and then in a couple different buildings.

"Have you ever been here before?" Nate asks as we stroll by some small tanks with various fish inside.

"No, I've never been to an aquarium or zoo or anything before," I say simply as I watch two clown fish that remind me of *Finding Nemo*.

"Never? First no video games, now this. What else have you missed out on?"

I walk to another tank that has some weird flat fish in it, not looking at Nate when I answer.

"Clearly a lot. I didn't even leave the state until I was in college, and even then, it was only to Washington. I've never even been on a plane," I shrug.

I don't look at him, but I feel his eyes on me, and I know he's thinking about why I've missed out on so much that would seem so normal to most people. I never questioned it before, I just accepted it's my life and I was meant to miss out on things as a kid. I figured some of it will happen as an adult.

"Aylin…" He starts, and I hear the sadness in his voice. I don't want his pity; I just want to enjoy our time together. That's all I've focused on lately. I don't know how long this will last, so I'm trying to live in the moment and enjoy it as it is.

"Don't." I turn to face him to cut him off, placing my hand on his hard chest, my pulse rising at the contact. "Don't feel bad for me, just show me what I've missed."

He smiles, I can tell he still feels bad for me, and probably wants to ask why I've missed so much, but I won't let him. He wraps his arm around my shoulder, pulling me against him. "You got it, sweetheart."

We pass by more tanks when we come up to a tank of jellyfish. I always thought they were so cool but have never seen any in person. I like the way they move in the water. I pull us to a stop as I stare at the little creatures.

"There's a type of jellyfish that's immortal, you know?" Nate says.

"How?" I question. I don't think anything should be immortal, life needs a cycle, no one wants to live forever.

"Well, it basically resets its lifespan, making it immortal. It's pretty cool if you think about it."

I shake my head, "I don't think so."

"Why?" He looks down at me, his dark eyebrows pulled together. *God*, he's attractive, I hate it.

"Well, they don't really do anything other than survive. So, not having any enjoyment and just having to survive forever with essentially no payoff? That sounds terrible."

"If they don't even know what enjoyment is, then are they really missing out, when all they know is survival?"

"So just because you don't know about something, you feel like it's worth living without? Because I've lived to just survive and I wouldn't want to do it forever, it's exhausting." I shake my head because I need to look away from his intense gaze that makes my knees weak.

"What do you mean you've lived to just survive?" he questions.

"Don't worry about it, I just wouldn't want to be immortal, that sounds awful." I try to move on, I shouldn't have admitted what I did to him.

I'm thankful he doesn't ask again; he just pulls me closer to him as we make our way to some exhibits outside.

I took Mel's advice, kind of, and opened up a little bit more and I hate it. So, I'm stopping again. It makes me feel vulnerable, like he's already looking at me differently. I don't like it.

We walk through an area with penguins, and laugh as they dive into the water. They are cute.

We pass by a tank that supposedly has an octopus in it, but it's dark and hard to see. Nate tries to find him since he's able to see more in the large tank due to his height, but he can't find it.

Making our way through the aquarium we come up to the otter tank, and I think they are my favorite. They look like little stuffed animals, and it makes me want to cuddle them.

I know I have a huge stupid grin on my face while I watch the fuzzy little creatures. I feel Nate's eyes glued to me, but I can't look away from the otters floating around in the water.

"You know, they hold hands while they sleep so they don't

float away from each other?" Nate asks, wrapping his arms around my chest, pulling me back against him as he rests his chin on the top of my head.

"That makes them even cuter," I say with a huge grin still plastered on my face. I think I have a new favorite animal.

"Where should I hold you to make sure you don't float away from me?" Nate asks jokingly.

I scoff. "Don't be cheesy, it's not a good look on you."

Suddenly, his arms move to my waist to turn me around quickly to face him, our chests pressed against each other now. I clench my thighs together because he affects me too easily, it's honestly a little annoying.

"What is a good look on me then, sweetheart?" He raises an eyebrow to me.

"Maybe I'll tell you later." I rise up on my tiptoes to press a kiss to his cheek before turning around to continue exploring through the exhibits.

We get to another inside part, and once we go in, I see a map indicating what's inside, which is multiple massive tanks with tunnels you walk through. We get to the first one, and I'm amazed. We are essentially in a room that is a giant fish tank. The lighting is filtered through the water giving the area a soft blue glow.

I walk ahead of Nate, amazed at everything.

I see sharks, one of them is pretty big as it swims over me, I watch, captivated at what I'm seeing. I probably look ridiculous as I gawk at my surroundings, turning in circles. I feel like I want to see it all at once, but I can't, so I have to keep turning to take it all in.

Finally, I look forward, seeing Nate leaning against a wall, his arms folded across his chest and his perfectly white teeth shown by his huge smile as he stares at me. His face is illuminated by the soft light around us, but I can see his eyes fixed on me like I'm the most interesting thing in here, when I definitely am not.

"This is amazing," I say because I feel like I need to break the silence between us, especially with the way he's looking at me.

"You're so beautiful," he says in response, pushing off the wall, striding over to me.

I feel the blush start to spread on my cheeks as I look down, I don't know what to say anytime he compliments me, let alone when he looks at me like that.

He closes the distance between us, cupping my face so I'm forced to look up at him. I feel his thumb pull my lip from between my teeth, I didn't know I was chewing on. I need to be more aware of these things.

"I could watch you like this for hours," he says softly. I try to look away again, but he won't let me.

I don't know what to say, sweet Nate is harder for me to talk to because I don't know what to do with it. When he's dominant, a bit demanding, or kind of an asshole, I handle that a lot better. This leaves me completely speechless and terrified.

I think Nate sees my internal struggle as he brushes his lips against mine softly. "Stop thinking so much."

He kisses me and I melt into him. I may not know what to say to him a lot of the time, but my body reacts to him no matter what. He pulls away too quickly and I remember where we are. Luckily no one else is in here right now, but anyone could come in any minute and that would be embarrassing.

We walk through the other tunnels, Nate holding onto me. I continue to be awestruck by my surroundings, whoever thought of this was a genius. I'm disappointed when we get through them all and end up back outside. It's less magical to be in the cloudy Oregon air than in the middle of a fish tank.

After a while we head back to Mel and Zander's house. I think about what Mel said earlier about giving Nate a real chance. I'm really trying, but sometimes I don't realize how closed off and damaged I am until I get scared.

While we are driving back Nate says something I've been dreading for a little while.

"They are sending me in next week." He squeezes my hand he's been holding as he drives.

"Oh, when?" I already told him it sounds dangerous; I know expressing my worry won't do anything. I may be scared to get close to Nate, but I'm also scared of him getting hurt.

"I'll find out on Monday when exactly. We aren't supposed to have any contact with our real lives while we are in," he says solemnly.

I don't like the pang in my chest as he says this. Is that why he brought me here? To have a nice last weekend together and then whatever this is will be over? I knew it would be at some point, but I don't like how I'm feeling about it right now.

"Okay, so this," I point at him and then back to myself, "will be done then?"

His head snaps over in my direction, "Is that what you want?" he asks sternly. It doesn't sound like that's what he wants, but isn't that what he just said?

"You just said you can't have any contact with your real life." I am trying to keep all emotion out of my voice.

"I said we aren't supposed to, but if anyone thinks I'll stay away from you they are insane," he says matter of fact.

"Isn't that dangerous? I mean I'm sure there's a reason they say you shouldn't."

"Do you trust me?" he simply asks.

I so badly want to say no. I've trusted less than a handful of people my entire life, and it has always taken me a while. For some reason Nate is different, and even in this short period of time, I do trust him. I just don't ever want to admit it because I feel like if I do, then it gives him a free pass to hurt me. Like if I admit it, then I give him permission because I made myself vulnerable enough to be hurt.

I want to lie, I really do, but Mel's voice is in my head telling me to give him a fair chance.

I sigh, and shrug, not giving a definitive answer either way. And because I can't say the word.

"Well, trust that I will keep us both safe and this," he copies my motion from before pointing to each of us, "is far from over, sweetheart."

My chest tightens at his words, and it scares the shit out of me. I haven't recognized any of the feelings I continue to try and bury. I've just been accepting that an extremely attractive man is giving me attention, and that's about it. This makes it feel like more, and it makes me want to retract.

He squeezes my hand again when I don't say anything. I hate that I do trust him, but I can't help the worry that comes from this. I don't know what he's going to be doing undercover, but there's no way it's going to be good.

I also would never dare bring it up, but I don't think he's dealt with whatever happened to him months ago that brought him into my office. I don't see him processing or anything, and he doesn't open up to me about it at all. I feel like he's just avoiding it, and that will only lead to an explosion later. I don't know if I can handle his explosion when it happens.

24

Present

Aylin and I go back to Mel and Zander's house after the aquarium. When we pull up, the garage is open with Zander sitting inside working on something at a workbench. We both get out of my car and walk toward him.

"Hey, how was it?" Zander asks us as we approach.

"It was great, what are you doing?" I ask him, examining the wood pieces around him.

"Mel wants some floating shelves, so I'm figuring out how to do that," he shrugs. I can see if from the short time here this man would do anything for her.

"Want some help?" I ask.

"If you're offering, I'll take it." He chuckles.

"Where's Mel?" Aylin asks, looking around for her best friend.

"She's down by the beach either reading, writing or possibly both." He smiles just at the mention of Mel.

"I'm going to find her," Aylin says to both of us.

She turns to walk around the house, but I reach out for her

arm and pull her against me to press a kiss to her lips first. I don't care that Zander is right there, I kiss her gently before smiling down at her as I see the pink tinge on her cheeks. I let her go as she leaves to try and find Mel.

"They have a way of getting to us, don't they?" Zander says once Aylin is out of earshot.

I turn around to assess what he's doing, trying to see if any of the wood scattered around can be salvaged.

"You have no idea," I say.

I've never been so into anyone before Aylin, the mystery around her just keeps pulling me closer.

"Oh, trust me, I do," he laughs.

"It's crazy how close Aylin and Mel are when they are so opposite," I comment.

"I think they bring out the best in each other, and they met when they both needed someone like that in their lives," Zander says, examining one of the pieces of wood.

I can't help but think about how what he says applies to me as well. Maybe, Aylin and I also met at a time when we both needed someone like each other in our lives. Even though I really am fine from what happened that night a couple months ago, having Aylin around has helped me in a lot of ways. I don't think about it as much, and it's been nice.

I watch Zander try to figure out what he's doing with the makeshift shelf and can't help but laugh at his previous failed attempts before jumping in to help him.

ZANDER and I hung out in the garage for a while, talking, drinking some beers and he really is a cool guy. It's kind of funny how well he and I get along, and how much we have in common considering he's technically a criminal.

I've never been one to judge people based on their past, so it didn't bother me at all. But the irony isn't lost on me.

Aylin and Mel had some time together that I didn't want to interrupt because I know how important their friendship is to each other. As it started to get later Zander and I made our way inside, expecting to see them there. We searched the small house and couldn't find them anywhere.

"I'll head down to the beach to look for them," I tell Zander as he starts to call Mel.

I make my way down the path to the water, hoping they didn't walk far. The four of us are going out to dinner, and I thought they would have made their way back earlier.

Of course, my mind goes to worrying about their safety. I can't help the different scenarios that flash through my mind of someone hurting them or trying to take them from us.

My steps speed up as my thoughts get darker as to why they aren't back yet I'm practically running once my feet hit the sand. I try to keep a calm composure as I take inventory around me, looking for any signs of them.

To the right there's some rock formations that would make it difficult to get around without climbing, so I decide to go left down the beach with quick steps. In the distance I see two figures, their long hair being blown back behind them. Even though I can't make out their faces, I know the slightly taller one is Aylin.

My nerves start to diminish as I see they are okay, and I was overreacting being so worried about them. I continue my quick pace toward them. They are both smiling and laughing at whatever they are talking about.

When I get close enough, I can't stop myself from grabbing Aylin, wrapping my arms around her waist to pick her up. She lets out a squeal because I don't think she expected that. I hear Mel laughing next to me.

"We didn't know where you both went," I say.

"Aw you do care," Mel replies with a fake sniffle.

I refuse to put Aylin down as we continue to walk back toward the house, even though I can see in her face she isn't happy about it.

"Zander was trying to call you," I say to Mel, ignoring Aylin's protests that I put her down.

"I don't have my phone, I like to keep him guessing," she shrugs.

"Keep him guessing or give him a heart attack?" I ask.

"A healthy dose of both."

"Last I checked, my legs work," Aylin says from my arms.

"Don't try to do that to me, I'll end up tearing apart everything to find you," I say, ignoring her comment.

"Put me down so I can run and test that theory," she says with a hint of annoyance in her voice, and I like it.

Mel is chuckling at our exchange. I don't know them very well, but I know Zander has a similar mindset as me and that he would stop at nothing to find her if she went missing.

"No can do, sweetheart, I officially have to be touching you at all times," I say as I hoist her over my shoulder and give her a quick swat on her ass.

She lets out a frustrated growl. "Mel, are you not going to help me? There's two of us and only one of him, we could totally take him."

"I know we are bad ass bitches, but I don't actually know if we could," Mel says, looking me up and down. She's at least a foot shorter than me, and it's funny to watch her weigh the option of trying while I have Aylin draped over my shoulder.

The three of us get back to the house, Mel walks quickly inside, I assume to see Zander. I finally set Aylin down where I'm met with narrowed blue eyes staring at me as she folds her arms over her chest.

"That was very unnecessary," she says, clearly irritated with me.

"I think it was completely necessary." I raise my eyebrow in amusement.

"You can't just manhandle me whenever you want," she huffs.

I can't help the laugh that escapes my throat as I lean closer so I can speak directly in her ear. I'm glad she doesn't try to pull away as my lips touch her ear softly. "I know you like it when I manhandle you, sweetheart."

I smirk as I pull away, watching her face flush with the truth of what I said. Yeah, Aylin doesn't like to admit a lot of things to me, but I know for a fact she likes how I handle her body. She doesn't deny it as she rolls her eyes and pushes past me to go inside the house without a word.

Following closely behind her we head inside where I expected to see Mel and Zander, but they aren't in the living room. The house is small, so I hear the shower running from the one bathroom and can assume they are both in there.

Aylin heads right into the guest room we are staying in. She tries to shut the door, but I open it before it shuts so I can follow behind her. She won't look at me as she starts going through her bag, pulling out the rest of her clothes.

I sigh before stepping behind her, wrapping my arms around her waist and nuzzling into her neck. She stiffens slightly at my touch like she's actively fighting against trying to lean into me like she normally does.

"Are you trying to fight me, sweetheart?" I ask against her hair.

"Nope, just trying to change so we can go to dinner," she nonchalantly says, continuing to pretend like I'm not holding her.

"I think we have time." I kiss her neck lightly, and she turns slightly to give me better access, which is how I know she isn't actually mad.

"No way, we aren't doing anything here." She shakes her head, turning around to face me.

"I'm pretty sure Mel and Zander are too distracted to care." I lean down to continue placing kisses along her neck.

"Nate," she sighs.

I hum against her neck, still not looking up to her as I increase the pressure of my kisses and graze my teeth along her sensitive skin.

"Nate," she groans, as more of a warning this time.

"Yeah, sweetheart?" I murmur against her skin.

"You have to stop," she whispers, as she raises her hands to grip my biceps, pulling me closer.

"You have to stop lying," I say, bringing my lips to hers, but not kissing her yet.

I half expect her to push me away while our breath mingles between us, lips barely touching.

"Make me," she rasps quietly, and my eyes shoot up to look into hers. Those bright blue discs staring right into me. I question whether she really just said that, but the look she's giving me confirms it.

I slam my lips onto hers, and she finally melds her body to mine meeting my feverish kiss. Our tongues collide as we fight to deepen the kiss. I push Aylin's bag off the bed so I can lay her down on it. I hold myself up on my elbows to keep most of my weight off her, other than grinding my hips down against hers resulting in a moan she releases into my mouth.

"How should I make you stop lying to me?" I say against her mouth at the same time I grind my hips down so hard she gasps.

"Figure it out," she snaps, pulling my mouth back to hers.

I groan, back to kissing her just as desperate as before. I slide my hand down her body, stopping at her breast to squeeze hard. Which earns me a moan mixed with a growl from her, as she arches her back to push her chest into me.

I continue to slide my hand down her body until I reach her waistline where I slowly unbutton her jeans, then her zipper. I'm deliberately moving as slow as possible as she bucks her hips toward me but doesn't say anything as our mouths stay fused together.

Continuing my slow movement, I push my hand inside her jeans, staying over her underwear that are soaked, just as I figured they would be. I don't bother taking any of her clothes off, she's about to be even more annoyed with me. I push her drenched panties to the side before sliding my finger over her slit which makes her let out a moan.

I put my free hand over her mouth. "You're going to have to be quiet unless you want them to hear you."

She narrows her eyes at me as I move my other hand lower to press a finger inside her. I feel the vibration of her sound against my hand as her eyes roll back. I keep my hand over her mouth as I pump my finger in and out of her pussy that is quickly soaking my hand. I press my palm against her clit as I slide another finger inside her.

I feel more noise against my hand on her mouth. "What's that? You want me to stop?" I taunt against her ear, taking her lobe in between my teeth briefly.

She shakes her head furiously.

I pick up the pace of my fingers inside her, feeling the beginning of her orgasm.

"Do you want to come?" I nip her neck.

I hear her whimper as she nods.

"Liars don't get to come," I whisper directly into her ear before pulling my hand from her pants and her mouth before standing up.

"What the fuck, Nate?" Aylin fumes, standing up after me, but wobbles a bit on unsteady legs from her denied orgasm.

"You told me to make you, so that's what I'm doing," I smirk. "Get changed."

She watches as I slowly take my fingers into my mouth to taste her. Her mouth slacks as she watches me.

Then, I turn around before removing my shirt, so she doesn't see how satisfied I am with myself. I grab a fresh shirt from my backpack on the floor by the closet.

Once I turn back around to face her, I pull my shirt down and see her still standing at the side of the bed, arms folded across her chest. Her pants are still undone but held up by her hips. It is physically hurting me not to grab those fucking hips. I refuse to give in. I'm making a point.

"Two can play this game, you sure you want that?" she asks, raising an eyebrow at me.

One side of my lip curls up as I crowd her space again. She doesn't move other than to look up at me. "No one else I'd rather play with, sweetheart. Get dressed, and don't think about finishing what I started."

I walk out of the room, leaving her to change by herself. She might make the rest of my night a pain in my ass, but it'll be worth it. Maybe, she will finally learn her lesson. Or maybe I get to keep trying, I'm fine either way.

WE ALL CLIMB into Mel's Crosstrek since both Zander, and I have cars that are too small to be practical. Honestly, I don't know how Zander fits in his tiny Porsche, he's a big guy and it looks like it could be a toy car for fucks sake.

Aylin and I sit in the back, I purposely sit as close as possible to her even though she hasn't spoken to me since I left the bedroom. I place my hand on her thigh, and she doesn't shoo me away.

That's something I've learned with her, she can appear one way, but it's not real. There so many layers to her I'm figuring out. For now, I just leave my hand on her thigh, rubbing my thumb up and down against her jeans absent-mindedly.

I watch her pull out her phone, but I don't look to see what she's doing. Zander and Mel are pointing out different places they like as we drive down the dark streets.

I feel my phone go off in my pocket, so I reach down to pull it out when I see a text from Aylin. I don't open it right away, I look over at her, she's not looking at me, but I see the slightest smile on her lips.

As tempting as it is to not give her the satisfaction of opening the text I decide to anyway because I'm a curious bastard.

> Aylin: You should move that hand a little higher to finish what you started back at the house.

I smile before replying.

> Nate: Don't tempt me, sweetheart. I will fuck you back here in front of your friends, I'm not shy.

I press send, and grip her thigh tighter, moving up slightly higher.

Aylin glances at her phone to see my response, and I'm too focused on watching her facial expressions to pay attention to what Mel and Zander are saying so I really hope they don't want a response. I watch Aylin type something before putting her phone back down, refusing to look at me as she looks out her window.

> Aylin: Neither am I. Maybe I'll take your cock our right now so you can fuck my mouth instead.

My eyes shoot up to look at her, but her eyes are still fixed out the window like it's the most interesting thing she's ever seen.

To say she took me off guard would be an understatement. Who the fuck is she? She never talks to me like that. Even at the thought of what she said, my dick is so hard I have to adjust in my seat, so it isn't painfully pressing against my zipper.

She looks over to me with a smirk, "You okay?" She licks her bottom lip slightly and I bite back a groan.

"I'm great, sweetheart." I wrap my arm around her shoulder to pull her against me as I lean down to whisper directly in her ear, so her friends don't hear. "Keep it up and see what happens."

I kiss the top of her head, while keeping my arm around her so she can think about what my threat might mean. I notice her thighs tighten slightly, and I can't help but smile.

We get to the restaurant without Aylin tempting me further, though I am beyond distracted and want to whisk her away from her friends to show her what she does to me. I resist the temptation because I know she wants me just as badly as I want her.

The restaurant is a seafood place right by the ocean. It's casual with a lot of knick-knacks, coast themed pictures and souvenirs around. Even though I've lived in Oregon my whole life, I never got to go to the coast much.

When my dad actually had enough time off from work to go on a vacation he always wanted to go somewhere outside of the state, even if it was just California.

The hostess takes us to a table next to a window that looks out onto the water. Aylin and I sit next to each other, opposite from Mel and Zander. I place my hand back on her thigh under the table as we all look at the menus.

"They have this lobster melt that is amazing," Mel says. "Oh, and the seafood artichoke dip."

"We come here a lot," Zander chuckles.

"I'll get whatever you suggest then," I announce, putting the menu down.

"They are famous for their clam chowder, so you have to try that," Mel says, seriously.

"Done." I nod before turning toward Aylin. "What sounds good to you, sweetheart?"

"Probably that lobster melt Mel mentioned," she says, closing the menu and placing it on the table.

I squeeze her thigh before turning back to face Mel and Zander. Suddenly, I feel my phone vibrate in my pocket. I look to see Aylin texted me again. I narrow my eyes at her as she places her hand lightly on my thigh, dangerously close to my dick.

> Aylin: What sounds good right now is you.
> Your cock. In my mouth. Inside me.
> EVERYWHERE.

I clear my throat and adjust slightly in my seat as I harden at her words yet again because I can't get the images out of my head. Her on her knees in front of me, my dick deep in her throat.

Goddammit. I swipe my hand over my face to regain focus. I can't believe her right now, this is new.

The conversation at our table is going between the three of them, but I haven't paid attention. The waitress came to take our orders and I try to control my thoughts. Mel and Aylin are making jokes about something that happened in college that clearly Zander is aware of. I mostly listen, enjoying the joy radiating from her..

Suddenly, I feel her hand move and without warning, it's over my hardened cock, feeling me through my pants. I try not to react as her hand tightens around me, but now I really can't think. She doesn't miss a beat in her conversation as she rubs me through my jeans. I grab her hand to still her, but it makes her hold tighter resulting in a grunt from my throat I couldn't prevent.

"You okay?" Mel asks.

I grab my drink to take a big gulp. "Yeah, sorry felt something in my throat."

Aylin squeezes tighter again, and I jolt slightly as I grab her hand away from my dick to hold tightly. I glance over at her to see a slight fire in her blue eyes. She's challenging me, and she's loving what she's doing.

I lean over to act like I'm pressing a kiss to her cheek, but whisper so low only she can hear, "You'll regret this."

I pull away smiling, she looks directly at me, the fire still there as she says loud enough for Mel and Zander to hear, "No, I don't think I will."

ONCE WE GET BACK to Mel and Zander's house Mel decides we are drinking as she pours shots for everyone. Aylin fights her on it, insisting she's not going to drink, but Mel has a way with persuading her.

Now, the girls are at least four shots deep, dancing around the living room with a Breathe Carolina song blasting through the speakers while Zander and I watch them as we lounge on the couch. He has some whiskey while I drink my beer.

Aylin is definitely tipsy and watching her be so liberated is amazing. She laughs with Mel as they belt out the lyrics to the song playing. I would never have guessed this to be the type of music Aylin likes, but she is full of surprises tonight it seems. They spin each other around, dancing like we aren't even here.

As the song ends and moves to the next one Mel looks like she whispers something to Aylin as they both look over to Zander and me. A small smile spreads across Aylin's lips before they come over to us. Mel pulls Zander up off the couch, pulling him to the center of the living room while she starts dancing on him. Aylin comes over to me, climbing onto my lap, straddling me. I'm taken aback while I place my hands on her waist.

"What are you doing, sweetheart?" I ask with a chuckle as she wraps her arms around my neck and looks at me with glassy eyes.

Yeah, she's drunk.

"I wanted to sit down," she says, shrugging.

"Yeah?" I chuckle.

"Yup, and I wanted to sit down right here." She swivels her hips once for emphasis, and I grip her hips tighter as I grow hard beneath her.

"You feeling okay?" I ask, my voice laced with desire even I can hear.

"I'm feeling great, but you have unfinished business with me." She swivels her hips again, while she raises an eyebrow at me.

I grip her hips hard enough to keep her still. "You owe me a truth first."

"Ugh," she whines. Aylin doesn't whine and it makes me laugh. I forget we aren't alone, but I don't even care. Mel and Zander appear to be in their own world anyway.

"One truth and I'll give you what you want." I run my teeth across the side of her neck.

She sighs, her body melting into my touch. She leans forward so she can speak directly into my ear, "I like you so much I'm scared you'll leave if you really get to know me."

I'm shocked by her confession, and I feel a little bad she admitted this to me while intoxicated. I want her truth while she's sober, so I don't push to ask the questions that I now have from what she said.

"I'm not going anywhere, trust me," I say, pushing some of

her long brown hair behind her ear before pressing my lips against hers gently.

"Take me to bed," she whispers against my mouth.

I nod, standing up while she stays wrapped around me.

"Night, guys," I announce to Mel and Zander who are too busy wrapped around each other to even notice us as I carry Aylin to the guest room.

As soon as I step into the room, I kick the door shut behind me, turn around with Aylin still in my arms as I press her against the closed door while I crush her lips with mine. She returns my deep kiss instantly as she rocks her hips against me the best she can with her back against the door, her legs wrapped around my waist.

We kiss until we are both breathless when I pull my lips from hers to travel down her throat. I continue to kiss and bite her sensitive skin while she gasps and moans, pulling me closer to her.

I reluctantly set her down because we are wearing too many clothes. As soon as her feet touch the ground, she slides down to her knees in front of me.

Aylin looks up at me while she undoes my belt, then the button and zipper on my jeans, pulling my pants and boxers down at once, freeing my rock-hard cock. Her eyes never leaving mine as she licks her lips before wrapping them around me. I'm overwhelmed by the warm wet feel of her mouth and I groan. With one hand braced on the door I take my other hand to wrap around her hair as she sucks me deeper.

"*Fuck*, sweetheart," I groan with my hips jerking forward as she continues to run her tongue all around the head of my cock before taking me deep into her throat.

She continues teasing me by pulling back, running her tongue along the entirety of my shaft before sucking me back into her mouth again. I hold onto her hair tightly as I control the urge to thrust my hips forward like I would be if I was fucking her perfect pussy.

It's embarrassing how fast I feel like I can come from what she's doing with her mouth. I pull her up to her feet because when I come it's going to be in her cunt, and I need to be inside her right now.

I turn her around, so her back is pressed against my chest while I lift her shirt over her head and free her from her bra quickly. I reach around in front of her to unbutton her pants, pulling them down as I press kisses down her spine and over her round ass, biting lightly while I get her naked.

I stand, hooking my shirt over my head before turning her around to kiss her deeply, her naked body pressed against mine, my cock pressed against her stomach as I push her back toward the bed.

Our lips never leave each other as we fall onto the bed and I balance myself above her to not crush her with my weight. As soon as her back hits the mattress her legs wrap around me, pulling me closer.

I take her bottom lip between my teeth as I slide my hand down her body to her soaking sex. I dip my finger in her wetness and begin rubbing her clit in the perfect pressure that makes her back arch while she moans.

I keep rubbing her before pushing one finger inside her tight wet heat. She rubs herself against my hand, chasing her orgasm I already know is starting to take over her body.

She presses her nails into my back harder as she begins to explode around my hand. I quiet her moans with my mouth, kissing her with so much purpose it's like I need it more than I need air.

Once she comes down from her high, I pull my lips away to press against her ear chuckling while I say, "Just so you know, I like you a lot too." I press into her, feeling her tightness all around my cock as I continue to thrust inside her.

She throws her head back with a gasp as I fill her. Groaning into her neck, "I love how perfectly you grip my fucking cock."

She whimpers with need as I speed up my thrusts. Her legs are wrapped around my hips as she pulls me into her. Her nails digging into my back as she begs for more. "Harder," she gasps.

I do what she asks, my thrusts getting harder, faster as I feel her starting to writhe beneath me. I feel like I never want to leave this moment. I don't know what she's doing to me, but I never want it to stop.

Aylin's moans grow stronger while another orgasm starts to take over her body. She gasps loudly as I tilt my hips slightly to hit her deeper. I want so badly to have all her noises, but I take her mouth again with my own to keep her quiet because of where we are.

She tightens around me, and I know she's close. Suddenly, I flip our positions so she's on top. I grab her hips, pushing her harder onto me, and grinding her body against mine.

"I want to watch your body while you ride me," I say as I slam her hips down onto me.

It doesn't take her long until her orgasm is about to take over again. She grinds against me harder, her nails digging into my pecs as she climbs higher and higher. I feel her tighten around me with her release and a moan as I flip us back so I'm on top and can take her mouth again.

She practically screams into my mouth as I switch our positions so I'm in control. Her legs are wrapped around me so tight while her nails dig into my back and I'm thrusting into her with a purpose.

With a particularly brutal thrust, I don't think I can hold off any longer, I let go. Both of us moaning into each other's mouths, our breaths are heavy and hot as we come.

Once we come down, I pull out of her, rolling to the side, pulling her against me. I need her close, I need to touch her, to feel her.

I need her.

We settle under the covers, my arms wrapped around her as she rests her head against my chest.

Neither of us say anything, we don't need to. Sometimes our silence and the way we hold each other says more than words can. It doesn't take long after I feel her breathing slow that sleep takes over for me as well.

25

Aylin

Present

The next morning, I feel my head pounding before I even open my eyes. Damn Mel and her powers of persuasion to get me to drink more than I should. I swear it's her superpower.

Slowly, I open my eyes, bracing for the onslaught of light from the giant windows. Luckily, I notice it's cloudy, so the sun is hidden enough to not assault me. Aside from my pounding head, I'm slightly disappointed to realize this is the day we go back home.

And with that, Nate is about to go undercover, and I have no idea what that is going to mean for us. He says we are still going to continue whatever we are doing, but I just don't see that being reality.

I notice Nate isn't next to me in bed, the man wakes up too early for his own good.

Eventually, I pull myself out of bed, cradling my head and adjust to sitting up before I try walking. I stop by the bathroom to dig around for headache pills before heading to the kitchen where Nate hands me a cup of coffee with a smile. I try to give him a small smile back, but I think I end up scowling as I take the coffee from him.

"I'm sorry," Mel says from over my shoulder. "I'm a bad influence."

I look over at her and nod as I take the pills with a giant gulp of coffee. Nate wraps his arms around me, pressing a kiss to my hair. At least he's learned to not have a conversation with me first thing in the morning.

"Who wants to continue the party?" Zander's booming voice says as he comes out of their bedroom.

I shrink back against Nate, while Mel glares at her boyfriend. "Have you ever had a hangover before?" she snaps at him.

Zander holds up his hands in surrender with a quiet, "My bad."

Nate continues to hold me against him, and normally I would want to push away from him. Something about knowing this might be one of the last times he will hold me like this makes me want to stay in his embrace as long as I possibly can.

"You're lucky I already love you," Mel says as she reaches up to kiss Zander on the cheek.

"When do you want to head back home, sweetheart?" Nate asks quietly into my hair.

I shake my head and nuzzle into him more. "Never," I say, my voice muffled by his shirt. Nate chuckles as he pulls me tighter.

"Thank you both for letting us come stay here by the way," Nate says to Mel and Zander.

I finally manage to pull myself away from Nate's warmth and instantly regret it, which is a weird feeling.

"Thank you for dragging her out here, I've only been trying since we moved like three months ago," Mel says, shaking her head.

I shake my head and roll my eyes. We've both been busy, and she knows it. I down the rest of my coffee before rinsing the mug out.

"I'm going to shower if that's okay," I announce quietly.

"Of course, do what you need to do, there should be extra towels in there." Mel waves me off.

I give her a small smile before heading to the guest room to grab my clothes to change into when I feel clean, and hopefully human again.

Once I'm in the room, I hear the door shut, I look up to see Nate is standing there with a grin.

"Why are you looking at me like that?" I ask, continuing to find the t-shirt I want.

"Like what?" I hear humor in his voice.

"Like—" I turn to him, waving my hand around gesturing to his body, "that."

"I just came in here to see if you needed help with your shower." He smirks.

I roll my eyes, searching through my bag again. I really thought I grabbed that shirt, but I'm thinking maybe I didn't. I pause for a moment before grabbing Nate's backpack without a word and grabbing one of his t-shirts instead.

"You could ask," Nate smiles as I try to walk past him out the door.

"Can I borrow your shirt?" I ask sweetly.

"Any time." He leans down to kiss me softly before opening the door.

I'm going to miss his kisses. Once I'm in the bathroom, I feel like reality hits me like a ton of bricks. The reality that I know everything is about to change between us, and I'm likely going to lose Nate to his job.

It's okay, it's better to lose him to his job than to lose him because he saw the real me and didn't like it. It's better this way. Especially before I have a chance to actually fall in love with him because I know how easy it would be, and that's the scariest thing of all.

WE SPEND the rest of the day with Mel and Zander. We all go down to the beach together enjoying the day, even though it's cloudy and the wind is whipping my hair all around, I truly love being here. I love being with my best friend and seeing her so in love.

Emotionally, I am pulling away from Nate. He keeps holding me close, and I let him, but I'm slowly putting my walls back into place. I'm trying to create distance between us so that when the goodbye that I know is coming happens, it won't be as difficult for me.

By the early afternoon Nate and I decide we should head back to Portland. I'm sad to be leaving Mel, but I'm glad we had this time together. Her and Zander walk down to Nate's car with us.

Mel pulls me into a tight hug as she speaks directly into my ear so the guys can't hear from the other side of the car, "I really like him for you Aylin."

"I'll be back soon," I say, ignoring her comment about Nate.

She pulls back to look at me skeptically. "I just want you happy, you know that."

"Yes, ma'am," I roll my eyes.

"Hey, leave the sarcasm to me," she jokes. We both chuckle before hugging again quickly.

Nate and I get in his car and as we start to pull out of the driveway, I wave goodbye to Mel and Zander as they stand, watching us go. Nate rests his hand on my thigh, where it stays for the remainder of the drive.

I can't bring myself to say anything to him, so I lean my head against the window, closing my eyes to try and sleep, but it doesn't happen. I'm too wrapped up in my worry about what is going to happen next.

Even though I didn't fall asleep, Nate clearly thinks I did, since he squeezes my leg slightly once he's parked before speaking softly.

"Wake up, we are back," he says, his free hand moving hair from my face.

Slowly, I turn my head to look at him, his bright smile on his face. I'm going to miss that smile. His hand is still on my thigh, the warmth has seeped through my pants, and I feel it in my entire being.

I'm going to miss that too.

I give Nate a small smile as we climb out of his car. He grabs my bag from the trunk as we make our way to my front door. I dig my keys out of my purse to unlock my door, Nate walks in behind me to set my bag down before cupping my face in his hands. I melt into his touch.

"I want to stay with you, sweetheart, but we both should probably rest before work tomorrow," he says.

I nod, licking my dry lips before speaking, "Are you going undercover right away?"

He sighs, "I don't know, I'll learn more tomorrow. I meant what I said, Aylin. This. Us. We are continuing this."

I bring the corner of my lip between my teeth with a hesitant nod. I know he means that, but I just don't think that's how it's going to be, but I won't say anything.

Nate brings his face down to mine, pulling my lip from my teeth with his own as he presses his lips against mine. Just like I melt into his touch, I melt into his kiss more. He kisses me softly; his tongue slowly caresses mine and this is one of the sweeter kisses we've shared. It's not hurried, it's not urgent, it's just feeling each other.

We pull away from each other's lips, Nate presses his forehead against mine, looking into each other's eyes. Neither of us says anything, but I feel like there's silent words passing between us. We just don't say any of them.

"Rest, we will talk later," he says softly, his eyes continuing to search mine like he wants me to say whatever I'm thinking.

I just nod.

Slowly, Nate lets me go before walking out my front door. I lock it behind him. I really do want to rest, my body is never happy with a hangover, and I need to be prepared for this next week.

I make my way to my bedroom, throwing myself onto my bed, but I still can't bring myself to fall asleep. I wish I knew why, but I feel like it's the culmination of everything. Fear for Nate, fear for us, stress, and just overall questioning what the hell I'm doing.

Now, it's Monday and I don't want to admit how anxious I am all day thinking about Nate and the information he's going to get today. I do everything in my power to not think about him at all because I don't want to reach out. I want to get used to the distance because I know it's about to get worse. I can do this. I'm strong, and I knew this was coming.

Plus, I need to focus on school. I still have my thesis, and everything else going on in my life, I don't need to be worrying about him. He's fine, and whatever will happen between us is going to happen. I just want to know when he's undercover, then I'll let it go.

Yeah right, Aylin, you'll let it go.

I don't actually believe that, but I'm going to try.

26

2 Months Ago (The Incident)

I'm working a double shift tonight to try and get some overtime, while also hoping this will help with that detective promotion that I'm more than ready for.

The night has been calm so far, not much going on when dispatch lets me know about a call to an apartment I'm way too familiar with at this point.

The Phillips' residence.

I let them know I'll head over there.

When I pull up and park in the parking lot of the apartment complex everything looks the same as it always does. I don't hear yelling or anything, though I never usually do.

As I'm getting out of my patrol car, I hear the loud bang of a gunshot.

My head moves quickly to identify where the sound came from, and the place it seems most likely is that apartment with the number four on the door.

Quickly, I call in backup to dispatch, but I'm not going to wait for anyone to show up. Call me stupid or whatever the fuck, I can't just wait out here when I know lives are in danger, especially when I know it's likely Rebecca and Layla's lives.

I pull my gun out of the holster, holding it toward the ground, ready to aim any second as I make my way to the apartment door.

In normal circumstances, I would need to knock and announce I'm here, but I have reason to suspect someone is in danger which means I can knock it the fuck down, which is exactly how I know I can explain myself later.

I kick the door down on the first try before announcing, "Portland PD!"

Entering the apartment, I keep my gun aimed in front of me, ready to eliminate any threat that presents itself. The apartment is eerily quiet as I make my way through the mess. The smell is terrible, like the booze, cigarette smoke and body odor have embedded themselves in every surface. It takes everything in me not to gag.

I'm looking around, waiting, someone is in here they have to be. I'm making my way further into the apartment when I hear a crash in a room off to the side. I storm in where I'm met face to face with Murphy, gun in his hand, swaying back and forth.

"Drop your weapon!" I exclaim at him.

The weapon thunks to the ground, I watch as it falls, my gaze falling on the body already on the ground. Rebecca. She's lying in a pool of blood.

"The bitch deserved it," Murphy says without remorse. He continues to be unsteady on his feet like he's drunk, but his eyes are dilated and glossed over like he might also be on some sort of drug.

I call into my radio needing an ambulance as I continue to watch Murphy's movements.

"Where's Layla?!" I scream at him, my gun trained on the spot between his eyes, my fingers begging to pull the trigger.

"Probably in hell with her mom," he slurs, and that catches my attention.

"Did you kill her too?" I ask, but there's no other body in this room.

"Not yet, but I'm about to."

Quickly, he storms toward me. I don't want to open fire, not knowing where Layla is. I tackle Murphy as he comes toward me. I whip the butt of my gun across his face as he continues to try to fight me. We both get off the floor as we continue to fight.

It almost seems like whatever he's on makes him immune to the pain I'm inflicting as I continue to pummel my fist into his face. He continues to fight me back, and I want to kill him, I want to so bad, but I want him to fucking suffer for all of this. All of the pain he caused for Rebecca and Layla, I want it given back to him ten times over.

"You're going to burn alive," I say to him with a punch I'm sure broke his nose.

He turns his head back to me like he didn't feel it as he smiles, knocking the gun from my hand as it goes flying across the floor. I'm too focused on wanting to beat his face in and I became careless, this isn't like me.

We continue fighting, I want to at least knock him out before detaining him because I want to enjoy his pain. He seems like he will never give up. Fists are flying, mine are split from the fight and he's breathing hard from the struggle which is the only sign this is affecting him at all.

Murphy grabs the gun he dropped earlier, and I'm fighting it from his grasp. Before I can do a damn thing about it, he turns the gun on himself and pulls the trigger.

I watch his body slump over as he falls to the ground, dead from the single shot to the face. I take a moment to take in the scene around me.

What the fuck just happened?

I shake my head staring at the fallen bodies around me. I

wanted this motherfucker to suffer and just like that he took the cowards way out.

There's a sniffle behind me, I look up to see Layla peeking around the door frame. I shoot up to stand and move her away from the scene before she sees anything, assuming she hasn't already.

I move quickly toward her which I can see scares her a bit. "Hey, it's okay. I'm going to help you, okay, Layla? Remember me?" I say softly as I reach my hand out so she can choose to take it if she wants.

I see her hesitate, but she finally nods, just once. I pick her up to take her out of the apartment right away. She nuzzles into my shoulder as I carry her outside. She's sniffling, and it sounds like she's crying, but trying to hide it. I can't help but think about the fact that her dad probably got mad at her for crying which is why she's trying to hide it. I hear the sirens coming closer as I step outside.

The air outside feels better in my lungs as I'm able to take a deep breath outside the muggy space now filled with death. I watch as the parking lot fills with cars with lights, and I almost forget the tiny human snuggled against me until I feel the wetness from her tears along my neck as she silently cries.

The next moments are filled with chaos as officers and paramedics storm inside the apartment while I continue to stand outside. Layla holding onto my neck so tight it feels like she's trying to suffocate me, but I know she's just refusing to be put down.

She's not saying anything, just crying silently against me.

"Officer Greene, what exactly happened here?" Someone I don't recognize comes up to me.

I gesture to Layla, refusing to answer anything while she can listen. She knows, but I don't think it would be beneficial to a five year old to hear me recount everything without emotion to another officer, like her parents' lives meant nothing.

Even though Murphy's really didn't.

The social worker from the first visit, Grace I think, shows up and she tries to get Layla from my arms, which only makes her hold onto me tighter. I've never been a guy that likes kids, but there's something about her not having anyone anymore, and knowing what she's gone through in her short life, that makes me want to keep holding onto her as long as she will let me. Knowing I make her feel safe, and that no one knows what the rest of her life is going to look like now.

The rest of the night is a mess. Finally, the paramedics get Layla to agree to look her over to make sure she's okay, but she only does so while sitting with me, not letting me leave.

Eventually, Layla falls asleep in my arms after being cleared of any injuries by the paramedics, that's when Grace comes up to me again.

"She's going to need to go to an emergency placement tonight," she says to me.

"Like some sort of orphanage?" I ask, unsure what an emergency placement is for a child with no parents.

"No, I mean we can try to contact any known family, but with how late it is, she will likely go to a temporary foster home until a more permanent placement can be identified," Grace explains.

"She has grandparents, she was staying with them for a little," I say quickly, remembering what Rebecca told me during one of my visits when Layla wasn't here.

"We will try to contact them; do you want me to take her until we get something figured out? I'm sure you have a lot to do because of all this." She waves her hand around referring to the chaos around us.

I shake my head. "No, I'll keep an eye on her, I can deal with everything else later."

Grace nods before walking away while dialing on her phone. I continue to hold the sleeping child to me and watch everyone move around me. I'm reminded of a similar scene when I finally got to my parent's house after they died. I know what it feels like to have them ripped away so suddenly without any warning.

Why does history have to repeat itself like this? Why do shitty things have to keep happening to people that don't deserve it?

I look down at the sleeping child in my arms. Her messy blonde hair is fanned out over my arm, her face is so peaceful as she sleeps, and I feel a pang in my chest knowing how her life has been altered. I know this moment of peace will never be the same for her. Nothing for her will be the same, and I hate that there isn't a damn thing I can do about it.

27

Present

I got my undercover assignment. My identity, my back story, my temporary home, car, phone, everything. They don't want to take any chances with this assignment. They've made that extremely clear through all the briefings just how important it is that they don't find out anything about who I really am.

These guys are good, and even knowing my real address or car could lead to them finding out I'm a cop, and then I'm dead.

My new name is Trevor Pratt. I'm still twenty-nine, but my birthday is now September 9th if it comes up, though it shouldn't. I even have a fake social security number, but the positive to criminals is they usually don't care about these types of identifiers. They generally expect everyone they deal with to be using a fake name anyway. The difference here is if they found out my real name, I'm fucked.

Going in at all is dangerous, there's always the chance I've run into them while on patrol. It's a risk any officer takes when changing roles like this. I was told to grow my hair out ever since this started to look "less like a cop". The short sides are now at an awkward length, but it won't be long until I can cut it all the same length and look a bit better.

Though, I'm not supposed to look "good". In fact, I'm supposed to dress and do everything in my power to look as shitty as possible.

We have three guys (that I know of) already initiated in the gang that I'm going to be working with, and my understanding is that I'll be brought in by one of them or another confidential informant under the guise I need money to pay off my fines from my last arrest, which was for possession of drugs and assault. I'm also not from Portland, I'm from Salem, about an hour south which is also where I was arrested and where I spent my time in jail.

I've had to digest so much information about who I am, what I'm doing, and what not to do under any circumstances, but the only thing I can think of is Aylin and when I can see her again. I know I can focus when I'm in it, but I get bored just talking about it, and I need to distract myself with thoughts of her.

She hasn't reached out to me since I dropped her off at her house. I noticed she was distant all day. I can feel when she tries to pull away from me. I know she's scared about me going undercover and what that will mean for us, but I meant what I said. This isn't over with us; I can't let her go even if I wanted to. I don't know what is wrong with me because I've never been so consumed by anyone, ever, but I can't lose her.

I leave her alone for the day, hoping that she might reach out, but also, I'm respecting her space and trying not to push her too much. I did that a lot in the beginning, and I recognize that she has to want to be with me, even when she fights it.

I went to what will be my new apartment and looked

around the simple one-bedroom place with plain, cheap furnishings. Fine with me, I don't need a lot anyway.

The one thing I am sad about is giving up my car for the time being. I plan to ask Aylin to drive it every once in a while, so it isn't just sitting there. Or I may see if she wants to borrow it while I'm undercover since her car is on its last legs anyway from what I can tell.

This all feels so surreal, I've worked my entire career for a chance like this, and I know I won't do anything to mess it up. I know there are so many things that can go wrong that are out of my control, and the one thing I can't stand is things being out of my control.

It's all been a waiting game for me.

Waiting for Aylin to reach out.

Waiting for the next steps of the assignment.

I can be a patient person, but I'm done waiting for something to happen. It's Wednesday and I'm just chomping at the bit for anything to happen.

I'm about to reach out to Aylin and let her know I'm done waiting for her to reach out to me when my burner I was given for the assignment goes off with a text. My heart pounds, this is it. It's time.

The text is simple with an address and a time later tonight. I'm expected to be there, and I'll be approached by one of our guys, which will start the ball moving. We don't know much about what will happen from there other than I will be tested because no one in the gang will trust me. I will likely have to do some things to prove myself, but I'm ready.

I know Aylin is in class all day today, and I don't think I'll be able to see her before tonight, but I decide to stop waiting and reach out to her anyway so she can know what's going on.

> Nate: Going in tonight. I will reach out when I can, but I still mean it, we aren't done.
>
> Nate: Also, want to borrow my car while I'm in?

I should have asked her sooner, but I really did want to give her space, even though she's about to get a lot of it since I'm not entirely sure how I'm going to make this work, but I just know that I will.

She replies quicker than I thought she would, but it's not how I would have liked for her to reply. I groan, running my hand down my face.

> Aylin: Why?

> Nate: Because I want you to have something to remember me by in case I don't make it out alive!

I'm joking, though, it is always a possibility.

My phone rings, and I see it's her. She probably didn't think that was very funny.

"Hey sweetheart," I greet when I answer.

"Are you serious?" She sounds genuinely concerned and I feel a little bad.

"No, I was joking, but it got you to call me."

She groans, "Why do you want me to borrow your car, don't you need it?"

"No, I have a beater I have to drive, this assignment is a lot to explain, but I would rather my car not sit around to die," I explain.

"I mean I guess, but I'm in class all day, you know this." I'm noticing she's talking quietly so I'm wondering if she's in class or snuck out somewhere to call me. I also am realizing how much I missed her voice.

"I'll take care of it, I can park outside your apartment and meet you quickly to pass off the keys." I could just hide them somewhere, but I am desperate to see her, and kiss her at least once.

She's quiet for a few moments, I look at the phone to see if we got disconnected.

"Yeah, I can meet you around lunch time, there's a coffee shop by campus I usually go to during my breaks."

I don't want to admit I know exactly what coffee shop she's talking about, she's only told me once, but it seems a little much for me to remember something so trivial she mentioned in passing.

"I'll be there. Noon?"

"Yeah," she sighs, and doesn't seem happy about it.

"Hey sweetheart, I'll be okay," I try to reassure her.

"I know you will, I have to go," she says quickly before we hang up.

I don't want her worrying about me, she has so much to focus on herself, but I won't deny it feels good to know that someone cares. Ever since my parents died, I haven't felt I had someone completely in my corner, not until Aylin.

I SEE Aylin in the window of the coffee shop before I walk in. I can see the stress written all over her face as she stares at her laptop on the table. A better man might let her walk away in our situation.

A better man wouldn't want to add to the worries she already has. I'm not a better man, but I still don't want her worrying about me. I'm just too selfish to let her go.

She doesn't look up when I walk through the door, so as I make my way over to her, I wrap my arms around her from behind, pressing my lips against her ear, I feel her stiffening against me.

"You're too tense, sweetheart."

"I don't have much time before I need to go, Nate." She sounds cold and detached.

I tense my jaw at her dismissiveness. I want to push back, but I don't want to add to her stress. I want to be her solace, like she is mine.

"Are you okay?" I ask instead, even though I know she's not going to be honest.

"I'm fine, I'll drive your car around but I need to go."

I want to press as she gathers her things to put in her bag. I'm not going to push it. I fish my keys out of my pocket to hand to her. I took an Uber here and will have to take one back since I left my car outside her apartment.

She takes the keys I'm holding out to her, but I grab her hand as she tries to bolt. I pull her body against mine; she lets out a puff of air at the sudden contact. Aylin isn't looking in my eyes, she's just staring straight ahead at my chest.

I hook my finger under her chin to force her eyes up to meet mine. Her bright blue eyes lock onto mine, but there's a disconnect, a distance in them I don't like.

"I will be fine, don't worry about me," I tell her. She softens against me slightly.

She chews at her bottom lip for a moment before whispering so quietly I almost don't even hear her, "I'm going to miss you."

I pull her lip out with my thumb. "Nothing to miss, sweetheart." I give her a little smile before pressing my lips against hers softly.

"I really do have to go," she says, and it's almost sad.

I run my fingers through her hair, Aylin closing her eyes at the sensation. "I will see you soon I promise," I whisper against her lips.

I watch the shiver run through her before she nods slightly.

I kiss her again before releasing my hold. I don't move from where I stand while I watch her leave the small coffee shop. I feel like there's more going on with her than just school stress and me stress.

Something is weighing on her. I'm making it my next mission to find out what it is. I'm going to find out everything about this woman, but first I need to take down some dangerous motherfuckers. *No pressure, right?*

I'M WEARING a loose-fitting hoodie even though it's a little warm, but no one will question me. Junkies wear jackets no matter the weather to hide track marks, I know I won't look out of place. I'm also in jeans and old Vans I pulled out from the back of my closet I haven't worn in forever. My hair is disheveled, and I didn't even have to try to sleep like shit to get the dark circles under my eyes, it just happened.

I met up with Jason, who I learned is one of our confidential informants before heading to the address. Jason was involved in Trent Moore's operation and cut a deal to be a CI to avoid jail time. I don't know him well, but I do know it's best for him to bring me in since he's been involved in the gang for a while.

No one trusts the new guys, so even though we have other undercover officers working this, they aren't as trustworthy to the higher ups of the gang since they are still so new. Which is why I'm about to walk into this place with Jason.

Before we round the corner to walk to the house, I ask Jason if there's anything I should know before we go in.

"Don't talk too much, don't ask questions and go along with whatever they say," he says gruffly. Jason isn't a big guy; he's lean with dark hair that hangs in his eyes.

"Done." His instructions seem simple, and what I expected anyway.

We walk to the "house" which is definitely a trap house. It looks to be practically falling apart and I'm a little worried my feet will sink through the floor as soon as I step in. I also recognize that I'm about to step into something I can't turn away from.

This is it.

All my other worries, everything with Aylin, the shit that happened with my parents, and what happened a couple months ago goes on the back burner in my mind. I have to be more present than ever while I focus purely on the task at hand. This is the only thing I'm thinking of as Jason and I walk through the door.

There are more people in here than I would have thought. Smoke is everywhere, and the smell is a mix of tobacco, weed and booze. I take in my surroundings as I try to be subtle. I'm hunching over as I walk attempting to make myself seem smaller than I am. Also, trying to walk with less of an authority, after years it's something that comes naturally, but I'm having to retrain my body, my posture and everything.

"The fuck is this?" Someone asks behind a plume of smoke. I know he's talking about me, but I'm not going to be the one to respond.

Jason leads us closer to the man that just spoke, and I can see him. He's covered in tattoos, sitting against a couch with two women on either side of him. He has a blunt in his hand as he looks at me skeptically.

"This is Trevor, my boy I told you about that could help us out," Jason says easily.

I lift my chin slightly in greeting while the guy on the couch continues to stare me down, no doubt in intimidation. I stay quiet, and I don't cower. I also don't meet his eyes because I know that would be considered a challenge.

"You a fighter, Trevor?" The man asks me finally.

I shrug, "When I need to be."

He continues to stare daggers at me, clearly unsure what to think about me, and whether he should trust me.

"Not a junkie, you're too big for that shit. What's your deal?" He's perceptive, but I guess my baggy clothes didn't do as good of a job hiding my physique as I thought.

"Just got out of lockup, and I need to make some money," I say calmly.

"What were ya in lockup for?" The guy asks, blowing out another huge plume of smoke.

I shrug, "Possession and assault."

He grunts, continuing to look me up and down, he's trying to intimidate me, I know that much. I don't cower, but I don't challenge him either.

"Ya know ya can't just walk in here and start makin' money with us. Ya gotta prove yourself." He starts to stand up, and he's probably a couple inches shorter than me when I'm not hunched over.

I still don't even know this guy's name, but I assume he's one of the ones in charge. There's always a couple of "lead" guys that report to the big boss who probably isn't even here.

"I know," I nod.

This guy continues to size me up, blowing smoke in my face and not saying anything.

Finally, he turns to Jason who is standing off to the side. "Bring him with tonight, see if he can handle it."

I watch Jason nod slowly before this guy pushes past me, deeper into the house. I'm confused, I thought there would be more of a test or something, this seemed too easy. I turn to Jason who gestures his head toward the door before walking toward it again.

Once we are outside, I feel like I can take a deep breath, and I promise to never take fresh air for granted again. I think I just shaved off a good five years from my lungs from all that smoke. We continue walking until we are out of view from the house to speak a word to each other.

"What's tonight?" I ask finally.

"Everyone meets up at one of the houses, they look like parties but it's all business and there will be deals, assignments being doled out, fights, you'll get the whole experience," Jason answers cautiously and I can tell he's nervous about this whole thing. Pretty typical, no one wants to be a snitch. Especially one working with the cops.

"Great," I say sarcastically.

I WENT BACK to my fake apartment for the rest of the day until Jason and I had to meet up again. He's driving us since I don't know where to go. As we get closer, I recognize the neighborhood we are in, and I begin to panic.

This is Aylin's neighborhood. We are right by her apartment.

I guess it makes sense, college students buy drugs and party, it's the perfect place to fit in with the norm, but it also makes Aylin too close for comfort to some extremely dangerous people.

We continue driving, and that's when I see it. My blue Camaro parked right outside Aylin's apartment. Then, not even two minutes later, we pull up to the house. I could walk to Aylin's apartment.

I am not comfortable with her being so close to this shit, I'm going to have to figure something out, and I'm sure she's not going to be happy about it.

Pushing those thoughts to the back of my mind Jason and I get out of the car and walk to the house. This one is a little nicer than the one earlier. This place looks a bit more like a house that is actually livable.

We head inside and it is just like a party, I'm a little confused. I feel like I have had the wrong picture in my mind about this entire lifestyle. This is seriously just a college party. Jason nudges me toward the back of the house where there's a door, he opens it, which reveals stairs clearly leading down to a basement.

Walking down the narrow stairs, the familiar smell of nicotine and marijuana fills my lungs once again, as we descend into the basement. This is more of what I figured we would be walking into. I guess it makes sense to have a real party going on upstairs, no one suspects anything, plus I'm sure it's a prime crowd to sell to.

The basement is all cement with some shitty couches around. People are spread out talking and there's a few women, all draped across a guy. Then, I see the same guy from earlier talking to two other men who look like they could be his security with their matching stocky builds, short hair and confident stances.

"Trevor, came back, eh?" the guy says, and dammit I should've asked Jason what his name is.

I nod.

"Still wanna prove yourself to work with us?" he asks.

"Sure, I'll do what I gotta do," I say, shrugging.

"I think I like ya. No fucks." He claps me on the shoulder forcefully, if I was smaller, he would've knocked me over. "We wanna see how you can hold your own."

Huh?

I look over to Jason for any sort of clue about what this guy is talking about, and he gives a slight shake of his head like he doesn't even know. This doesn't look good for me.

When I face forward again this guy (I really need to find out his name) is holding out a blunt for me to take with an expectant look on his face. This is a common way to snuff out cops, they know we can't take what they offer, even if weed is legal. Lines can get blurred, and it was drilled into my head before going in. I was told to make an excuse and make it good. Luckily, with my back story I have the perfect excuse.

"Can't, my PO drug tests me and that shit sticks around." If that is weed then it's a decent excuse since that shit will stay in the system for a long time.

Lead guy gives me a skeptical look, then smirks before nodding. "Ya ready?"

"For what?" I ask a little too forcefully before remembering I'm not supposed to question this guy.

He hands the blunt to Jason casually, I watch to see if he actually takes a hit, wondering if it could possibly be laced. He smokes it like normal, so I assume it's fine, unless he does the harder shit, which wouldn't entirely surprise me.

Lead guy walks further into the basement, which is way bigger than I would've assumed. We get to another open room, and this one has a crowded circle around something in the middle. There's the sounds of fists flying and flesh hitting flesh filling the air. The various smoke and alcohol smells are now mixed with the metallic scent of blood in the air as well.

I lean over toward Jason so only he can hear me ask, "Is this some sort of fight club shit?"

"I don't know, I don't deal with this side of the club," Jason replies, shaking his head.

Internally I scoff at him calling it a club, what a nice way to label a gang. But I wonder what he means that he doesn't deal with this side. I thought everyone would be involved in everything...this is new information I file away for later.

"You're up next Trevor," Lead guy says to me.

"What? Why me?" I question, and the furrow of his brow

reminds me once again I shouldn't question him, but I'm swimming in confusion right now.

"I told ya, prove yourself then we can talk about ya makin' money with us." His tone takes on a harder edge to it, clearly asserting his authority in this moment. I don't have a choice.

"I gotta win?" I ask.

"If ya don't, then ya didn't prove yourself," he answers before walking over to the other side to talk to someone.

Shit. I can fight but didn't really expect to actually need to. Not tonight.

I also can't forget that Aylin is just down the street completely oblivious to all the danger so close to her. Oblivious to me and what I'm doing so close to her. I have to get her away from here as soon as possible.

The crowd cheers, and it seems like whatever fight was happening is over as I see them pulling one of the guys out. He's clearly knocked out, or at least I'm hoping he is, because he's not moving and with those injuries he could be fucking dead for all I know.

"Trevor!" My fake name is called, and I push through the crowd easily as I get to the middle. It's concrete here too, blood stained and disgusting. I whip off my sweatshirt and t-shirt underneath. Fighting in jeans is not ideal, but this isn't ancient Greece, I'm not getting naked.

"Dragon!" The same voice calls, and I see someone walking through the crowd to the center.

I wonder for a second why they call him Dragon until he takes off his shirt as well to reveal the giant dragon tattoo spanning his entire chest, and wrapping around, I'm sure covering his entire back as well.

This guy is big, he definitely has a couple inches on me, he's broad and muscular. He's also obviously fought here before, giving him an advantage. My usual confidence wavers slightly as I take in his snarl, already busted knuckles and natural comfort in this place.

"First knockout is the winner," a voice calls. I prepare myself. I have to win. "Go!"

Dragon attacks first, clearly used to using his brute strength to take down his opponent right away. I maneuver away just barely before he tackles me completely. I take the brief opportunity of being slightly behind him to shove my elbow down into the back of his neck.

He swings out right away catching me in the gut. I hold my stomach, but don't let it slow me down. We are facing each other again, clearly both learning each other's style and how to use it to our advantage. He might be stronger and more experienced in this, but I'm more observant.

I notice he's favoring his left side, but he swung with his right which means he's at a disadvantage being weakened on his stronger side from some previous injury, I'm sure.

He comes at me again, and instead of avoiding this time, I jab my fist out quickly, connecting with his nose. The crunch is hard to stomach but he just shakes his head slightly before righting himself, like he barely felt it. He's probably broken his nose so many times he does barely feel it.

I won't attack first, that's his move, and probably something he expects, but it would put me at a huge disadvantage with someone like him.

Like I expect he comes at me again, and this time it's obvious he's trying to finish this. Fists are flying, I'm hit in the face and the gut again, but I refuse to let it slow me down. I return his punches and I notice him starting to slow down from the exertion. He's not used to going against someone who is able to stay standing for very long.

We continue the all-out brawl, knuckles connecting with flesh, blood flying and neither of us letting up.

Finally, I notice him starting to sway on his weaker side

and I take the opening I have by punching him right in the temple. He goes down instantly once my fist connects with the bone. My fist fucking hurts. My knuckles are shredded to bits, I'm bleeding from my nose and lip at least. My lungs are burning, and my stomach hurts so fucking bad, but I won.

I stare down at the large man on the ground, I'm breathing heavily, covered in sweat when Jason comes up to me. "You won, man."

I look up to find the lead guy staring right at me from his slightly elevated spot at the back of the room. He has a sinister smile on his face as he nods to me. Jason pulls me out of the center of the room, and back behind the crowd right as they are announcing the next fighter.

"I think you did it," Jason says quietly. I shush him as the lead guy comes up to us.

"Nice, I haven't met a good fighter since I met Dragon," Lead guy says nodding toward the guy I knocked out.

I shrug like it's not a big deal.

"Come by tomorrow, we'll see about you helpin' out," Lead guy says before walking away.

Once he's out of ear shot, I turn back to Jason. "I'm getting the fuck out of here."

He nods, handing me my shirt and sweatshirt back. I use my shirt to wipe off my face before putting my sweatshirt back on even though it's a million fucking degrees down here. We head upstairs to the normal party, and I make a beeline right outside because I need fresh air.

The cooler air outside hits my face and it feels so much better than a stuffy house. Jason and I head back to his car so I can go home.

"Who even is that guy?" I ask finally.

Jason hesitates a second before answering, "Everyone calls him Cap. I don't even know his real name."

I think on that for a second before shaking my head. I'll deal with learning more about that later.

Right now, I'm going to clean up and then I need to talk to Aylin and somehow convince her she needs to get the fuck out of here. I know where I want her to go, but I know my little mystery is going to fight tooth and nail against the idea. Too bad I will drag her there if I have to.

28

Aylin

Present

"Absolutely not! Are you insane?" I exclaim to Nate as he stands just inside my front door casually.

He texted me saying he's coming over. It wasn't a question; it was a statement which already annoyed me.

Then, he showed up with cuts and bruises on his face that he won't explain and is demanding I move my shit into his townhouse in Vancouver.

"Sweetheart, I'm really not fighting you about this. You don't realize how dangerous it is around here and I need to know you're safe," he expresses.

"Nate, I've lived here for years, and nothing has happened. I can take care of myself. I like my apartment. I don't want to stay at your place. Plus, it's so far from school."

"Good thing you have my car to use then, huh?" he says smugly and I can't decide if I want to punch him or kiss him. His face looks like he's already experienced getting punched recently, but still.

I groan, "You can't just come in here and start controlling my life, that's not how this works."

"How what works?" He smirks. We haven't established any sort of "official" relationship because...well honestly, I don't know how, but I can tell he wants me to open up.

"This," I gesture between us. "You can't control me or force me to live somewhere else or tell me what to do, or— " He cuts me off with his lips on mine and I want to push him away, but I let myself enjoy it for a second, even if I hate whatever this is that he's trying to do.

"I'm not trying to control you, I'm trying to keep you safe," he murmurs against my lips, and I really do hate how easily my body gives into him.

"Keep me safe while I live here then," I try, but he just shakes his head.

"Sweetheart, you don't know the shit that is happening just down the street from you. There's some fucked-up stuff going on, and I can't keep you safe here because I shouldn't even be here. Someone could see me, and that makes you a target."

I don't like that what he's saying makes sense. Obviously, I don't want to be in danger, but I really don't want to move into a place I don't know, especially his place. Even if he won't be staying there it's too close to living together for my liking.

I'm shaking my head, and Nate cups my cheeks. "My house is far enough away that no one in this world runs the risk of seeing you with me or seeing you at all." He rests his forehead against mine. "I would never forgive myself if something happened to you."

I sigh, the fight leaving my body. I want to keep pushing him about this, but he makes sense, and I do recognize that it could put both of us in danger, and he isn't able to watch me twenty-four-seven.

"Fine," I sigh reluctantly.

A smile spreads across his face as I relent, even though I'm still not happy about it.

"I'll help you get some stuff together then we can go."

"Wait, you expect me to go *now*?" I gape at him. I said I would go, but I didn't mean right this second.

"Yeah, you think I'd be able to sleep tonight knowing you're still here. No way." He shakes his head.

"I don't..." I stop myself, re-thinking how I want to argue this. "How can..."

I come up empty on any good excuse. Groaning, I finally start throwing a bag together full of some clothes, and my school stuff. As I pack up quickly, I realize how little stuff I have that is actually personal.

Sure, I have some decorations, but not much. I don't have any pictures, or sentimental items. I realize how sad that seems, out of the twenty-seven years of my life I have nothing that means anything to me, and it hits me, just how pathetic I am.

"Ready?" Nate asks, slinging my packed bag over his shoulder like it weighs nothing.

I look at him, his hair is longer than when we first met, starting to look shaggy, light scruff covering his sharp jawline. His hazel eyes are bright against his tan skin and I realize he's the only thing in this apartment that means something to me.

And that thought scares the absolute shit out of me.

Before I'm able to dwell on that thought any longer, I mumble, "yeah," as we leave my home for the last three years.

We pull up to Nate's house, and I've been here once before, it's a nice place in some suburban area of Vancouver. It's pleasant, kind of like Sam and Jeff's, so I immediately feel like I don't belong. Like I'm not good enough to stay here, and someone is going to stop me. Instead, Nate looks over at me with a smile as he holds onto my hand, walking into the front door.

Nate said the area I live in isn't great, and I knew that, but he doesn't know that I've lived in more dangerous places, where the danger was in my home with me. He doesn't know anything about what I've been through, and I know that's my fault. He will never know because if he did, then I know he wouldn't look at me like he's looking at me right now.

"Make yourself at home while you're here, this place could use it," Nate chuckles, as he takes my bags to the master bedroom.

His place is sparse, it makes mine look like a furniture store, and that's saying something. I know why I don't have much, I mean I can't really afford it, but I know why I don't have personal effects. I don't understand why he doesn't. I'm sure he makes a decent living so he can afford it. Plus, he has people, friends, and I'm sure he has some family, unlike me.

I don't even realize that I'm staring off into space until Nate comes up behind me, wrapping his arms around my waist, kissing the side of my face.

"You okay, sweetheart?"

I try to scrunch my shoulders up, but he doesn't let me, resting his chin on my shoulder.

"I don't know, Nate, this is a lot," I shake my head.

He moves his hands to my hips, turning me around to face him. When I won't look up at him, he tilts my face up with a finger under my chin.

"Talk to me," he practically whispers, and I'm taken aback by his softness.

"I told you, I was fine at my apartment, and this is your place and it's a lot."

"And I told you why this is best for now. It's not permanent, it's for your safety."

I don't realize I'm chewing on my bottom lip until he pulls it out with his thumb.

"What aren't you telling me, sweetheart?"

Everything.

I'm broken. I don't deserve to be saved. I'm not worth his efforts. I'll never be who he wants me to be.

I don't belong here.

I don't belong here with *you*.

I don't say any of that, instead I press my lips to his. It's meant as a distraction, and I don't actually intend for it to go further, but it's like once we make contact everything else disappears in the background, and nothing matters at this moment.

Nate groans as I slip my tongue past his lips, his grip on me tightening, bringing me flush against his hard body. All my softness melding to his hardness and God, do I love it. Suddenly, everything turns heated between us, his hands becoming rougher as they slide up my shirt until it's on the floor.

I do the same so I can feel him, I want to feel every warm part of him against me because even if I don't deserve any of this, I'm going to enjoy it while I can.

It doesn't take long until our clothes are on the floor, but we haven't made a move toward the bed, just kissing and touching. I could almost be content with just this.

Almost, but not quite, because when I feel his fingers slide through my wetness I arch into his touch immediately, moaning into his mouth, and it's like any sort of restraint Nate had snaps in that moment.

"Get on the bed," he commands, low and intimidating. My knees buckle at his tone alone.

I obey him, moving to lay on the bed on my back, watching him the whole time I do. He doesn't say anything, but he shakes his head while his hand is palming his dick.

I want to have him in my mouth again. I swear, I hated blow jobs before. I have only given less than a handful in my life, but something about him has me changing my mind.

I sit up and look at him confused, but before I'm able to ask what he wants, he grabs my ankles, using them to flip me onto my stomach. I let out a yelp at the sudden movement, but then he's wrapping an arm around my waist to lift me to my knees. I stay like this, anticipating his mouth on me, or fingers, or cock, but nothing happens.

I look over my shoulder to see him standing behind me, hooded eyes as he just watches me with a slow pump of his fist around his length.

"Nate," I complain because I feel like I could explode from the anticipation.

"Yes, sweetheart?" he asks, almost taunting.

Suddenly, I'm feeling exposed and almost embarrassed in this position. I want to move, I want to walk away, but I can't do anything. It's like I'm hypnotized by this power he has over me.

"Nate, come on," I groan.

What is he trying to do?

"I want to play a game," he says lazily, like he doesn't even have a naked woman in front of him, beyond ready to fuck him as he continues slow strokes on himself.

"*Now?*" I snap at him, turning to face him again.

"Don't move," he commands, and I stiffen at the authoritative tone he takes on. It's not cruel, it's not loud, it's just strong. I usually react to tones like that and shut down, but not right now. I feel myself grow weaker with need instead.

"Every truth you tell me, I'll give you something you want."

I already hate this game, but Nate does something to me that commands me in a way I've never experienced in my life.

"I want you to touch me," I say.

Nate laughs, "I want a truth I don't already know."

I scowl at him over my shoulder, dying to be in a less

exposed position. I know he's doing this to make me more vulnerable, and I want to hate it, but I don't.

"I don't think I'm worth all this effort you're putting in for me," I say through clenched teeth.

He's silent for a moment, and I think I should've said something else. Anything else.

Then, I feel him behind me. I feel his large hand running down my spine, it makes me shiver under his touch.

"I think you're worth so much more," he says into my ear before pressing a finger inside me. I gasp, and rock my hips against his hand, seeking more friction as he pumps his finger in and out of me.

"You want more? You know what to do," he growls.

"I've never fully trusted anyone." The words fall out of my mouth without me even thinking about them.

Nate presses against me harder as he inserts another finger inside me, and I buck against his touch, wanting more. *Needing* more as I moan his name.

"Do you trust me, sweetheart?" he asks as he nips my earlobe.

I refuse to answer, biting my lip as I continue to push my hips back against his hand, chasing my pleasure instead of answering. I'm so close, I feel the pleasure building low in my belly as I press against his fingers harder. I'm right there, then he pulls his hand away.

"What—" I turn around to see Nate has stepped back, arms folded across his chest, eyes narrowed at me.

"Answer me."

"Nate, it's not a simple answer," I try, turning to sit down and face him.

He leans down, bracing his arms on either side of me, his face inches from mine. "Yes, it is. Do you trust me?"

I feel the panic starting to rise within me and I feel the urge to run. I can't do this; I can't let him in. Then, I look into his eyes boring into mine and I feel like I'm stuck in this spot, and he won't let me out without an answer.

"Yes," I whisper, hoping maybe he didn't hear me. I feel more exposed by that one word than the fact that I'm sitting here naked, and still teetering on the edge of an orgasm.

That word sets him off again, his lips on mine and I never want it to stop, but more than that, I want him to touch me again. I reach down to wrap my hand around his shaft, he groans as soon as my skin touches his. I only pump him once before he's pulling me off and pushing me back onto the bed.

I go willingly this time, lying on my back, looking up at him as he lowers himself between my legs, placing kisses along the inside of my thighs. I throw my head back on a moan as I silently beg him to put his mouth on me, but other than his hot breath ghosting over my soaked center for a moment he doesn't touch me yet.

"Another one," he says, and I'm so worked up and can't think straight, I don't even know what more to tell him.

"You're the best I've ever had," I moan.

Nate chuckles as he sucks my clit into his mouth, the combination of the vibration from his laughter and the suction sends my hips shooting off the bed. He bands his arm to hold me down as I moan.

"I told you I want truths I don't already know." Nate nips at me with his teeth, and I swear I almost blackout from the sensation.

"You're such an asshole," I moan. He just smiles.

I feel his tongue lick my entire opening before spearing inside me, and I'm already so close again. He moves his mouth back to my clit, flicking his tongue against me, and I feel like I'm about to be hit with a train of pleasure when he pulls away again.

"Nate!" I scream at him.

"If you want to come, you'll give me one more, and make it

good."

I groan, I hate this stupid game.

"I've never felt like I deserve anything good or deserve to be happy at all because I know it won't last." I let the words fall out again, not thinking about what I'm saying, not second guessing how I feel just putting it out there.

Nate pauses for a second before rising to hover over me, looking into my eyes intently, I see the worry there, he doesn't like that truth, but too bad, it's what he asked for.

"Are you happy when you're with me?" he asks.

I nod.

"And you don't think that will last?"

I shrug.

"Aylin." My breath hitches because he never calls me by my name, and that's how I know he's serious. "Listen to me. You deserve so much more than you let yourself believe, and I don't plan on going anywhere, so sorry to break it to you, but the happiness you feel with me isn't going away."

I want to argue, I want to fight back about this. I want to believe him, but my brain won't let me. I don't say anything else, as I pull him back down to me again with his lips on mine. This kiss is softer, and it's almost too much emotion in one kiss for me. I need the level of aggression, and roughness Nate gives me. This is too much. This feels like...*more*.

I reach down to grab his hard cock. He grunts as I squeeze him, his teeth grab onto my bottom lip, pulling it into his mouth. I moan, squeezing him again, harder this time.

"What are you doing to me?" he asks against my mouth as I feel him line up at my entrance, pushing in slightly.

I wish I knew what he was doing to me too.

Then, with one strong thrust he's inside me and I moan at the stretch. God, he feels so good. Nate snakes his hand between us to massage my clit as he pumps his hips against me. As soon as his fingers touch the bundle of nerves, I explode from all the previous buildup. Clenching around him, I wrap my legs around his waist tighter, moaning his name.

"*Fuck*, Aylin," he growls, moving his hand onto my hip and pressing down while his hips snap against mine roughly.

"Oh, God, yes, Nate, *yes*," I moan at all the pressure from his hands pushing me down, his hips slamming against mine, rubbing and hitting me in all the right places to induce another almost immediate orgasm.

I pull his mouth to mine as the second orgasm takes over my body, needing his mouth, his tongue, every point of contact with him I need at this moment.

"You're fucking perfect," he says against my mouth right before flipping us so I'm straddling him. I feel his dick so deep inside me I swear he's in my stomach. "Ride me," he demands.

I can't deny him as I start to move my hips against him, rubbing myself against his pelvic bone as his mouth is on my nipple sucking so hard, I might have a mark. I don't even care as I start to build yet again.

Nate's hands go to my hips, pulling me against him harder until I scream out with another orgasm, this time I feel him tense as his own release takes over.

We are both breathing hard, our skin slick with sweat, but we don't move for a few moments, just being together.

When Nate pulls out of me, he pulls me against him as we roll over while I stay in his arms. It's almost like he can't let go of me, and I don't want him to.

Nate presses a kiss to the top of my head before murmuring, "Are you ever going to stop fighting this, sweetheart?"

I lay there, unsure of what to say.

Unsure of how to tell him that I've been fighting all my life, and it's all I know, so I don't know how to live differently.

Instead, I don't say anything. I just press a kiss against his chest, snuggling closer, enjoying this moment with him, letting myself live and enjoy something for once.

IT'S BEEN a couple of days that I've been staying at Nate's house. After he brought me over here, he stayed the night before having to leave in the morning to get back to whatever he's doing with the case.

We can't really communicate since he's left his real phone here and only has his burner phone in the field, and I haven't seen him since he left.

I would like to say it's been weird being in this house, but there's a level of comfort being here, being surrounded by his things and his scent, that has a calming effect on me.

Now it's Sunday morning, I'm having my second cup of morning coffee while working on my thesis when my phone rings.

I'm a little surprised to see that it's Sam. She calls me, but for some reason I always expect her to just stop reaching out, it's not like she has any obligation to continue talking to me. I know she's never seen me that way, but I will always see myself as a burden I put onto her and Jeff for the two years I lived with them.

"Hey," I answer.

"Hey Aylin, how are you doing?" Her cheerful voice asks.

Sam really is awesome, both her and Jeff did more for me than I could have ever asked for. I know once I moved out, they continued to foster teenagers, and never had any kids of their own. I'm not sure if that has been by choice, or if they weren't able to. I never wanted to ask because it's not my business.

"I'm good, working on my thesis." I drink the last bit of my coffee, holding the phone to my shoulder as I go to the sink.

"I am so proud of you, and everything you've done." I can hear her smile, and it makes my shoulders scrunch up.

"Thanks," I reply quietly.

"I was calling because I'm actually heading to Portland

today for a conference there this week, and I was hoping we could meet up, I miss you."

"Sure, when would you like to meet?"

"I can come by your apartment around five if that works for you?"

I look around this place that is not my apartment, and I don't think I want to even attempt to explain this to Sam. I guess I could go by there, meet Sam and grab more clothes when I leave.

"Yeah, sounds good."

"Awesome, see you then."

We hang up, and I think about whether I should tell Sam about Nate or not. It's also this moment I realize how weird I am about relationships with anyone. Sam and Jeff aren't my parents, not even adopted, and I don't see them in that way either. I guess I see them as distant cousins or family friends or something.

Then there's Nate, we aren't like "boyfriend and girlfriend" which just seems weird.

Does anyone even ask that anymore?

Who knows, we sleep together and I'm staying at his house while he's off doing god knows what.

What is my life?

BEFORE I LEFT Nate's house, I cleaned up the little mess I made of my clothes and dishes, just in case he comes back while I'm gone. I would most likely know if he was going to since we set up a bit of a system so I'm not taken off guard with him coming back, which is something he suggested, and I couldn't even fully explain how thankful I was for it.

We have code words he will text that if anyone were to see his burner, they wouldn't know what it means. He also doesn't have my number saved, and the fact that he has it memorized is hot in a way I would have never even thought about before.

Blue means he's coming over, and everything is fine.

Purple means he's coming over, and there's a problem.

Yellow means I need to leave, and he will tell me when it's safe to return.

I'm really not sure why a "yellow" text would happen, but he insisted we have this as a "just in case".

I brought back my luggage to repack more clothes, so while I wait for Sam to come by, I grab the rest of my clothes from my closet and throw them into the bags. I also throw in some other various items I figure I might want with me at some point since I still don't know how long I'm supposed to stay at Nate's.

There's a knock on my door right at five which isn't surprising since Sam is always on time. When I open the door she's standing there, and it's amazing how she hardly looks any different than she did when I first met her when I was fourteen.

She's only in her early forties now, but I still think she could pass for her twenties. She's always been pretty, and I always have felt out of place next to her, but her calming presence has always eased those thoughts when she's around.

"Aylin, you look amazing," she says with a wide smile on her face before outstretching her arms for a hug, but she doesn't wrap her arms around me first. She never has, she always lets me accept or deny physical affection from her. It's the small things like this that have always helped me be more at ease.

I smile back at her, and accept the hug. I've gotten more comfortable with physical affection as I've gotten older. I'm still not a huge fan of it most of the time, but it doesn't make my skin crawl anymore. For some reason I've been okay with touching Nate from the start, and even wanted to touch him back.

"Thanks," I cringe at the compliment, "So do you."

"I feel like I haven't seen you in so long," Sam says, holding me by the shoulders, and running her eyes over my face.

"It's been like a year I think." I gesture for her to come into my apartment, so we aren't just standing in the doorway.

"I'm sorry, it's just been so busy, we got a set of three siblings placed with us for a while, it was quite literally a full house." Sam shakes her head as we both sit on my small couch.

"I think it's great you guys are still helping kids that need it," I tell her, and it's true. I wish I could do something to help kids that were in similar situations as I was, but I am still learning how to take care of myself. I can't imagine helping take care of kids that are traumatized like I was.

There's a reason I chose not to focus on children in my therapeutic studies, I know my limits and I know there's no way I could handle it.

Sam nods, "I'm a helper by nature, you know this. So..." *here we go*, "what's new with you?"

I shrug, "I've been doing my clinical as a therapist for the Portland PD, and just excited to finish, but not sure what I'm going to do next."

"You'll figure it out. I know it can seem overwhelming to almost be done, but you will be surprised how easily something may fall into your life."

I'm not so sure about that, I don't think anything has ever just "fallen into my life". I've had to work really hard for what little I have.

Sam is glancing around my apartment, I know she likes to examine environments, it's something I do as well, learning about a person without them telling you. Even though she already knows me well enough that my apartment won't tell her anything.

I notice when her eyes catch on something, and when I look to see what she's looking at it's my overstuffed bags just outside my bedroom. Shit, I should've hidden those.

"Are you going on a trip or something?" Sam asks.

"Um...yeah, well kind of, I'm...um staying somewhere else for a little while. No big deal." I feel like I'm a teenager trying to get away with something. Which is stupid, I'm twenty-seven, but I can't tell Sam everything that's going on.

"Oh? Where are you staying?" she questions, and I would like nothing more than to melt into this couch right now.

"Just with a friend, there's some stuff going on in the complex, so I'm just going to stay there for a little," I try to keep my voice even, but I do not want her to ask me anymore about this.

"Isn't Mel living on the coast?"

"Oh, yeah, she is. This is a different friend...um you don't know them," I shrug.

Sam is quiet for a moment, I know she's waiting for me to say more, but I'm not going to. I will sit here in an awkward silence until she chooses to leave.

"Aylin, you don't have to tell me, but are you seeing someone?" she asks suddenly, my eyes shoot up to hers.

"I...um...it's not, I'm not— "

"It's okay, you don't have to tell me, but I do want to know if he treats you well. I worry about you here by yourself."

I know why she's asking. I'm aware of the statistical probability of me getting into an abusive relationship due to my past. It's something that came up in my college classes a lot, and how hard it can be to break the cycle of abuse. I know she cares, and she's concerned I could end up stuck. She also knows I wouldn't reach out to her for help if I needed it.

I nod, "I'm okay, and he treats me really well." A small smile appears on my lips as Nate's face flashes through my mind. I may have quite a few hang ups about whatever he and I are doing, but I can admit that he treats me better than I deserve.

"Good, now enough heavy stuff, take me to a place we can get a good drink," Sam says, hopping off the couch.

Whenever she comes to see me, we tend to get a drink or two, and it never ceases to be a little weird, but I appreciate her being more like a friend than any sort of authority figure to me.

Sam and I go to an upscale bar that Mel once described as a "parent's night out" type of bar, which made me laugh, but when she explained it, I guess I understood why. There are nice circular tables with fresh centerpieces. It's a big place that has a selection of food that is a step up from bar food but is just nice appetizers.

"How's Jeff?" I ask after we have sat down, and Sam is examining the large drink menu.

"He's great, just got another promotion so I'm really proud of him." Sam smiles every time she talks about Jeff. I lived with them for two years, and it was the first time I actually saw two people in love.

I remember living with them for about a month and they hadn't fought. I asked Sam about it, and she told me they have disagreements, but they don't yell or hurt each other, not ever. I was sixteen and knew that people who were supposed to love each other didn't hurt each other, but I had never actually seen it.

"That's great, tell him congrats from me," I say before we tell the waitress our drink orders.

"I will, of course." She smiles at me.

"How did you know you wanted to be with Jeff long term?" I ask suddenly.

She gives me a slight smile that tells me she knows exactly why I'm asking, but she doesn't embarrass me by calling me out.

"You know, I don't think I've ever told you how much you remind me of myself when I was younger."

I shake my head slightly. "There's no way."

Sam chuckles, "Oh yes there is. I didn't have an ideal childhood either, Aylin, not as...hostile as yours." I cringe at her words and the reminders they bring up, but I know she's not trying to hurt me. "When you first came into my office, I saw myself in you, I also saw your strength and resilience."

She's always told me how strong and resilient I am, but I've always thought she was just being nice.

"I knew you'd have a long road ahead of you when it comes to trust and love because you'd never experienced it. I recognized that within you because I was the same. I refused to let anyone close to me emotionally for a long time. Jeff was the first to ever take the time to break down the walls I'd spent years building, and he refused to give up."

I internally laugh at that. I'm all too familiar with someone refusing to give up.

"I fought it, Aylin. I refused to let go for so long because I knew this would just end in heartbreak, and I couldn't take any more pain. But Jeff wouldn't let me go, he wouldn't give up on us, and finally I let go. I let go of my reservations and let myself feel for him, and I have never regretted it, not a single time over the last fifteen years."

I feel my eyes starting to blur with tears that I don't want to fall.

"How did you let go, though?" I ask softly because I don't think I could even if I wanted to.

Sam takes a drink before answering, "I just decided the potential heartbreak is worth it, everything would be worth it, and I just let myself feel."

I sigh. It's not like I expected the answer to life or something, but I wanted a little more than that because I just don't think I'll ever see the potential heartbreak as worth it. I'm not good enough for anyone, and I'll end up all alone no matter what I do. No matter how hard Nate fights, and I don't think I'll ever be able to just let myself feel.

29

9 Years Ago (Age Eighteen)

Today is move in day at the University of Oregon, and I'm so ready to be finally starting my life on my own. Sam and Jeff have been fantastic the last two years I've lived with them, but it's time for me to grow solo.

I'm excited I get to start over here, no one knows who I am. No one knows my past or anything about me. I can be whoever I want to be.

I know my roommate's name is Melody, and that's about it. We were randomly assigned dormmates, and I'm just glad I only have one roommate. I know some people get stuck in dorms with 2 or 3 people, and that just sounds way too crowded for me.

Sam and Jeff drove me to Eugene to help me move in. I feel weird referring to them as "foster parents", but I guess technically that's what they were, and they were the best ones I could've asked for.

They said I could come back to their house for the holidays, but honestly, I never want to step foot in that town again if I can help it. They did say they would check on me with phone calls and texts every so often, which I appreciate. I know I can reach out to them anytime as well.

I shooed them out of the dorm once we brought in all my stuff. I didn't want to deal with an awkward first meeting with Melody and the questions I know will come up because Sam and Jeff look very young to be my parents, even though they are barely younger than my bio parents. We also look nothing alike, and I would rather not deal with questions or assumptions up front. I told them we could go out to eat before they started the five-hour drive back.

There's a crash at the door, I quickly go open it to see what's going on. I see a girl a little shorter than me with long auburn hair staring at the ground where the boxes I assume she was just carrying now lay.

"Well fuck," she says, bending down to start collecting her stuff.

I kneel down to help her as well, grabbing one of the boxes.

"Are you Melody?" I ask once we stand up.

"Oh, call me Mel! Sorry, what a great first impression." She shakes her head as we both bring the boxes inside the dorm.

"It's okay, I'm Aylin," I put my hand out to shake which she does.

I helped her and her dad bring the rest of her stuff into the dorm. She shoos her dad out quickly just like I did to Sam and Jeff. We work on organizing and decorating the room while learning about each other.

I learned she's an English major, she's from Portland and she's outspoken and funny. I'm a little afraid that we might be too different to become close friends, but I'm hopeful. I tell her I'm a Human Services major and I'm from Pendleton. When she asked if my parents came with me today, I just nodded.

"Oh, I should warn you I do have a little issue with nightmares so if you have earplugs or headphones or something you might want to sleep with them in or you'll end up hating me," I tell her because I can't imagine how mortified I'll be if I woke her up screaming one night.

The nightmares aren't always consistent, but when I have a major life change, they tend to be worse, and this is definitely a major life change.

I go meet with Sam and Jeff for an early dinner before they head back home. I have to reassure them about fifty times that I'm okay, that this is what I want, and I will let them know if anything changes.

Mel and I end up staying up most of that first night just hanging out, talking, and getting to know each other. I knew that first night that any concerns I had about this mystery person were not valid, and she might end up being my best friend.

Over the first term at UO Mel and I got really close. I learn more about her family, how she's lived with her dad since her parents got divorced when she was ten, and how her relationship with her mom isn't the best.

When the holidays come around after our first term, I start to open up a little bit about my family situation even though I'm terrified to share anything about my past that I'm trying to constantly move on from.

"You going home for winter break?" she asks one night we are hanging out in our room.

I shift in my seat, "No, I was just going to stay around here."

"Why? There's not going to be anyone around."

"Yeah, that might be nice."

"You saying you're sick of me?" She pretends to be offended.

"Well, I wasn't going to say anything…but since you brought it up…" She throws a pencil at me while I laugh. "No, it's just not worth the distance especially when I don't have a car."

"I'm sure your parents want you home though, I mean most usually do. I think mine are indifferent, but still," I chuckle. Mel didn't have the easiest or most "typical" home life either, but as far as I know it wasn't abusive.

"Oh, mine don't care," I shake my head.

"You never really talk about them. I don't think you've ever talked about your family actually," she realizes.

"Yeah, it's complicated." I twist my hands in my lap, I don't really want to talk about this. I like Mel, she's the best friend I've ever had, she's different from my high school friends. I feel like they weren't real friends since I haven't even spoken to them since I left, but this is just a lot.

"It's all good, you don't have to tell me, but would you want to come to my house for the holidays then? You'll be more entertaining than my dad, that's for sure."

"No, I couldn't do that."

"Uh, yeah you could. Actually, you might be saving me a bit if you did," she sounds like she's excited about the idea.

"Would your dad mind though?"

"Hell no he wouldn't! Come on, please?" She gives me puppy dog eyes that make me laugh.

"Okay, fine."

I went with Mel to Portland for the holidays, and on the drive there I finally told her about Sam and Jeff, who she knew I talked to, but didn't know who they were.

I told her about my parents, how they had me young and when I was sixteen, I was taken from their care because they hurt me. I didn't go into details, still to this day no one knows the full extent of the abuse I went through in my time of living with them.

No therapist, psychiatrist, not even Sam could get me to fully open up about *everything* and I intend to keep it that way. No one needs to know everything I went though, it's not their business and I don't need anyone's pity more than I already get. Not from Mel, though, she doesn't pity me even after she learns about my history. She just calls me a badass, and we move on which I appreciate more than she will ever realize.

Throughout our freshman year Mel and I only grew closer. I learn more about her life which has been monumentally more interesting than mine. She tells me about a guy named Zander. They were best friends when they were super young, then he moved away and came back her junior year of high school when it turned into more than friends until he had to leave again before senior year.

She was drunk one day when she told me about him, she said how badly she regretted how they left things when he had to leave. She blew up on him, and now it's been almost two years with no contact. I tried to convince her to reach out to him, but she waved me off by saying he wouldn't want to hear from her after the shit she said to him. She wouldn't tell me what it was, but it couldn't have been good.

This happened right around the start of spring term, which is also when I noticed a change in Mel, she wasn't as happy-go-lucky as she usually was. I was a little concerned, she wouldn't give me much information until I came home one day, and she was on the floor crying.

"What's wrong?" I ask frantically, as I sit next to her on the ground by her bed.

"I just don't know what to do anymore," she stumbles through her sobs.

"About what? Is it school? What's going on?" I know she's been struggling a bit, but I didn't think it was this bad.

"God, I don't even know. I just feel like I have the world's biggest weight on my shoulders, and I don't know what I'm doing anymore. I don't know what I'm going to do, and I feel like I just fuck up all the time and that's all I'll keep doing." She drops her forehead onto her arm as she hugs her knees to her chest.

"Why do you feel like you don't know what you're doing?"

She's always so confident when it comes to her schoolwork, and she wants to be a writer. She carries around a notebook and pen wherever she goes because she will get random inspiration from the smallest things, and she insists she has to write it down right away or the idea will be lost.

"I just don't. I feel like the whole world is against me and I'm fighting an uphill battle, I've felt like this for a while. Then, I talked to my mom who just made me feel worse about myself and now I just...I don't know," she sniffles.

"Look, I think that's just life. We have to fight some battles, we deal with people that suck, but we find our passions and our reasons along the way so no matter how hard things get, we will have these reasons to keep going. It's like...a key. We find our keys to life, and they keep us going."

I continued to console Mel during this time, and we decided later that day we were going to get tattoos to remind ourselves of that.

Well, Mel decided this, and I decided to go along with it since it's not something I would ever usually do.

We ended up getting matching tattoos. Mel got hers on her inner wrist, a small key, I got the same design on my ankle because I wanted to make it a little easier to hide if I needed to for my career of choice.

We knew we had keys to our lives and we have reasons to keep going, no matter how hard shit gets and no matter what is thrown at us, we have our passions, our drive, and we have each other. We will get through it, no matter what.

"I want to be you when I grow up," Mel says to me that night as we are laying in our beds about to go to sleep.

I chuckle, "What do you mean?"

"You've gone through more shit than anyone I've ever known and you're still the strongest, most motivational and put together person I've ever met. I want to be like that. Thank you for being my best friend."

I couldn't even reply. I didn't know what to say. I smiled, glad she felt that way because I certainly don't. I don't think I'm particularly strong or put together, but I guess I can appear that way. I go to bed that night thinking about what my keys to life are to remind myself why I keep going.

30

Nate

Present

It's been a few days since I moved Aylin into my house, and it has helped with my focus on the case because I know for a fact, she's safe there. I know she's far enough from the bullshit I'm dealing with, that I don't have to worry about my worlds colliding.

I do hate that I can't check in with her, but I had to leave my real phone back at my house just in case. Plus, it's too much of a risk to text her on the burner phone all the time, so I'll have to make time to see her at some point.

The last few days have been mundane, meeting with Jason at one of the many houses the gang has and just observing. Nothing interesting has happened since the weird little fight club they have going on, and I still don't exactly know what that was about.

The other odd thing about all of this is Cap hasn't been around at all, but I still feel like I'm being watched or examined whenever I'm around these people.

Some might think I'm just being paranoid, but I know that's

not it. I've always been hyper aware of my surroundings, and that increased when I became a cop. I notice the small glances from around the room, the quiet conversations around me just so they can hear what I'm saying to someone else.

The worst part about it being so boring, is that I still have no idea what they are really doing. I know what Sarge talked about in the briefings, about them trying to expand like some kind of fucking mafia, but I haven't seen or heard anything that even hints to that.

Honestly, I haven't even seen much drug dealing which is the one thing that was known for sure, thanks to Trent and Zander, but that isn't enough for a bust of this caliber. I'm feeling my frustration because I hate being stagnant like this, I need something to happen, and I need it to happen soon.

My burner phone rings as I'm just getting ready to meet up with Jason again. I half expect it to be him, but when I answer I'm a little surprised to hear Mitch's voice. We haven't talked much recently.

"What's up?" I say nonchalantly.

"How's it going?"

I shrug even though he can't see it. "Fine, I guess, nothing exciting."

"Can you meet up later?" Mitch is hard to read, he always has been, which is good for this line of work, but annoying for me at times.

"Sure, I guess, where?"

"Probably best if we meet up at your real place."

I hesitate for a second. Mitch doesn't know about Aylin at all since we haven't really talked, and I'm not a guy to sit around and gossip like that with my buddies. So, he would be really thrown off to not only meet Aylin, but to see her *staying* at my house.

"How about your place? I'll make sure I'm not followed."

Mitch sighs before agreeing and we hang up. He probably

knows I'm hiding something, but it's probably something he feels like he has to be concerned about. I'll tell him about her tonight. He will probably tell me I'm being stupid, but that's fine. He can think what he wants, it's not his life.

Jason and I meet up at a neutral location not far from my fake apartment. He's smoking a cigarette while leaning against the side of a building as he waits for me. We have to be discreet in any conversations we have out in the open like this because we never know who might be around listening.

I've been pretty impressed with Jason as a CI. At first glance he seemed a little sketchy, and I wasn't sure about trusting him. After these last few days, I think he's just as done with this shit as I am and wants out so badly he's willing to actually help the cops.

"Anything new?" I ask casually, kicking my foot up against the building to stand next to him.

Jason lets out a cloud of smoke. "Nothing much, Cap told his guys he wants you back tonight."

I raise my eyebrow to him, "Back where?"

"The place by campus," he replies, throwing the cigarette butt on the ground and crushing it with his shoe.

"Is there any info on what the fuck that's about?" I ask, running a hand down my face.

Jason shakes his head, "Nah, but the guys made it sound like Cap has some sort of plan for you, they just won't tell me what it is."

I nod once, "Thanks, I'm going to head there alone tonight, it's going to raise too many questions if you're always with me."

"Wasn't planning on it anyway, they have me out on a job later." He pushes away from the wall.

"What's the job?" I question because this is news to me.

Jason kicks at the ground as he hesitates for a moment. "Feels weird to tell you 'cause…ya know, but it's a drug run. Picking up product and bringing it back."

"You sure it's only drugs?" I feel like I have to ask because I'm looking for anything else with this group, and when there's a shipment it could be anything. Weapons, women, stolen product, counterfeit money.

I. Just. Need. Something.

He nods, "Yeah, I mean I won't know for sure until I see it, but it's always just drugs."

"Okay, anything else?"

Jason shakes his head before we go our separate ways. I rake my hands through my hair, frustrated at how hard this is turning out to be. It's not like I expected to walk in and have everything laid out in front of me, but I just assumed I would have at least some small info on anything else going on.

I decide to drive around a bit to make sure no one is tailing me before I let Mitch know I'm coming over. I do debate going by my house to see if Aylin is there but decide not to. I know I'll get a chance to see her at some point soon.

After almost an hour, I'm sure no one is following me, so I head to Mitch's house. He lives in a quiet neighborhood in Beaverton, outside of Portland. I park in his driveway and give one final visual sweep before knocking on his door.

"Wow, you look like shit," Mitch greets me.

"Thanks, fucker," I walk past him inside.

His place is way different than mine, he actually has decorations. I'm pretty sure his mom helped him with it because nothing in here looks like something he would pick out, but it has a homey feel that my place is missing.

"So," I plop my ass onto his couch. "Why'd you want to risk my life meeting up with me?"

Mitch scoffs, "You're risking your life doing this anyway, meeting with me hardly changes that."

I shrug, "Just know if they find my body, you're the one to blame."

He rolls his eyes, "Nope, if anyone finds you, I know it was your own stupidity that got your ass killed."

"Damn, what did I do to you?" I question. We always give each other shit, but Mitch seems more on my ass lately, and it's starting to piss me off.

"Honestly? You took on this case when I still don't think you're ready."

I groan, "Seriously? You're still on this? I. Am. Fine."

"You're not, did you even give the therapist a chance? Did you take it seriously at all or did you just use her to make her clear you?"

My hands ball into fists at him mentioning me using Aylin. Yes, that might have been my plan before I met her, but then shit changed when it came to her.

"I didn't use her, she believed in me, and if it helps anything I'm still technically seeing her."

Mitch looks at me skeptically. "You're still seeing her...how?"

"Okay, look, I know what you're thinking, but it's not like that. I really like her, there's just something—"

"*Dude!*" Mitch shakes his head at me. "You're sleeping with your therapist."

"Okay, well yes, sort of, but I stopped seeing Aylin as a therapist before anything even happened, and *it's not like that*."

"What's it like then, Nate?"

"I like her, okay? I didn't use her, I wanted to get to know her, and then I just wanted to keep seeing her, just not as a therapist."

Mitch is quiet for what feels like forever, and I know he's pissed at me. He's convinced I haven't been okay since what happened to my parents, and yeah, I changed that day, but I'm fine. Then for some reason he got on my ass more after what happened with Layla and her family, and he just won't let it go.

"You're a jackass, you know that right?" He finally says.

"Why? Because I finally found a girl that I actually like, and can hold my attention?"

"No, because even if you don't see it, you did use her. It just happens that you ended up liking her."

"Well, she doesn't see it that way, and neither do I, but I don't know why my supposed best friend is so against me being fucking happy."

"That's not what I'm saying, but are you really happy? Like actually?" He softens his voice slightly, so I don't feel like I'm being scolded like a fucking child as much.

"I am. A case like this is everything I've wanted, and I'm going to finally get a promotion from it. Plus I finally found someone who seems like she fucking gets me."

"I mean, it's kind of her job to *get you*." He rolls his eyes at me.

"You don't believe she's into me? Because trust me, she is."

Mitch sighs, running his hand down his face. "Look, I'm sure she is, I'm just worried about you. I feel like you went into all of this too quickly and you're going to get yourself in some fucked up situation you can't get out of and end up really hurt or fucking dead."

"Thanks for caring," I say sarcastically. "But I got this, I'm going to be fine, I'm careful when I need to be, but I take risks to get shit done."

"Unfortunately, I do fucking care, which is the problem, and I'd be kind of sad if you died."

"Nah, you'd throw a party," I joke, and I feel the tension lifting slightly.

"Only because that's what you'd want." I see him relax a little, and I feel like my friend is coming back around.

"True."

"One more thing, have you considered checking on that little girl you helped?" Mitch asks cautiously.

My smile fades and I look down at the floor at the mention of Layla. I hadn't even considered checking on her, I felt like it would be better if she didn't have some kind of reminder from that night to show up, and possibly ruin any progress she's made.

I shake my head in response, really wanting him to drop this too.

"Maybe you should think about it," he suggests.

"Yeah, maybe," I say, but only to get him to drop it. "Look, I gotta go, I have some shit to do on the case tonight."

Mitch nods, "Just...think about it."

I nod once before heading out to my car. I don't tell him that I can't go see her, I don't want to be a reminder to her, but I also can't stand the thought of her possibly *not* doing well, and what that would do to me.

Shaking those thoughts from my mind, I head toward the house by campus because I'm ready for a distraction, and ready to know what the fuck this Cap guy has planned for me. I know I'm more than prepared for whatever it is.

I walk into the house, this time I'm alone. It feels odd to be completely on my own without Jason, but it also makes me feel more in my element, like I can really do what needs to be done without having a shadow.

The house is exactly the same as it was last time I was here, full of people, smoke and who knows what else. I make my way back to the same door that leads downstairs because I'm sure that's where I'll find Cap who is supposedly waiting for me.

The area is set up just like it was the last time I was here; another fight is happening with people surrounding the area to watch. I notice something new this time, and that's a smaller guy walking around taking money from people, I assume for bets on the fight. I can't help but consider how many people probably betted against me my first night here, and the thought makes me internally smile.

On the other side of the room, I see Cap standing with his arms folded, cigarette in his mouth as he watches the current fight. Slowly, I make my way over to him like I'm just watching the fight so as not to seem too obvious.

I'm standing a few people away from Cap when I stop moving, standing with the crowd acting like I'm watching the fight, but really, I'm watching Cap in my peripheral vision.

The fight going on doesn't take long to be over as one of the guys is dragged out of the area, and the other one celebrates. I hear Cap say something, unsure if it's to me at first until I notice he walked slightly closer to me.

"Ya hear I had a job for ya, or did ya come back on your own?"

I turn to look at him, but he's still staring forward as the next two guys enter the fighting ring.

"Does it matter?" I shrug.

Cap is quiet for a few moments and I wonder if my answer was a little too cocky, but I know I can't be a "yes man". That's one way to get stomped all over in this world.

I feel a heavy hand slap down on my shoulder as I hear Cap's raspy laugh. "I think ya got potential, Trevor, let's go."

I follow Cap and two of the guys that were standing by him as they make their way out of the basement. One of the guys slaps someone on the back who automatically stands up to follow as well. I really wonder what I might be involving myself in right now, but I continue to follow.

Once we are all outside Cap gestures to a black SUV parked on the street, and simply says, "Get in." While the three other men that followed all piled into the car as well.

I wonder if I'm about to get taken out to a field to be shot or something. Maybe I've been caught, and this is how they deal with their problems. I could take Cap if I needed to, but the rest of these guys are bigger than me, which is not easy to do.

This is what I wanted; this is what I have to do. If I refuse, then I'll definitely be out before I'm even in.

I will have failed.

I know I have to do this. So, with a deep breath, I get in the SUV sandwiched between two of the guys in the back seat while the third sits in the driver seat, and Cap in the passenger seat.

"Comfy?" he asks with a sinister smile.

"Never better," I reply sarcastically.

With another raspy laugh he turns to the driver saying, "Let's go, Saw."

The guy—Saw—takes off down the street. I might have been thrown around the car a bit if I wasn't being held in place by the two giants next to me. This car was not made for three 6-foot-plus men in the backseat.

Against my better judgement because I've always been a curious mother fucker, I open my mouth to ask, "Saw?"

Cap turns slightly so I can see his profile when he speaks, "Ya ever seen the movies?"

"The Saw movies? Yeah." I nudge my right arm slightly to try to get a little room from Tweedle-Dee next to me, and I hear a deep growl come from him, but I can move my arm now.

"Saw here takes some...inspiration from those movies when it comes to dealing with people," Cap says with a sinister smile.

I want to be a smart ass and say the guy from the movie is named *Jigsaw* not just Saw, but figured I'll save my snarky comments for when I'm sure they are going to kill me, just in case that's not what's happening.

I turn to Tweedle-Dee on my right. "You got a name from a movie too?"

He grunts but doesn't respond beyond that. His bald head is

so shiny the lights from outside reflecting off it I decide I'll call him Cue for cue ball in my head. Probably not out loud.

I try again with the same question to Tweedle-Dumb on my left, "What about you?"

"Nah, I'm Kill Switch."

"Seems like a long nickname," I say under my breath.

"Wanna find out why?" Kill Switch snaps.

"Calm down, K," Cap says from the front. "This one might be helpful for us."

Maybe I'm not being taken to a field to be murdered, that's good news. I want to ask where we are going, but I feel like I might have pushed the limits on my questions for this car ride.

The rest of the ride is silent as we drive about twenty minutes away, pulling up to some strip club. Not my type of scene, even if I didn't have Aylin back at my place, I've never been a guy that enjoys strip clubs. Respect for the women that have that power and confidence, it's just not the type of entertainment I find myself going to.

Saw parks the car right up front, Cap turns back to look at me and says, "Have my back."

Before I'm able to ask him any questions he, and the rest of the guys are getting out of the car. Clearly, this is some sort of test. He doesn't know me, which means he doesn't trust me enough to actually have his back. That would be why the three other guys are here as well, but clearly Cap has some sort of plan for me.

We head inside, and I can feel the air of the place thickening with tension as the five of us walk with purpose through the entire building toward the back. I'm walking slightly behind Saw and Cue while Kill Switch and Cap walk ahead of us. They are walking like they own the place, and for all I know, maybe they do.

We reach a door, and when KS swings it open, I see a few

girls scurry away before the five big men barrel through the door and continue going toward the back of the building.

No one is saying anything to us, and the guys aren't saying anything to anyone. All the girls have looked away as soon as we walked by. It's a weird feeling to be so adamantly ignored by every single person, it makes me uneasy because I know the avoidance has to do with one thing. Fear.

Once we are at another door that says, "DO NOT ENTER" KS proceeds to open it immediately where I see it's a small office space.

"Can you fucking read?" The guy sitting behind the desk says before swinging around, his face dropping as soon as he sees who it is. "Leave."

I think for a second, he's talking to us, which makes me inwardly cringe because I know that is not how anyone should talk to them. Then I see a topless woman stand up from where she was clearly blowing him before we walked in.

She rushes past us, but not before Cap smacks her on the ass. I ball my fists tightly to prevent me from punching Cap for the blatant disrespect but hold back and offer a sympathetic look to the woman, but she doesn't glance my way.

"To what do I owe the visit, gentleman?" The man from the desk asks once he's standing and his pants are zipped up. He looks like a typical slime ball. Probably mid-sixties, stomach hanging over his belt line, greasy hair slicked back. Every single stereotype I can think of for a strip club owner, this guy would be it.

Cap rounds the desk to sit in the chair, I can't help the grimace as I think about the fact that this guy's bare ass was probably just on that thing and I wouldn't touch it with a fifty-foot pole, but Cap doesn't seem to give a fuck.

"Don't be dumb, Rob, ya know why I'm here," Cap muses nonchalantly.

We all have crammed into the small office that was definitely not made for 6 grown ass men to be in at once. Saw and Cue are standing in front of the closed door so there's no way to leave. I'm standing off to the side, arms folded, trying to appear like I know what's going on.

"I...uh...oh, the money," Rob says like it just occurred to him.

Cap doesn't say anything, just gives Rob a knowing look.

"I have the money, of course, it's in the drawer right there," Rob points to a filing cabinet next to the desk.

"Tell me why I'm here to collect instead of ya giving the money to Deuce when he came by last week...and yesterday?" Cap appears calm, though I can tell he is anything but.

Rob hesitates as he looks around to Cap's guys and me before he speaks again, "Okay, I didn't have the money before, but I do now—"

Cap quiets him as he slams a gun on the desk.

I'm aware that I am going to see a lot of things. Shit, I've seen a lot of things in my career as it is, but at this moment, I am unsure what I'm about to witness. I continue to keep my face neutral, arms crossed while I just watch everything that is happening around me.

"Rob, ya know I don't like coming to do other people's jobs," Cap announces, I can hear the annoyance and boredom in his voice.

"I-I know Cap, look, the money is in the drawer. All of it is there just—"

"I'll get the money but this is also about a lesson. When my guys come here, you pay them. Got it?"

Rob seems confused considering Cap hasn't moved, and what he's saying almost seems like he's going to let him go without injury. I don't see that happening.

"Y-Yes," Rob clears his throat. "Yes sir."

Cap nods, "Good, get the money."

Rob looks around the room at all of us before moving back

around the desk toward the drawer he says has the money. He's clearly nervous, I can see his hands shaking from where I stand. I continue to watch with a hardened expression.

As soon as Rob leans down to open the drawer of the filing cabinet everything happens in a flash. Cap slams Rob's head down onto the metal, KS and Cue rushing over to grab Rob before he even hits the ground.

Cap picks up his gun, flipping it around in his hand like he's inspecting it while the two guys hold up Rob who has blood gushing down his face, groaning in pain.

I sneak a glance at Saw to see that he has a knife in his hand. He's flipping it between his fingers like he's just waiting to use it.

"Do ya think I'm a fuckin' idiot?" Cap asks calmly.

Rob groans in response, resulting in Cap slamming his gun across Rob's face. I hear the crack as the metal hits bone.

"Ya must, since I'm here with my guys and ya act like I ain't got a reason to be." Cap shakes his head, still speaking calmly right before raising his foot to slam into Rob's sternum.

KS and Cue continue to hold him like the kick didn't even faze them, but I saw Rob's body bow at the force, that shit had to hurt.

"I don't! I really don't!" Rob screams, I can hear the blood gurgling in his throat.

"If I come back here again, ya don't leave alive," Cap states as he stands up, moves to the drawer Rob was headed to, pulling out stacks of cash.

I take in the whole scene, Rob gurgling and groaning while blood pours from his face. The giant men holding him up stand still as statues while Saw and I watch.

Cap doesn't say anything as he counts the cash, the only sounds are coming from Rob. I'm thankful I don't have a weak stomach because this would make anyone else sick.

Once he's done, Cap takes the cash, stuffing it in a bag that I didn't notice before. No one says anything, Rob continues to groan in pain, but they don't let go of him.

Cap gestures toward me to follow him, "Take care of him," he says to the other three.

I hear the wet sounds of flesh hitting flesh as I follow Cap out of the office into the main part of the strip club. I have so many questions, but I know I need to keep my mouth shut. I walk behind him, and continue to stand up straight, arms folded, my face telling everyone looking our way to "fuck off".

I catch some of the girls looking our way, perusing me up and down with interest, but I don't look at any of them. Cap leads us toward the back which I assume is some sort of VIP booth just for him.

He grabs two girls and pulls them along to join us, they both drape themselves on him as he sits down. I sit on the other side of the booth, another girl comes over trying to sit on my lap, but I wave her off, but that doesn't stop her as she runs her hands up my chest, and around the back of my neck.

I realize what she's doing, these girls are told to check for wires and she's checking me. I let her for a few moments before waving her off again, this time she listens. Before walking away, I see her give a small nod to Cap, telling him I'm clear.

"Not interested?" Cap chuckles as he messes with the strap on the top of the blonde to his right.

"Nah, I have a girl and she'd kill me," I say seriously.

"They never know, we can get away with whatever we want, Trevor." He winks in my direction before untying the blonde's top revealing her naked tits to us both.

I shrug, "I'm good. Do you own this place?"

Cap turns his attention to the brunette on his other side as the blonde nuzzles against his neck, her whole body pressed against his side. "I run a lot of places around here."

Not really an answer, but I nod.

"Portland has the most strip clubs per capita in the US.

They got lots of uses, and ain't looked at too closely," he simply says.

I log that info in my mind for later. What other uses does he have for these places, and he says he *runs* them, but doesn't own them? So, who does?

I decide to be bold with my next question, "So, was this some kinda test for me?"

A slimy smile spreads across Cap's face. "No bullshit with you, huh?"

I fold my arms across my chest, "Nope."

"I know I could have some use for ya, but I needed to see if ya could handle it."

"Handle what? Some blood? Thought the fight the other night would prove that."

Cap chuckles as his hand slips between the blonde's legs. I keep my eyes anywhere else because I really don't need to watch this guy finger fuck someone right in front of me.

"I think ya could be useful to me Trevor, and I needed to make sure. We have a lot of shit goin' on around this city, and I always need someone to make sure it's all...handled."

"Handled?" I question.

Cap smirks, "I need guys makin' sure business is runnin' how it should, and fuckers like Rob ain't takin' advantage."

"You want that to be me?" I furrow my brows. I don't even know the extent of the businesses, no one has told me shit.

Cap laughs loudly making the girls jump. "Don't get ahead of ya self, maybe one day Trevor, but ya ain't even initiated."

I feel like this guy doesn't make any sense. First the fighting, now this. It's like he's giving me mixed signals and I thought I was just going to be doing drug runs for a while until I built up trust, but I have barely seen any drugs exchanging hands at all.

"How do I get initiated?" I ask because I know I can't question anything else he's said without raising some red flags.

"Just stick around and it'll happen. I got big plans for ya, don't worry."

I'm not necessarily worried, but something about the way he said that makes the hair on the back of my neck stand straight up.

I don't trust this guy, I don't trust anything he says, but I have a feeling he does have "plans" for me, and they probably won't all be good.

31

Aylin

Present

School has taken over my life.

It always does as the term progresses, but I am feeling the pressure and stress tenfold this time around, I think because I'm so close.

Oh, and my thesis is kicking my ass. Whoever thought this was required to get a Doctorate degree deserves to be castrated.

Or was it a woman? No, there's no way, a man is definitely behind this.

On a brighter note, there's only a few more weeks left of this term, then I have a holiday break, not that the holidays mean anything to me, but it's a break.

I hope Nate won't want to do anything special. He doesn't have his parents, and doesn't mention any other family so at least I won't have to deal with any awkward family celebrations or weird traditions.

I shake my head of the thoughts, it's only the beginning of November, I don't have to stress about any of this yet.

Nate hasn't been able to come back to his house much, and

when he does it's only for an hour or two, he claims just to check on me. I roll my eyes because I'm used to being independent and I don't need to be "checked on".

Though, it is pretty cute.

He hasn't been able to tell me anything he's been doing, but I notice when he does come over his knuckles are busted, and he has bruises on his body.

I worry about him.

I don't want to, but I can't help it and that's probably also the source of some of my stress.

He tells me not to worry, but I'm completely helpless when it comes to him.

I've become more comfortable in his house, and it's a little scary. He noticed because last time he was here he made a comment about it.

"You look like you've started to put your mark on this place...I like it," Nate says smiling, looking around the living room.

I haven't done much, just put some of my throw pillows on the couch and one of my favorite fuzzy blankets.

I also put up some string lights in the bedroom because I like to read or work on my computer in bed, and I like having softer lights when I do.

"I'm sorry, if it's too much I can take it back to my apartment," I say, walking toward the kitchen to stack up the stuff I can take back.

Nate reaches out, grabbing my hand in his to pull me against him. His other hand reaches up to pull my bottom lip from between my teeth. *I swear, I never noticed having a nervous habit like this, until him.*

"I like it, I like this place looking like it's lived in. I like how it looks like you *live in it*."

"Temporarily," I roll my eyes.

"Of course." He winks before pressing a chaste kiss to my lips.

. . .

I look around the bedroom, I'm lying on his bed, over the covers with just my fuzzy blanket over my legs. Other than the string lights I really haven't done much in here, but it is more... comfortable.

I rub my eyes, it's late and the light from my computer is starting to hurt my head so I decide to go to sleep. I think I've exhausted my writing capabilities for the night. Closing my computer, I set it on my nightstand before settling under the blankets to try and fall asleep.

As I feel myself drifting off, I hear some noise at the front door, my heart rate automatically picks up. Nate would be the only person coming here, and he always texts me before showing up using our code words.

I double check my phone, and don't see anything from him. I begin to panic at the thought of someone coming into my space unannounced like this.

Even though Nate's house still doesn't necessarily seem like it's *my* space it makes the uneasy feeling caused by the ratting front door even more heightened.

Quickly, I dial 911 preparing to press "call" at any second as I jump out of bed and make my way downstairs. I'm approaching the front door cautiously as the doorknob rattles like someone is repeatedly trying to open it, despite the lock.

All the alarm bells are going off in my mind as I get closer to the door until I'm able to look through the peephole. When I do, I gasp so loud I'm sure he heard me. Then I hear his voice, it's strained, and I can tell he's struggling to speak as he calls my name.

I rip the door open to reveal Nate hunched over, barely standing as he grips the door frame, which it looks like is the only thing keeping him upright.

"Oh my God," I breathe, as I reach for his arm to sling around my shoulder to pull him inside.

He stumbles in, my small frame nothing compared to his,

he's dragging us both down, but I refuse to give up.

He's covered in blood; I think it's all his. It's getting all over me, but I don't even care. I need to clean him up so I can see the extent of his injuries.

I'm pulling him along as his body grows weaker. Just a few more feet to the guest bathroom downstairs, I know we can make it.

After what feels like an eternity we make it into the small bathroom. Nate's breathing is choppy, he hasn't said anything since I grabbed him, and I'm too focused on keeping both of us moving to ask any of the thousand questions racing through my mind.

I turn the shower on, planning to wait for it to warm up, but Nate has other plans, it's like if he stops moving, he will collapse. Instead, he uses me for support as he pulls us both into the freezing water before I see him start to go down. I lean myself against the wall of the shower and hold on to him for dear life as we slide down to the ground.

We are sitting on the floor, the door of the shower open with Nate's outstretched legs not fitting inside. He's sitting in between my legs, his head resting back against me. His breathing is shallow, I'm panting from the exertion of holding him up, mixed with the panic I'm still feeling.

"Where are you hurt? We should get you to the hospital," I finally say as I rip at Nate's shirt beginning to examine for injuries.

"No hospitals, I'll be fine, I just need to rest," he says, and I can tell how much of a struggle it is for him to speak.

"No, if you have a concussion, you can't rest." I finally get his wet shirt off him to reveal the massive bruises, cuts and scrapes covering his normally beautiful torso. I do my best to hold back my gasp, the angry colors blooming on his skin have me shaking.

I try to focus on helping him, and not freaking out as I

remember all the times my body resembled something similar to this, but I didn't have anyone to take care of me back then.

Nate isn't alone like I was.

He has me.

I watch as the blood swirls around, the water cascading all around us, washing all the red down the drain.

Blood.

Nate's blood.

A memory flashes in my mind of myself watching my own blood swirl down the drain. So much blood dripping from my skin...

No, my focus is on Nate.

I turn my attention to his head where it appears most of the blood is coming from. It's hard to fully see the extent of his injuries from this angle and through all the blood gushing from various places, but I see some gashes by his eye, his lip, and his cheek. I recognize these types of gashes; these are from fists. Possibly fists with ring covered knuckles. The bruises on his torso look like they could be anything: feet, hands, weapons.

"Nate, please look at me," I plead into his ear so he can hear me. His eyes are closed, breathing shallow, but I know he's awake by the grimace of pain on his beautiful and broken face.

With a grunt, Nate rolls his head to the side so he can look at me. He slowly opens his eyes, the hazel is dull, his pupils dilated, clearly from the trauma his head has sustained.

"We have to get you to a hospital, or seen by someone, you could have internal injuries." I'm holding back sobs.

I move to stand up so I can grab a phone, but Nate stops me. "Just stay here with me, I'm okay, baby, I promise." His voice is gravely and I can hear the struggle as he speaks.

He's not, but I'm not going to start a fight with him right now. I just hold him. His bleeding has slowed down, the water around us that has warmed up is now running with a pink tinge.

I want to ask how this happened.

Who did this?

Why isn't he doing anything about it?

I need to know so much, but I know it won't help him. He just needs me. I know the feeling, sometimes I just wanted someone.

Anyone to hold me.

Anyone to save me.

Anyone to love me.

And I had no one.

Eventually the water becomes cold again, and I know we need to get out of here. I reach up to turn off the water, my fingertips barely able to push the lever off.

Once the water is off the silence is almost unbearable. The soft dripping of the water as it turns off fully is the only noise in this small space. Nate is only in his jeans, I'm still fully clothed with freezing wet clothes sticking to my skin.

"Can you get up?" I whisper softly.

He grunts, but nods.

I continue to help him stay steady as he stands, slowly, careful not to make any sudden movements that could hurt his head further.

We make our way up to the bedroom, leaving puddles along the way from our soaked clothes. The stairs are a struggle, but Nate amazingly pushes through.

Once we get there Nate sits on the edge of the bed, neither of us caring the blanket is going to be wet from his jeans.

He's still not talking, and it hurts because other than the obvious injuries this is how I can tell he's not okay. Nate is so full of personality, always has something to say and for him to be like this is painful.

I grab some boxers for him, and one of his t-shirts for me before helping him out of his pants that have suctioned themselves to his skin.

"Please let me call someone," I plead softly once I finally pull his pants off, and hand him the clean boxers.

"Call Mitch, use my phone," he says gruffly. He doesn't even sound like himself, and my heart hurts to see and hear him like this.

I nod before going to his nightstand where he keeps his real phone while he's out. I peel my clothes off as I wait for it to power on. I continue to keep an eye on Nate as he pulls on his underwear, so painfully slow. I want to help him, but I don't want to suffocate him by overdoing it.

Once his phone is on, I go to his contacts to dial Mitch. He answers after the second ring.

"What's up?" He sounds slightly alarmed, probably because Nate shouldn't be contacting him right now.

"Um, Mitch it's Aylin, I don't know if you know who I am, but— "

"Oh, I know who you are. Where's Nate?"

"He's here, at his house and he's hurt, he needs someone, but he keeps telling me no to the hospital."

I hear Mitch sigh on the other end of the phone. I look over at Nate who has now laid back on the bed, his feet still planted on the floor, I would almost think he's sleeping.

"Stubborn fucker, let him know I'll be over with Jack soon."

"Who's, um, Jack?" It seems stupid to ask given the circumstance, but I don't love the idea of random people coming around while Nate is like this.

"He's a paramedic, and a buddy of ours, he can help. Thank you, Aylin."

Mitch hangs up, and I go over to Nate, slowly sitting next to him. I run my hand along his forehead, pushing some of his hair off his head.

"Mitch is bringing Jack here to help you," I say softly.

I take the opportunity of Nate laying back like this to get a better look at his injuries on his torso. I ghost my fingers over the beginnings of all the bruises. I try my hardest to keep my tears back, but I fail as I feel the warm liquid running down my cheeks.

    I'm so scared for Nate.
    I hate this.
    I'm so scared seeing him hurt like this.
    What if it gets worse?
    What if he gets killed doing this?
    I know I have continued to fight this thing between us, whatever it is. I refuse to acknowledge the extent of feelings I have for this man in front of me, but I am so scared of losing him.

    He's the first and only person in my life I have trusted so completely. I trusted Sam and Jeff, but even then, it wasn't fully. I was always wondering if they resented me, and if at some point they would turn around to kick me out because I wasn't worth their kindness.

    I trust Mel, I really do, but for some reason there's always a part of me that holds back with her, and that maybe she's just my friend because she feels bad for me.

    I've also never really loved anyone. I thought I loved my parents, but I didn't, I couldn't. I have love for Mel, but this is different. Looking at Nate right now I would give up anything and everything for him to just be okay at this moment.

    I need him.
    I love him.
    I love him.
    The realization makes my chest burn. The tears continue to fall, and Nate opens an eye to look at me like he just realized I sat down next to him. He reaches his hand to me in offering. I take it cautiously because I do not want to hurt him. He doesn't seem to care as he pulls me against him, letting out a sigh I thought might be from pain, but when I look at his face, I can

see the peace that's settled over his features. It was a sigh of relief.

I want to tell him what I just realized but the words get caught in my throat. Plus, I don't want him to think I'm just saying it because he's hurt. I bury my face into his neck softly as I try to telepathically share my thoughts with him.

Share all I'm feeling.

Share all my love with him.

Instead, neither of us say anything. I think Nate might have fallen asleep, so I nudge him softly.

"You need to stay awake until they get here," I whisper softly, hoping he won't hear that I'm crying.

Nate grunts, "I'm awake."

It's silent again while I debate saying anything, but decide I need to know.

"What happened?" My voice cracks as I fail to hide my crying.

I don't think Nate is going to answer me. He stays silent and unmoving until his arms tighten around me for a second, then he speaks.

"It was a part of their fucked-up initiation," he starts before taking a shaky breath. I can tell how difficult it is for him to talk right now. I'm about to tell him to stop before he continues. "They held me down and took turns beating the shit out of me. I couldn't do anything to fight back except wait for it to be over."

I can't help the sob that escapes me as the visual I have of Nate being held down, helpless against the assault. The onslaught of my own memories of a similar situation takes over my mind before I can stop it and I continue to cry.

I hate this.

I hate this is his life.

I hate what my life was.

I hate all this fucking pain.

"Nate, why can't I take you to the hospital?" I ask.

"Because they will take me off the case if they know."

I furrow my brow, sitting up to look him in the eye to reply, "You mean you're *not* done with the case?"

He snakes his hand back around to pull me down again. "No. I'm initiated, now it will just get easier and I'm okay. I'll continue to be okay, sweetheart."

I shake my head, "Why? Why do you feel like you need to do this so badly?"

"As long as these people are out there others are going to continue to get hurt. I want to make sure this stops."

"What about you, though, Nate?"

"What about me?"

"Your safety. I can't..." I trail off. I don't think I can voice my thoughts. They are there, but I can't say them, it's too vulnerable.

"You can't what, sweetheart?"

I sigh, closing my eyes and bracing for any impact these words are about to have on me. "I can't lose you."

Nate is silent, and I want to take it back. I'm going to take it back; tell him I didn't mean that.

"You're not going to lose me, I promise."

I'm crying again, or maybe I never stopped. Either way, my cheeks are soaked from my tears.

Mitch and Jack arrive soon after I confessed more than I ever have before. I get up to let them inside the house while Nate continues to lay back on his bed.

As I walk behind the two men into the bedroom, I feel the pang in my chest seeing how broken Nate looks like this, and I hate it. I stand in the doorframe debating if I should stay in the room or leave. I'm about to turn around to wait in the living room when Nate calls me over again.

"Aylin, I need you."

He needs me.

I've never heard him so broken, and this whole ordeal is

tearing me apart. I've also never had anyone *need* me. I'm not needed. I've never been needed.

Nate needs me.

I nod once before walking back over to the bed and sitting next to Nate while Jack starts removing supplies from a bag he brought with him.

Mitch stands off to the side, watching everything. He looks scary intense; I can't even look at him as his eyes bore into Nate's like he's angry at him. Which he might be, if I wasn't so scared, I might be a little mad at him too.

I place my hand in Nate's, as Jack pours liquid on some wipes, and warns Nate it's going to sting before wiping on the cuts on Nate's face and torso. Other than squeezing my hand slightly he doesn't have any reaction.

"You could have broken ribs, you know?" Jack says.

"Any cure for that?" Nate huffs.

"Not like a cast for any other broken bone, just taking it easy," Jack replies, and I can tell from his tone he's not too happy with Nate right now either.

"Then, I guess I'll be fine."

I roll my eyes. "What about internal injuries?" I ask Jack.

"He could have those too," Jack shrugs as he continues cleaning Nate's wounds.

My head swings over to the stubborn man lying on the bed before he squeezes my hand again. "I don't have internal injuries, sweetheart."

I hear Mitch scoff from where he's standing off to the side. "You're such a jackass."

"Are you really trying to pick a fight with an injured guy?" Nate snaps.

"I just want the injured guy to pull his head out of his ass before he gets himself killed," Mitch snaps back.

I want to fold in on myself, I hate when people fight around me. Raised voices and harsh words make me want to crawl and hide. I don't even realize I'm squeezing Nate's hand as hard as I am until his eyes lock onto mine.

"I'm fine," Nate says and I'm not sure if he's trying to convince me, Mitch or himself, but they stop snapping at each other for the moment while Jack continues his work of bandaging Nate's injuries.

The room is full of silent tension until Jack announces that he's done.

"Seriously, man, you need to take it easy for a few days. I know telling you to go to a doctor would be wasting my breath, but you really should," Jack says, putting all his stuff back in his bag.

"Thank you for coming," Nate says, wincing as he sits up.

I put my hand lightly on his back to help him ease up before he scoots back on the bed so he can lay on it fully.

Mitch looks like he wants to say something else before they leave but shakes his head as he walks out of the bedroom. I follow both men out so I can lock the front door behind them.

Jack leaves first, but Mitch hangs back, and I'm not sure I want to know what he has to say to me. I wrap my arms around myself as a defense mechanism because for some reason this entire night has made me feel like I'm a little kid again. I don't like all the feelings this is bringing up within myself.

"Thank you for helping him," Mitch says, and my eyes shoot up to his in confusion.

"I-I didn't do anything except call you."

Mitch sighs, "Not just tonight, he's a stubborn asshole as you know, but you don't know how he's changed."

I stare at him, "What do you mean?"

Mitch looks back toward the bedroom where Nate is, contemplating, "He'd kill me if he knew I told you any of this, but I think you should know."

My heart rate picks up, because I don't know if I want to know anything about Nate without him telling me himself, though he's not exactly the most open person. Neither am I, so I think we just accept it about each other.

"Nate used to be different before what happened to his parents, then he turned into this other person. I thought he needed to work through some shit, and for a while it seemed like he was in his own way, not necessarily a *healthy* way. It was *Nate's* way. Then, the incident a couple months ago happened, and I feel like he fell even deeper into his bullshit, and I didn't know how to help him."

I would seriously like to stop crying tonight, but it keeps happening. I am desperate to ask Mitch about all of these mysteries surrounding Nate that I still don't have answers to, but I refrain. I know Nate has to tell me these things himself.

"Then he started seeing you, and it might seem stupid or cliché, or whatever, but I feel like I saw glimpses of the old Nate again. I think you make him want to be better, even if he doesn't notice it. Clearly, since he's still doing dumb shit like this, but I know you can get through to him. So, thank you."

I don't know what to say, I really don't. I'm not doing anything special for Nate, so how could I possibly be helping him in any way? I'm a freaking therapist and I don't even see how I'm possibly helping him.

I nod to Mitch before he turns to leave. When he's almost out the door he turns to say one more thing, "Don't be afraid to push him a bit, I think you're the only person who he will let in."

With that he's gone.

I lock the door, shaking my head. I can't push him because then he might push back, and I don't think I'm capable of letting anyone in like that.

Mitch's words are swimming around in my mind as I reach the bedroom again, pushing the door open. Nate looks like he's sleeping, and I know I need to monitor him to make sure he's okay.

Carefully, I climb into the bed next to him, keeping my distance so I don't accidentally hurt him, but it's like an instinct that he knows I'm here now, as he snatches me by the waist to pull my body against his. I settle against him, my ear pressed to his chest as I listen to the soft beat of his heart. The sound is so comforting knowing he's here, knowing he's with me.

I know I should leave it; I know I should wait until another time when he's feeling better, but the words fall out of my mouth before I can stop them, and I feel like I just need something from him. Something to prove Mitch is right, maybe Nate will let me in.

"What happened to your parents?" I squeeze my eyes shut as I feel Nate tense up next to me.

This is now the second time I have shoved my foot in my mouth tonight and I hate myself for it, but this is so much worse than the first time.

The next few moments go by without an answer, the air is thick, and I feel like I'm going to implode from the tension. Then the last thing I ever expected happens and he answers.

"They were murdered."

"Oh my God, Nate, I'm sorry. You don't have to tell me anymore; I shouldn't have asked-"

"It's okay, I want to tell you," he says, but doesn't continue, and I'm not going to ask him to. Then, he does.

"Right before I left for college my dad got sick, cancer, so he had to retire earlier than he wanted. The doctors told us with chemo he had a good chance of survival. I wanted to defer a year to stay home with him, but they both insisted I go. It took a lot of convincing, but eventually I agreed on the condition I would come home every single chance I got."

I listen intently as Nate speaks, and I almost forget how injured he is because he doesn't sound as pained as he did earlier. I wonder if Jack gave him something for pain, I was too distracted to watch everything he did to help Nate.

I'm envious of the relationship he clearly had with his parents. They all loved each other, that's so obvious, and I wish I knew even a fraction of that feeling.

"I told you before that my dad was a cop too, a detective, who worked some pretty high-profile cases. Unfortunately, this made him some enemies, though he was never afraid of anything happening. He didn't think anyone who was so desperate to hurt him would ever be able to find him. It was probably arrogance on his part, but I get it because I feel the same way.

"It was the week before I was going to come home for spring break, I got a call from my dad's old boss that something happened, he wouldn't tell me what, only he was sorry, and I needed to come home. I was only two hours away at school in Washington. I made it home in half that time to see all the ambulances, cop cars and fire trucks outside my parent's house."

He pauses, and I run my hand along his chest softly in comfort because I can tell where this story is about to go, and I want to tell him he doesn't have to tell me anymore, but I'm not able to say anything.

"They wouldn't let me inside, they said I wouldn't want to see it. I didn't listen, of course, so I pushed past everyone until I got inside and saw them. They were covered in blood-stained sheets, but I saw the scene and that was enough. I didn't stay inside long, I couldn't because I ended up throwing up all over the front lawn, and I don't remember the rest of that night. I just know that a part of myself died with them. I wasn't the same after that night."

"Do they know who it was?" I ask cautiously.

"No, they don't know exactly who did it. They narrowed it down to a few suspects, but never had enough evidence against anyone to convict so the case went cold."

I realize I haven't looked at Nate this whole time he's been talking, so I adjust myself so I can look up into his eyes. "Nate, I am so sorry you went through that."

He holds me against his chest tighter, even though I have to be hurting him, but I couldn't move even if I wanted to.

"I don't know all the details; I didn't want to. The one thing I know is my dad secretly dialed his old boss, even though he knew he wouldn't save himself he wanted to try to save my mom. That was one of the reasons I was so adamant about teaching you to defend yourself when we first met. I may not have known you, but I know I wanted you to be able to protect yourself. My mom was the softest, sweetest woman, and unfortunately that left her defenseless when it really mattered. My dad was weakened by all the treatments so he couldn't do anything to protect either of them except try and get help for my mom."

I see the pain in his face, and I don't even think it's physical pain at this point, just reliving what had to be the worst day of his life.

"Nate," I say, reaching my hand to cup his cheek. "You don't have to save everyone else just because you couldn't save them."

He flinches at my words, and I wonder if I should've kept that to myself. I can't help it; I can tell that's what he's doing. He wants to save me; he wants to save everyone. I don't even know what happened months ago that was the whole reason we met, but I would bet it has to do with him saving someone that might not have been able to be saved.

Nate wants to be the hero for everyone. Everyone except himself.

32

Present

"You don't have to save everyone else just because you couldn't save them."

Aylin's words are on repeat in my mind as I continue to hold her against me. I feel like all the pain I felt when I first stumbled in here has faded into the background to just a dull ache.

Is that really what I'm doing?

No, I just don't like to see people getting hurt.

It doesn't have to do with my parents, does it?

Fuck, I don't even know. I just want to forget about this entire shit show of a day.

I have no idea if Mitch is going to tell Peters about what he saw tonight, and I wouldn't put it past him. Who knows if I'll even still be on the case by morning, but right now I just want to focus on the beautiful, strong, intelligent woman currently curled in my arms.

"Thank you," I say with my lips against her hair.

She looks up at me, "Why is everyone thanking me tonight? I didn't do anything."

I chuckle, but it hurts my ribs, "You need to give yourself more credit."

Aylin's face scrunches up like she doesn't believe me, and I can't help my urge to kiss her. I press my lips against hers softly. She kisses me back, and I feel like everything from tonight fades away in the background.

I pull away for a moment to just look into her bright blue eyes. I could stare into those eyes forever and find something new about them every time. How the blue is slightly darker around her pupil. How she has flecks of green that are so slight I can only see them when our noses are pressed together like this.

"Since we are sharing things, you share something with me," I say softly, trying not to scare her because I know how she can get when it comes to opening up to me.

I see the panic in her eyes as I tighten my arms around her before saying, "Just tell me something, anything, no matter how small it is."

I see her think for a moment before sighing, "Have you seen the tattoo on my ankle?"

I nod, it's small, but I think at this point I've seen every little thing about her.

"Mel and I each have one, it matches, and we got them during our first year of college together."

I press my lips to the side of her head. "What does it mean?"

"Everyone goes through stuff in their life, and it is how you handle it that shapes you. Sometimes you have to find that thing to hold onto to help you get through it. It can be your key to life, and you can have as many of them as you want. They are the reason you keep going."

I tilt Aylin's chin up so I can look into her eyes again. I can see her unease written on her face, probably because she doesn't want me to ask her anymore about that, and for now I won't. My fatigue is catching up to me.

Instead of saying anything else I press my lips to hers gently. I lick the seam of her lips, and I can tell she's hesitant to let me in, but she does. Our kiss deepens and I almost forget I'm even hurt; I forget we are potentially in danger being here together. I was *not as* cautious about getting here as I should be after I left the initiation. I forget it all. Aylin is all that matters.

"Nate," she pulls away, but I continue trailing kisses along her jaw and down her neck because I can't stop. "We aren't having sex, you're hurt."

"Who said anything about sex, sweetheart?" I chuckle against her neck, even though I know she can feel my thickness against her thigh.

"Nate," she groans, pushing me away.

"Fine," I lay back, but continue to hold her against me, because I'm not letting her go. "No sex tonight."

"Not for at least twenty-four hours," she corrects.

"Twelve," I counter, and hear her huff.

"You're such a pain in the ass," she says, but I hear her laughter.

"You love me anyway." I don't even think about what I just said, but I feel her tense up in my arms.

Neither of us say anything, and I don't know if I freaked her out. I really didn't mean it like that, or I didn't think I did, but the more I think about it maybe I did.

I've never told someone I love them besides my parents. Girls have said it to me, but I've never said it back, never even thought about it. Not until now. As I drift off to sleep, I consider the very real possibility that I have fallen in love with Aylin.

It's been three days since I came home. I haven't heard from Cap or any of the guys about what they want me to do next, but I also haven't heard from Sergeant Peters that I'm off the case.

Luckily, I'm not in a ton of pain thanks to my concoction of Ibuprofen and Tylenol, though the bruises look pretty shitty.

I know I should show up to the fight house one day to show that I'm alive. Now that I'm initiated, I'm not going away, but there's one thing I want to do first.

It's like after that night when I finally told Aylin about my parents, I felt a weight lifted off me with her knowing the truth. I also can tell it has made her more comfortable with me.

Well, I'm thinking it has to do with knowing the truth, it might also have to do with her fear of losing me. Either way, I've enjoyed it.

I keep thinking about what Mitch told me, and how I should go see Layla. I feel like maybe if I do see her, then things can really start to get better. Maybe I can start getting better.

I called Mitch last night to get the info for Layla's grandparents, and I called them this morning, told them who I was and asked if they thought it would be okay for me to see her. When I spoke to her grandma, she seemed happy to let me come over. I asked if Aylin could come with me because I truly don't know how this is going to make me feel.

She's still sleeping, and I haven't told her what I want to do. I hope she will be okay with this, and not shut down on me again. I look at her sleeping so peacefully in my bed, and I love this view of her. Long brown hair splayed all over my pillows, her body covered in one of my t-shirts and tucked under the comforter.

I glance around my room appreciating the little touches of *her*. It's nothing big, but the living room has more color, and this room looks more lived in. It's the subtle things that make me the happiest with her here.

I bought this house years ago with the help of the life insurance money from my parents. It always felt weird and useless to do any decorating or personalize it at all, but having Aylin here makes me feel differently.

I can't stop the smile that tugs at my lips seeing her so peaceful like this. Aylin sleeping is the only time she's unguarded, her face is so calm I can't help but remember the realization from the other night that I love her. I haven't told her yet, but I want to get through this first so she can know about all the dark corners I've kept hidden.

Kneeling next to the bed, I look at her up close for a few seconds longer before I push her hair back from her face softly.

"Wake up, sweetheart," I whisper, running my knuckle down her jaw to her collarbone.

Aylin groans, and shifts her face into the pillow. "It's the weekend."

I lean up to kiss the side of her head, "I know, I want to take you to meet someone."

She moves her head to the side so I can see one of her bright blue eyes narrowed at me. "Who?"

"This conversation is going to take some coffee first," I say, standing up.

I may not know everything about my little mystery, but I do know that she doesn't like mornings and needs coffee before I have any sort of real conversation with her.

She sits up, looking at me skeptically. "What's going on?"

"It's not bad, I'll tell you once you're up."

"I'm up." She steps out of bed, and I can't help the way my eyes rake over her body, and how I love seeing her in my shirt, but I want to rip it off her at the same time.

"Coffee first," I smirk before turning around to go into the kitchen.

Once she's on her second cup she demands I tell her what I'm hiding.

"Okay, remember how I first came to see you because I was involved in an incident while out on patrol?"

I see her hesitate before nodding.

"Do you still want to know what happened?" I'm not as nervous talking about this as I thought I would be. I was extremely nervous telling her about my parents, and I hated reliving that because I don't talk about it with anyone. For some reason the thought of telling her this has me calm.

"You don't have to if you don't want to. I'm not trying to force you to tell me anything you don't want to tell me."

"I do, though, I want you to know everything."

I see her swallow roughly before nodding, "Okay."

I tell her everything from the first contact with Rebecca, Murphy and Layla up until the last one. I don't leave any details out as I let it all out for the very first time. I haven't told anyone what happened out loud, only wrote it in a report where I was able to detach as I typed the words.

Aylin listens without saying anything. I watch her face carefully to make sure she is okay hearing about this. I can tell she's using her therapist skills because her face stays completely neutral through the entire retelling.

"Mitch thought I should go see Layla to see that she's okay. I talked to her grandma, who she lives with, and they said we could go see her today."

Finally, Aylin speaks for the first time since I started talking, "Are you sure you want me to go?"

I take her hand in mine. "Yeah, I'm man enough to admit I need you to go with me."

She sighs before nodding, "Okay, I'll go."

I cup her face before pressing my lips against her. I feel her melt into my touch like she always does. "Thank you, sweetheart," I rasp against her lips.

33

Present

Nate finally told me what brought him into my office in the first place, and I have so many thoughts and feelings flying through my head.

Relief he finally told me.

Fear he wants me to go with him to see this little girl, Layla.

Nausea from all the memories this has brought up for me.

I couldn't say anything as he told me the whole story because I know exactly how it feels to be stuck in a house like that. He never said if Layla was hurt or not, and it sounds like her mom actually cared about her to try to keep her safe.

I never thought I would envy a little girl who lost both her parents, but I do. Because she was able to get out of the toxic household while still young.

I agreed to go with Nate, but I'm regretting my choice every passing second. We are in the car, his hand is on my thigh, but I'm not talking. I haven't said much at all since he woke me up today.

These last few days with him have been amazing, and as

always, I knew something would make it end. I have a feeling this will be the cause. My false happy bubble is about to pop, and I have no idea the explosion I'm going to cause.

As we pull up to the modest house on a quiet block, Nate parks the car on the street, I turn ready to tell him I should just stay in the car when he speaks first.

"I'm really glad you agreed to come with me." He smiles, giving my thigh a squeeze.

Well, shit.

He also told me he needs me.

Again.

This is the second time in a few days he said he needs me. For some reason I never realized that would be a weakness for me, but it is.

I don't say anything in return, I just give him a small smile as we climb out of the car. Nate takes my hand in his, intertwining our fingers as we walk to the front door. I'm thankful for the contact to ground me as my heart races while I panic, but I also feel anchored to him so I couldn't run away if I wanted to, which I'm very close to doing.

The front door opens to reveal an older woman, I would guess in her mid to late sixties, she looks tired, but dressed nicely with her gray hair pulled back from her face.

"Hello, you must be officer Greene," she greets with a smile, looking Nate up and down. It's hard not to be drawn to his physical appearance, clearly age doesn't matter when it comes to him, and I get it.

"Please, ma'am, call me Nate." He smiles his bright, perfect smile and I feel even more out of place next to him, even though he's holding my hand tightly. "This is Aylin."

I give the woman a small smile.

"I'm Nadine, it's nice to meet you both. Layla is upstairs in the loft if you would like to go see her."

I feel the sweat on my hand that's holding Nate's and I want to let go to wipe it on my pant leg, but he refuses to loosen his grip as we walk inside.

"Layla, sweetie, you have some company," Nadine calls as we ascend the stairs.

Once we reach the top I see a little girl, she looks to be around six with long blonde hair and as she looks up at us her brown eyes are bright and...happy. She smiles as she stands up and skips right up to Nate.

"I remember you, you're the policeman that came to my house." She's smiling, but I'm nervous at the mention of her remembering Nate because that likely means she remembers...everything.

Nate smiles at her and drops down to his haunches to be eye level with her. I watch, frozen in my spot to see this interaction.

"I am. My name is Nate, and you're Layla, right?"

"Yup!" Layla exclaims proudly, "Do you wanna see my dollhouse?"

"I would love to," Nate says. Layla beams at him before skipping back over to the dollhouse on the floor.

Nate gives me a wink before following her. I'm still frozen in my spot as I take in the whole scene. This little girl was exposed to horrendous conditions and violence, and here she is seeming...fine. I think about everything Nate told me he saw, the fear she had. How she held onto him like he was her lifeline, how he saved her.

No one was there to save me. I had to save myself.

I watch Layla show Nate around her dollhouse and introduce her dolls to him by name. He listens intently, asking questions like it's the most interesting thing he's ever seen. I forgot Nadine was still standing by me until she speaks quietly.

"Your boyfriend is so sweet."

"Oh, he's not...I mean...we—"

Nadine holds her hand up with a smile, stopping my rambling.

"You don't have to explain, but I can see it all."

I want to ask her what she means, but a little voice is calling my name, and I realize it's Layla.

"Aylin, come here, Nate says you have to see this!" She's so excited to show us her toys even though we are complete strangers. Well, I am, I guess she might have some sort of trauma bond to Nate.

I hesitate before walking over to where they are both sitting on the floor. I do my best to fake a wide smile as she gives me a tour of her dollhouse. I feel the panic rising in my chest. I feel the memories beginning to assault me from all angles as I think about what her life has been until this point, and what mine was for so long.

I can't break down, not here, not now. I have to hold it together, at least until I'm alone. I take a deep breath, focusing to put a calm, confident mask on so no one can see how close I am to losing it.

Nate's hand rests on my thigh, giving me a squeeze before whispering in my ear, "Thank you."

Those two words help calm me slightly as I watch Layla describe the drama of her dolls like she doesn't have a worry in the world.

Layla continues to want Nate and me to play with her and her dolls, and I can't seem to get over how...adjusted she is. I know trauma manifests in different ways, and that sometimes it doesn't affect people until later. I'm about to have my doctorate in mental health counseling, but for some reason seeing this little girl so...normal has me feeling all sorts of emotions.

Obviously, I'm happy she's not broken into pieces over what she went through, she's clearly happy and taken care of. I just can't help the jealousy I feel and the hatred I have for myself for feeling that way.

After about an hour Nadine asks if she can talk to Nate for a minute. I get up to go with them as well, but I feel a little hand grab mine and pull lightly.

"No, stay with me a little longer, please?" Layla asks so sweetly, and I hate myself even more for how I'm feeling.

I look to Nate to see if he wants me to come with him, but he just smiles as he says, "It's okay, stay with Layla, it'll just be a minute."

I hesitate as I sit back down, her and Nate have been the ones running the show this whole time, I've just been in the background, as I always am. Now, I feel like I have pressure to interact, and the panic is beginning to resurface.

"You know, Mr. Police Officer Nate saved me," Layla states so nonchalantly I have to think about if I just heard her correctly.

"Yeah?" I hesitate, really not sure of what to say. "He's pretty good at saving people."

"Did he save you too?" she asks, sweetly, looking up at me. Her eyes are so expressive, and it takes me off guard a bit.

I smile, and this time it's genuine as I answer her, "Yeah, I guess he kind of did."

"Was it because your daddy yelled too?" Her question wipes my smile off my face quickly.

"What?"

"Nate saved me because my daddy would yell a lot. Did he save you from your daddy yelling?"

The panic overwhelms me as my mind goes back to when I was younger. I can't stop the memories hitting me from all angles, knocking all the air out of my lungs.

"Aylin, you okay?" I hear Nate ask from somewhere, but I feel like I have tunnel vision, and I can't breathe. I just need to leave.

I don't remember standing, I don't remember walking, all I

can see is all the hitting, all the yelling, all the name calling. The screaming in my head gets louder.

"Worthless!"

"Useless!"

"Piece of shit!"

"Whore!"

I hold my hands over my ears to get it to stop, but it doesn't help because it's only happening in my mind.

I don't remember how we got outside, but suddenly the air feels less thick and I'm able to take a deep breath in, but it doesn't help the tightness in my chest, and it doesn't quiet the yelling. I feel arms wrapped tightly around me, and words are being whispered in my ear, but I can't make them out.

I want to run, but my feet feel like they weigh a million pounds and I'm stuck. I can't breathe, I don't know if I'm speaking. I don't know where I am or what's happening. Suddenly the words being whispered in my ear get louder.

"Sweetheart, calm down, I'm here, just breathe."

Nate.

I'm with Nate.

Nate is safe.

Nate is calm.

I'm not at my parents house anymore.

I'm safe.

Once my breathing has slowed, and I'm able to see we are outside in an unfamiliar neighborhood, I'm mortified at what just happened.

"Oh my God, Nate, I don't know what happened I'm so sorry," I begin, and the panic starts to take over my body again.

"Shh," Nate says calmly, smoothing my hair on the sides of my face. "Let's just go home, okay?"

I nod, but I feel so bad. I blacked out, I should apologize to Nadine and Layla, *oh my god*.

Nate continues to calm me as we get in the car and drive

back to his house. He's telling me it's okay, everything is fine. Layla is fine, I'm okay.

I don't feel like I'm okay, I feel like I've officially lost my mind. It really was a matter of time until I snapped, I mean it should've been expected. I just can't believe the trigger was as simple as a six-year-old asking if Nate saved me from my dad.

How I wish he did.

It feels like we are back at Nate's house in the blink of an eye, but I think my panic attack has altered my perception of all reality around me because I feel weak and confused altogether.

Nate scoops me up out of the car, and I want to protest since he's still hurt, but I just don't have the strength to fight anything right now. Instead, I bury my face closer to his chest so I'm surrounded by his scent and it can take over all my senses and calm me.

I focus on the feel of his arms around me.

I look at how his shirt is tight around the muscles of his arms as they hold me up.

I breathe him in.

I feel the softness of the fabric against my skin.

After we are inside, Nate sits on the couch with me on his lap. As I'm coming back to reality he holds my face in his hands, searching my eyes with worry.

I let out a long breath I feel like I've been holding forever, and it makes my muscles feel like jelly. I'm convinced my entire body would collapse onto the floor if Nate wasn't holding onto me right now.

"What happened, sweetheart?" Nate asks softly, and I have to close my eyes because the way he's looking at me with so much concern has me continuing to feel overwhelmed.

"I-I don't know," I say, but it's not true. I know exactly what happened. I haven't had a panic attack in *years*. The last real one I remember was at Sam and Jeff's house. I was convinced they were going to kick me out and I would have to go to a foster home. *I lost it.*

"Did something happen?" he questions, and he cares so much. Too much. This just shows how broken I truly am.

"No, well," I pause, looking into his eyes. I have to tell him, he has to know how messed up I am so he can run far, far away from me. I know it will be the end of us, but I can't keep going on like this with him. I love him, and as painful as this is going to be, I need to do this. "Yes, a long time ago." I can't look at him.

"Tell me please. I've told you everything, I want to help you like you've helped me."

I feel the tears about to burst out of my eyes at his deep, gentle voice. I love this man and can't even tell him. But I can tell him this.

I take in a deep breath, "Okay, um, when I was a kid, I was…" I pause again. I have never said these words out loud. I have always said something else; my parents hurt me, I went through stuff as a kid, no one in my family wanted me, etc. I've never said the next three words that come out of my mouth. "I was abused."

I flinch in preparation for how Nate is going to react. I expect an outburst of some kind. Him telling me to get out, he can't even look at me, I'm damaged goods, something, but it doesn't happen.

His arms tighten around me, as he pulls me closer to his chest. "Tell me whoever hurt you is dead before I find them and kill them myself." He says the words so calmly, but I can tell he means them.

"I have no idea, I didn't want to know after I left their house at sixteen." I feel myself relaxing into his hold again.

"Can you tell me what happened?" he asks softly, his fingers running through my hair gently. The simple touch lulls me into a sense of calm that I'm able to tell him.

I can't tell him everything, mostly because a lot of the abuse I blocked out, but I tell him the major points. How they would hurt me, why they would hurt me, the words they would say, the names they would call me.

Then, I tell him what happened today.

"Layla asked if you saved me from my dad yelling and for some reason I just...lost it. It felt like I was her age again, stuck in that house with them, being hurt by them. I couldn't take it, *ugh* I must have scared her so bad." I hide my face in my hands at my embarrassment and shame.

"Hey, it's okay you just froze until I got you outside. I will call Nadine to check on Layla and we can let her know you're okay." He comforts me, even though I don't deserve it.

I nod, "Okay, thank you."

"So, this is why you struggle with getting close to people isn't it?" he asks.

"Yeah, I know you probably want to run for the hills now that you know about all my damage, and I don't blame you."

"What?" He pulls my eyes up to his again, "The last thing on my mind is running from you, Aylin I—" He stops, bringing his forehead to mine. "I can't let you go. I could never let you go. I've never felt like this with anyone before..." He pauses again, and I feel my heart rate pick up again. Then, his next words send me into a spiral all over, "I'm in love with you."

My heart drops into my stomach.

I feel another panic attack coming on.

I'm hallucinating, this is all one giant panic induced hallucination because I have no other explanation for what is happening right now.

"What?" My voice is weak because the tears and panic makes it feel like my throat has been ripped apart.

"I love you, Aylin."

Yup, I definitely heard him correctly that time.

"I-How? I just told you how fucked up I am, and you think you *love me*?"

Nate chuckles, "Sweetheart, you're not fucked up, we both have been through our shit, and I think it's safe to say we understand each other's shit. Yeah, I love you."

If someone told me, I would have someone saying those three words to me at any point in my life I would have never believed them. Let alone, having them said to me by this man I still don't think I deserve, and he said it *three times*. This man who doesn't think I'm worthless, or useless or anything my parents called me.

Nate loves me.

I pull his mouth to mine so I can show him everything I'm feeling but can't say in this moment. I kiss him hard and deep, giving everything I have over to him. I'm officially done fighting all the emotions I have for him.

He has me.

He has every single part of me, and I tell him with my lips on his. He takes it greedily like I'm about to rip it all away from him.

Maybe it's because we are both damaged, fucked up and broken.

Maybe we do understand each other's shit.

Maybe it's time to finally be who I really am, and fully embrace it for the first time in my whole life.

Nate wasn't there to save me from my dad yelling like he was for Layla, but he did save me from myself.

I move to straddle Nate's lap while our mouths stay fused together, tongues tangled in the best way as his hands land on my hips, holding me against all his perfect hardness.

Pulling my lips away, Nate continues to kiss my jaw, down my neck, pulling my shirt to the side to run his tongue along my collarbone.

"Nate, you're still hurt," I moan, not wanting him to stop. I haven't let things go too far for the last few days since I have been worried about his injuries.

"No, I'm fine now. I need you." He nips at my throat, and I melt like a putty in his arms. Something about him saying he needs me makes me instantly submit.

"We have to be careful; I don't want you hurting yourself even more," I say breathlessly because Nate hasn't stopped kissing, licking, and biting up my neck to my jaw.

"I'm fine, there is no way this will hurt me in any way." Nate pulls away so I can see the smirk on his face. I roll my eyes, "You trust me?"

Swallowing, I nod slowly.

I see the mischievous smile spread across Nate's beautiful face, his hazel eyes shining with something so foreign to me it could only be his love. He scoops me up in his strong arms. I am always amazed he can pick me up so easily when I'm not small. My legs wind around his hips as his lips land back on mine.

He carries me to his room that has temporarily become my room as well. Adding to the list of things I can't bring myself to admit to Nate; his home has begun to feel like my home.

He has begun to feel like home.

I don't get the chance for my spiraling thoughts to take over before Nate has thrown me onto the bed. I gasp as my body bounces on the mattress. Nate continues to stand at the end of the bed staring at me, the hunger evident in his eyes making my thighs clench together.

For some reason, I feel the need to scoot away from the intensity in his eyes. I move until my back hits the headboard, but Nate reaches out to grab my ankle and pull me back down instantly. I yelp as he climbs over me, his hips settling between my spread legs hitting me at just the right spot, I bite back a moan.

I reach out to run my hands along his chest, but before I'm

even able to make contact he's snatched both my wrists in his large hand and pins them above my head.

"Keep your hands here, or I will tie them to the headboard. I have my handcuffs around here somewhere," Nate's voice is deep and husky with his command. I can't stop my legs from winding around his waist. "I'll tie those to the bed too."

I gasp, dropping my legs back to the bed. Nate smirks, "Good girl."

I feel like with anyone else those two words would've made me annoyed, but not Nate. I melt for him, wanting to please him. I want to do everything he wants.

He slides off the bed, and I instantly miss the warmth and weight of his body on mine as he moves so slowly to stand in front of me. He reaches my hips to agonizingly slowly remove my pants and underwear. He pulls the fabric down my legs as his rough hands caress my soft skin. I squirm under his touch wanting more. Wanting him to move faster, press harder, just give me *more*.

Nate stops with my pants around my knees, lifting his eyes up to mine. "I mean it, stay still or I will make it so you can't move."

I bite my lip with a whimper, I feel myself get wetter with every word he says, and I don't know how or why this is turning me on so much. Nate unleashes some side of me that is still so new and scary, but I love it.

I love everything he gives me.

I love who I am with him.

I love *him*.

Nate bites my thigh before continuing the slow process of removing my clothes. I don't think I've ever struggled to stay still so badly until this moment. My arms outstretched above my head; I'm fisting my hands together so hard I feel the circulation cutting off in my fingers.

After what feels like an eternity Nate has removed my pants

and panties. My arousal dripping onto the bed beneath me as I struggle with the urge to push my hips up and beg him to touch me.

Suddenly, I feel his hot tongue running up the length of my leg, and my fight to not move becomes even harder. I groan at the feeling as he ascends higher to my throbbing pussy but doesn't move his head between my legs like I want.

His breath is on my soaked center, barely an inch away, but not touching as his hands run up my thighs, to my waist as he pushes my shirt up just as slowly as he was before.

"Nate," I moan both in pleasure and protest and I want him to do more than this. I want him to be rough with me because this slowness is sure to be the death of me.

"I'm being careful, sweetheart," he says with a kiss to my stomach. "I can't run the risk of me hurting myself now, can I?"

Oh, I get it. He is trying to torture me because of what I said, and probably for my excuses the last few days of not wanting to hurt him.

To be fair, it didn't stop him. We didn't have sex, but we did almost everything else.

"That's why you can't touch me, I could get hurt." He smirks up at me with my shirt bunched just below my breasts which are heavy with the need to have him touch them.

"Ugh," I throw my head back. "I get it, you're fine, just touch me."

He pushes my shirt up slightly higher, "I am touching you."

"No, touch me *for real.*"

My shirt is now over my breasts, his mouth descends over one of my nipples still covered by my bra. "I am." He growls.

"Nate," I moan.

He has my shirt up to my neck before his hands run along my covered breasts, slipping behind my back to release my bra.

"You'll have to let me move to take off the rest of my clothes," I say smugly.

"Maybe, the rest of your clothes are staying on," he replies.

"Nate, *please*," I beg because he has driven me to a point of insanity.

"Say it," he taunts as his mouth lands on my bare nipple and sucks so hard I gasp.

"Say what?" I snap. I'll say anything at this point.

"What you want." He moves to my other nipple, sucking just as hard.

"Nate, fuck me *please*."

He pulls back, a smile on his smug face, "Well, when you ask so nicely."

Before I'm able to take a breath, Nate flips me onto my stomach and lands a smack onto my ass. He pulls my hips up, then his mouth is licking all the way from my clit to my ass. I clench at the thought of him being back there.

"Nate, no!" I exclaim. No one is getting back there, I may love the man, and he doesn't even know it, but no way.

He chuckles as he licks up my dripping arousal. "Sweetheart, you have to know I love every single part of you, and I want you in every single way I can."

I want to fight back, but I can't. The way Nate licks up my entire opening before pushing his tongue inside me. I drop my head to the mattress with a moan.

"I love those sounds you make." He licks me again and I feel myself about to combust. If he even breathes against my clit again, I'm going to lose it, but he doesn't. He continues to focus on just licking up my wetness dripping from me.

"I love your perfect fucking pussy that gets so wet just for me."

I moan in agreement, my sounds muffled by the sheets.

"I love how you taste," he emphasizes his point with a long languid lick up my entire seam.

"I love that you fight me," he bites my inner thigh before soothing the bite with his tongue.

"I love that you care so fucking much," he squeezes my ass in both his hands almost to the point of pain before kneading the skin.

"I love when you let your guard down and show me who you really are."

I'm sitting at this peak of pleasure just dying to be pushed over the edge, but Nate is continuing to keep me teetering right there. My head is fogged by the pleasure so I can't even fight him on everything he's saying.

He knows I would never hear his confessions if I wasn't drugged by the pleasure only he can give me. As much as I want to deny the fact that he knows me. He does, better than anyone else.

He knows how to drive me crazy.

He knows how to bring me pleasure.

He knows how to push me to my absolute limits.

He knows *me*.

Nate grabs my hips to flip me onto my back, settling his weight between my legs, his thick erection that is contained in his pants settled against me in almost the perfect spot, if I just shifted a little bit...but I'm frozen with his next words and the intensity at which he says them.

"I love *you*, Aylin. Everything about you, I love it all."

I want to say it back, I desperately want to, but my voice won't come out. For the second time today, I react the same way I did when he first told me. I show him with a kiss how I feel since I just can't say the words.

We come together in a hard kiss, our lips bruising each other, tongues in each other's mouths, teeth nipping at each other's lips. It's untamed, wild and *us*.

I grab at Nate's shirt needing to have all his clothes off. I need to feel his warm skin against mine, and he lets me, finally letting me touch him again. I have him naked in record time, pushing his pants down with my feet, and he's inside me before they are completely off.

My hands fly up to his back, nails scratching down his muscles before pushing on his ass so he can push into me harder. I need to feel everything only Nate can give me.

"Fuck, Aylin, I will never get tired of this. Never," he groans with a hard thrust, my eyes rolling back as I hear the headboard slam against the wall.

"Nate...*God*," I moan as my pleasure builds, and I know I'm seconds from coming harder than I ever have. It's like everything I'm feeling is about to explode, all the feelings I can't admit to are taking over my body.

Nate's thrusts grow slower and harder as I dig my nails into his back just trying to hang onto him as I feel myself about to explode. His mouth is on mine capturing all my moans as his pelvis hits my clit perfectly in an absolutely mind blowing rhythm.

"I'm so close..." I breathe into his mouth.

"Give it to me sweetheart, show me how much you love me."

With that I explode in pleasure. I scream out his name as I clench around his cock still driving into me as he chases his own release. I feel like everything I've felt with Nate takes over as I let go and release it all with the hardest orgasm of my life.

Nate isn't far behind with his own release as he groans, driving into me at a punishing pace until I feel him swell inside me and fill me with his release. I bite down on his shoulder as I come down. I hold him so tight because I don't want to let him go.

He knows I can't say it back to him, he can see how hard it is for me to admit that I love him, but he knows.

He knows me.

He knows how I'm feeling.

He knows I love him.

We lay together for a few moments before he pulls out of me, rolling onto his back and pulling me with him. I lay my head on his chest, just listening to his rapid heartbeat, our legs tangled together and sweat covered bodies latched onto each other.

"I'm never letting you go," Nate says with a kiss to the top of my head.

Suddenly, everything catches up to me, the exhaustion from my panic attack. The exhaustion from my release, my eyelids are heavy, and I can't help but drift off while being warm and comfortable in Nate's arms.

34

Present

I couldn't bring myself to tell Aylin about what Nadine wanted to talk to me about. I still don't even have my brain wrapped around what she's asking of me. It's something that I don't think I can worry about right now. I need to get through this assignment, then maybe I can talk to Nadine about it more, maybe have Aylin with me.

Then, I saw Aylin panicking and I couldn't focus on anything that wasn't her. I knew she needed help, and I knew she needed me. I didn't plan on telling her I love her, but in that moment, I needed her to know. Even though she couldn't say it back, I know she feels the same.

I also know the reason she can't say it back is because of her past, which makes me see red just thinking about it. I'm going to have to look into her parents to see where they are. They better be dead because they don't want me to find them if they aren't.

She told me some stories of the abuse, which was enough to know both her parents were at fault and she didn't deserve any of it. It all makes sense now, though. Her being so guarded, how she pushed me away for so long, her self-doubt, how she couldn't trust me. All of it makes so much more sense now.

It feels even better now that we don't have any barriers between us. She knows my past, and I know hers. The good, bad and the ugly. I love her for all of it just as much.

Aylin fell asleep with her head on my chest, and my arms wrapped around her. I know she was probably worn out from everything, and I want her to keep sleeping, but I also want to check on Layla like I promised Aylin I would.

As slowly, and carefully as I can, I remove myself from her body that's completely tangled around mine. I pull the blanket around her naked body as she cuddles deeper into the pillow, I was resting my head on.

I grab my phone before pulling on some boxers, then dialing Nadine as I quietly make my way downstairs.

She answers after only the second ring. "Hello?"

"Hello Nadine, this is Nate, I just wanted to check in to make sure you and Layla are okay?"

"You are so sweet. Yes, Layla asked about you both after you left, she was worried about your girlfriend." I smile, I never thought I would be happy or so proud to call someone my girlfriend. *Mine.*

"Aylin is okay, she just started not to feel well. I hope we can come back another time if that's okay?" I don't want to push this on them, but I liked spending time with Layla. I liked seeing that she's okay.

I hate to admit that Mitch was right, but...he was kind of right.

"Of course, you both can come back any time, I hope Aylin feels better soon."

"Yeah, I think she's starting to feel a bit better."

"I hope I didn't scare you off too much with what we talked

about; I just want to know that Layla will have somewhere to go."

Shit. I wasn't sure if she would want to talk about this more, especially since this is something that I can't think about right now.

"No, you didn't, I just have a lot going on right now, but I'm sure it's not something to worry about for a long time, if ever," I tell her seriously.

"I'm sure you do, hun, and I feel bad even bringing it up at all. We don't have anyone else, and I just know you'd make sure she's okay."

I have never thought about kids for myself, let alone needing to take care of someone else's child. Not to mention, a child that has been through so much shit in her short life. For some reason Nadine thinks it would be best that if her and her husband die, *I* am the next best choice to take Layla in.

I didn't say yes or no because I had to help Aylin, but I don't even know what to say anyway. Nadine said her husband's health isn't doing well, but she seemed extremely healthy, so I'm not overly concerned about something happening. Plus, if it gives her peace of mind then I guess I'll agree, though I'm sure it will never come down to that.

"I get it, yeah, it would probably be better than letting her be lost in the system." I run my hand down my face. I really should talk to Aylin about the possibility because I don't see my life without her, but I'm sure this is just a precaution.

Nadine lets out a sigh of relief I can hear through the phone, "Thank you, Nate, feel free to come see Layla any time."

"Thank you, ma'am, have a good evening."

We hang up, and I shake the thoughts away of anything happening that would result in Layla coming to live with me. That's ridiculous, I'm not going to worry about it.

All my focus goes back to the woman in my bed as I head up the stairs, cradling her warm body against mine as I settle both of us back under the blanket. She squirms to nestle closer as I wrap my arms around her and slide my thigh in between hers.

"Where'd you go?" Aylin mumbles.

I kiss the top of her head, "I called Nadine to check on Layla. She's okay and was worried about you."

Aylin buries her face deeper into my chest. "I feel bad," she whispers.

"Don't feel bad, she's okay. You are okay. *I* am more than okay, it's all good," I joke. I hear a small chuckle come from her.

I squeeze her tighter. I know I should bring up the other thing Nadine said, but that can wait. We have time and I just want to enjoy this moment with her because I need to get back to the case tomorrow. I know everything is about to be more serious now that I'm initiated.

One more night with my girl where it's just us, the outside world doesn't matter.

Our pasts don't matter.

The future doesn't matter.

It's just Aylin and Nate in this moment. I'm going to enjoy this for just a little while longer.

IT'S BEEN a couple weeks since the initiation, and I've been in so deep in the case I have only been able to see Aylin a handful of times, and even when I have, it's only been for an hour or two. I barely sleep, and I still feel like I'm not any closer to a big bust than I was weeks ago.

I've been working as an enforcer of sorts. I go with this guy Deuce (who I call Douche to myself because he's the textbook definition of it). He collects from the various businesses around town, mostly strip clubs, a couple of mattress stores and a pawn shop. I go with him when we need to collect, and I come back with Saw if they don't pay.

I'm not proud of the things I've had to do while I'm with Saw, and on occasion Douche at times because I have to rough up the guys a bit before they give up the money, but I know it's just a part of the job.

I've learned the strip clubs are fronts for human trafficking and drug dealing. The girls working there are a mix of legal and illegal ages, and there's always VIP areas where the girls of all ages are expected to do whatever the customer wants. The girls are also the ones dealing in those places.

There are back rooms where supply is kept, and girls push it on the customers that come in while also getting hooked themselves. It makes me fucking sick.

The mattress stores and pawn shops are fronts for money laundering, which is more common than people expect, and although it's illegal, it isn't really what this case is focused on.

The one thing I've been able to report back to Sergeant Peters is the strip clubs. Unfortunately, the only option they have is to raid and get the girls out, but in all honesty, they will get new girls in there in less than a week because we don't know who's actually running anything. That's why we have to wait a bit longer before conducting a bust or it would be pretty easy to figure out that I was the rat.

I thought it was Cap who ran it all, but he just *thinks* he does, and he might be high up in the rankings, but he isn't who everyone reports to. I can't even get any info from him without seeming suspicious and aside from nights at the fight house I never see him.

The fight house is another thing that I have been looking into. I learned what that is about for the most part. They test guys wanting to be brought in with a fight. If you do well then you are used more for the muscle, hence why I am where I am.

Depending on how well you do depends if they bring you in at all, even if you lose.

At the end of the day, it all comes down to if you'll be useful or not, in any way.

There is also a bigger fight ring that is used as an underground cage fighting space where various gangs come together and go against each other in a way that doesn't cause an all-out gang war, but money changes hands and sometimes arguments are settled.

Of course, everyone fighting is just a pawn in the game, the higher ups control everyone and everything. If they have an issue, they send in fighters to go against another higher up's fighter. They keep their hands clean, and don't give a shit about who gets hurt. It's a win-win for them.

Everyone is working for somebody. They just don't know who I'm really working for.

I realize it's the week of Thanksgiving, and the only reason I know is because of all the signs around the holidays. I don't care about any holidays since my parents died and considering Aylin doesn't have any family either I don't think it's something she cares about as well, but we haven't been able to talk about it.

The holidays don't matter in the crime world, so nothing is going to change with the case, but considering most of the work I do is at night it's been pretty shitty having to be freezing all the time. Especially tonight while I'm standing back as Deuce is watching this guy count out the money he owes.

This club has a storage room you can only access from an alleyway, with the only door being outside. Seems like a shitty system to me, but I didn't design the place.

I keep my arms folded in front of my chest as a way to appear intimidating, but I'm also trying to keep myself fucking warm.

It feels like forever until the guy is done counting, and

Deuce grabs the bag from his hands he was dumping the money into.

"Next time don't take so fuckin' long," Deuce growls before pushing past the guy to head back inside.

Rolling my eyes, I follow behind him as he storms through the strip club. This is something Deuce does that made him earn the title Douche Deuce to me. After we finish business, he decides to indulge in some pleasure.

Sometimes, I'm able to get him to leave with some bull shit about Cap needing us somewhere else, or on another errand. Though, there's nights like tonight where that isn't the case, and he isn't hearing it from me.

He doesn't even give me the chance to catch up to him until he's pulling a girl into the VIP room. Even though he has the bag of money with him no one here is stupid enough to try and steal from either of us. They all know who we are and who we work for.

I catch a glimpse of the girl he pulled away and she looked legal, not by much, maybe twenty, but that's the only reason I don't intervene despite wanting to so we can just leave.

Since I know I'll have to kill some time I head to the bathroom, but when I turn down the hallway that leads there, I hear a sniffle over the muffled club music.

As I go deeper down the hallway, I peek into one of the alcove areas from the awkward building shape. It's dark, so I can barely make out the tiny figure curled up, holding her knees to her chest as she sits on the ground.

"Hey, are you okay?" I ask softly, bending down to be at her level.

Her red puffy eyes look up at me, and even in the dim lighting I can see her face a bit better. She's young, there's no way she's a day over eighteen, if even that.

It looks like she recognizes me, or is just scared of men in general because as soon as she looks at me, I see her try to tuck herself deeper into the darkness without saying anything.

"It's okay, I promise I won't hurt you." I try to calm her down. I raise my hands in the air to show I don't have anything and that I'm not going to try to touch her.

I can tell she's still skeptical of me, but if something happened to her, I want to make sure she is okay, and possibly stupidly, get her some help.

"Did something happen to you?" I ask quietly.

I hear her sobbing again, clearly conflicted if she should tell me anything.

"You're one of them," her voice is much higher than I would've thought, and it makes me think she has to be younger than eighteen.

I know the next thing I do is definitely stupid, but I am fighting an internal battle of right and wrong. All I can think about is Aylin and Layla, how they were hurt so young, and if this girl is being hurt, I can't let it continue. I know it puts me at risk, but I need to help her.

I shake my head, "No I'm not. I can help you."

She starts to cry harder, "You're lying, all of you lie."

"What's your name?" I ask, hoping I can make her feel more comfortable so I can help.

She hesitates, tears streaming down her cheeks while she examines me. I know what she sees. I do look like one of them, my hair is unkempt, I'm in an oversized sweatshirt and jeans. I have bags under my eyes from the lack of sleep. Plus, I'm a big guy, and I know it. I can tell she's wondering if I have alternative motives because I'm sure that's what she's used to.

"Mila," she practically whispers, and I'm not even sure I heard her right.

"Mila? Is that your real name?" I know they tell these girls to use fake names, so they are harder to trace.

After another moment of silence she nods, though I'm still not sure if I believe her or not.

"How old are you, Mila?"

"Twenty-one."

"No, you're not."

She flinches at my tone that came out harsher than I intended. I think about how Aylin has to remain calm with everyone all the time in her position, and my respect for her grows even more.

"Sorry, but there's no way you're twenty-one," I try to say more calmly so she will continue to open up to me.

Mila looks down before answering me, "I'm eighteen."

I still am not fully convinced but decide to leave it for now.

"Did someone hurt you, Mila?" I ask gently.

She cries harder before nodding her head. *Fuck.*

"Shit, look, Mila, I need you to trust me for a minute because I'm going to help you, but I need you to make sure you don't tell anyone what I'm about to say,"

Mila looks up at me, and nods.

"Promise me," I say sternly. I'm taking a huge risk right now, but I can't just leave her like this, and I don't know another way to help.

"I promise," she whispers through her tears.

I look around to make sure there's no one to overhear me.

"I'm an undercover cop, and I need you to go to the Portland PD office and ask for Mitch McDowell. Tell them Nate sent you to ask for him, and tell him everything, okay?"

She hesitates for a moment before nodding. I wish I could take her myself, but there are eyes everywhere. I'm already taking a bigger risk than I should even talking to her for this long, let alone telling her who I really am.

"Promise me you'll go, and you won't tell anyone else who I am or that we talked, okay?" I say, standing up.

She watches me carefully before nodding again. "I'll go tomorrow, and I won't tell anyone else."

I really hope she means that. She seems like a terrified little girl, and I'm choosing to believe she trusts me enough to go get herself help without ruining my cover in the process.

I might do stupid shit at times, but it usually works out for me, and I hope this won't be any different.

I head to the bathroom, and once I'm out I see that Mila is gone from her hiding spot. I hope she left the club. I go back out to the main floor acting casual as I keep my eye out for her. I don't see her. I just hope she left to go somewhere safe or right to the police station. I need to let Mitch know she will be coming in.

Deuce makes his way out of one of the back rooms, fixing his belt as he does. I nod in his direction as we both head out the front doors to the car we took here. I get into the driver's seat, him in the passenger as he dumps the bag into the backseat.

Without a word to each other I drive us back to the house where I first met Cap and the guys. This is usually where we drop off the money we collect, usually to one of Cap's guys. After that's done, I can only hope I can go back to my fake apartment to pass out for a few hours.

I want to go to my real house and see Aylin, it's been too long since I've slept with her soft body wrapped around mine, but it's too late for me to show up. I know she likes my texts alerting her I'm coming over, and I wouldn't want to wake her up either way.

Once the money is dropped no one says anything to me, which means I am free to leave. I head straight to my shitty fake apartment, dialing Mitch on my burner phone as soon as the door is locked behind me.

"What?" He answers the phone, his voice groggy. I clearly woke him up, but I don't give a shit about his sleeping pattern.

"There's a girl, Mila, she's going to come in asking for you. She needs help and she knows who I am, so I need you to help her."

I hear him sigh. "You know, I would've thought you'd stop doing dumb shit, but here you are doing more dumb shit."

"Helping a potential trafficking victim is dumb shit to you?" I snap.

"No, but blowing your cover to do so is."

"Agree to disagree on that. She won't tell anyone, she seems like she really needs help."

"You know I'll help her; did you get any other info?"

"She said she's eighteen. I don't know if I believe her, but that's all I got. We weren't exactly in the best place for me to ask too many specifics."

"No, just in a good place to blow your cover to her." I can hear his eye roll through the phone.

"She won't out me. Don't worry about my shit."

"I always worry about your shit. Between the other night when Aylin had to call me, and now this. Maybe you need to get out."

"I can't, you know I can't. I'm fine, I'm good."

Mitch sighs, "I like Aylin for you, and I know you care about her, so at some point you need to stop with your bullshit so you can be safe so *she* can be safe."

"She is safe, and I'm fine. This is a dangerous job, no matter who you are, but we do it anyway."

"Fine, just maybe think about shit before you do it sometimes, yeah?"

I chuckle, "I always do."

"I'll let you know if the girl, Mila, comes by," he says, his voice sounds resolved like he knows he's not going to get anywhere with me, and it's true.

He won't. I'm fine, I'm safe, and so is Aylin. He's worrying for no reason.

"Thank you, go back to sleep, you sound like shit," I attempt to joke.

"Fuck you," is his reply, but before he can hang up, I tell him to wait.

I think about what he said about Aylin being safe, and I just want him to double check, "Hey, could you, uh, check on Aylin for me? Just call her before you go there, she needs a heads up."

"Yeah, I got you." I can hear his smug smile through the phone.

"Thanks." We hang up, and I feel better knowing he will have eyes on my girl since I can't be there for her as much as I wish.

Suddenly, the night hits me as I fall onto the uncomfortable mattress and pass out instantly.

35

Present

I miss Nate.

    I hate admitting that, even to myself so I haven't been able to bring myself to say it out loud. I know I'm an independent woman, but I also recognize I am at my best and most comfortable when he's around.

It doesn't help that I know he's in a dangerous situation and I just want to know he's okay. I know he can't be coming home all the time or reaching out to me constantly to let me know because that would be more dangerous for both of us.

I check in with Mel, and even call Sam myself a couple times just to talk to her. I'm trying to be better about nurturing my relationships with the important people in my life.

I'm just trying to be better.

Nate's friend Mitch called me earlier to ask if it's okay for him to come by after his shift. I hesitated because I don't really know him very well, but I know he's close with Nate, and in the spirit of trying to be *better,* I agreed.

My days at clinical have gone well, Dr. Tanvers always has

positive things to say and good feedback to give me. Sometimes being there makes me miss Nate more, as I think of the times he came in there, pushed my limits and bulldozed his way into my life.

Every time I look at the desk he took me on, and have to clench my thighs together as I remember how good he felt. How good he always feels. I think of where we started compared to where we are now. I never expected to fall in love with the arrogant, pushy, and handsome man that strolled into the office, but here I am.

I wouldn't change a single thing that happened. Maybe opening up to him sooner, but I know if he did, then things would be different, and I don't want that for either of us.

I got this week off from going to clinical since it's Thanksgiving week, so I've been able to focus solely on my assignments and thesis, which has been nice.

Mitch texts me that he's heading over. It's silly, but it makes me crave one of Nate's code word texts more than I would've ever thought.

There's a knock at the front door that I know is Mitch, but I still look through the peephole to make sure before opening the door for him.

"Hi," I say, moving to the side so he can come inside.

"Hey, how are you doing?" Mitch asks as I shut the door.

"I'm okay," I shrug. "How's Nate?"

Mitch chuckles, "Nate is Nate, but he's okay, I think. He saved a young girl yesterday. She came into the station today scared out of her mind asking for me. Said Nate sent her."

"This seems to be a theme with him," I joke.

"Yeah, he's rough around the edges, but has good intentions."

I smile, I remember thinking he was all rough edges when we first met, but Nate's heart is much bigger than he lets on, and it's just one of the many things I love about that man.

"Thank you for telling me to push him, by the way. He opened up to me." I probably wouldn't have asked what I did that night if it weren't for Mitch telling me to push.

"Yeah? With everything?"

I nod. "Thank you for helping him connect with Layla again too, I think it really helped."

"Yeah, you know, I give him shit, but he really is my best friend and I just want him to think about his own safety for once and realize he has things to live for," he pauses, "people to live for." He gives me a pointed look.

"I don't think it's that he doesn't take his own safety into consideration, I just think he wants to save everyone over himself." I told Nate that's what I think, and I feel like it might have put some things into perspective for him. At least I hope it did.

"That makes sense, have you ever thought about being a therapist? You might be good at it," he teases, and it makes me chuckle.

"I've considered it."

Mitch seems like a good guy, and a good friend even if he can come off as abrasive at times. I can tell he really does care about his friend, and I'm glad he came over to check on me. Not only because he was asked to, but so I could know Nate is okay too.

"I should head home, but feel free to reach out if you need anything while Nate is busy."

I nod, it makes me feel good to know he would help me if I needed. He doesn't know me very well, but clearly knows how much Nate cares about me, and it feels good to have people, to have support.

I don't think I've ever felt so surrounded by people that care. I have Mel, Nate, Sam, Jeff and now Mitch. For the first time ever, I know with complete certainty I'm not alone.

Mitch leaves, and I make sure all the doors and windows

are locked before heading up to the bedroom. I look at the bathtub in the en-suite and decide to take a relaxing bath for the first time in...a long time.

Once I'm settled into the warm water, I decide to call Sam, and ask something I haven't asked before. It's completely out of my comfort zone, but I'm pushing myself out of that a bit lately. I know I need to grow, and this is the way to do it.

"Hey, Aylin, good to hear from you," Sam says as she answers the phone.

"Hi, how are you and Jeff?"

I can hear her smile as she answers, "We are doing well, how about you?"

"I'm good, I was wondering...um...are you both busy for Thanksgiving? I know it's short notice, and it's okay if you are I just—"

"We are just home as always, why do you ask?" I can hear her hopeful tone, but it doesn't make me any less nervous to ask.

"What if we...um maybe spent the holiday together?" I haven't spent any holidays with them since I moved out. They used to ask, but that stopped after a couple of years.

"Of course! Yes, oh you know how much we would love that," she sounds so excited it makes me smile.

"Okay, I could maybe go there..." my voice trails off. I haven't been back to Pendleton since I left for college. I had no desire to, and even suggesting it has my heart rate elevating as I think about seeing the familiar places that caused me so much pain.

Sam must hear my hesitance. "You really don't have to, we could always come there, I'll bring the food and you don't have to worry about cooking a big meal or anything."

It would be easier for me if they came here, but I feel weird inviting them to Nate's house without talking to him first, but my apartment would be pretty cramped, even with just the three of us.

Should Nate meet Sam and Jeff?

Would he even want to?

This was a mistake, I don't know what I was thinking. "You know, never mind, it was a stupid idea, I'm sorry."

"It's not a stupid idea, I just want you comfortable, but we would love to spend a holiday with you, and we would be willing to come to you, just let me know."

I nod even though she can't see me. "Yeah, I'm sorry, I'll think about it. And let you know. I'm sorry."

"Don't be sorry, Aylin, I am happy you even thought to ask."

"I'll talk to you later."

I hang up before sinking down into the bathtub until I'm completely submerged. I used to do this when I was younger. The silence under the water helped me pretend I was somewhere else. Anywhere else.

The difference now is I don't want to be anywhere else. I don't wish I was someone else, or anything, but the silence still brings me peace. I'm going to ask Nate if it's okay for Sam and Jeff to come here even if he can't be home to meet them. Or doesn't want to.

Home.

There's that word again.

My lungs start to burn before I lift my head out of the water.

Once I'm out of the bath I send a text to Mitch asking him if Nate will know when he can see me again. I hate how that makes me feel like a needy girlfriend, but I just don't want to bring people he doesn't know into his house.

Girlfriend.

Another word that comes up.

I guess that's what I am, I know Nate has referred to me as his girlfriend, it's just weird for me to accept. Sometimes none of this feels real, and I feel like I'll wake up one morning in my apartment, all alone and this was all a dream.

My phone pings with an alert, and I wonder if it's a coincidence because I would be shocked if Mitch got ahold of him this fast.

Nate: Blue.

I feel the excitement building as I think about seeing Nate soon. I am like a giddy little kid when it comes to him. Even though we've only been able to see each other a handful of times, for only a few minutes at a time since he said he loves me, I feel the love I have for him bubbling over whenever I see him.

I still haven't said the words to him, but I know he understands why, and I will. It's just every time I try, I can't get them out and end up kissing him instead. I'm getting better, but I'm still far from perfect.

I put on one of his t-shirts and some underwear, my ideal sleepwear. I like that all his shirts smell like him, so even though the scent tends to fade from the bed since it's been so long since he's spent the night, his shirts still linger with it. Plus, I use his detergent to wash them. Which may make me seem crazy, but I don't care.

It's not long until Nate is here, I jump into his arms immediately once I see him. I don't even know why.

Well, yes, I do. I missed him, but it just feels good to be held by him.

"I missed you too, sweetheart," he says with a chuckle, and a kiss on my lips.

I love that I don't have to say the words for him to know how I'm feeling. That used to be something that scared me, which is why I would hide behind my masks, but not anymore. Not with him.

"Did Mitch talk to you or are you here on your own?" I ask.

"I was already on my way when he called me, I know when my girl needs me."

His girl.

"How long can you stay?" I'm afraid it won't be very long, like usual.

"I probably shouldn't stay long, but when you're looking at me like that, I can't leave."

"Like what?" I ask innocently. I know exactly how I'm looking at him.

"Oh, sweetheart, I love you," he chuckles with another quick kiss on my mouth.

I run my hands along his stubbled jaw. He's been growing it out so it's more like an actual beard now, and his hair has gotten a lot longer than when we first met. He's still the hottest guy I've ever seen.

"I wanted to talk to you about something first," I say quickly because I know how easily it is for us to get lost in each other.

"Anything," he says easily.

"I told you a little about the couple that took me in after... everything. Sam and Jeff." I watch his reaction, and he nods in acknowledgment. "I asked about spending Thanksgiving with them, I've never done that before, and I thought I would go to Pendleton, but I just...can't."

"Do they want to come over here?" He asks casually.

"Is that okay?" His thumb pulls my lip from between my teeth.

Dammit, I'm still doing that.

"Of course that's okay, sweetheart, I want to meet the people who helped you."

"You can be here?" He usually doesn't know when or where he will be on a daily basis and Thanksgiving is in three days, so it seems weird he can say he will be here.

"I will do whatever I need to so I can make sure I'm here," he's smiling his bright, panty dropping smile at me.

"You'll be safe though, right?" I think back to my conversation with Mitch earlier about Nate and his regard for his safety.

"Of course, I'm earning trust with the guys, I'll work it out, stop worrying about me," he kisses me again, and this time I'm lost in him like I always am.

He doesn't stop touching me the entire night, and I don't want him to. I'm able to fall into a peaceful sleep, completely wrapped around him.

It's the morning of Thanksgiving, and Nate hasn't been back since the other night when he said he wanted to meet Sam and Jeff. I'm hoping he does show up, but I understand if he doesn't.

Sam called me early this morning to tell me they are on their way since it's a bit of a drive. I cleaned up the house, took a shower and put on some nice jeans and an off the shoulder sweater.

I'm surprised when I pull my phone out, and see Nate texted me, "blue". I smile, he really is going to be here.

He walks through the door, and instantly insists he needs a shower. "I hate that I look like this when I'm meeting your not-parents for the first time."

I chuckle, I still think he's insanely attractive, but considering I met him fairly clean shaven, and with a much shorter hairstyle I can only imagine this new appearance isn't the most comfortable for him, especially when he wants to make an impression.

"Don't worry, they will like you," I tell him, following him upstairs as he heads to the shower.

Nate pulls off his shirt, revealing his drool worthy body to me, and I have to fight my arousal because I already got ready, and that is two seconds from going to shit if I keep staring at him.

"You going to join me, sweetheart?" Nate smirks as his hands fall to the buttons on his jeans, and he starts to push them down his muscular thighs.

My mouth waters as I think about what is underneath those boxers he's wearing, but I know we have to wait.

"Later.. and then that," I point toward his crotch, "is going in my mouth."

"Fuck...you sure I can't convince you for that right now?" Nate groans.

"Nope, that's dessert," I wink before kissing him quickly.

He tries to grab me, which we both know will quickly change my mind, but I manage to move out of his way, laughing as I shut the bathroom door behind me.

"Killing me, sweetheart!" Nate calls from the bathroom.

I laugh as I get downstairs. I know Sam said I didn't have to cook, but I wanted to try to make one thing, which was a corn casserole I found online. It looked fairly easy, and the ingredients were cheap enough that it didn't break my bank.

I'm putting the dish in the oven when Nate comes downstairs looking hot enough to melt the clothes right off my body if he wanted to. He cut his beard slightly shorter, which gives him a more mature presence and I may want him to keep it even after this assignment is over.

He's wearing dark wash jeans and a black t-shirt that hugs his muscled torso perfectly.

Sweet Jesus, what is he doing to me?

"That smells good," he says, leaning in to kiss my cheek, but he nibbles on my neck slightly, making me giggle. *Who would've thought I would ever giggle?* "But you smell better," he bites my neck slightly harder, making me yelp.

"You are going to torture us both if you keep doing stuff like that you know?" I taunt.

"Maybe, but I like you all wound up for me, sweetheart."

I roll my eyes, I know what he likes from me, he likes pushing my buttons, thus pushing me to my limit and out of my comfort zone.

"They will be here any minute," I tell him, looking around quickly to make sure there's nothing else needing to be cleaned up at the last minute.

"Are you nervous?" Nate asks, leaning against the counter, extenuating his long, perfect body.

"Nope," I answer honestly. I know I have nothing to be nervous about. They will like Nate. I'm sure he will like them. Everything is fine.

There's a knock at the door, Nate peeks to make sure it's not someone unexpected before opening the door. They both have insulated bags of food in their hands, and I know Sam probably went a bit overboard with cooking, though we agreed no turkey because that's just too much work. She made chicken instead.

"Come on in," I say while both Nate and I grab bags from their hands to lighten their load.

I introduce them both to Nate, and Sam smiles in my direction when Nate wraps his arm around my waist. I lean into him which shows my comfort level, and I know she notices.

This feels good. Natural, even. Like in another world Sam and Jeff are my parents, and they are coming over to meet my boyfriend like it's the most normal thing in the world.

I help Sam with heating up the food, and finishing my corn casserole. I will admit looks really good and I'm proud of myself.

Jeff and Nate put the football game on, even though Nate keeps trying to help us in the kitchen Sam keeps waving him off. It all feels so...*normal*. I almost forget how so not normal our lives really are.

This is easily the best holiday I've ever had. Even the two I spent at Sam and Jeff's when I was younger don't compare to this. Nate is always touching me like he can't stand to be away from me. Sam and Jeff both seem to really like Nate, and everything is relaxed.

The evening turns into night, and as we are all just sitting around talking, I can't look away from Nate, so enamored with him and with how we got to this place.

For once, I do feel like I deserve the happiness I'm feeling, and maybe it won't be taken away from me. Maybe I've finally endured all the pain slated for me in this lifetime.

I smile, snuggling closer to Nate's side on the couch as he holds me. I feel so at peace in this moment, and nothing has ever felt better.

36

Present

I hate leaving Aylin the morning after Thanksgiving, but I need to get back. I didn't tell anyone I wasn't going to be around on the holiday, but no one tried contacting me either, so I figure it's fine.

I did learn that Mila went to Mitch like I told her to. Turns out she was honest; her name really is Mila, and she really is eighteen. I'm not sure who it was to convince her, Mitch or someone else, but she agreed to be a confidential informant.

Since she doesn't have charges to work off, she actually can be paid to be a CI, which is usually pretty appealing to someone who really wants to get out of the life, and get away. No one wants her to be in extremely dangerous situations, but she is our ears on the ground of the club to listen out for anything extreme, especially big shipments of anything.

A lot of the guys are dumb and talk openly in front of the girls because they figure they aren't going to do anything. Mila is extremely brave for being willing to do what she is, and I said

I would check in with her fairly often to make sure she stays safe.

Jason reached out a couple days ago that we need to connect about something, so I texted him to let him know where to meet. It's one of the neutral areas around town. We switch up where we meet so no one questions seeing us in the same place repeatedly.

Even when it doesn't seem like someone is watching you, I know someone is.

I get there first, looking around while I wait for Jason until I see him round the corner, and he looks like shit compared to the last time I saw him. He's been a skinny guy with bags under his eyes, but his face looks more sunken in, and he looks slimmer.

I hope he isn't falling deep into doing hard shit because he's a good CI, it would suck to lose him to addiction.

"You good, man?" I ask once he gets closer.

"Yeah, shit's been rough lately." He runs his hand through his greasy hair. He looks like he hasn't been sleeping or showering, but he seems sober right now, and not jittery like he needs a fix.

"What's going on?"

He sighs, "Some shit is going down that's being kept under wraps, but it's not good."

"What does that mean?"

"I don't know much, no one tells me shit, I just overhear loud fuckers that can't keep their mouths shut, and I can just tell someone is planning something big, and it's probably not going to be good."

The fuck?

"Who?"

"I don't even know that, man. Maybe Cap, he always has his fucking hands in everything going on, but I don't even know what is being planned just that they are telling everyone to be ready."

"Like a fucking gang war, what is it?" I snap.

Jason shakes his head. "No, I don't think it's that, if it was they'd want all of us to know and hit them first. This is something internal, I just don't know what. Could be an expansion, could be a promotion, could be a cutting, I don't know."

"A cutting?"

"Yeah, when an initiated member has to get cut it's a whole thing, doesn't happen often but it's fucked and because you're going to ask, no they don't live."

"Any word on who would be getting cut?"

He shakes his head again. "No, I don't even know if that's what it is. Just make sure you watch your back extra carefully, and don't trust shit from anyone."

I scoff, "I don't trust anyone but my girl." I don't care if that makes me look weak to anyone who's not me, it's the fucking truth.

Jason nods, "Good, none of these fuckers can be trusted, but be careful."

"You too," I tell him before we go our separate ways.

As I'm climbing back into my shitty loaner car, I get a text from Cap telling me to come to the fight house.

Fucking great.

I am not looking for a fight today, but I am wanting to know more about what Jason might be talking about.

I get to the house, going straight downstairs like I always do. It's early in the day so there's no actual fights happening, just a bunch of guys hanging around, drugs being passed about and smoked.

Cap is in his usual spot toward the back of the room, I make my way over to him.

"Sup?" I ask, folding my arms across my chest.

"I wasn't sure about ya when I first saw ya," Cap says, cutting out any bullshit.

"Let me guess, you're still not sure," I said smugly.

Cap laughs, "Nah, I've been impressed by ya, and I want a bit more for ya."

I perk up at what he's saying, hoping for more than just money runs with Deuce and Saw, so I can maybe start learning about the actual behind the scenes shit going on.

"Yeah?" I ask.

Cap nods, "How 'bout ya come with me to meet one of the suppliers for the clubs, and we can work out something for ya?"

I shrug like it's not a big deal, "Sure."

Cap smiles, and it's a creepy as fuck smile as he says, "Good, we will meet up with him later, first I wanna see what ya think about some new recruits."

I know he means guys that will be fighting since that's how all potential recruits are judged, and that's fine with me. I'm about to start moving up. I can feel everything about to come together, fucking *finally*.

37

Present

It's been about a week since Thanksgiving, and I can honestly say my life has never been better.

I feel like everything is going well with my classes, at my clinical, and the end of the term is quickly approaching before I get three weeks off. Then, it's my final term of my doctorate and I am so ready to be done.

The only thing that would make the break better would be if Nate was done with his assignment so we could lock ourselves away somewhere and not leave each other's side.

Yup, that sounds perfect.

I can only hope.

I'm packing up my stuff at the end of my late class. I'm ready to go home, take a warm shower to warm up my chilled skin from the weather, then curl up under a mountain of blankets on Nate's bed, and pass out.

It's been nice driving Nate's car around since he went undercover. I was against it at first, it felt weird.

Well, I was against a lot of things for a while because it felt weird, but this was one of those things. Now, I like it. The car is fast, easy to handle and way better than my shitty, but reliable Toyota.

I get into the blue sports car, peeling out of the parking lot as I make my way to the highway that takes me to the bridge into Washington toward Nate's house.

Driving through the city, there's never a time where the number of cars on the road decreases a ton. Maybe in the middle of the night, but even though it's late-ish on a weeknight there's a decent number of cars on the road.

A flash of light from behind me grabs my attention as I see a big SUV behind me driving way too close for comfort.

"Pass me then, jackass," I mumble to myself as the driver continues to ride my ass.

I push down on the gas as far as it will go to speed up, and the car takes off from underneath me. I like the rush it gives me.

The annoying SUV behind me falls back fraction, but remains close enough that I remain on edge.

I cross the state border, glancing back to see if they are still following me, and they are. My awareness heightens with each mile I drive, and the car continues to follow closely.

Something is wrong.

Something doesn't feel right.

I remember hearing about some test whenever someone is following you to make four right turns in a row, and if they are still behind you, they are definitely following.

The next exit comes up, I quickly move over to exit, even though it's not the one I would usually take.

The SUV does the same, despite the fact that we both had to cut across three lanes to do so.

I take the first right and turn quickly. So does the SUV.

I narrow my eyes to see if I can make out anything about the driver, but their bright lights are practically blinding me. I can't even see the people in the car.

I whip around the second right, and turn faster than I probably should have considering the roads are a bit icy from the freezing weather.

The SUV is close to me once again.

My heart is pounding from the panic and adrenaline running through my blood. Quickly, I take the third turn without even hitting the brake.

The SUV is *still* there.

I tighten my hold on the steering wheel, knowing if they take this next turn with me, I'm about to drive faster than I've ever have before.

The turn approaches me quickly, and just like the last time I take it without slowing down. I feel the back of the car fishtail a bit before evening out once again.

I floor the gas as soon as I'm clear of the turn, then look back, waiting for the lights to appear again. For a moment I don't think I'll see them as I continue to speed down the streets.

Then, suddenly they are there again. I know it's them because those bright blue lights are hurting my eyes as they continue to drive way too close.

As dangerous as it is, I grab my phone and text Nate's burner phone.

> Aylin: Purple.

I know the code words weren't for me, and this isn't exactly how we agreed to use them, but it's the best I can do.

I hope he understands how scared I am. I could have said yellow, but I'm still convinced I can outrun whoever this is, and that's exactly what I'm about to do.

I make my way back to the highway. As soon as I'm on the on ramp I floor the gas, pushing the car above hundred miles per hour, and take off. I should probably have turned around to drive back toward Portland where I'm more familiar, but I am afraid they are familiar with that area as well. Whoever they are.

Racing down the highway, I'm hoping no cop tries to pull me over, because I doubt they will care about any excuse I have when I'm currently felony speeding.

I weave through the cars on the road, not slowing down. I keep glancing in the rearview mirror to make sure the SUV is long gone and won't catch up to me again.

Finally, it's been a few miles since I've gotten a glimpse of the black car, and I feel like I might be in the clear. Though, I'm still on edge and panicked, I feel like I might be okay enough to head back.

As I make my way back toward Nate's house, I keep looking behind me to make sure I'm not followed again. There aren't many lights that appear in my rearview mirror, and the ones that do aren't the bright blue ones attached to a black SUV.

I'm still cautious as I drive back to the townhouse, and even more cautious as I pull into the garage, shutting it as soon as the car is parked inside. I watch the door close to make sure no one sneaks in.

Making my way inside, I lock the garage door, then run around to check every single door and window to make sure they are all locked. I'm extremely paranoid, but I don't know what that was about, maybe it was completely random, but I refuse to believe that. I'm not that ignorant.

Once I double check every single door and window downstairs to make sure they are locked, I hesitantly make my way upstairs to check those windows. They are all locked as well.

Finally, I look at my phone, but Nate hasn't replied. He could be rushing over. I want to tell him I'm okay so he doesn't panic, in case he hasn't seen the text, but I'm still not sure if I really am okay. I send him another text anyway.

Aylin: Blue…I think.

Again, this isn't the exact system we set up for the code words, but I'm hoping he will understand what I'm trying to say.

Even though I doubt I'll be able to go to sleep for a while with my paranoia so high, I still change into my sleepwear so I can at least feel comforted by Nate's t-shirt on my body.

As I'm climbing into the warm bed I hear a shattering downstairs, and all my panic comes roaring back. My heart is beating so fast I feel like it might bust out of my chest, and I feel like I can't catch a breath.

I grab my phone before quietly going toward the stairs and looking to see what window was busted. It's one right by the front door. I fumble with my phone as I try to unlock it and dial 9-1-1.

Another window shatters, and I can't hold back the scream that escapes my throat. Then, I see the dark figure climbing through the second busted window. I press "dial" on my phone, but the figure sees me, and rushes toward me.

I race up the couple stairs I walked down and run toward the bedroom. As I try to slam the door shut, I'm pushed back as the figure pushes in. I throw my phone at the man's head since it's the only thing in my hand. I hear it make contact with his skull, but I don't stick around to see if it did any real damage before I'm racing down the stairs toward the front door.

Suddenly, I'm yanked back by my hair just before I get to the door. I scream again as I'm slammed down to the ground.

"Fucking bitch," the man growls as he climbs on top of me attempting to pin me.

I fight with everything I have, not letting him grab ahold of my arms as I punch and kick, flailing my entire body like a fucking maniac, just so he isn't able to get a good grip on me.

I manage to hit him in the face a few times before bringing my leg up and kneeing him right in the spine. I wiggle away from underneath him as I try to run again. He grabs my ankle before I can get away, and I fall onto the ground, all the air rushes out of my lungs.

Screaming, I kick my feet back finally making contact with his face, so he lets go. I stumble as I try to get up again and the slight mistake was enough time for this mystery guy to get up, grab me, and fling my body across the room. I hit the coffee table with a groan as it collapses under my weight being thrown onto it.

"Stop fucking fighting, it'll be easier," the man spits blood onto the floor.

I don't say anything, and it hurts to get up as he continues to come toward me, but this motherfucker doesn't realize I've been beaten before, and pain doesn't mean anything to me anymore.

Even though my side is killing me, I get up to try and run toward the door again. Instead of giving this guy the chance to grab me again, I duck out of his way and kick him when he gets too close to me.

"God fuckin' dammit," the guy growls as he lunges for me again, but I duck out of his reach, and instead of running toward the door, I run toward the kitchen.

I grab one of the knives from the block on the counter, holding it in front of me. I feel warmth seeping down the side of my face, I know I'm bleeding, but I can't even feel where it's coming from.

The guy laughs at me holding a knife in front of me.

"You think it's funny I'll cut you?" I taunt.

"Nah, I think it's funny you *think* you'll cut me."

I tighten my grip on the handle despite my sweaty palms making it difficult to hold.

"Your little boyfriend didn't mention how feisty you are," this mystery man says, and I'm immediately taken aback. He knows Nate and he's trying to fucking kill me?

No.

"What the *fuck* are you talking about?" I snap as I try to hold onto the semblance of sanity I have while I figure out what's going on.

Nate wouldn't do this. Nate wouldn't hurt me. He loves me, he's not like that.

"Your boyfriend *Trevor*," he says the name like it annoys him. "Said he has a girl, but never mentioned you were a fuckin' fighter."

Trevor?

Then it hits me, this guy knows Nate as his undercover identity.

Wait, but how are they here? How do they know about me? I have so many questions I don't know what is happening other than this guy is trying to hurt me, and I doubt Nate knows anything about it.

"What do you want?" I scream at him, pointing the knife higher at him.

"Your boyfriend has fucked up, and now you're going to pay for it."

Before I can even form another thought, the man lunges at me. I swing the knife at him, cutting his arm. He releases a hiss of pain but doesn't stop coming at me. He grabs my wrist, slamming it onto the counter until I drop the knife.

I keep fighting back because now I can, but he doesn't let up. I'm flung around the room so many times I can't keep track. I'm bleeding from so many places, and my body is sore all over, but I refuse to give up.

I feel how weak I'm getting as I'm thrown onto the floor again. When I try to get up one more time my arms give out under me, and I know I can't take it anymore.

Luckily, I got in some good hits, and this guy isn't going to walk away from this unscathed. I can't even think about the damage around Nate's house, all the blood, broken furniture and shit everywhere from the scuffle.

I let out a sigh of defeat as I know I'm not going to be able to push myself up again. The man leans down over me, and chuckles, "I'll make sure to tell him how feisty you are, it'll make you more fun to play with."

I'm not able to reply before there's a sharp sting in my neck. Then everything goes black.

38

Present

I get what Jason was talking about, something is up. Cap is bringing me along when he does shit, and he acts like it's because he wants me to move up in the rankings.

Though, nothing is happening beyond that and I'm starting to get suspicious. I notice all the other guys keep their distance from me, which normally wouldn't bother me. The fact that this seemed to happen overnight is weird.

I'm with Cap, the other guys are out doing who-knows-what, when my burner phone goes off in my pocket. I usually don't check it around him just in case it's something him or the guys shouldn't see.

Cap isn't looking at me, so I glance down to see the number I haven't saved, but know by heart as Aylin's. It says "purple", and my heart rate instantly kicks up in my chest.

The code words have been for me, but her sending that means something is wrong. I need to get away from Cap, and back to check on her. I don't know how long he's planning to be here supervising this shipment of cocaine, but I need it to hurry. The fuck. Up.

I'm bouncing on the balls of my feet, looking around as I try to think of any scenario that Aylin would send me the code word without something being wrong, and I come up blank.

Time is moving so slow, but I know I can't get away from Cap right now since we drove in the same car, and he won't leave until they are done unloading the stupid fucking shipment. I should just leave anyway and deal with the consequences later, at least I'll know Aylin is okay.

Fuck, for the first time I'm actually conflicted on what I'm supposed to do.

My phone goes off again and I see another text from Aylin's number that says "Blue...I think" I release a half sigh of relief. I want to believe she's okay, but she doesn't even seem sure.

I need to get the fuck out of here, and over to her.

Finally, Cap is done, and we are able to leave. I speed back to the fight house where I get out of the car as fast as I can to jog over to my own car.

"Where ya goin'?" Cap calls after me.

"I got something to deal with," I call back before getting in my car, and racing toward my house.

While I'm driving, I call Mitch.

"Yeah?" He answers.

"Get over to my house, something is wrong," I demand.

"Should we call backup?" He asks, and I hear his keys shuffling in the background, so I know he's coming to help me.

"No time, get there *now*," I tell him before hanging up so I can focus on getting there myself.

"Come on, baby, please be okay," I say to myself, but it's for Aylin as I race down the streets.

As soon as I pull up to my house, I can see the busted windows in the front.

No.

I jump out of the car before I've even turned it off, running up to the front door that I quickly realize is unlocked.

As soon as I step inside, I'm brought back to the night my parents were killed. The house is a mess, the coffee table is busted, there's drops and smears of blood all over the floor. That better be from the fucker that broke in here because I know my girl is a fighter.

I usually pride myself for being able to remain calm under pressure, it's one of the things that makes me good at my job, but not right now. At this moment, I can't think about anything other than where Aylin is and needing to see her, to make sure she's okay.

"Aylin, it's me!" I call out just in case she is hiding somewhere waiting for someone to come.

There's no response.

I hear Mitch approach behind me with a quiet, "*Fuck*". I don't say anything to him as I start rushing around the house. I can't even give myself a moment to think about how it looks like a tornado came through here and how much it closely resembles what my parent's house looked like.

Aylin is still alive; I know she is.

This won't be like that night; I won't lose her.

I won't.

I can't.

I'm racing through my entire house, opening every door while I continue to call out her name, but there's nothing. No response, and I don't see her. I check the garage, only to see my car sitting there which means she didn't leave on her own.

Once I get to our bedroom, I see her phone on the ground with the screen shattered. I pick it up to see if it still works, but it doesn't.

"Fuck!" I yell, throwing the phone against the far wall.

"What?!" Mitch bounds up the stairs quickly.

"She's not fucking here!" I'm pulling at my hair in frustration while trying to figure out where she is, and who I have to rip apart with my bare hands.

"Come on, man, who would've taken her? Are you sure she didn't go somewhere with friends or something?"

"Dude! Did you see the fucking shit show downstairs, her phone is up here with the screen shattered and you want to try, and fucking tell me she went out with *friends*?!" I scream.

"Fine, probably not. Who do you think took her? You have to keep your head on straight so we can find her. You can't flip out like this."

"Don't fucking tell me what I need to do right now! You have the one person you fucking care about taken from you and see how you react!"

Mitch nods, "We will get her back, you know we will, but we need to call in some backup."

"No, fuck that, we don't have time. I'm going to go find her."

"Nate! Think about this for just one second. We have to report this and get more guys to help out. I know you don't want to, but we have to."

"You call backup if you want, but I'm not sitting on my ass waiting for anyone to show up, I'm going to find her. You can help me or not I really don't give a fuck."

I don't even wait for him to respond before I'm rushing back down the stairs, the keys to my car Aylin was driving are on the floor of the living room. I scoop them up because I'm not driving the other piece of shit anywhere right now.

I don't give a fuck about my cover.

I don't give a fuck about anything other than getting her back.

"I'm in." Mitch says as I'm opening the door to the garage.

I turn to him with narrowed eyes. "The fuck do you mean?"

"You're not about to do this alone, I have your back, man. We will deal with everything else after we have your girl back."

I would've smiled if I was capable of it at this moment. I'm just glad Mitch came to his senses enough to help me, without worrying about what he's "supposed to do" for once.

I nod as we both get into my car. I barely wait for the garage door to open before I'm barreling down the driveway and heading south toward Portland. I throw my phone at Mitch as the car skids getting onto the freeway.

"Call Jason, I think my cover is blown anyway see where he's at. I want to see if we can get info from him first."

Mitch doesn't say anything as he nods and starts dialing on the burner.

Hang on, sweetheart, I'm coming to get to you, and I'll kill anyone who laid a single finger on you.

39

Present

My eyes feel heavy, and my entire body feels like I've been hit by a bus, or maybe a train. I hate that this isn't the first time in my life I've woken up in a similar state.

The biggest difference this time is the overall sluggishness that I'm sure is from whatever that asshole injected me with.

As I start to wake up a bit more, I feel tightness around my wrists, and my shoulders are killing me. I try to wiggle around only to figure out my arms are pulled back, almost unnaturally with my wrists tied behind my back.

I try to move my legs around, but of course those are tied together as well. I drop my head back with a frustrated groan. I'm lying on a mattress if it can even be considered that. It's only a couple inches thick and feels like I'm lying on the cold ground anyway.

I'm still in what I was wearing when I was attacked, Nate's t-shirt that now has blood on it, and some sleep shorts since I opted for more than just underwear due to my paranoia and

I'm slightly glad for that now, but it is doing nothing to keep me warm.

The room I'm in is pitch black, I can't see anything and it's freezing. There's no windows, no sliver of light from a door or a curtain. Nothing. Just black.

I wonder if this is what death feels like. Painful, tired and dark. I used to think about what it would feel like to die a lot. When I would be in bed at night after my parents hurt me, I would wonder if that would be the night I wouldn't wake up.

I always knew I would die young, and at the hands of someone else. I just never thought it would be like this.

I guess my worries were always right, I never thought I deserved happiness and any sort of happiness I felt would be ripped away from me. Just like this.

I finally love someone, and he loves me.

I'm finally happy with where my life is.

I'm almost done with my degree.

And it's all going to be ripped away like I always knew it would.

And I never told Nate I love him.

Now I'll never get to.

That's the thought that makes me start to cry. Not the thought of dying, not the pain I'm feeling, but the fact that I will never be able to tell Nate everything I feel for him. I know he knows, but I wish I told him. I wish I was able to say the words.

I wish I did a lot of things in my life; I should've traveled, even though I didn't have the money, I should've figured it out.

I should have lived without the constant fear of things going wrong.

I cry harder realizing all the things I'll never get to do.

I hear a door slam in the distance, then the room illuminates with blinding lights. I have to close my eyes at the onslaught of brightness that makes my retinas burn and my head throb.

There are heavy footsteps coming closer, and I wish I could get into more of a defensive position, or just have any advantage at all in this situation, but I am completely vulnerable and I hate it.

"Look at ya, awake. That shit hit ya harder than it should've," the guy says, and I can hear him getting closer.

I'm still not able to open my eyes, I can feel how much they are burning behind my eyelids.

"Not gonna say anythin' to me?" The guy asks.

I stay silent. I don't even sniffle, though I really need to from all my crying.

"Fine, I'm Cap, and I know your boyfriend which is why ya are here, in case ya wondered."

I still don't make a noise.

I hear this guy, Cap, huff out a breath before I feel his foot on my side pushing me off the mattress onto the hard ground.

I guess I was wrong about the mattress, the ground is slightly harder.

I let out a groan as my sore body hits the floor, and the position I'm in now is way worse, as I lift up my head to get a look at him despite my eyes burning.

"There ya are, now we can talk."

"I have nothing to fucking say to you," I snap at him. My voice is hoarse, and it hurts my throat to speak.

"Ya are feisty. I like it. Look, we know *Trevor* is not who he says he is. I know he's a cop. Known it for a while now, just wanted to see if we could play with him a bit."

My head drops to the ground so he can't see my face as I know all my emotions are written all over it. They know Nate is a cop, and I don't even care about my own safety anymore, I know they aren't going to let him get out of this either.

I just hope he doesn't find me, then maybe he can get away and live.

"Then," Cap continues, "we were gonna take him, but one of my guys saw ya instead and well...ya seemed more fun to play with. Then we could get...Nate, is it? Two birds with one stone and all that."

"Just kill me, but don't hurt him. Killing me will hurt him enough," I groan. I know it would hurt Nate. I know he would hold the guilt and I hate that, but if there's any chance of him surviving this, I want to make sure it happens.

Cap laughs, "Ya both will die no matter what, don't worry. Let's send him a pic, I'm sure he wants to see ya."

His hand grabs the back of my head that's still sore from the scuffle before, as he pulls me up by my hair, I grit my teeth through the pain as he guides me to sit up on the ground. I scowl up at him. He looks intimidating from my angle on the floor with his broad body, tattoos and face contorted in a wicked smile.

I might have a hard time fighting him off, but I know Nate could do it, this guy doesn't have anything on him. Too bad I think he has other plans for both of us.

Cap snaps a picture of me a few moments before I hear the phone start ringing in his hand.

"Didn't take long," he winks in my direction, and I fight the urge to vomit.

I can only hear one side of the conversation, but Nate's voice is loud on the other end of the phone, I just can't make out what he's saying.

"Don't tell me ya are stupid enough to call in ya other cop buddies," Cap says nonchalantly.

"Yeah, I got her here, she's fucking hot, I see why ya want her back." Cap winks at me again and this time I don't fight the gag that comes out.

"Shut the fuck up, I know everything and if ya want her back ya gotta come get her ya-self."

"Nate no!" I scream because I know he's going to agree to that, but I know we both aren't going to make it out of this, no matter what this guy says.

"Ya wanna talk to her? Here," Cap says before the phone is put on speaker, and he's holding it in front of me, but far enough I'm not able to try something like bite him.

"Sweetheart, are you okay?" I can hear the panic in his voice, and it makes the tears well in my eyes again.

"I'm fine, Nate, please don't come here, they are going to kill us both. For once just save yourself, *please!*"

"You know I'm not going to do that, I love you I'm—"

Cap takes the phone off speaker so I can't hear the rest of what he's saying.

"No!" I scream again.

"Ya have six hours to find her, or I can't promise she will still be here, or alive," Cap says with a laugh before hanging up the phone.

I can't help the tears from falling again. I know he's going to try to find me, but I've already accepted my fate, I just hope it's over quickly. I've endured enough torture in my life, I just want it all to end.

"I'll be back *sweetheart*," Cap says with a mocking tone, and hearing him call me that makes me gag again. I hated when Nate first started saying that to me, but it grew on me, and I'm going to miss it.

Without another word Cap walks back the way he came, turning the lights off right before the door slams. Once again it's pitch black, cold and I'm alone. Tied up on the floor, and the sobs overtake me.

I curl up on the floor, not even bothering to get back on the paper thin mattress, as I cry myself into oblivion.

Who They Are

I DON'T KNOW how long it has been since Cap came in here, but I'm woken up by the door slamming again. I scramble to sit up despite the protests from my sore body.

This time there are two voices, and my heart rate picks up when neither of the voices sound familiar. I know it's not Nate, but neither of them sound like that guy Cap from earlier either.

I use all the strength I have to try and scoot my body back, away from the sounds and hopefully to a wall. It's harder than I thought it would be, my body is not holding up from all I've had to endure. Plus, I haven't had any water or food in who knows how long, so I'm even weaker.

Suddenly, the lights come on again, and I groan, they are so bright I don't know who put them here, but they were an asshole.

I see the two guys that came in, and I know I'm fucked. Especially with how they are both looking at me right now.

They are both massive, the slightly taller one is twirling a knife around between his fingers. The other one is clean shaven, and might have been attractive at one time, but the scowl on his face makes him look as evil as I'm sure he is.

"This is it?" The clean shaven one says, and I furrow my brows. *This,* like I'm literally nothing. I guess to them I'm not. People don't matter to assholes like them.

"I heard you fight back, I like when they fight," the one with the knife says, and I cringe at his voice. If the devil exists that's what he sounds like.

"Trevor was always so fucking annoying acting like he's better than all of us, makes sense he's a fucking cop," clean shaven one says.

"Never wanted to get his hands dirty either, should've fuckin' known," knife guy says with a nod.

"Fucker is going to get what's coming to him, but first we can have fun with his girl," clean shaven says.

I don't get why all of these guys refer to "having fun" with me. They are sick bastards. Every single one of them.

"Don't worry, we won't go easy on you. We are going to fucking ruin you. If he ever finds you, all you'll be is a bloody mess. He won't even recognize you," knife guy laughs as he describes the scenario.

I try to move back away from them again, but clean-shaven grabs my ankles pulling me down toward them before climbing on top of me. I scream as loud as I can despite it feeling like my throat is being ripped apart at the force of my scream.

"I'll go first," the guy on top of me says, as he nods toward the other guy. "Saw will kill you before he's done with his turn."

I scream louder as I try everything to get this guy off me. It's a lot harder to fight without the use of my arms or legs, but it doesn't stop me. I'm screaming, bucking my body as I feel his hands start to roam down my chest toward my shorts.

I keep screaming, and wiggling my body, I won't give up, I might have accepted death, but I will fight tooth and nail against being violated like this. Even if I'm going to die, I'm not going to die with these men being the last ones to touch me.

"Grab her fucking legs," the guy on me yells to the other guy—Saw, I think.

I continue to try and fight them both as his hands reach my shorts, pulling them down. I scream louder, but I officially can't move anymore with the combination of their weight on me.

I know there is nothing I can do anymore.

Nothing except accept that this is going to happen.

I can't stop them.

I can't fight them.

This is it for me. I close my eyes and hope I'll never have the chance to open them again because they are about to take everything from me.

40

Present

Even though I'm annoyed at the stop, we end up picking up Jason during my search for places they could have taken Aylin.

We went to the fight house first, and I went on a rampage, but didn't see anyone I recognized, and didn't see her in any of the rooms I checked. I busted through every single door in that house, even interrupted some shit I wish I didn't have to see, but I don't care. I'm blind with rage.

Jason, Mitch and I are headed to one of the clubs when my phone dings with a message. Mitch is holding it for me, so he sees what it is before me.

"Uh, man you might want to pull over to see this," he says nervously.

I whip the car to the side of the road immediately, hearing Jason "thunk" in the back from me slamming on the brakes. I snatch my phone from Mitch's hand at the same time I throw the car in park.

My blood boils at what I'm seeing. Aylin has her hands

behind her back, probably tied up, but I can't see that part. Her legs are tied at the ankles. She's sitting on a dirty floor, and everything around her is concrete.

She has dried blood on her face, in her messy long brown hair, on the shirt she's wearing—my t-shirt. She's a mess, and my heart hurts as I look at how pained her face is. She's always beautiful, but I am about to lose it at the pain she's so clearly in. And the fact that she's with that grimy motherfucker.

Instantly, I press "call", and Cap answers right away. I can hear his smug smile through the phone, and I wish I could reach through it to throttle him.

"Don't tell me ya are stupid enough to call in ya other cop buddies," Cap says nonchalantly.

"Nah, I can handle you myself. Where's my girl? Are you with her right now?" I snap loudly.

"Yeah, I got her here, she's fucking hot, I see why ya want her back."

"Don't say a fucking word about her you piece of shit! When I see you, I'm going to enjoy taking my time ripping you apart piece by fucking piece," I scream at him.

"Shut the fuck up, I know everything and if ya want her back, ya gotta come get her ya-self."

"Nate, no!" I hear Aylin cry out in the background.

"Put her on the phone!" I demand

"Ya wanna talk to her? Here."

"Sweetheart, are you okay?" I rush out because I'm not sure how long Cap will let me talk to her.

"I'm fine, Nate, please don't come here, they are going to kill us both. For once just save yourself, *please!*" She begs, and it hurts me to hear how broken she sounds, her voice is hoarse as she pleads.

"You know I'm not going to do that; I love you I'm—"

"No!" She calls in the distance, and I know Cap took away the phone.

"Ya have six hours to find her, or I can't promise she will still be here, or alive," Cap says with a laugh before hanging up the phone.

"FUCK!" I yell, throwing the phone on the ground.

"Come on, maybe we can use that picture to figure out where she is," Mitch says, trying to calm me down again, but I am so far gone in my anger nothing will calm me except having Aylin back in my arms.

"It looks like a fucking concrete box, there's nothing that will help us, but knock yourself out." I pick up my phone from the floor to toss over to Mitch before pulling back out onto the road.

I continue speeding down the streets when Mitch passes the phone back to Jason. We are getting closer to the club I want to check next. The shitty thing is, since I was kept in the dark about so much, I'm limited on where I should even check.

It makes sense now why I was kept in the dark. They knew I was a cop. I wonder how long they knew. I wonder *how* they knew.

Glancing back at Jason I can't help but wonder if he ratted me out, maybe he shouldn't be with us right now. I narrow my eyes, maybe he's helping them. God fucking dammit I can't trust anyone right now.

"I think I might know where this is," Jason says from the back seat.

I'm skeptical, maybe he's just saying that to throw us off. I don't have very much time, and we can't afford to waste it. Though, I have zero leads, and if he's working against me, he's fucking dead.

"Where?" I snap.

"There was this place I went with Trent once while he was trying to work with these guys and they were trying to combine resources so—" I cut him off.

"Fucking WHERE, Jason?!" I scream.

"There's a warehouse Cap and Trent wanted to convert into some sort of new club, it's south of Portland," he says as I whip the car in the other direction.

"Tell me where to go, and don't waste any fucking time," I threaten.

It takes us about twenty minutes before I'm pulling up to a building that looks empty. There are no lights, no cars I can see. Nothing.

"You fucking with me?" I ask Jason, narrowing my eyes through the rearview mirror.

"No, this is it, but it's just a guess. I remembered the basement freaked me out because there were no windows or ways to get out except a single door that locked from the outside."

I wait for a beat just staring at him through the mirror before speaking again, "You working against me, Jason?"

"The fuck? Like some sort of double agent? No."

"Then how the fuck did they know I'm a cop?" I snap at him.

"They know you're a cop? Shit," Mitch mumbles from the passenger seat.

"Who the fuck knows? These guys are good, man, but it wasn't me," Jason defends. I watch him as he speaks to see if I can get a sense of him lying, but I don't.

"Fine, let's go," I say to both of them before getting out of the car.

I still want to know how they figured it out, maybe I'm just shit at being undercover. Maybe, it was that night of the initiation, someone followed me without me knowing. Maybe I was being followed in general and never knew it. I'm usually aware of my surroundings, but these guys are good, they could've been hiding in plain sight or stationed at places I went. So many fucking possibilities and maybe it is all my fault.

Aylin being taken is all my fucking fault.

Jason takes the lead as the three of us walk around the

building to a side door Jason says leads to the basement. I still don't fully trust him, but it's the best I can do right now. If the slightest chance she's here I need to check.

I try to pull open the door, and I'm shocked to find it unlocked. My heart rate increases as I realize that must mean if she is being kept here, someone is in there with her.

Or this isn't where she is.

Pulling the door open there's a set of steep stairs and as soon as I'm stepping in, I hear a scream. I know it's Aylin.

I run down the stairs, skipping two to three at a time until I'm at the bottom where I see the giant open basement, and at the far end of it I see people. Aylin is screaming. I see someone on her, and I run over there as fast as I possibly can.

When I get closer, I see it's Saw and Deuce, Saw is on her legs while Deuce is on her body. I knock Saw off first before Deuce. A half a second later, I hear a gasp come from Aylin, but my focus is solely on killing these two motherfuckers.

I'm seeing red, I can't even see her right now as my fist is driving into Deuce's face over and over again. My haze is broken for a moment when I hear Aylin scream my name. I look up just in time to see Saw swinging that stupid knife toward my face.

I move out of the way before he's able to make contact, but Deuce is on me, driving his fist into my stomach to try and knock me off of him. It doesn't work and I punch his face a few more times when I see Mitch finally fucking helping me and is knocking back Saw.

Deuce and I continue to fight, but I have the advantage in size and experience. It doesn't take long until I've knocked him out. I go to help Aylin who looks terrified against the wall. She shakes her head at me and gestures with her head behind me.

I look to see what she was signaling, and I see Mitch on the ground with a knife pressed to his throat by Saw. I look back at her, dying to get her out of here, but I need to help Mitch.

With a sympathetic look in her direction, I turn toward Saw and Mitch wondering where the fuck Jason is and why he's not helping. I knock Saw off Mitch. He wastes no time getting back up coming toward me, knife still in hand. I've seen what he can do with that thing, and I do not want to be on the other end of it.

"You really think you're leaving here with her, rat?" Saw spits at me.

I see Mitch getting up and wiping the thin line of blood from his neck. It's not deep enough to be concerning.

"I know I am, but you think you're leaving alive after touching her?" I taunt.

Saw laughs before lunging toward me, knife first. I grab his wrist, twisting it around to attempt to get him to drop the knife. It doesn't work, and I feel him punch me in the side. I continue twisting his wrist to get him to release the knife.

He's knocked from my grasp, and I turn to see Mitch on him. He has the arm with the knife held down with his knee as he fights.

"Get her out of here!" Mitch calls.

"I'm not leaving you alone with this," I tell him.

"Back up is coming. *Go.*"

I don't know when he called back up, but I look over at Aylin who is staring wide eyed at the scene in front of her covered in tears and blood. I run over to her, pulling the tie from her wrists loose before scooping her up in my arms. I can't help but ask something that will make or break my decision to come back down here and kill them.

"Did they touch you?"

She shakes her head, "You stopped them before it went too far."

Seeing how much blood is on her, knowing some of it is hers and knowing they did touch her is too far for me. But my focus right now is getting her out, making sure she's safe and then never leaving her side again.

Holding her close to my chest I run up the stairs, I see Jason standing just outside the door.

"The fuck are you doing?" I ask him. I feel Aylin tense in my arms.

"Mitch told me to keep watch to make sure no other guys showed up," he answers quickly.

"Did he actually call backup?" I ask because I'm not sure if he was lying to me or not just so I would get Aylin safe.

"Yeah, he said he did right before running down there after you."

I nod, then see the lights in the distance coming toward us.

"Help is coming, sweetheart, I'm not leaving your side, but they are going to want to take you to the hospital," I tell her softly.

She shakes her head at me, "No, please don't make me go, I'm not hurt enough to go to the hospital I just want to go home, *please*."

"Sweetheart, no, you need to be checked out by doctors. I need to know you're okay."

"Nate, please just take me home. I just need you; this isn't anything I haven't handled myself hundreds of times before."

That subtle reminder of her childhood feels worse than any punch I received tonight. I disagree with what she's saying right now, but I can't fault her for it. I didn't want to go to the hospital when I was hurt either, even when she begged me to.

I sigh, but agree, "Okay, let's get you home." Turning toward Jason, I tell him, "Tell Mitch I'm taking her home."

Before he has a chance to answer I'm jogging with Aylin in my arms toward my car, knowing they both will be able to get a ride back with someone else.

I lay Aylin in the front seat, pulling the rope from her ankles off before closing the door and climbing into the driver's seat.

Peeling out onto the dirt road, I race out of the lot in the opposite direction of the oncoming backup, so they don't try to stop me.

Once I'm out onto the main roads I peek over at Aylin, she's leaning against the window, eyes closed. I lightly place my hand on her thigh because I need to touch her. I need to know she's really here.

She flinches when my hand makes contact, and I go to pull it back but she's placing her hand over mine to hold it there. That little touch means more than any words could right now. She's scared, she's been through more than I even know about, and yet she wants me close.

I relax slightly at the thought as I do what she asked of me and drive us home.

41

Aylin

Present

I'm staring out the window as Nate drives us back to what I thought would be his house, but I soon realize he's driving us to my apartment. I squeeze his hand tighter thinking he's about to leave me.

He's going to take me to my apartment, and then be done with me.

He must sense my fear because he's quick to soothe me. "We can't go back to my house sweetheart, the windows are busted and too many people know about it now."

I nod. He's right. Neither of our places are ideal, and something we are going to have to figure out, but for right now I just want to be locked away somewhere safe. Somewhere with him and forget the rest of the world. Forget the evil in the world and forget the pain I've endured.

It's not long until we are in my apartment, locked inside. It feels weird to be back here. I didn't realize how much of my stuff I'd brought over to Nate's house until I'm standing in the living room noticing all the little things that are missing.

My couch is bare, everything is neat and tidy because this place hasn't been lived in. Being here now, I notice how it doesn't have that same comfort feeling it once had. It doesn't feel like my home anymore.

Nate goes straight to my bathroom and starts the shower for me as I stand in the living room lost in my thoughts. I feel his hands touch my waist tentatively. I can tell he's being gentle with me after I flinched in the car. I really didn't mean to; I was just surprised he wanted to touch me, so I didn't expect it.

"Come on, sweetheart," he says softly.

I let him lead me into the bathroom, even though this doesn't feel familiar to me anymore. His house became my house, and now I don't even know where we can stay and be safe.

Shaking those thoughts from my head I start to lift the t-shirt from over my head, but wince at the soreness in my arms and side as my arms lift.

"Let me help you," Nate offers, and I nod.

He moves the shirt up carefully before helping me slip my arms through the arm holes without me having to raise them too much. Once it's off, he moves to help me out of my shorts. He doesn't try to push anything further, but for some reason I want him to. I want to feel him. I want him to help me forget everything that isn't him.

As Nate ushers me into the warm shower I grab his arm. "Join me," I say quietly, my throat raw from the screaming.

"Sweetheart..." I can see his conflicted expression.

"Nate, please, I need you," I say the one thing that he has said to me that always makes me give in.

And it's true.

I need him.

He sighs before quickly pulling off his own clothes and stepping into the shower with me.

Without saying anything Nate grabs the almost empty

bottle of body wash, putting some on his hands since I don't have anything else to use in here as he slowly and carefully washes my body. His touch isn't sexual at all, it's caring and loving as he washes every inch of my skin.

Finally, everything hits me all at once and I start to cry. The hot tears streaming down my face without me being able to stop them.

"Aylin, sweetheart, talk to me please, what happened? Did I hurt you?" Nate panics as he holds my face, wiping my wet hair away, searching my eyes.

I shake my head, but the tears don't stop.

"No, you're…you're perfect. It's just everything… I was so fucking scared Nate, I thought I was going to die. I was resigned to dying, but I couldn't stand the thought of anything happening to you and I'm *terrified*. I can't feel like that again. I can't be so scared like that again, I can't lose you Nate." The tears are stronger now as I confess to him. I bare myself to him fully for the first time.

Nate pulls me into him, holding me close. I feel his erection digging into my stomach, but we both ignore it. I know this isn't about that.

"You weren't going to die; I wasn't going to let anything happen to you. I will *never* let anything happen to you again. You won't lose me and if you think I'm ever leaving your side willingly again, you're wrong."

I continue to cry into his chest as he runs his hands down my soaked hair, down my back, soothing me. Just holding me under the warm spray of water. The feeling of him starts to consume me.

I want to get lost in him.

I want to feel only him.

I want to forget everything that isn't him.

"Nate, I need you," I say, looking up at him.

"I'm here for you, I'm always here for you."

"No, I *need* you. I need to feel you. I need you to take it all away. Take away the pain, take away the feeling of their hands on me, take it all away. Show me how much you love me."

I see the conflict in his features, clearly unsure if this is a good idea, and maybe it isn't, but it's what I want. It's what I need. Those men didn't get far enough to rape me, which I know was their intent, but their hands were still on my body, and I want Nate to take that away.

I want to forget about what we will have to face once we leave this shower. I want to forget about what the future holds for us, for his job, for my school, for everything. I just want it to be Aylin and Nate for a little while longer.

"Please," I say softly, and he gives in with a light kiss on my lips. A kiss I quickly deepen.

His hands are on my waist, sliding around to my back to pull me flush against him. I slide my arms up his chest to the back of his neck, pulling the hair on the nape of his neck so he will lean into me more.

My tongue licks the seam of his lips, and with a groan he opens up for me, our tongues tangling instantly. It's like the last bit of his control snaps in that moment. Nate slides his hands to the back of my thighs, lifting me up, pressing my back against the cold shower wall.

I gasp at the feeling but tighten my arms around the back of his neck as he devours my mouth. Both of us are getting more and more desperate as the kiss turns frenzied, like we need the other to survive.

Rolling my hips against him I feel his hot erection rub against me, and I moan at the feeling, desperate to feel him everywhere. I need it. I need him.

Reaching down, I grab his thick cock in my hand, and squeeze. He groans into my mouth before biting my bottom lip briefly.

"Nate," I moan into his mouth as I guide the head of his erection to my dripping center. "You love me?"

"I love you more than I ever thought possible. You're fucking everything, Aylin."

I flick his top lip with my tongue, "Prove it."

With that, Nate's lips are back on mine, kissing me harder than before as he presses against me. I arch my hips to guide him inside me. We both moan in each other's mouths at the feeling before he thrusts hard, so he's buried to the hilt.

The feeling of him stretching me, filling me, *loving me* is all I feel. We hold onto each other desperately as he thrusts into me, pressing me harder into the wall each time. He's not hurried, he's not frantic.

This isn't fucking.

This is making love, and it's something I've never felt before.

Our mouths don't part from each other as we continue to feel each other so deeply, my body lights up with impending release. I grind my hips against him, so my clit hits the perfect spot on his pelvis with each thrust.

"God, Nate, you feel.... ah," I can't even finish what I'm saying when I explode around him with an orgasm that takes me by surprise at how sudden and hard it hits me.

"*Fuck*, sweetheart," Nate groans as his lips move down my neck, and bites lightly.

His thrusts become harder as I can feel him close to his own release. His lips are back on mine, hard and demanding as we take from each other everything we need. We breathe in each other's air because it's how we will survive.

I feel him swell inside me before his orgasm takes over his body, and with a guttural moan he fills me with his release, resulting in us sinking into each other even more. Even though he's holding me up I feel like we are both supporting each other in this moment.

Tomorrow isn't guaranteed, and neither of us know what is going to happen now, but the one thing we know is that we aren't letting each other go.

"Nate," I say quietly, pressing a kiss to his neck.

"Hm?" He mumbles, pulling his forehead to rest against mine.

Looking into his hazel eyes, I see everything I need from him, and I finally say the words that have been continually caught in my throat when I look at him.

"I love you," I practically whisper, but he hears me.

His eyes light up, "Say it again."

I light chuckle leaves my lips, "I love y—"

He cuts me off with a kiss, and I can't help but laugh. Even though we have a lot of shit to deal with, I know everything is going to be okay.

42

Present

Shit. Is. A. Mess.

It's been two weeks since I got Aylin back, and there was so much that needed to happen, so much that still needs to happen, but the one constant has been her.

We have barely left each other's side for the last two weeks, and I wouldn't have it any other way. When I don't see her, I panic, and maybe that's unhealthy. Call it what you want, but I refuse to lose her again.

They were able to arrest Deuce and Saw the night we found Aylin. With the help of Jason, Mila and myself they had enough evidence on various crimes to arrest Cap as well as bust a couple of the strip clubs for a list of drug and trafficking charges which led to more arrests.

This wasn't even close to the level at which we were hoping for when this case started, but at least we know some of the bigger players have been taken out, and this will at least set them back business wise for a while.

The FBI is now involved due to the level of operation

spreading further than we originally thought, which means it's their case now anyway.

I talked to Mitch after that night as well, and he was fine with a few cuts from Saw's knife. I told him I owe him my life, and I do. He's my best friend, despite the rough patch we went through because I can be an asshole, he's a genuine guy.

Aylin and I both agreed we didn't want to go back to my house in Vancouver. It brought on too many memories for both of us, we need a fresh start. I got it fixed up and put up for sale immediately. Luckily, I got multiple offers quickly and should be closing in about a month.

We both also agreed her apartment wasn't the best option to live in either. Nothing felt safe anymore. I offered her anything she wanted, we could live at the fanciest hotel or shittiest apartment she wanted as long as she was happy and safe.

We were able to find a month-to-month apartment outside of Portland in Clackamas which increased her commute slightly, but she said she didn't mind. She sublet her apartment quickly, so it was out of our hair.

Aylin was able to explain to her professors and Dr. Tanvers what happened. Luckily, everyone was understanding about the...situation. She didn't ask for any sort of extensions on her work or excuses; she just wanted to make sure she wasn't punished for the work she missed.

My girl is strong as shit and determined. She's on winter break right now, and we've tried to take this time to our full advantage and spend every second together.

I told Sergeant Peters I needed some time off after I met with him, and he laid into me about a lot...but surprisingly, I wasn't actually in trouble. He praised me for putting the job aside for once and helping my girl instead.

To say I was shocked would be a bit of an understatement. I did not expect that from him, but apparently Peters is a bit of a family man, I would've never guessed. He told me there's things more important than the job, and for the first time in my life I understood.

That's also why I'm thinking about what I'm going to do next.

I love being a cop, but I don't think being undercover is really the thing for me. Peters said when I'm ready to come back, there's a detective spot open for me. I thanked him but told him I was going to think about it.

He was surprised by my response, but said he understood.

I've thought about what Aylin said, her fear of losing me and my need to save everyone without regarding myself, and I want to be better. I still want to help people, it's who I am. I can't sit back knowing people are getting hurt and just do nothing. But I know I can't be put in situations like I was before.

I can't risk putting *her* in those situations either.

I think I know what I want to do, but it's going to take a bit of work, and I haven't told Aylin what I'm thinking yet. I think she would be happy about it, but I want to know it's happening before telling her.

I look down at the beautiful woman wrapped around me as she's sleeping, completely unaware of how caught up in my thoughts I've been. I examine her face that has mostly healed by now. I lean down to press a kiss to each spot I know was hurt. I've done that every day for the last two weeks. I'm not sure if she knows what I'm doing, but it doesn't matter. I feel responsible for her getting hurt, so I need to know she's okay.

She stirs at the contact of my lips on her skin. Her bright blue eyes flutter open, looking up at me as a small smile graces her lips.

"You okay?" She asks me. She asks me that a lot, but I don't mind because I ask her too. We both hid too much from each other when this all started, and now there's nothing hidden between us, and never will be again.

"I'm amazing, how are you?" I kiss her forehead again.

She shrugs, "I could be better."

I frown. "Why?"

With a smile she says, "Well, you woke me up kissing the wrong part of my body."

I laugh, "Sweetheart, you know that's my favorite way to wake you up."

She chuckles as I climb over her, kissing down her whole body making my way to one of my favorite places. As long as I can do this the rest of my life, I'm going to die a happy man.

43

Aylin

6 Months Later

I did it.
I did it.
I fucking did it!
I graduated with my doctorate!

There were so many emotions I felt seeing that stupid piece of paper in my hand for the first time. Of course, I cried, but I felt like a weight was lifted, not only because I didn't have to write anymore papers or worry about grades or anything.

No, the weight that was lifted was all the self-doubt put on me from the day I was born. All the comments that I would never be good enough and never be able to do anything with my life.

But I did it.

I proved them wrong.

Now, trying to figure out what to do next.

Nate's birthday is June thirtieth. We agreed we needed to do something in celebration for my graduation and his birthday. Though, he tried to deny making his birthday any part of it.

He asked what I wanted, and I just said I wanted to do something I've never done before. Lucky for him, that's a lot of things. I didn't expect what he chose, which was a weeklong cruise in the Caribbean.

His reasoning, he wanted to take me somewhere new and couldn't settle on just one place. The cruise allowed us to go to three places, so that's what he went with.

Nate sold his house, which I felt bad about at first until he told me he didn't have any sort of emotional connection to it other than the pain it caused him when he found out I was missing, and he didn't want that reminder every day.

We've been living in a small one-bedroom apartment that lets us do month-to-month without costing an arm and a leg. Which is good because I can't contribute much, even though Nate apparently has a decent amount in savings and insisted I didn't have to contribute at all.

I refused to freeload off him, and I've been paying what I can.

After he took some time off, he continued to be on admin leave while he actually went to counseling, not with me, obviously. But he's said it's been helpful, and I haven't said, "I told you so", but I mean...I did.

I feel his large presence behind me before his arms wrap around my middle, and his head rests on my shoulder.

"What are you doing, sweetheart?" Nate asks, nuzzling into my neck.

I'm standing on the balcony off our room because Nate decided to be fancy with this cruise. Looking out into the open ocean is peaceful and terrifying at the same time.

For once, I woke up before Nate and couldn't help but come out here to look at the sun rise over the ocean. It makes me think about how I would've never guessed I would be here. How I almost wasn't. How the world is so big, so unpredictable and sometimes we just need to live without worrying about the consequences or repercussions.

Sometimes, we just need to let ourselves love without the fear of heartbreak because it could result in us losing out on the best thing to happen to us.

"Just thinking," I lean my head back against him.

"About?" He asks with a gentle kiss to my neck.

I know before I would've tried to distract him from the question, or wave him off, but I don't do that anymore. It's hard at times to be open with Nate, but I've done better. I also started seeing a counselor myself, and I'm glad I did.

"How happy I am," I say honestly, and it's also an unfamiliar thing to feel like this without the lingering fear of it being taken away. It's liberating.

"Well, I hope I can make you happier with my news then," Nate says with another kiss to my throat.

I turn around in his arms to look at him, this is the first I'm hearing he has news for me.

"What is it?"

We just left on the ship yesterday, and we don't have any service in the middle of the ocean so whatever it is he has to have known since before we left.

Nate smiles, and if he wasn't holding me up right now, I might have fallen over, he never fails to make me weak with his perfect, bright smile.

"I was offered a job, a detective position with the Oregon State Police."

"That's amazing!" I jump up on my tiptoes to wrap my arms around his neck and pull him down to me as he chuckles. "But weren't you also offered a detective job with Portland?"

I pull back to see him smiling still, as he holds me close to his body. "Yes, but *this* position has a specialty that is pretty important to me."

I narrow my eyes at him in confusion, he seems really excited about this, and I swear if he's about to tell me about some crazy dangerous specialty, I might consider pushing him off this balcony.

"This job would be as a detective with a focus on crimes against children," he says softly, holding me tighter, probably anticipating my reaction.

My jaw drops as I stare up at him. "Like...you mean kids that...like...me?"

"Yeah, sweetheart, I want to help people, you know that, and I want to make an actual difference, this position is perfect."

Tears well in my eyes, whenever I think he can't get better, he does. I knew he didn't want a detective job that put him undercover again, but the fact that he wants one to help kids is just...

I can't stop myself as I wrap my arms around him tightly, pressing my head to his chest as the tears fall.

Nate's arms wrap around me tightly, soothing me. This probably isn't the reaction he expected, but I am so happy, I know he will be amazing. There are so many times I wish Nate was able to save me when I was younger, even though it's ridiculous since he's only two years older than me.

I look up at him, taking him in. Taking in everything about him. "I love you so much, Nate."

He smiles, pressing his lips to mine before pulling away just slightly whispering against my mouth, "I love you too, Aylin. I didn't get to tell you the best part yet."

I pull back to look at him. "There's more?"

Nate nods. "Since it's with the state police I will have to travel around the state for different cases."

I furrow my brows at him. "How is this the best part? Are you trying to get rid of me?"

Nate laughs, "Never, sweetheart. Since you're still looking at jobs and exploring options, I'm letting you know you can expand your search a bit."

"I'm so confused. What do you mean?"

"We don't have to stay in Portland, or even close to it. Technically, the offices for the state police are in Salem, but I can choose to live anywhere in Oregon. So, where will it be?"

My jaw drops again. I really didn't want to stay in Portland after what happened because I'm paranoid and anxious about us being found again, and Nate is now saying we could go anywhere? I don't even know...*well it would be nice to be close to people I know.*

"Is Newport an option?" I ask, not wanting to get my hopes up. I mean, he may not even want to live there anyway.

Still smiling he answers. "Of course, wherever you want."

I feel the tears preparing to make their appearance again. "Really?"

Nate chuckles, pulling me to his chest. "Yes, sweetheart, if you want, we can start looking for a place there when we get back."

For some reason that makes my eyes flood with tears again.

"Is that a yes?" Nate asks.

I nod frantically against him.

"Perfect," he murmurs against the top of my head.

He's right, everything about this is perfect.

THE WEEK WENT by way too quickly as we explored the tropical islands, and ate way too much every single day on the cruise. We enjoyed sunsets over the ocean and made love more times than I could even count. There were nights we barely slept because exploring each other's bodies was more important.

I feel like we will never get tired of each other, it's like everything has fallen into place in our lives.

Now we are back, and some people are disappointed when they come back from a vacation, but I feel even more excited because I know we are about to have some thrilling changes.

I'm going to look for jobs near Newport. I was already considering doing work as an online therapist for a while.

Now, it just makes the most sense while I figure out if I want to focus on any certain specialty myself, and maybe at some point work with a nonprofit or something.

That's the beauty of life, I have the freedom to choose whatever I want to do now. Plus, I know Nate will always support my decisions.

We get off the ship and turn our phones on for the first time in a week. Of course, my phone is flooded with texts from Mel, even though I told her I wouldn't have service.

> Mel: I miss you.
>
> Mel: How am I supposed to survive without talking to you for a whole week?!
>
> Mel: This is some sort of punishment, isn't it?
>
> Mel: Some best friend you are...
>
> Mel: I don't mean it! I take it back! Take me back! Please!!!!
>
> Mel: Wow...this sucks. I hope you're having so much fun!

I chuckle at all her messages, knowing she's just joking around because that's who she is. I'll call her once we get back to Portland.

Looking over at Nate I see he has his phone to his ear and a shocked look on his face. My own smile falls as I look at him because he looks more than shocked, he looks...*panicked.*

"What's wrong?" I ask, my heart rate instantly kicking up in my chest.

Something is wrong, I can tell, but Nate continues listening to voicemails and staring at his phone before meeting my eyes, and I am not sure I want to know what happened.

44

Shit.
    Shit.
        SHIT!

We just had the best time together, and I can't even believe what I'm hearing on my voicemail.

Since everything happened, I never really had the chance to talk to Aylin about Nadine and Layla. I really thought it wouldn't be something that would ever come up again, but damn was I wrong.

The first voicemail is from the caseworker, Grace, "Hello Nathan Greene, this is Grace with the Department of Human Services. I know this might be difficult to hear, but Nadine Harper the guardian to Layla Phillips has passed away. In her will she stated no other next of kin, and that you would be the best placement for Layla. We are working on a diligent relative search, but if you could please call me back."

The next voicemail is from Sergeant Peters, who is still technically my boss since I just put my notice in before we left. "Greene, DHS is calling me wondering where you are, something about a placement? I don't want to know details of your life but sort it out."

If I wasn't so panicked about how I'm going to explain this to Aylin I might actually laugh at how I might miss that cranky bastard.

I have texts from Mitch too.

> Mitch: Why is Peters asking where you are? What did you do?
>
> Mitch: Did you leave without actually telling anyone?
>
> Mitch: I know you're leaving all of us here, but you're not done yet.

I can't even muster a laugh or snarky response to Mitch right now.

"What's wrong?" Aylin asks me. I know she can see the panic all over my face.

"Um...there's something I forgot to tell you and now we have a bit of a situation," I finally tell her.

Running my hands through my hair I lead her away from the crowd at the port because I know I can't keep this from her any longer. I didn't even mean to keep it from her in the first place.

"Nate, you're scaring me, what's going on?" She holds onto my bicep, squeezing tightly.

"So, remember when we went and saw Layla, and Nadine wanted to talk to me for a minute before you had your panic attack?"

I see her flinch at the memory, I run a soothing hand down her arm as she nods.

"So, she told me her husband was pretty sick, and she wasn't sure how long he would be around. It made her worried if something happened to both of them, where Layla would go." I pause to take in her expressions, wondering what she's thinking.

She doesn't say anything so I continue, "She asked if I would consider taking Layla in if they weren't around to care for her anymore, and I didn't want to say yes without talking to you. I figured it was such a long shot of it actually happening, I just agreed. Then, everything went down with you, and the case and honestly, I forgot about it."

"And now?" Aylin asks quietly. I can tell she knows what's coming but needs me to say it.

"Now, apparently that did happen, and they said her will states me as Layla's guardian, so they are trying to get ahold of me. I'm so sorry I didn't tell you before. I know this is a lot, and I'm sure we could figure something out with them, she did say something about looking for relatives," I explain.

Aylin is quiet for a few moments, looking deep in thought. I can't tell how she's feeling, even though we both have been more open with each other, she is still a pro at keeping her emotions masked when she wants to.

Finally, she asks, "Do you want to help her?"

I look into her eyes, questioning why that's her response. Then, I think about the question. I answer truthfully. "Yes. I saw just a fraction of what she went through, and I want her to have the best life possible."

Aylin nods, "I do too."

My jaw drops. "So, you're okay with it? I mean, it's not like we are adopting her I don't think, but you'd really be okay taking in a six-year-old right now?"

She nods again. "Obviously the timing isn't ideal with us wanting to move, and both having big career changes, but she needs people to care for her. I want us to help her."

"Have I told you you're amazing lately?" I kiss hard before wrapping her up in my arms and crushing her to my chest.

"I don't know what we are going to do while we are still in

the apartment though," she says, bringing her bottom lip between her teeth, which I know she does when she's nervous.

"We will figure it out, sweetheart, we will get a new place soon."

This was not the ending I was expecting of our vacation.

45

Aylin

To say I was shocked by what Nate said would be a bit of an understatement.

If I had to guess a hundred things it could have possibly been, that would not have even crossed my mind.

We got back to Portland way too late for him to call the caseworker back last night, but neither of us were able to sleep. We got online and started looking for houses in and around Newport. Unfortunately, we won't be as lucky as Mel and Zander to have a house on the water.

It's okay, though, we found a few we like and sent them to the realtor Nate used to sell his house, letting her know we would like to look at them.

I did mention to Nate we need to ask Layla if she's okay moving away because this is already going to be a huge transition for her, maybe she doesn't want to start off next year at a new school. Maybe she likes it here.

There's so much more to consider now.

Nate is pacing while he talks to the caseworker, I'm not paying attention until I hear him ask, "Today?"

I look up to see he's already looking at me.

"Yeah, we could um...pick her up today." I can tell he's nervous. I'm nervous too, neither of us know what we are doing. Maybe this is a bad idea.

I widen my eyes at him as he says bye to the caseworker and hangs up.

"We can pick her up from the temporary foster home she's been staying in around noon," he states.

"What does she need? Do we need to go get her stuff? Like clothes? A bed? Oh my god, where can a bed go for her?" I start to panic as I look around the living room. This apartment is not big, and it only has one bedroom.

What were we thinking, we can't do this!

"Hey, it's going to be okay. Yes, we should probably get her a bed and I let the caseworker know our home situation. She said it's okay since it's temporary. She will need to come see our new house once we get it, but everything is going to be okay, sweetheart," Nate soothes me, and I'm impressed with how calm he is right now.

I have no choice but to nod and accept what he's saying. I can't freak out; he's right we will figure this out. It will be okay.

WE PULL up to the house Layla has been staying in. We went to the store earlier, got a little plastic princess bed that didn't take up too much room in the living room once we moved some stuff around so she would have her own space.

We also got a booster seat for the car, and some clothes for her I hope she will like.

My palms are sweaty as we stare at the house, neither of us rushing to get out of the car yet.

"Are you really okay with this, sweetheart?" Nate asks.

I lick my lips before nodding. I really am, I'm just nervous.

"Okay, let's do this," he says with a squeeze to my thigh before we both get out of the car.

Nate knocks on the front door. I can't stand still, but he's holding our intertwined hands up to his chest, and it's helping to feel his heart pounding in his chest.

He may seem calm and collected, but I can feel how nervous he really is.

A woman that looks to be in her mid-thirties opens the door. "Hello, are you Nate and Aylin?"

"Yes ma'am, nice to meet you," Nate says so smoothly it almost throws me off.

"You too, I'm Jane. Layla is just in her room, she's been taking all this change pretty hard," Jane explains, and my heart drops for Layla and how she must be feeling.

"Is it okay if we go talk to her?" Nate asks gently.

"Of course, it's the third door on the left," Jane says as we walk down the hallway.

I'm not sure how Layla is going to feel about seeing us, and I'm terrified we are about to make things worse, especially if she's already struggling.

Nate taps on the door softly before saying, "Layla, it's Nate and Aylin, can we come in?"

He presses his ear to the door waiting for a response. I can't hear anything, but after a second, he nods to me, so I assume she said yes.

We enter the room slowly. It is a cute set up, all neutral colors with a simple twin bed, white dresser and a mix of white and beige blankets and pillows. I hope she will be okay with her very...different set up at our place.

Layla is sitting on the bed hugging a stuffed animal. I can see her eyes are red, she's clearly been crying, and I can't help the pain in my chest as I think about how much she's gone through in her short life. I remember feeling jealous she was able to get out when she did, but all those feelings are gone. I just want to help her.

"Hey Layla, do you remember us?" Nate asks, kneeling next to her bed, and I follow his lead, doing the same.

She looks at us, fresh tears in her eyes as she nods, clutching her stuffed animal tighter.

"I know you've had a lot of things going on lately, but I think it's going to get a bit better; would you want to come stay with us?" Nate asks gently.

Layla is quiet while it looks like she's thinking. She's so small, but something in her eyes makes her seem so much older as she tries to process what Nate said, and really think about it.

"Are you going to take care of me?" She asks so quietly I almost miss it. My heart breaks at her words.

I get why she asks. It's a valid question when you haven't been taken care of before, and the fear that it will happen again. I completely get it.

"Of course, we are," I answer quickly, because I can tell her words hit Nate hard. He can be so tough, strong and protective, but he has a gentle heart, and I know this is hard for him too.

She seems to think for another moment before looking at Nate. "You won't yell like my daddy?"

I think I just felt my heart physically rip apart in my chest. I try not to show a reaction, and luckily this time her words don't send me into a spiral. I really have been working on my triggers, I know they will come up. I need to work through them.

"Never." Nate promises, and I know it's true. The only people I've seen him yell at were people hurting me. I know he would never hurt us.

"Okay," she nods before slowly scooting off the bed.

"Do you have anything to bring with you?" I ask, glancing around the room for a bag or anything.

"Miss Jane has my stuff I think," Layla sniffles, wiping her nose with the back of her hand.

"Do you want to do anything before we leave?" Nate asks.

Layla shakes her head no.

The three of us go back out to the hallway and Nate wraps his arm around me, pressing a soft kiss to my temple as we follow Layla.

Jane has a little suitcase that she told us has Layla's clothes in it. *That's it?* That's everything she has? That can't be right.

I think Jane sees the confusion on my face because she clarifies the social worker has more of Layla's things in storage at the office. They knew this would be temporary, and we will be able to get all of her things.

Once we get back to our apartment, I can see how nervous Layla is. We show her the bed we got, and the princess sheets we picked out.

"We were actually going to move to a bigger house soon, but it might not be here in Portland," Nate tells her.

"If that's okay with you, though Layla, we know you have school here, and we can live anywhere." I say quickly. I know this is a lot to put on her right now, we are probably overwhelming her.

"Where are you moving?" She asks.

"Have you been to the beach before?" Nate asks.

She shakes her head.

"Well, that's kind of where we were thinking, would you like to see if you like it?" He is so gentle when talking to her it makes me melt each time.

She nods.

"Good, we were going to look at houses tomorrow if that's okay with you?" He checks in with her.

She nods again.

Nate looks up at me, and I nod too.

WE GO to Newport the next day to look at the houses we liked online. I let Mel know, and she knows the situation with Layla since I called her freaking out when we found out, but I told her it might be too much for her to meet two new people right now.

She totally understood, and since we will likely be moving closer to her soon anyway, she was okay with it.

Out of the three houses we ended up only liking one, there was a sunroom on the second floor that had the perfect view of the water in the distance. It's not on the beach by any means, but up on a hill and we liked it.

Most importantly, Layla liked it.

She seemed to be in a much better mood than she did yesterday, even claiming one of the rooms as her own. Nate couldn't say no after that, and let the realtor know we would put in an offer on it.

I know he got life insurance from his parents which he bought the townhouse with, and after selling that, he has enough to pay for this house, but I still told him I would be helping.

He waved me off like he always does about me paying for stuff, but no matter what, I'm going to help.

Now, we took Layla down to the water. She's never been to the beach, but it looks like it's where she's supposed to be.

Luckily, the weather is nice today, sunny and a little warm, even though the water is freezing. She's running all around the sand, chasing the waves as they crash onto the surface, running away and screaming when they get too close.

Nate and I stand back just watching her be carefree and having fun. A couple dogs come up to her with a ball in each of their mouths, she throws it for them and giggles.

Nate wraps his arm around me, pulling me against his side as we watch her.

"Are we crazy?" Nate asks..

"Probably, but we are going to give her the best life possible," I promise.

He nods, "Yes we are, it might not always be easy, but we can do this."

"Yes, we can."

I continue to lean against Nate as we both take in our new reality. As much as we went through, I wouldn't change a thing because it put me right here, right now, right where we are supposed to be. Who we are supposed to be.

EPILOGUE

Layla

Two Years Later (Age Eight)

It's been two years of living with Aylin and Nate. We all moved to the beach not long after I started staying with them.

I was scared to move somewhere so far, but I love the beach. The water is cold, but it's fun to run through, plus there's always dogs at the beach and I like to play with them.

I've asked Aylin and Nate for a dog, they've said yes, but I have to be patient. I'm not good at being patient, but I still get to play with dogs at the beach while I wait for one of my own.

It was hard when I started living with them. I missed my grandparents, and my mommy. I know they are all together in heaven watching over me. I know they would be happy I'm with Aylin and Nate because they are so nice.

Nate saved me before, and I don't remember a lot about the night he saved me, I just know he felt safe, and I didn't want him to leave me. I was a little scared to live with them because I didn't know if Nate would yell at me and Aylin, like my daddy yelled at me and my mommy.

He hasn't, and he is always touching Aylin like holding her hand, or touching her face, whispering to her or kissing her —*gross*. But I never see them mad at each other, and they never get mad at me.

A couple months ago, I thought I was in trouble because I called Nate "Dad". They both looked at me with their eyes big, and I thought I did something wrong, so I got scared and ran to my room.

When they came to check on me, they let me know I wasn't in trouble, it just surprised them.

"L*AYLA, we want you comfortable with us, and that means you can call us what makes you comfortable. Don't feel like you have to call us anything you don't want to.*" Aylin says to me.

"It was an accident, I didn't even mean to." I tell them.

"It's okay, if you want to call me 'Dad' then you can. If you want to call me 'Nate' or 'the greatest person I've ever met'—"

Aylin pushes against his shoulder lightly at the last one which makes me giggle.

I shrug because I don't know what I want to call them, it's always been Aylin and Nate, but I mean...they are basically my parents.

I'VE CALLED NATE "DAD" a couple times after that, but Aylin has just been Aylin. Not because I don't like her or anything, I really do. It's just I had my mommy, and she loved me, I know she did, and it's a little weird to call someone else mommy.

My dad wasn't very nice, and Nate is nice. I want a nice dad, which is why it is so much easier to say it to him.

Sometimes I have nightmares that wake me up, and they come in to check on me. Aylin told me she has nightmares sometimes too.

Tonight, I just woke up from a really bad one. It was so loud, there was yelling, hitting, and a loud bang. I woke up screaming, and Aylin was right next to my bed soothing me, telling me it's okay.

She sits on the edge of my bed pushing my blonde hair away from my face. "You're okay now, Layla."

I grab for my stuffed kitty, holding her tight to me. My mommy gave her to me.

"Do you remember when you asked me if my dad used to yell too and if Nate saved me from him?" Aylin asks.

I nod, I remember she looked very scared and left after that. I thought I did something wrong. Grandma Nadine said I didn't, but I still felt bad.

"Well, he did. Nate wasn't old enough to save me yet, but my dad used to yell, and I went to live with someone else too, just like you."

"Really?" I ask, sitting up higher in my bed.

"Yup, you know Sam and Jeff?" She asks. I've met them on holidays, Aylin said they are friends.

I nod.

"They took care of me for a while after my dad yelled really bad at me," she says.

I didn't know this about Aylin, she's like me. She's always been good at understanding me, but I know her job is helping people, I didn't know she knew what it was like.

"But now you're a grown up, and it's okay, right?"

Aylin smiles, "It took some time, but yes, I'm okay now. I can tell you what helped. I actually have something for you. I was going to wait to give it to you another time, but I think it might help you now."

I nod, I really hope it's the puppy I want, but I doubt it.

Aylin gets up, goes through my bathroom that connects to another bedroom before coming back with a small black box in her hand. She sits down on my bed again before opening it. There's a small key on a chain inside, she pulls it out and I see it's a necklace. It looks like the key she has on her ankle.

"Sometimes, you have to remember important things in your life that make you happy. I call those things keys to your life, and I wanted you to have a key so when things get tough you can think about the things that make you happy, your keys."

She reaches out to put the necklace on me. Once it's clasped around my neck I look down at the gold, it's super pretty, I don't want to take it off.

"I think a puppy would be one of my keys," I tell her, which makes her laugh.

"Don't worry, you'll get a puppy, I want one too," she whispers.

"Good. This is really pretty, thank you...Mom," I say the last word so quietly, but I hear her small gasp. I flinch thinking I might be in trouble again.

They told me what felt right, and it does. I can have two moms. I know my mommy wouldn't mind. She would want Aylin to take care of me and be my mommy now.

"Layla, you know we love you so, *so* much, right?" She brushes my hair from my shoulder.

I nod, "Yeah, I love you both too, Mom," I say it again and it feels right.

Aylin starts to cry as she reaches out, and I wrap my arms around her neck as she hugs me tightly. I had some bad stuff happen to me, I know that, but I think I'm pretty lucky to have Aylin and Nate as my new parents.

~

Nate

I didn't think it was possible to fall more in love with Aylin, but I just did.

I'm watching her comfort Layla after a nightmare; she doesn't know I got up too. I've been standing outside the cracked door just watching their interaction. Layla has called me "Dad", but this is the first time she called Aylin "Mom", and I am extremely close to crying.

Especially as I watch them hug, these two amazingly strong girls that have been through so much they never deserved, and now they have each other. I know no one would've been able to understand Layla better than Aylin. I think tonight proved that.

Aylin comes out of Layla's room, I can't help myself as I wrap my arm around her waist, pulling her against me as she yelps.

"You scared me," she whisper-yells. "How long have you been standing here?"

"The whole time," I say honestly.

"Did you hear everything?"

I nod. "You're amazing."

She shakes her head at me, "No, I think I just...I understand what she's been through. Maybe not exactly, but I get it."

"Which is why, again, you're amazing," I kiss her cheek, her jaw, then her neck.

"Okay, maybe this should continue anywhere except right outside her bedroom," Aylin chuckles, trying to push me away lightly.

"You're right." I nod before scooping her up in my arms, catching her by surprise before carrying her into our room.

Something about seeing her being so perfect to Layla makes me feel like I need to claim her, make sure she knows she's mine.

We haven't really talked about kids of our own together, I think we are both happy to just focus on Layla, giving her everything she could ever want, that we don't necessarily need to have any of our own kids.

Though, of course practicing making them is more than fine with both of us. I toss Aylin onto our bed after shutting the door behind me before climbing over her body, hovering above her as she reaches up, running her hands across my stubbled jaw, down my chest then around to my back wrapping herself around me.

"Thank you for everything, Nate."

"No thanking me, everything is for us. The three of us. I love you."

She smiles before leaning up to press her lips against mine. "I love you," she whispers against my mouth before we are lost in each other.

∽

Aylin

Today is Mel and Zander's wedding day.

I don't think I have ever seen Mel so stressed out. Even though her wedding is really small she is so paranoid about everything being perfect I swear she's going to rip her hair out.

"Mel, do you love Zander?" I ask.

"What? Of course I do, I wouldn't be here if I didn't. Why? Did he say something?" I see the panic rising within her.

I hold back a laugh. "No, I just wanted to remind you that this is about you two and your love for each other. As long as it is you two saying 'I do' then it's going to be perfect, right?"

She sighs, "You're right."

I smile. She looks beautiful. Her curves accentuated in the white dress with just the right amount of sparkle. Her long red hair is curled around her shoulders, she opted for no veil.

I'm her maid of honor, wearing a light green floor length dress she picked out, that I actually really like.

Layla is her flower girl, who looks so cute in her dress that's the same color as mine, but has a flowing skirt that doesn't quite reach the floor. I curled her long blonde hair then pinned some of it up.

"Are you ready?" I ask Mel as I know it's about time.

She nods. "Yeah, yes. I can do this."

"Just think of Zander," I tell her to try and help.

"Okay, just think of Zander...*nope*, see if I do that then I only see him nak—"

Luckily she cuts herself off as she glances over to Layla. "Never mind."

I can't help the laugh that comes out of my mouth. "You have a problem," I shake my head at her.

"Are you kidding? I know you are the exact same way with Nate," she accuses.

I just shrug.

"Let's do this," I say before ushering Layla over to where we are going to walk.

The ceremony is up on a hill where there's a grass area and a perfect concrete spot for Mel and Zander to stand that looks out onto the ocean because, of course, they wanted to get married here in Newport.

I instruct Layla to walk out first, throwing the petals onto the ground. She's smiling at everyone, even though she doesn't know them. I'm so proud of her.

Next, I go out, my eyes immediately finding Nate's who is standing off to the side by Zander. His eyes lock with mine as his gaze roams my entire body making me feel exposed, but I keep walking until I'm at the front, waiting for Mel.

I can feel Nate's eyes on me the rest of the ceremony, through Mel and Zander's vows, through their kiss, then finally when they were announced as officially married.

Nate offers his arm to me so we can walk back together. Layla coming up to Nate's other side to take his hand in hers, I imagine we look like a little family, which we are.

My little family. I never would've thought I'd have this.

At the reception Layla is having a great time dancing with practically everyone. Nate danced with her for a bit, then Zander, Mel, and she even let Mel's dad dance with her a little. It was easily one of the cutest things I've ever seen.

I'm sitting at the table watching the whole thing when Nate saddles up next to me, having shed his jacket, and rolled up his shirt sleeves up to his forearms giving me my favorite view.

"You okay, sweetheart?" He asks, wrapping his arm around my shoulders. I instantly lean into his shoulder as we both watch Layla on the dance floor.

"I can honestly say I have never been better."

We are both quiet for a moment before Nate asks, "Is this something you'd want one day?"

I sit up to look at him.

"What? A wedding?" We haven't talked about that before, not that I mind, I'm extremely happy with our lives, I haven't seen a need to change anything.

Nate nods.

I shrug. "Maybe someday, but honestly, it's not super important to me. I love you; you love me, we have Layla and I'm so extremely happy, I don't need more than this. Do you?"

Nate pulls me against him again. "I want you forever, whether that's with a piece of paper making it official or not."

"Well, I have good news for you then, with or without a ring or a piece of paper I'm already yours forever. You're stuck, Officer Greene."

"Hey, whoa, it's Detective Greene, Dr. Porter." I lightly swat my hand against his chest. I still hate being referred to as a doctor. It doesn't make me as upset as it used to, but I just don't like it.

"Well, *Detective*, you have me forever no matter what," I smile at him.

With a kiss on my lips, he replies "You've had me since the first time you turned me down."

I laugh, I love this man with my whole heart, and I know this is it for me.

I've finally accepted that I can be happy, and this won't ever be taken away from me.

THE END

WHAT'S NEXT?

Read Trent's story, "What They Feel".

A dark enemies to lovers romance in the Falling series.

"What happens when everything comes falling down?"

BLURB:

NOW is the time. Everything he's worked for is within reach.

He can move out from his fathers shadow and prove himself.

Until he's faced with his biggest challenge yet when he meets her.

She challenges him in a way he never would have thought.

And makes him question everything he's ever believed when it comes to feelings and love.

NEVER in a million years did she think she would be in the middle of a storm as strong as him.

Despite her clear distaste there's something pulling her in.

But when it all comes to a head is WHAT THEY FEEL even worth it?

Download Here: What They Feel

ABOUT THE AUTHOR

Madi is 20 something trying to figure out what "adulting" is. Madi has been writing stories since she was a teenager she continues to express all her emotions in her writing. She's also an avid reader, especially of dark romance. Madi lives in the PNW where she attended college after moving from the unforgiving heat of Arizona. Madi spends her free time with her husband and family of pets (4 dogs and 2 cats).

If you want to be kept up to date on news regarding my next release, follow me on Instagram, TikTok and my Facebook reader group!

Instagram: @madidaniellewrites

Tiktok: @madidaniellewrites

Facebook Reader Group: Madi Danielle's Reader Group

If you enjoyed I would be forever thankful for your review on Goodreads and Amazon. As a new indie author it helps me a ton for you to spread the word!

ACKNOWLEDGMENTS

I just want to say I am so happy with the group of people I have in my corner! This book was a lot harder to write than my first, and I don't think I ever saw that coming. But you all made me keep going when I saw the love for Mel and Zander, and the excitement for Aylin because I wanted her story told. Aylin's story was something I thought deserved to be out in the world, and something important to see that you can overcome your demons. I have worked in human services, and seen the darkest parts of human nature. Because of that I wanted to write a story of survival, and redemption, hoping it can help others struggling to know it can and will be better.

Of course this story wouldn't be here like it is without my best friends Ashley and Julia who are always supporting this crazy journey, providing input and loving on the male main characters! I love you guys, but you already knew that.

I want to thank Megan and Sarah for being some of the first to get to know Aylin and Nate, and loving them as much as I do. Plus, Sarah for creating the most beautiful teaser and graphics! I'm seriously obsessed.

And of course, Cat from TRC Designs for yet another beautiful cover. This woman is the best, and the absolute sweetest! I couldn't imagine more beautiful covers for this series, and she makes them come to life.

Thank YOU for getting this far, reading, and hopefully enjoying. I have many more stories to come so stick around and come along this journey with me.

www.ingramcontent.com/pod-product-compliance
Lightning Source LLC
LaVergne TN
LVHW011942060526
838201LV00061B/4186